DREAMS
OF THE
DARK
SKY

THE LEGACY OF THE HEAVENS
BOOK TWO

DREAMS
OF THE
DARK
SKY

TINA LeCOUNT MYERS

Night Shade Books
New York

Night Shade books may be purchased in bulk at special discounts for sales promotion, corporate gifts, fund-raising, or educational purposes. Special editions can also be created to specifications. For details, contact the Special Sales Department, Night Shade Books, 307 West 36th Street, 11th Floor, New York, NY 10018 or info@skyhorsepublishing.com.

Night Shade Books® is a registered trademark of Skyhorse Publishing, Inc. ®, a Delaware corporation.

Visit our website at www.nightshadebooks.com.

10 9 8 7 6 5 4 3 2 1

Library of Congress Cataloging-in-Publication Data

Names: LeCount Myers, Tina, author.
Title: Dreams of the dark sky / Tina LeCount Myers.
Description: New York : Night Shade Books, [2019] | Series: The legacy of the heavens ; Book 2
Identifiers: LCCN 2018042910| ISBN 9781597809559 (hardback : alk. paper) | ISBN 9781597809566 (pbk. : alk. paper)
Subjects: | GSAFD: Fantasy fiction.
Classification: LCC PS3612.E3365 D74 2019 | DDC 813/.6--dc23
LC record available at https://lccn.loc.gov/2018042910

Cover illustration by Jeff Chapman
Cover design by STK•Kreations

Hardcover ISBN: 978-1-59780-955-9
Trade paperback ISBN: 978-1-59780-956-6

Printed in the United States of America

For Jürgen

A cast of characters and two glossaries, one for English and another for Jápmemeahttun terms, can be found in the back of this book.

Dreams of the Dark Sky is the second book of the Legacy of the Heavens.

The first, *The Song of All*, introduced readers to the worlds of the Jápmemeahttun and the Olmmoš.

~

First among those created by the gods, the Jápmemeahttun lived in harmony on the fringes of the tundra until their numbers grew so large that they overwhelmed their lands. As they struggled to survive, the gods took pity and gave them a gift. The Jápmemeahttun would live their lives in two halves: the first as female and the second as male, and as one soul prepared to leave the world, another prepared to give birth. The life force of the gods would pass through the old soul into the unborn, giving the baby life and turning the mother's gender to male in the process. In this way, balance was soon restored to their population.

~

When the Olmmoš humans walked out of the east with their odd ways and their strange animals, the Jápmemeahttun welcomed them and taught them how to live upon the ice and snow and find light in the endless darkness. But over time, the humans grew wary of their guardians, whose lives seemed to stretch on forever.

What started as an affinity between two peoples ended in enmity as the humans rebelled against the authority of those they called the Immortals.

For generations, battles between humans and Immortals raged on, until the Immortal Elders discovered the Song of All. Believed to be a gift from the gods, the Song of All acted as a veil to shield the Immortals from human eyes so the two tribes could live in the same world and never interact. This fragile peace held for almost a hundred seasons of snow, until the Brethren of Hunters began to seek out the reclusive Immortals to regain their wartime power, now challenged by the priestly Order of Believers.

Raised by the Brethren, Irjan had avenged his family, slain by rogue Immortals, by becoming the most skilled among the Hunters. He eventually grew weary of bloodshed, though, and fled to live a peaceful life as a farmer, husband, and father. But when he came upon his wife and infant son moments before they died, Irjan suspected the Brethren. Even as he mourned his wife's death, Irjan tracked the Immortals deep into the snow-covered forest in the hope that their legendary powers would bring his infant son, Marnej, back to life.

The Jápmemeahttun life bringers Aillun and Djorn had journeyed together to their Origin to give birth. The inherent danger in this sacred ritual was compounded when they heard a human voice within the Song of All. As Aillun started to give birth and Djorn, the ancient warrior, began to die, Irjan ambushed them. Thrusting his infant son into the light emanating from the old Immortal's body, Irjan brought Marnej back from the dead. But Aillun's subsequent death left Irjan responsible for Dárja, the infant Immortal she had birthed.

Dávgon, the Brethren leader, dispatched his best hunters to bring back the traitor Irjan to serve the Brethren's cause or forfeit his life for his earlier betrayal. Irjan, to elude his former comrades, set off for the Northland, where he had once safely traveled. But Irjan's skills as a Hunter had not prepared him to care for two infants, and he was forced to rely upon the aid of strangers. Drawn into a Brethren trap, Irjan's life was saved by Kalek, an Immortal healer who had been heart-pledged to Aillun. Together, Irjan and Kalek protected the infant Dárja, but could not prevent the Brethren from kidnapping Marnej.

Kalek soon learned that Aillun had made Irjan Dárja's guardian. Torn between his duty to his people and his lost love, Kalek brought Irjan to the Immortal Elders and what he thought was safety. The Elders knew what Irjan had not yet accepted—the human Hunter, in fact, had dual heritage, and possessed the unique ability to enter the Song of All as if he were a Jápmemeahttun. But his arrival among them bound the Elders to choose between protecting their kind from the humans and respecting Irjan's right to live as one who had both human and Immortal blood. Their compromise to imprison Irjan temporarily staved off discontent.

While imprisoned, Irjan consoled himself with his friendship with Kalek and his responsibility for Dárja. However, he continued to harbor plans to rescue Marnej from the Brethren, who would turn his son into a killer. Irjan escaped at the first opportunity, forcing Kalek to choose between his new friendship and his tribe. Convinced by Irjan that his son's freedom would serve the Immortals, Kalek fought alongside his friend until he was wounded. When it became clear there was no hope of rescuing his son, Irjan chose to save Kalek's life, returning with him to the Northland, where he and Dárja were reunited. Irjan spent the next sixteen seasons of snow as a prisoner, teaching Dárja what he knew best—how to fight.

Dávgon, the Brethren leader, aware of Marnej's Immortal blood and the unique abilities he possessed because of it, used Irjan's now-grown son to track the Immortals and foment war between the two tribes. When Marnej entered the Song of All, the Immortal Elders realized there was no hope for peace. Dárja, who had grown into a skilled fighter, ardently supported the call to war. However, the revelation that she would never experience a fully Immortal life because of Irjan's interference in her birth confirmed her fear that Irjan had always loved his son, Marnej, more than her. Determined to prove herself a true Immortal warrior, Dárja secretly joined the warrior ranks to confront the humans, unaware that Irjan had also joined as a last attempt at redemption.

When the Immortal warriors used the Song of All to attack the human soldiers in the Great Valley, Marnej pushed his way into the mêlée, anxious to demonstrate his loyalty to the Brethren. While Dárja fought her way through the human ranks, Irjan gave his life to protect his Immortal comrades when the tide turned against them. Decimated by the human victory in the Great Valley, the remaining Immortal warriors withdrew into the Song of All while Dárja was taken prisoner. At the Brethren's fortress, Dárja and Marnej confronted their shared past and discovered, to their surprise, the potential of their tenuous future.

DREAMS
OF THE
DARK
SKY

Part One

LOST TO <small>THE</small> SONG

CHAPTER ONE

KALEK PICKED AT THE meager meal of stewed rabbit and bitter greens. He ate out of habit, out of a healer's instinct to sustain his body, but, more and more, he wondered why he bothered.

A suppressed giggle broke through the hushed atmosphere in the dining hall. Kalek looked up from his bowl. Two young nieddaš sat with their heads together. One had a hand over her mouth. Her shoulders shook with laughter. The boaris scattered about the dining hall continued to eat. The old showed no interest in the lives of the young.

Once a lively center for sharing meals, the dining hall had become cheerless in the moon cycle since the battle with the Olmmoš. It was impossible to enter a common area and not think of those who had died defending their kind in the last battle. The Jápmemeahttun had believed the power of the Song of All would preserve peace by keeping them safely hidden. But the Olmmoš could not live in peace, and Kalek cursed the day they had walked out of the eastern dawn. He had not been born yet, but he knew the songs from before, when their kind had thrived in balance with the world around them.

Look at us now, he thought. The few Taistelijan warriors who had survived the battle stood out among the nieddaš and the boaris. They were thankful to be alive, but they lived with the heavy burden of guilt. Indeed, it seemed that those who sought out healers, like himself, suffered less from an illness of the body and more from a sickness of the spirit. Increasingly, the old spent more time alone, listening to the Song of All, waiting for their time to end. They seemed to prefer the chorus of the wider world to the melancholy of their own immediate one. Yet, when called upon, they honored their duty as life bringers. They traveled to their Origins without complaint. Old and wise, they must have known that when their spirits left this world, new souls would likely not replace them.

But what alarmed Kalek most was not the pervasive sadness among the old, but the changes wrought among the young. Although the youngest still ran about playing innocent games, the older ones left childhood behind for hard work.

Wood for fires still needed to be chopped. Metal and leather still needed to be wrought. Animals still needed to be butchered. And fields still needed to be plowed. The survival of their kind depended on these tasks, which meant survival depended on the nieddaš, who were now the majority.

The necessary new duties had made many of the older and more capable nieddaš sullen and silent. They exhibited a harshness that had not existed before the battle. Still, when the time came for these nieddaš to return to their Origins and give birth, they struggled, restless and fearful, because what had once been a rite of passage had become, to their minds, a death sentence.

No one wanted to speak about what was happening, but none could ignore the fact that few nieddaš returned from birthing. Once, a nieddaš could expect to be a guide mother in the course of her life. Now she could only hope to be one. Kalek had seen the sidelong glances of those who still had no babe to love and nurture. And they all felt the palpable desperation as the songs of the guide mothers were sung less and less.

Despite his calling as a healer, Kalek found it hard to offer counsel to those nieddaš who came to see him. In their sad faces, he saw Aillun, his beloved first heart-pledge, who had traveled to her Origin what felt like a lifetime ago. Believing she could save them both from sorrow, Aillun had not shared the truth of the quickening within her. At the time, Kalek had told himself his wounded heart justified his harsh last words. But really it was his injured pride that had made him growl like a trapped bear. Later, though, when Aillun failed to return from her Origin, he would learn what real heartache was. He would not be the one to send these innocent nieddaš to their death in the Outside.

"You have pushed your food from one side of your bowl to the other many times, Kalek."

Startled by the voice, Kalek looked up.

"Lighten your heart and be done with your meal," Okta said.

Kalek dropped the wooden spoon. He looked deep into the eyes of his mentor. A milky whiteness grew in them now, but the ancient healer's gaze was still sharp and penetrating. He could not lie to his mentor, his friend.

"What are we doing?" he asked, hopelessness flooding his question.

Okta raised his unruly eyebrows. "We are surviving. As we always have."

Kalek's despair turned his gut sour. "To what end, Okta? We are defeated."

∼

Okta patted his apprentice's hand. This was by now an old conversation between them.

"Kalek, even in defeat, there can be life."

The young healer shook his head, his focus on the bowl in front of him. "We are all just waiting to die."

"It has always been so," Okta said gently.

Kalek's head shot up. His pale, feverish eyes bore into Okta just as they had the day of the battle, when Kalek had found Irjan's body. Nothing in the young healer's training had prepared him to see his friend and lover broken and bloodied. It did not matter that Irjan was part Olmmoš and had once hunted their kind. He had fought and died like a true Jápmemeahttun warrior. Then, as now, Okta knew that Kalek's giant frame could bear much, but anguish threatened to crush his soul.

"Fine words meant to play with one's thoughts," Kalek said. "They are not an answer."

Okta nodded his head, allowing the reproach to stand.

The old healer lifted his cup. He wished he could ease his apprentice's pain. He wanted Kalek to regain his spirit, to see beyond the death of friends and comrades, and the death of those he had loved. Aillun first. Then Irjan. Okta drained his tea, then placed the cup down.

"There are no words I can offer you, Kalek, that will be sufficient," he said. He stood and gathered his bowl and cup. "I will return to my chambers and then go out to gather herbs."

The ancient healer did not wait for his apprentice to answer, and Kalek did not try to stop him.

~

The knock upon the apothecary door stopped Okta at the garden's threshold. He considered ignoring it, longing to be outside where the rhythm of life pulsed, unchanged and welcoming. But a healer could not ignore someone in need. He backtracked through the crowded room filled with pungent herbs and distilling tinctures. He opened the door, surprised to see the Noaidi.

"Einár! This is unexpected. Are you feeling unwell?"

The Elder shook his head. "May I enter? I wish to speak with you."

The formality of the Elder's request placed Okta on guard. While the two shared a friendship that spanned ages, Einár was the head of the Council of Elders and the gods' Oracle. For the last several seasons of snow they had not agreed on much, but in the vast span of their lifetimes, this was but a small matter.

"I have not seen much of you since our return," Okta said, standing back to allow the Elder's hunched frame to enter the apothecary. *When did Einár become so thin? So frail?* he wondered.

"My time now is mostly spent with the gods," Einár said with a matter-of-factness that belied the onus of being the Noaidi. "I try to understand their wishes, and our future."

Okta hesitated. "And . . . what do they say?"

Einár clasped his hands in front of him. The sleeves of his pale-green linen robe fell down across his gnarled knuckles. "They say many things, but I am not here to speak of the gods. I am here to speak to you of Dárja."

Okta winced. The name cut him like a knife. His hand rose to his chest where the weight of responsibility rested heavy and immutable.

He was to blame for what had come to pass, at least in part. He had been angry and callous when he had last spoken to Dárja. He had told her she would always be a nieddaš. That she would never be a mother. Never be an almai. Never be a warrior. He had been blunt and brutal, and he had immediately regretted it.

Despite all his training as a healer, Okta had not understood what it meant to live a singular life. His had been a Jápmemeahttun life. He had been a nieddaš. He had given birth. He had handed his child to her guide mother, then embraced his life as an almai. When asked, he had become a warrior. He had experienced it all, as his kind was meant to. But Dárja was unique, and Okta had failed her. They had all failed her.

"I have heard her song," Einár said.

The calm pronouncement set Okta back on his heels. He braced himself on the edge of his scarred work table. Disbelief clouded his thoughts, but his heart pounded.

Dárja had disappeared the day the Taistelijan had marched to battle. He did not doubt she had wanted to prove herself worthy to be a warrior. To prove him wrong. And he was wrong. He was wrong to keep his doubts about her future to himself for as long as he had. He could have helped her. They all could have helped her. But the truth remained hidden for too long, too painful to relive.

Okta met the Elder's gaze. "She is alive, then?"

"Yes. I have heard her song."

Okta's elation made him eager to tell Kalek. The news would give the young almai the encouragement he needed. It would light the way back from the darkness that had consumed him.

Einár raised a hand to caution Okta. "There is more. I have also heard the song of Irjan's son."

Whatever hope had welled within in the ancient healer was dashed. "Marnej," he muttered, remembering Irjan's son, whose very existence had threatened what little peace remained to their kind. Silently, he blamed the boy, *So much life lost. So many lives changed. And Marnej at the root of it all*.

"I do not know what this means," the Elder continued, "but I leave you to make the choices you feel you must." He paused, then added, "The way you have always done."

Okta staggered back at the impact of this judgment. He glanced at Einár, expecting to see condemnation. Deep folds shaded the Elder's weary eyes. Okta's shame bloomed hot. He had just quietly denounced the Olmmoš boy when he should have castigated himself. Blame rested with him, not Irjan's son. Okta plopped down on the bench beside his work table. He was too old and he had seen too much to deny his attempt at playing a god. When Irjan had entered their lives, Okta had been adamant that, as half-Jápmemeahttun, Irjan deserved to live. But there was a part of him that now wondered if their kind might have been spared the recent tragedies had he just let the Taistelijan warriors track and kill Irjan in the very beginning.

"You have always listened to your heart, Okta," Einár said. "Sometimes for the betterment of us all, and sometimes to our detriment. But we are so few now." The Elder paused as if he chose his next words with care. "I am compelled to caution you. The actions of one will impact us all."

Okta nodded.

The Elder withdrew from the apothecary, closing the door behind him. Okta sat, taking stock of the news. The knowledge that Dárja lived was both a profound joy and a subtle agony. Self-ishly, he wanted to see her determined young face peer around his door again, if only to exonerate him for his part in her misery. But if that came to pass, he would once again have to cause her heartbreak. He would have to tell her of Irjan's death on the bat-tlefield.

Young. Headstrong. She will only see her part in it, Okta thought woefully.

He could not say Dárja had been wrong to blame Irjan for what had happened. Irjan's actions had altered the course of all their lives. In trying to bring his son, Marnej, back from the gods' embrace, Irjan had doomed the life bringers, Aillun and Djorn. The life force created by a boaris at death was meant to help the nieddaš give birth to her child and then allow her to transform to almai. Djorn did not have the power to sustain life for more than two souls. Marnej had been reborn, but Aillun died. And Dárja had been denied the life force she needed to mature fully as one of their kind.

When Irjan had pleaded to join the warriors leaving to fight the Olmmoš, Okta had recognized a man desperate for some kind of redemption. While he did not agree with the need for bloodshed, he respected Irjan's desire to be a part of it. He had not talked Irjan out of fighting. Rather, he had helped him, and embraced him, and watched him ride into battle. His heart had ached for the man. Half Jápmemeahttun and half Olmmoš, Irjan had labored to do what was right and had suffered for love.

Kalek was right to agonize over how to tell Dárja this truth, he mused to himself. *If she were to walk through his door right now . . .* The thought disappeared almost as soon as it formed.

Okta leaned forward to rest his hands on his knees. The antic-ipation kindled by Einár's news flickered briefly before reason snuffed it out. Dárja may be alive, but she could easily be a prisoner or pursued by the Brethren of Hunters, by Marnej even. Okta was certain that, despite the distant connection between Dárja and Marnej, if their songs were heard together, then it could only mean she was in danger. Marnej had been raised an as Olmmoš. Raised to be a Piijkij, like his father, he had sworn an oath to kill their kind. Marnej might be Irjan's son, but he was also a Hunter.

Okta wanted to act. He wanted to do something. But Einár's warning stung his conscience like summer nettles. In the past, Okta had sent Kalek out to meddle in the affairs of the Olm-moš, believing it to be the best course of action. And he knew if he told Kalek that Dárja's song had been heard, his apprentice would rush into the Outside to try to find her. Kalek was as much a guide mother to the girl as Irjan, even if Irjan was her chosen biebmoeadni.

Okta wrestled with his thoughts. The reasonable part of his mind said it would be futile to send Kalek out to save Dárja. She could be dead within days. But the truth was that he could not bear the thought of losing Kalek. He had risked his apprentice's life twice, believing the chance for peace was justified. But never again. Kalek was too dear to him and the future was now too uncertain to risk anything on some notion of pride.

~

Okta still sat with his hands upon his knees when Kalek entered the apothecary. If any misgivings persisted, they disappeared the instant he saw his apprentice. Framed by his pale, lank hair, the young almai's doubt-etched brow overshadowed his face. *If the gods possess pity they will place no more demands upon him*, Okta thought, then silently promised, *Nor will I.*

"I thought you had left to collect herbs," Kalek said, surprised to see Okta.

"Yes, yes. I became distracted and delayed," the ancient healer said, staying within the bounds of truth.

Kalek passed by his mentor, briefly touching Okta's shoulder. "Come, I will help you."

Okta watched Kalek's sure, fluid movement around the apothecary. How different their paths had been. He remained grateful that Kalek had not had to fight in the war. Too young for the ancient battles and too valuable for this last stand, Kalek had been spared. But even as he praised the gods for this small mercy, he knew that the young almai had not really been spared. To watch one's kind slowly die over a lifetime might prove to be a greater cruelty than witnessing comrades killed in battle.

"Thank you, Kalek," Okta finally said. "I much prefer your company to my own."

A feeble smile graced the almai's face. "That is only because you are so old and your own company so familiar."

"True," Okta agreed with a knowing laugh, "I find that, in your company, I need to bend less to pluck the right herbs."

Kalek took the thin woolen cloak from its worn peg. He held it out to Okta, who stood. Kalek's smile lingered, but it did not reach his eyes.

CHAPTER TWO

T HE HIGH PRIEST OF the Order of Believers felt the tingle of satisfaction as his bishops, soldiers, and servants bowed their heads and murmured their greetings. "My Vijns" rose up through the smoke-blackened rafters of the great hall's vaulted ceiling.

Bávvál offered a casual wave of his hand to acknowledge the deference of those gathered, then dabbed the sweat that beaded his closely cropped hairline. The summer's stultifying heat had pressed its way into the airless hall, but Bávvál still wore his full ceremonial raiment. The fox collar clung to his neck, as the woolen cloak dragged across the earthen floor. Even with the lightest weaves, the long length of blue cloth tugged upon the clasp at this neck, chafing him with each step.

Still, Bávvál would not have changed anything for comfort's sake. His robes were a sign of his power. He was the Vijns, the Breath of the Gods. He had been the one to prevail where his predecessors had failed. He had seen the end of the Jápmea Immortals. *Immortals*, he scoffed silently, the rancor of their ancient name upon his tongue. *Jápmea scourge, more like. A pestilence finally cleaved from this world. And the Brethren of Hunters will soon join them in obscurity.*

With no Immortals, there was no need for Immortal hunters. The Brethren's bid to wrest power from the Believers, from him, was at an end. Bávvál took delight in how easy it had been to manipulate the Brethren's honor and their oath to protect the Olmmoš from the Jápmea.

Their sacred Oath. Bávvál sniffed at the thought.

A few worthless concessions to the Brethren's leader, Dávgon—and a well-placed spy—and Bávvál had discovered the truth about their treachery. Whatever dreams of power Dávgon had envisioned for himself and his precious Piijkij, they would be crushed forever when it was revealed that the Brethren of Hunters had harbored among their ranks the very abominations they had sworn to kill.

Bávvál smiled to himself as he stepped onto the ornate wooden dais. The smell of warmed beeswax enveloped him. He approached the carved pillars that flanked the lone imposing chair. The pillars, with their snarling bears, were a fiercesome sight, but it was the chair that truly symbolized Bávvál's authority. He had ordered the blackened wood to be inlaid with bone. Light and dark, like life, where days and souls were measured by the light and the dark they contained.

If he were to remake the chair now, Bávvál would use the Brethren's bones in place of the reindeer and the cow horn that had been used. Indeed, he might yet do just that. It would be a testament to his achievements, and a warning to any who would challenge him. Pleased with this new idea, Bávvál turned and released the silver clasp at his neck. His robe fell with a heavy rustle. He looked out on the crowded-yet-hushed room before easing himself into his seat of power.

Slowly, those standing came to life once again with shuffling feet and overlapping voices.

"Rikkar," he called to a retreating figure.

The man came to a jerking stop, then turned on his heel, his downy hair a nimbus above his sloped shoulders. Rikkar looked to all sides to see who else had noticed him, then hurried toward the dais, hesitating at the edge. Bávvál waved him forward.

"My Vijns," he said, bowing before the High Priest.

Bávvál eyed the man's thin arms and boney wrists with distaste. He had known Rikkar since they were both acolytes. *Scarcely off our mothers' teats*, he recalled with nostalgia. His mother had chosen not to claim him when a better offer of a handmate had been made. The new man wanted nothing to do with the last man's seed, and the Believers gained another body to serve the gods. Rikkar, on the other hand, had been the cherished son of a Believer priest. Coddled and praised as a youth, Rikkar had grown up believing in his own ordained ascendance. Indeed, one could not deny he was a gifted orator and a passionate Believer. However, his presumption was not matched by an aptitude for advancement.

Rikkar had been clumsy in his efforts to rise above his position as village priest. He had sought to use one of the Brethren's disgraced Piijkij for his own gains and when that failed, he was compelled to ally himself more closely with the Brethren. Bávvál, in due course, forgave him his treachery. As High Priest, he respected ambition. In fact, he much preferred it to passion. Ambition was predictable, zealous faith rarely. Yet Rikkar had surprised him. *Throwing his lot in with the Brethren*. Now that, Bávvál had not foreseen. Still, as was the way with most fledgling conspirators, Rikkar had made mistakes, only to find himself caught between the bear and the eagle.

Rikkar had gaped like a fish upon land when Bávvál had confronted him. It was an amusing recollection. All the more gratifying for the outcome. Seventeen seasons of snow as a viper in the Brethren's nest. *And Dávgon none-the-wiser*.

"Has word been sent to the Brethren's fortress?" Bávvál asked, leaving the past for the present.

"Yes, my Vijns," Rikkar said through a thin-lipped smirk.

"I see this prospect pleases you, Rikkar." Bávvál kept his tone light. "There was a time when these Hunters were your brothers-in-arms."

The man's smile faded. "An error you helped me to realize. Through your grace I will sit upon the Court of Counselors."

"You are not wearing the Counselor's robe yet," Bávvál warned, his words clipped. He had forgiven the priest his trespass. He had not forgotten the betrayal.

"Yes, my Vijns." Rikkar inclined his head, revealing the pale scalp of his tonsure.

"And what is Dávgon's intention?" Bávvál asked, growing impatient with the man's fawning.

"They are preparing to journey here for an audience, my Vijns."

"In what numbers?"

"It is to be a large retinue. The Avr wishes to make an impression upon all who might see the Brethren."

Bávvál frowned, more from disgust than concern. "What of the Jápmea?"

"You can be assured he is bringing her." Excitement had crept back into Rikkar's voice. "The boy will likely be among the escorts, as he is often at Dávgon's side."

Rikkar's eager countenance annoyed Bávvál. "You will not be missed?" he asked with a hint of mockery.

Rikkar blinked, his eyes momentarily downcast. "I am tolerated, but not sought for my company or my joik," he said. Then, with a rueful laugh, he added, "They would be shocked to hear the story of my life sung." And, as if to himself, he whispered, "Indeed, I am."

"My Vijns," a penetrating voice from the crowd broke into the quiet.

Rikkar stirred.

Aware of his priest's shame, Bávvál looked out into those gathered. "Come forward," he said to no one in particular. Then, to Rikkar, he said with uncharacteristic kindness, "The gods thank you."

"As I thank the gods," Rikkar mumbled in a thick voice, then withdrew, swerving around an approaching servant, who momentarily teetered with his laden tray of food.

The servant knelt, presenting the tray to the High Priest with deference. Bávvál picked at slices of cold goose, leaving aside the dark bread and hard, pungent cheese. He had just taken a bite when his counselors appeared before him, each affecting a more dignified aspect than the next.

"My Vijns," the eldest in the group spoke up, his voice more of a croak. A weak attempt at a smile merged his wrinkles together, a look that most would mistake for an ailment. "We must address the matter of these soldiers."

The other counselors nodded in agreement, but let their deputy carry on.

"We cannot continue to quarter them within the Stronghold. There are too many. They have depleted our stores."

"I see no need to keep them," the youngest counselor interrupted, his impatience winning out over prudence. "The Jápmea are defeated."

Bávvál shifted his attention to Erke, the young counselor, regretting his decision to raise the thankless cur. "There is much you do not see," the High Priest commented, turning away from the sallow-faced youth to address the ancient counselor. "Your concern is noted. For the time being, we will maintain the soldiers at the Stronghold. Increase the requisitions from as far afield as you must go. When I am assured, then we will distribute the soldiers to safeguard the temples."

"Safeguard against what?" the callow youth blustered.

The comment, whether born of simple-mindedness or outright insolence, tested Bávvál's forbearance and coalesced his resolve to be rid of the young counselor at the first opportunity. No amount of coin or patronage was worth his irritating presence.

"The soldiers," Bávvál said, "will safeguard against any who dispute my power. And to make sure, Erke, you shall join their ranks. No doubt they will benefit from the wealth of your wisdom." The youth blanched, then looked as if he were about to protest. Bávvál cut him off with a curt dismissal. "The gods thank you."

Taking the cue, the counselors bowed their heads. "As we thank the gods," they intoned as one, then scurried away. Their flaxen robes flapped about them.

Bávvál picked up another piece of cold goose from the tray beside him. He popped it into his mouth and chewed thoughtfully as he considered his next step.

"Get me Áigin," he said to the servant standing just beyond his sight. When Bávvál heard no movement, he looked over his shoulder to see the boy anxiously craning his neck in every direction before running off like a startled deer.

"My Vijns, you wished to see me."

With a jolt, Bávvál swiveled in the other direction. "Áigin," he said, stifling his gasp.

The reed of a man inclined his head. His long, thinning hair fell forward to frame his composed face.

"Dávgon is bringing his pets to us," Bávvál began without preamble. "The march will likely be a gaudy display meant to impress farmers and villagers. Two regiments are to leave immediately. I want their fortress burned and every Piijkij in chains. Make sure the commanders know to stay well away from Dávgon's procession. I do not want the surprise I have planned ruined by carelessness."

"It will be done," the gaunt man replied with the assurance of one unaccustomed to doubt or disappointment.

Bávvál held up his hand to forestall Áigin's departure. "Make sure I never have to hear from Counselor Erke again. But allow his family to mourn his shocking accident." Then, almost as an afterthought, he added, "The gods thank you, as I thank you."

Áigin nodded, then slipped away as silently as he had appeared.

CHAPTER THREE

MARNEJ AWOKE FROM FITFUL dreams drenched in sweat. He sat up in his bunk, sliding his legs out from under knotted covers. The cool earthen floor beneath his bare feet reassured him. No thrum. No pulse. No voices in his head other than his own. *Thank the gods.* But even as he thought this, Marnej's gratitude foundered on the fact that these were the same gods who'd blighted his life. They had made him different. *Made him . . . what?* He didn't know.

The girl, Dárja, claimed he was Jápmemeahttun. An Immortal, like her. Marnej told himself that it was a lie. She was the Brethren's prize from the Great Battle. She would say anything to gain her freedom. Still, she knew about the voices. She heard them too.

Marnej shook his head to clear his doubts. *Just because I sometimes hear voices doesn't mean I'm a Jápmea.* But a part of him knew that he was deceiving himself. How else could he explain his visions before the battle or the strange way his world had dissolved into another—one where everything felt disturbingly alive? He shivered at the recollection.

She'd called it a gift. Marnej snorted. It was a curse that set him apart from the other Piijkij. They didn't trust him. He saw it in the way they looked at him. But he was loyal. Above all else, he was loyal to the Brethren of Hunters. Unlike his father, Irjan, who had betrayed the Brethren by walking away from his duty and his oath. Just like he'd walked away from Marnej.

Irjan had never cared about him, no matter what the Jápmea girl had said. Still, for one brief moment, Marnej let himself believe that his father had always loved him. He let himself envision a life where he was accepted. Wanted. Even now his heart leapt at the possibility. His breath was quick and ragged with longing. Disgusted, he pushed away the desire as he hastily propelled himself to his feet.

The girl's Jápmea. She'd say anything to escape, he reminded himself.

"I *am* loyal," he muttered as he tugged his shirt over his head, the cord lacing catching on his tangled hair.

Marnej stuffed his still-bare feet into his boots, whose worn leather fit like a second skin. He'd proved himself on the battlefield. The Avr had said so.

"You've honored the Brethren of Hunters," he'd said. "You are now a Piijkij."

This last part rankled. Marnej had been raised a Piijkij. He'd been raised to hunt and kill the Immortals. He'd taken the Oath like all the others, and he'd upheld his promise. It had been the Avr who'd asked him to use his gifts. He'd done what was asked of him, but there'd been a subtle change in the Avr after that. Marnej felt the man's eyes on him, as if he might prove treacherous, like his father before him. But Marnej owed his allegiance to the head of the Brethren of Hunters, if only for the fact the man had given him a home among the Piijkij, even after his father's betrayal.

~

Marnej strapped his miehkki to his side. Little more than a moon cycle had passed since his sword had been bathed in Jápmea blood. Now, it was cleaned and honed, resting comfortingly at his hip, waiting. Marnej fell in step with the other Piijkij. Those more senior than him grumbled about the High Priest of the Believers who had commanded their attendance.

"...as if we were his personal soldiers."

"It's thanks to us he sits on that pretty throne of his."

"I hear the one he shits in is even grander."

"Doesn't change the smell," the seasoned Hunter beside Marnej said, then elbowed him. "Cheer up, whelp."

Marnej snapped to attention, nodding with a half-hearted grin.

At the stable, Marnej saddled his horse before leading the beast out into the fresh morning air. The sun cut through the tops of the tall pine and larch trees, forcing him to shield his eyes. When they adjusted, he saw the girl seated on a horse with her hands tied together in front of her. Even so, she held her head high.

"What's she doing here?" Marnej asked, covering his surprise with disdain.

"A reminder to the people that we're the ones who saved their rotten hides from the likes of her kind," a voice replied, then Bihto's head popped up above the shaggy dun-colored back of a neighboring horse. A toothy smile split his square face as the aging Piijkij settled in his saddle with an appreciative grunt.

"Not much to look at, though," Bihto added with a nod to the Jápmea girl. "All gristle. Like a cockerel. They say they had to pry the sword from her fingers."

Marnej made a vague reply. He knew better than Bihto what the Jápmea girl was capable of. He had faced her once in a chance encounter. From the moment he'd seen her move, he'd known his father had trained her. At the time, Marnej had begrudged Irjan for stepping between them. But he now realized the gods had spared him that day. The girl was more skilled a Hunter than he was. It made him uneasy thinking he'd almost let her out of her cell to prove her wrong about his father. She'd been toying with him, just as she had when she'd wielded her sword against him.

"Only when the ravens have plucked out their eyes should you lower your blade against an Immortal," Marnej said, quoting an old Brethren axiom.

"True enough," Bihto agreed, nudging his horse into an easy walk beside Marnej.

~

Dárja squinted, but did not raise her bound hands to block the light. After the darkness of her cell, it took a long time to make out the shapes in front of her. Scents, however, assaulted her from all sides. Horse dung, leather, and the stench of the Olmmoš. Dárja was by now inured to her own rank odor, and though she wished to bathe, she wore the dried bloodstains with honor. No one could look at her and question her skill as a warrior.

A fresh breeze from the east momentarily banished the circling flies. Dárja shook the hair from her face. She caught sight of a familiar profile from the corner of her eye. Without turning her head, she observed Marnej riding toward her. He passed without a glance in her direction. Dárja sniffed. She should've expected nothing less. She'd offered him the truth and he'd run from it like a frightened rabbit. Nor had he revisited her. His alleged interest in his father, Irjan, had been nothing but idle curiosity. *He's not worthy of his father's love*, she thought contemptuously.

Dárja looked around at the ugly faces of the Olmmoš. Their eyes were too big, too wide. She looked for the older Olmmoš, the one who'd often come to stare at her through the crude iron bars of her cell. The one with a broad, furrowed brow and shorn hair the color of ash. His powerful bearing suggested he held standing among the Piijkij. What he thought of her, she couldn't tell. By torchlight, he would hold her unwavering gaze for a time, then walk away, taking the light with him.

After each of his visits, Dárja would close her eyes, weighed down by the leaden silence of the Olmmoš world. The torchlight would still flicker behind her lids for a few moments more. She'd shiver, overwhelmed by the lifelessness of everything around her. She would let her inner voice go out in search of the Song of All. In search of her kind. But she heard no answer. No other voice but her own. Desolation would incite her to try again and again to find that precious connection she so craved. And when that failed, she tried to fashion Irjan's face in her mind's eye. But the visions always faded before she could outline his features. She worried she was forgetting what he looked like. She worried she was forgetting the one who had loved and cared for her better than any guide mother could have.

Then the oppressive darkness would take possession of her. It would contort her doubts into deep-seated dread. *He's probably already forgotten you*, she'd taunt herself. And she deserved it. She'd said such terrible things to Irjan. But she'd been so angry. Her whole life had been shaped by his love for his son, Marnej. Her future traded for his. She'd left Irjan resolved to prove she was a warrior, even if her body would never change. The single-mindedness of her purpose had fueled her on the battlefield. It had made her relentless. It had kept her alive. But now, living meant little if she could not tell Irjan that she regretted her anger.

The squat horse beneath her jerked into motion. Dárja grabbed a hank of the horse's mane to keep herself from falling off. The reins, tethered to the Olmmoš rider in front of her, stretched taut. The horse's broad back was uncomfortable. She felt as if she were an unwieldy load. When she rode upon her binna, she and the reindeer were one. They rode quick and sure with their songs entwined. She would never understand why the Olmmoš would want to ride a creature like a horse whose spirit had been broken.

A wet splat landed on Dárja's cheek, jarring her once again. She let the spittle of the passing Piijkij ooze down her face. She glared at him, then raised herself to her full height. Her eyes ahead, she thought about all the Olmmoš she'd killed on the battlefield. She hoped a good number of them were Piijkij. *Dead in their own shit and offal*, she thought with grim pride. And if she got the chance, she would make sure more would follow their comrades before death claimed her. She didn't fear her death. In fact, part of her welcomed it. Better to die than to live among these people, as Marnej had done. Better that Irjan never know his love for his son had been so sadly misplaced.

Dárja began to hum to herself. At first softly, then, as probing stares turned in her direction, she raised her voice to recite the battlecry of her kind.

We are the Taistelijan.
We are the warriors of the Jápmemeahttun.
Our swords serve our kind in death,
Our knowledge our continued life.
We walk into battle to end what was long ago begun.

Dárja had never uttered these words aloud, outside of the Song of All. But it felt good to use her voice. Her next chorus grew even louder, demanding attention.

From farther up the line she saw Marnej turn in his saddle. Even at this distance, Dárja could see his shock. He gawked at her as if he had never seen her before. She sang a third chorus as a shout, as though she meant to be heard in the Pohjola.

"Shut her up," someone growled.

Dárja opened her mouth, then crumpled forward, grunting as pain exploded in her arm. She only just managed to grab hold of the saddle before her weight carried her over the side of the horse. She squeezed tight her eyes. Her breath was a shaky wheeze, but she willed herself to sit up. The blow to her arm had ripped apart the tender new skin that had formed on her battle-wound. Blood seeped fresh and red through the old brown stains on her sleeve. She did nothing to staunch the blood. Rather, she began to hum again, low and insistent, a new refrain forming in her mind:

I am the voice of one brought to life by truth.
And by my sword that truth shall be set free.
I am watched over by the stars, but my destiny is my own to make.

~

Marnej turned back around, his pulse racing. He'd heard that chant before. He'd been lost in one of his visions and one voice had built upon another until every fiber of his being had vibrated with the power of that chorus. *We are the Taistelijan.* The chant had wound its way through him, seeking out his doubts, his desires, his soul. He'd felt their heartbeats. He'd known the Jápmea pride and their power. He'd seen their flashing swords and green fields and felt the pull to join their ranks. *We walk into battle to end what was long ago begun.*

Marnej's stomach turned at the memory. He'd thought he'd glimpsed the future, but his visions had betrayed him, and he'd led the Olmmoš into an ambush. His hands suddenly felt slick. He released his grip on the reins and wiped his palms one after the other on his coarse linen sleeves. The fabric's rough weave snagged on his scabs, tugging them just as the Jápmea girl tugged upon his thoughts.

She'd known about the voices. She'd spoken of them as if he should understand her meaning. But he hadn't understood. He only knew the voices had always been there. They'd been a comfort in childhood, then a cause for concern as he grew up. Marnej thanked the gods the Avr had not asked him to seek out the visions again, because doubt now plagued him. He could no longer tell himself it was the gods working through him, nor would he accept that it had been the Jápmea.

CHAPTER FOUR

OR THE BETTER PART of two days, the Brethren of Hunters' procession had moved slowly through the countryside. They had passed fields and farms where families came forward to point or just stare at the Jápmea girl. In the villages, people lined the narrow path. They jeered as the prisoner passed, throwing whatever was at hand at her. Dávgon was pleased that the Jápmea girl reminded people that the Brethren's victory had finally made them all safe. *Our victory*, he thought. And it was *their* victory. *They* had tracked the Immortals. And *they* had led the soldiers into battle. Without the Brethren, all would have been lost.

Dávgon looked over his shoulder at the Jápmea girl who rode with a straight back. She sneered through muddied features, as if it were he and not she who smelled of rot and death. But no amount of pride could change the fact she was his prisoner. *Perhaps the last of her kind*, he speculated with some regret, loathing the prospect of giving his prize to the High Priest. Bávvál had so little vision. He would probably just kill her in some crude display, when there were so many more interesting possibilities.

Dávgon searched the company for Marnej. He spotted the boy's blond head amid the grizzled grey of the veterans. He watched the boy ride. Nothing about him seemed worthy of suspicion. Still, the matter of the Jápmea ambush at the outset of the battle disturbed Dávgon. At the time, Marnej had been as surprised as the rest by the trap. Were it not for that, Dávgon would have believed it a deliberate betrayal. But the young Piijkij had proved useful in the end. Jápmea blood ran through the boy's veins. How much, he did not know. Less than Irjan, to be sure. But the boy was no less talented than his father. It begged the question of what might come of mating him with the girl. *The secrets I could learn*, he mused. *The power I could wield.* The Avr turned forward again, determined now to keep his prize.

Ahead, the Believers' Stronghold loomed. It was a hulking structure above a barren morass. The great swaths of trampled marsh were the same lifeless brown as the defense picket and the inner palisade beyond. Indeed, the only color for a league around were the long banners of the tower. Dull yellow on a fading blue background, the Ten Stars of the Bear bent and twisted as the banners snaked across the cloud-dotted sky.

Dávgon held up his fist. The retinue came to a stop. At his signal, the advanced guard dismounted and approached the gate. Their footfalls thundered across the bridge planks. Dávgon sat astride his horse, noting with growing irritation that their arrival had gone unheralded. *Not even a sentry*, he thought as he followed his men through the arched battlement. It was just another example of Believer carelessness that he would change. Discipline would prevail under the Brethren's guidance.

A pair of dusty and disheveled soldiers came running forward with short pikes in their hands. As they neared, the Brethren's advance guard closed ranks to stop them.

"The Avr of the Brethren of Hunters enters for an audience with the High Priest," one of the Piijkij boomed.

"By whose order?" the larger of the two soldier's challenged.

Dávgon bristled at the insult. His men answered for him, casting aside the two soldiers as if they were nothing more than sacks of grain. The soldiers moaned and rolled on the ground but seemed unwilling to rise again. Dávgon rode forward, his advance guard clearing the way with weapons drawn. Some of the Believers' soldiers milling about took interest in the arrival of the men who had so recently led them into battle. More, however, hurried off, intent on avoiding the work the arrival of the Brethren entailed.

The mounted procession followed the advanced guard through the Stronghold until they reached the stables. At the long, overhung corral, Dávgon signaled for the rest of his men to dismount. The ground fairly shook as their boots landed on the dirt. A haze of billowing dust swirled around restive hooves and anxious feet, then settled back down on the unwelcoming earth.

The Jápmea girl sat upon her horse with her head held high as if she commanded the men around her. Dávgon's appreciation of her brazenness waned. He muttered to a man beside him to pull her down. The Piijkij nodded, stepped forward through the horses, and yanked the Immortal from her saddle. She writhed on the ground for a moment, then gathered her breath and released a stream of abuses that could not be ignored.

"Silence her," Dávgon called out.

Rough hands pulled the girl to her feet, but she ignored the two men at her side to stare fixedly at him as her voice rang out.

It is I. Truth calls me.
And by my honored blade, the honest word shall set me free.
I am safeguarded by the stars, but my hands shape my future.

Though her phrasing was old and stilted, Dávgon understood her well enough. "Keep her quiet," he said as he turned on his heel to march through the ornate doors that marked the sanctum of the Order of Believers.

～

The hall buzzed with interest as the normally smug clergy peeked over each other's shoulders with wide eyes. Parting just enough to allow Dávgon and his retinue to enter, the onlookers closed ranks in an awkward crush. The High Priest sat in his garish chair upon the dais at the room's far end. The man's finery was wasted on him. Sickly, with the aspect of a rat, Bávvál would have been culled early had he come up through the Brethren ranks.

Whispers trailed Dávgon's footfalls.

He stopped well short of the dais, greeting the High Priest with a curt nod and no further deference to the man's title.

The small man stood, overshadowed by the carved bears on the flanking pillars, then stepped forward, dragging his long cloak the length of the dais. Bávvál's dignity, however, was undone by the sweat that coursed down from his temples.

"What treasure have you brought me, Dávgon?" he asked.

The Avr's muscles tensed at the man's possessive tone. "We have *our* Jápmea prisoner," he said, emphasizing ownership.

The priest smiled coyly. "Just the one?"

"We killed the rest," Dávgon said, his rage at the priest's lack of respect building.

The High Priest nodded appreciatively. "Yes. Yes. The tales of the Piijkij are all I hear of these days."

"The deserving should be lauded when the Jápmea are defeated," Dávgon seethed.

"Indeed! And we wish to hear of your campaign in great detail. In fact, I have sent for my bishop to record the events for posterity." The High Priest looked over his shoulder. "Ah, here he is now. Dávgon, I believe you are acquainted with Rikkar. He has just become my bishop. A reward for his faithful service to the Believers and his Vijns."

Dávgon's hand touched the hilt of his sword, the bitter taste of bile rising in his gorge.

"Rikkar had the most interesting things to tell me," the High Priest clapped his hands in mocking delight. "He said you have within your ranks a Jápmea. Now, perhaps he meant this girl you bring me, but I think not."

The High Priest dropped all pretense. "Dávgon, did you really believe I would not find out that you rely upon a Jápmea for your battle plans? Or, have you been blind to their cunning infiltration of your company? Because, I know firsthand it is easier to gain access to your Brethren than to a woman's skirt."

"Lying rat!" Dávgon spat as he rushed the High Priest with his sword drawn.

~

Dárja kicked the Piijkij to her right in the knee. She pulled herself free from the other Hunter with a wrenching twist of her entire body. The effort carried her to the ground. She rolled backward, avoiding the crush of rushing boots as the whole room spasmed with men fighting and dying.

Dárja saw Marnej rooted in place, slack-jawed. She tore the gag from her mouth.

"Marnej, run!" she yelled, then sprang to her feet.

Dárja shoved her way through the tumult, crashing into a door at full speed. The stout barrier held. Someone grabbed her by the shoulders and spun her around. She raised her bound wrists to clobber her attacker and caught the corner of Marnej's chin. He staggered back but kept his grip on her.

Dárja writhed. "Let go of me."

Marnej held tight, his face grim.

Dárja's frustration boiled over. "Even *they* know what you are," she raged, trying to tear her arms free. "But I suppose you're still loyal." She said loyal as if it made her sick. "Loyal to men who want to use you. Men who've only ever used you."

Even in the torchlight, Dárja saw Marnej's face flush.

He pulled the knife from his belt, then raised its point at her. Dárja bucked and kicked, her eyes on the glinting blade. Marnej's face was a cold mask.

He raised his blade higher as he grasped Dárja by her wrists. Then, with a deft cut, her hands were free. Marnej reached around her waist without touching her. He pulled back the bolt on the door, then handed her his knife as he drew the sword at his side.

Stunned, Dárja trailed Marnej as he rushed into the courtyard just beyond the hall.

Marnej slashed at the unsuspecting guards.

Dárja grabbed a dead soldier's sword in time to slice upwards, across the soft flesh of an exposed neck. The man's throat sprayed blood into her eye. She wiped it away, but another soldier was already upon her. She swung wildly as her vision blurred. She heard a grunt, then lashed out again, swinging blindly at anything in her way. As she ran, Dárja wiped her face with her forearm, footfalls pounding behind her. She planted her foot, then turned to attack, nearly cleaving Marnej's arm as he fended off two soldiers. Dárja reeled with the momentum, but recovered herself in time to skewer one of the soldiers. Then she and Marnej fought their way past the palisade and picket, taking advantage of the confusion.

As they crossed into the open ground, Dárja sprinted ahead, despite her feet sinking deeper and deeper into the marshy ground. Arrows fell around her with deadly splats. Still, she ran. Her eyes focused on the distant trees. Their tall trunks seemed so impossibly far. Surely an arrow would find her before she found herself in their safety. Dárja ran—begging the gods, then cursing them. She ran until branches whipped about her, stinging her face and arms.

Bleeding and winded, Dárja turned back toward the way she'd come. Bent, with her hands on trembling knees, she watched Marnej. His arms and legs pumped back and forth as he labored to free himself from the fen's sticky hold. She looked beyond him to where the Olmmoš drew their bows. There were mounted soldiers behind the archers now.

Dárja stood up. She held out her arm as she shouted, "Run! Marnej! Horses!"

Then she felt the hot grasp of his hand in hers. He pulled her forward, and together they ran farther into the willow shrubs and downy birch that filled the gaps between larger pines.

"Wait," she cried.

Marnej dragged her ahead.

"We'll never outrun them," she said, breathless. "We have to find the Song."

He grunted. Dárja dug in her heels. She wrestled free her hand.

"We have to find the Song!"

Marnej rounded on her. "I don't know what that means."

"The voices," she said, searching for something he would understand. "We have to find the voices."

Marnej shook his head. "We don't have time." He started to turn away.

"It's the only way," she said, hating the precious moments they were wasting by arguing.

He spun to face her. "I can't just . . ." He stopped short. "Besides you said you couldn't hear them."

Dárja groaned, suddenly wanting to be free of Marnej's hesitancy. She could just find the Song herself and be done with him. But even as she thought it, doubt crept up. She pushed it back down. "That's when I was alone," she said, grabbing Marnej's arm. "But together . . . together we can find it."

"I can't just summon the voices like that," he hedged, shaking his head.

Still, he didn't pull away from her.

"Try," she implored, glancing back over her shoulder, catching movement through the trees. She faced Marnej, taking his hands in hers. "Do whatever it is you need to," she said. "I'll do the rest."

Marnej closed his eyes. Dárja thought he'd begun seeking out the Song. Then his eyes opened. Uncertainty lurked behind their pale suspicion.

"What if it doesn't work?" he asked.

Dárja met his gaze. "Then we'll fight and we'll die."

Marnej nodded, his mouth set with determination. He closed his eyes. Dárja said a silent prayer to the gods, then focused her mind on the Song of All. She repeated her song again and again, as if she could conjure all the other voices. Then she thought of the ground below and the trees around and the sky above. She was a part of it all. She sang her song for the ground, the trees, and the sky.

> *I am daughter of the gods.*
> *I am sister among the Jápmemeahttun.*
> *I started my life at my Origin, with sadness and joy as my companions.*
> *I have braved dangers and met enemies and can see the truth of friendship.*
> *I go into the world to meet my destiny, knowing that the stars watch*
> *over me.*

For a long moment, Dárja heard nothing. Then like the eagle's piercing cry she heard:

> *I am the vessel of a father's soul.*
> *I have journeyed into the realm of the dreams of the dark sky,*
> *And traveled back in a blaze of light.*
> *I enter into the world to meet my destiny,*
> *Knowing that I have been touched by the gods.*

Then all the other songs came flooding in. The trees. The rocks. The birds high on the branches. She felt the raven's breath as it swooped down across the marsh and felt the trees sigh in the new breeze. The earth pulsed like her own heart and she'd never been gladder or more relieved. Dárja wanted to stay as she was, to bask in the beauty and the power of being connected to everything. Most of all, she wanted to find Irjan's song. She longed to hear its strange sadness that she'd found a comfort in for all her life.

But she couldn't. There was Marnej. His presence tugged at her, as if he might pull her back into the Olmmoš realm. Then she heard his song again and this time it was strong and sure. Dárja opened her eyes. Marnej swayed before her like a sapling, then his eyes snapped open, and he doubled over, retching.

Dárja looked beyond his hunched, heaving body, to where the soldiers ran toward them. Their faded yellow tunics darted in and out of the farthest trees. At any moment they would be upon them. The chorus of surging voices swirled around Dárja in a heady mixture of comfort and confidence. She took her fighting stance, instinctively tightening her grip on her sword.

Marnej moaned but seemed to register the change in her stance. He pushed himself to stand just as the soldiers ran past them. He flinched. Gently, so as not to startle him, Dárja touched his shoulder. He turned to face her, swaying with the effort. The soldiers continued to run deeper into the forest. Their frustrated shouts of "Where'd they go?" and "They've disappeared!" overlapped with crushing steps and snapping branches.

"They can't touch us," Dárja said, as much to remind herself as to reassure Marnej. "Not as long as we stay within the Song of All."

Marnej nodded, but his eyes were unfocused.

"Listen to the voices," she urged him. "Call to them. They will protect us. They will guide us back to our kind."

Marnej opened his mouth to speak but his words came out thick and slurred. Then Dárja heard him say, "Our kind."

CHAPTER FIVE

THE TREES BLURRED AS Marnej ran. He caught sight of Dárja. Her face was flushed with effort. Her dark braid bounced against the small of her back. The sun dipped low in the sky but they had not run long enough to have escaped the soldiers pursuing them. Marnej turned back, his foot catching on a root. He staggered but kept his thoughts focused on the voices within.

It was only a matter of time until the soldiers caught up with them. *And then what*, Marnej wondered. *And then the voices will hide us—protect us*, he answered himself silently. *But would they? Would they really?* He glanced at Dárja again. If she was afraid and tired, it didn't show. And then it struck him that he didn't know her well enough to tell when or if she was afraid or tired. She was Jápmea—an Immortal. Maybe she could run forever and never grow tired. But he, despite his training with the Brethren, was afraid. And he was tired. He couldn't run much farther. He needed to rest.

Marnej's eyes searched for a place to hide. He knew he was thinking like an Olmmoš, but he couldn't help it. He was human, or at least most of him was, and he didn't truly believe the voices would protect him. Not after the way they'd fooled him in the past.

Nothing. No boulders. No caves. No hills. There was nothing but an endless expanse of birch and pine trees.

Then Dárja screamed.

Marnej lurched to a stop, circling in place. "Dárja!"

"I'm here." Her tight voice rose from behind low mounded crowberry bushes.

Marnej trampled the berry-laden shrub to find himself teetering on the lip of a pit trap. Dárja sprawled below him in a tumble of branches she'd brought down. The soft earth under Marnej's foot gave way. He dangled momentarily in mid-air before he hit the ground with enough force to knock the breath from his body.

Laying helpless on his back, Marnej blinked. The treetops above blended together. For an instant it seemed the world would collapse in on him. As the air rushed back into his body, he closed his eyes, overcome with relief, then rolled to his side to heave. But nothing remained in his stomach to expel. They'd not had a moment for a sip of water, let alone time to forage for food.

"We've got to get out of here!" Dárja said as she shifted beside him. "Hurry."

Marnej pushed himself up onto his elbow and tried to wipe the foul taste from his mouth. The world around him turned again as if it were shaking itself loose of him. Dárja struggled to stand, then collapsed with a whimper, grasping her ankle.

"Is it broken?" he asked, staring into her dark, welling eyes. He heard panic behind his question. With her dirt-smeared face and her hair tangled with twigs, Dárja no longer looked like a proud Immortal who had fought and killed men in the Great Battle. She looked like a scared little girl.

Dárja grimaced, shaking her head, as she cradled her ankle with muddy hands. "I don't think so," she said in a tight exhale. "But I can't stand."

Marnej hung his head. They'd just managed to stay ahead of the soldiers when they were at a full run. There was no way they could escape while hobbling on three legs between them. He raised his eyes to look at Dárja. "We can't run if you're hurt."

She stiffened.

"I'm not blaming you," he said quickly. "I'm just stating a fact. Even if you could run, I can't. I need to rest. I was looking for a place to hide when you found this." Marnej widened his arms to encompass the pit.

Dárja turned her back on him to crawl away.

"Dárja." Marnej drug out her name in exasperation. When she continued to move away from him, he called after her again. This time his voice shook with anger—the anger of eighteen seasons of snow with the Brethren, while Dárja had grown up cared for by his father, Irjan. Gods how he hated that man for abandoning him, his own flesh and blood, to live among the Immortals. Still, Marnej burned with jealousy.

Dárja looked up the length of the earthen wall. She used her sword to push herself to her feet, then tottered on her one good leg as she reached for the exposed roots. Her repeated and fruitless efforts acted to temper Marnej's acrimony.

"Come on," he cajoled, looking at the fallen branches and the surrounding trees. "You've found the perfect hiding place."

Dárja scowled at him.

Marnej rose to his feet. He circled the pit, regarding it from all angles. If she thought him insincere, so be it. He wasn't interested in soothing her feelings. He just wanted to secure their cover and get some rest.

"Hand me the branches we knocked down," he said.

Dárja continued to glare at him without answering.

"Look," he said. "You're hurt. I'm tired. This hole is well camouflaged. We can hide and rest and then figure out what we're going to do next."

Marnej began to gather the twigs and limbs displaced by her fall.

Dárja didn't say anything as she eased herself back down to the ground. She merely scooted on her hands and knees toward nearby fallen branches, pushing them over to him. The two of them worked in begrudging silence as he assembled a roof over the pit.

When he'd nearly finished, Marnej held out his hand. "Give me your belt."

Dárja sat with folded arms. "Why?"

"If we make it until tomorrow without getting caught, we'll need a way to climb out."

"The Song of All will protect us," Dárja said.

Marnej continued to hold out his hand. "You keep saying that, but it's meaningless to me."

"The voices," she snapped. "The voices will protect us."

"Are they going to get us out of the pit?" he argued, gesturing again for her belt.

Dárja's sullen mouth twitched. She shifted onto her knees and untied the leather band at her waist. Her tunic drooped open and her leg coverings sagged. Dárja grabbed her clothes to keep them in place as she tossed the belt to Marnej, who offered her no thanks. Taking off his own belt, he joined the lengths of leather, looping them around a sturdy root, then tested their strength. Satisfied, he edged back down into the pit, pulling into place the last bit of greenery.

When his feet touched the ground, Marnej's legs collapsed under him. He sank down onto the cool dirt. Seated, his breath escaped him in a long, heavy sigh. Then he leaned back, stretched out, and closed his eyes.

Despite his exhaustion, he was still curiously aware of Dárja beside him. They were strangers to one another. Enemies even. Except that their lives had somehow been bound together by the actions of his father.

Dárja shifted, grunted, and then lay still. He smelled her rank but musky scent above his own fetid odor as fragments of voices overtook his thoughts. He heard Dárja's voice within himself, like the faint whisper of an approaching dream. And then her voice filled every corner of the dark void around him.

I am daughter to the gods.
I am sister among the Jápmemeahttun.
I started my life at my Origin with sadness and joy as my companions.
I have braved dangers and met enemies and can see the truth of friendship.
I go into the world to meet my destiny, knowing that the stars watch
    over me.

Like a longing he could not control, his own voice rose unbidden from the depths.

I am the vessel of a father's soul.
I have journeyed into the realm of the dreams of the dark sky,
And traveled back in a blaze of light.
I enter into the world to meet my destiny,
Knowing that I have been touched by the gods.

Touched by the gods echoed in Marnej's thoughts as he prayed they'd remain hidden from the soldiers who hunted them. Making it safely to the Northlands of the Pohjola seemed too much to ask.

~

Dárja squeezed her eyes shut and concentrated on the Song of All. She tried to ignore Marnej's snoring. Then she counted her own breaths, one after another. It was pointless. Between Marnej's low rumble and her own aching ankle, she could no more escape into sleep than she could fly away from this pit. Annoyed, she stiffly rolled onto her side to stare daggers at Marnej. She hated him for his ease in sleeping.

Marnej's head lolled to one side, his mouth open and his lips slack. His otherwise sharp features softened. Dárja marked the slow rise and fall of his chest, feeling a growing uneasiness in her own. Weeks ago, even days ago, she would've gladly put her blade between his ribs. She'd been so sure of herself. So sure of her enemy—the Olmmoš. She'd done what she believed to be right.

The Olmmoš were never going to stop hunting her kind. They were never going to be satisfied until her kind were wiped from existence.

And Marnej was Olmmoš. More than that, he was a Piijkij. He'd been trained to track and kill her kind. Had he found her in this pit a few weeks ago, she had no doubt that he would've killed her without a second thought. Her pulse began to race. She'd seen him do it on the battlefield. He had plunged his blade into her comrades' hearts. They were dead while he was alive, and she felt the injustice keenly. Still, she could not ignore her part. If pushed to speak the truth, she would have to admit that when she closed her eyes to sleep, she could still hear the cries of those Olmmoš she'd killed in the battle. She could still see their faces.

Dárja winced as she rolled onto her back. She didn't want to look at Marnej anymore. But looking away didn't change the fact he was Irjan's son. Nor did it change the fact he was, at least in part, Jápmemeahttun. Was that why she had saved him? Or was it because he was Irjan's son and that by giving Irjan what he most wanted in life—his son returned to him—she could somehow make amends for what she'd said.

Dárja's breath caught. A lump welled in her throat. She would make it right with Irjan if she made it back to the Pohjola. What was done couldn't be undone, but at least she could forgive him. She should forgive him. He was her bieba. He'd raised her. And when she'd asked, he'd taught her everything about swordcraft and fighting. He'd made her into a Taistelijian. What did it matter that she would remain a nieddaš for the rest of her life? She'd proven herself. She'd killed Olmmoš. Many of them. What did it matter that her body would never change? She was a warrior.

But then, what did it matter that she'd even fought in the battle? She would probably never live to see her people again. Irjan would live out his life believing the worst of her, that she hated him. Dárja pressed the palms of her hands to her eyes. She was determined not to cry, determined instead to hear Irjan's voice within the Song. Again, she willed that familiar refrain to come forward, but she could not hear it.

Marnej stirred beside her. He mumbled, "How long have I slept?"

"Hours," Dárja said, turning to face him.

Marnej sat up. He ran his hands across his face, then through his dirty, straw-colored hair. He blinked as if he were caught between the worlds, then looked around, startled.

"Dárja?"

"I am right here!" she said, her annoyance flaring when she figured out he could neither see nor hear her. Marnej was no longer within the Song of All. *Just like every other Olmmoš*, she thought.

Reluctantly, Dárja pulled her thoughts back from the Song. Unrelenting silence gripped her. It brought her every fear to the surface. She had to fight the urge to turn back to the Song. Then, with a gut-wrenching shift, she succumbed to the leaden heaviness of the Olmmoš realm.

Marnej scrambled back in surprise.

"You left the Song," she said. "Why did you leave?"

"I can't control the voices," he said. "I'm not like you."

Dárja hugged her stomach as it dropped away from the rest of her body. "I don't like being out of the Song."

"Well . . . I don't like being in it."

"You didn't object when we were in the forest outside that Olmmoš fortress."

"And you didn't seem to have a problem being out of it when you were swinging your sword at me," Marnej answered.

Dárja narrowed her eyes, but said nothing more. What was there to say? Marnej was a thankless Olmmoš. She should've left him to rot with his own kind.

"Any signs of the soldiers?" he asked.

She shook her head.

"We need a horse," he said, with such an air of authority that Dárja wanted to contradict him, just for spite. But her ankle had resumed its insistent throbbing. She hadn't put weight on it since her first attempt to stand. Even if she could put weight on it, she couldn't run. She thought of her beloved reindeer, who'd carried her into battle. There would be no reindeer this far south and the Olmmoš preferred horses.

Marnej stood up slowly. Clumps of brown earth stuck to the back of his sodden leather vest and seat of his breeches. He crossed the pit in one long stride, then reached up and grabbed the belts.

"Wait," Dárja said. "You're not going to leave me here!"

Marnej didn't turn around. "You'll be safe here while I go and find us a horse."

Dárja struggled to her knees. "And what if you don't come back?"

Marnej spun on his heel. "Do you believe I have no honor?"

Dárja's hand went to her waist, where her sword should have been. She gripped the fabric at her side. "I know nothing of your honor. I know even less about your skill." That last part was a lie, but she straightened herself as she knelt there, and pretended to be more brazen than she actually felt. "What if you're captured by soldiers? I'd be left here to die. Get me out of this pit, then go get a horse. If you don't make it back, at least I can crawl away."

Marnej's hands balled into fists. A muscle in his neck flexed.

Dárja sensed her sword on the ground by her knee, but she didn't let her gaze waver from Marnej's eyes.

"Fine," he exploded as he released his breath. "But I can't carry you out of this pit. You're going to have to help me."

"Tell me what I need to do and I'll do it," she said.

Marnej tugged on the belts, pulling himself halfway up the side of the pit before dropping back down. He squatted in front of her.

Dárja let her relief turn quarrelsome. "I thought you said you couldn't carry me."

"I can't," he said, lacing his fingers together. "Put your knee in my hands and grab on to the belts. I'll lift. You pull."

Dárja picked up her sword and used it to limp forward.

"Can you climb with that?" Marnej asked, gesturing to her sword.

Dárja gave him a sharp look. She tossed her blade into the forest above, then put her knee in his hands, and grabbed high up on the tethered belts. Using her good foot to find purchase on the earthen wall, she pulled herself up as Marnej hoisted her toward the lip. Cresting the edge, her foot kicked loose a cascade of dirt down onto Marnej who sputtered and cursed.

Relieved to be on the forest floor, Dárja leaned against a tree trunk, her body shaking with the effort to climb out. She watched with bitter interest as first Marnej's sword landed in the crowberry bushes, then the top of his head emerged from the pit. His fingers grazed the gnarled tree trunk a moment before she heard the sound of roots snapping. Marnej fell from sight, landing at the bottom of the pit with a bone-jarring thud.

CHAPTER SIX

"ÁIGIN," BÁVVÁL BELLOWED AS he silently damned the incompetence of his army.

The lithe man wound through the uneasy groupings of clergy and servants who stood about the Great Hall.

"Were you aware a group of Piijkij escaped from the Brethren Fortress?" Bávvál asked.

Áigin gave a passing glance to the prostrated soldier beside him. "It is the first I am hearing of it, my Vijns."

Kneeling, the soldier looked up, adding, "It was only a handful of men."

Bávvál glowered at the soldier, who prudently cowered.

Before Bávvál could say anything, Áigin said, "I can assure you that they will soon be dead."

Bávvál was too hot and now too annoyed with the failings of his men to be so easily mollified.

"I don't want them dead. I want them in chains. Here. Before me. I will choose when and how they die."

Áigin inclined his head, seemingly unperturbed. The man's placid demeanor served to further irritate Bávvál.

"What information have you gotten from Dávgon?" he demanded.

Áigin rearranged his clasped hands. "As you know, my Vijns, the Avr of the Brethren of Hunters is not easily persuaded to speak. It will take more time to convince him to do so."

"No more time," Bávvál said with a finality that commanded the room's attention. Then an idea occurred to him. "How many of his Piijkij fill our cells?" he asked.

Áigin did not hesitate. "Near forty. Some men, but mostly boys and old ones."

Bávvál stood abruptly. The force of his movement nearly knocked back the heavy chair. Those closest to him flinched.

"Bring Dávgon to me," he said. "Now."

Áigin stood rooted in place. His piercing eyes roved about the hall. "Perhaps this is a matter that would best be served by a private audience," he said with a bow.

Bávvál did not let his ire overshadow the wisdom of the suggestion. "Then lead me to him," he said.

Stepping down from the dais, Bávvál ignored the still-groveling soldier and eschewed the assistance of eager acolytes. He followed Áigin through the flustered crowd, pushing aside those too slow to move out of his way.

Once outside of the Great Hall, Bávvál kept a quick pace across the short distance to the defense tower.

"He has said nothing?"

"He has not, my Vijns. I have put pain to him that would break the sturdiest of men. If I continue, I will kill him."

The two men passed through the prison's guarded gate.

Bávvál dismissed a soldier's bow with a curt wave, his plan coalescing. "I will break him. If he knows nothing of the Jápmea female and his own half-breed, then I will at least have the reward of seeing him in pain."

"He does not fear for himself," Áigin said.

Bávvál gave a mirthless laugh. "Dávgon has always prided himself on his fortitude. He will feel different when it is his beloved Piijkij who are made to suffer."

The hitch in Áigin's smooth gait told Bávvál that he had surprised his agent. But with those absurdly long legs of his, Áigin swiftly closed the gap. The two men walked abreast past the pit cells. The dirt walls muffled the defeated voices, but could not mask the stench of their bodies and excrement. Bávvál held his breath, releasing it when they came to the end of the passage at the base of the defense tower.

Áigin peered through the door's slit before lifting the wooden bar from its iron cleats.

"Haven't heard a sound from him," the guard said.

Neither man acknowledge the grim-faced guard as Áigin swung the door wide. Bávvál swept into the cell. Despite the summer heat, the rock walls seeped with moisture. The bare-chested man inside raised his head off the ground where he lay hunched. Thick shackles stretched his arms taut.

"Bávvál," he said, his voice a slur, "have you come to dirty your hands?"

Áigin lunged and grabbed a hank of the prisoner's hair.

The man's head shot up. A ragged gash of a mouth split the man's otherwise pulped and misshapen face.

Bávvál leaned in, relishing the damage wrought upon the man's body. "Could this be the Avr of the Brethren of Hunters? The man who led an Olmmoš army to victory over the Jápmea? You look much worse than the last time we met, Dávgon."

"The last time we met, Bávvál, you betrayed me," the man hissed like a cornered badger through his broken teeth.

If there was ever any doubt in Bávvál's mind about the need for this man to die, it was banished in that instant. Even beaten and bloodied, Dávgon looked ready to fight. Bávvál steepled his hands in front of his mouth, letting the curve of his smile show behind.

"Let us agree we were both the agents of betrayal. You simply had the misfortune to be less skilled in treachery's finer points. Perhaps, if you had spent less time practicing with your sword and more time observing the politics of the faithful, you would not be in this position."

Dávgon's face darkened behind its mottled, bluish hue.

"If I had not practiced wielding my miehkki, you and the rest of your faithful Believers would be dead by the Jápmea blade."

"That is true, Dávgon." Bávvál brought his hand to his heart before adding, "and the gods thank you, as I thank you."

Dávgon lurched upwards, straining the bonds of his chains. He lashed out with a kick that landed across the High Priest's face.

Stunned by the pain, Bávvál staggered back, pressing his hand to his cheek. He sensed more than saw Áigin jump forward. But he heard the satisfying sound of bones being broken. When his eyes stopped watering, Bávvál beheld with savage delight the heaving mass that had once been Dávgon, Avr of the Brethren of Hunters.

Bávvál wiped the oozing blood from his mouth and nose onto his sleeve. The streak of red was vivid on the white background. "Hold him up," he ordered.

Áigin grabbed Dávgon by his shoulders so that he sat in front of Bávvál.

The High Priest bent forward, his hands on his knees for support, but wary of the kneeling man. "The Jápmea and the half-breed, where are they?"

A cough burbled up through the prisoner's throat, followed by what sounded like a laugh. Bávvál's brutal kick to the man's stomach changed the tone of the laughter to a wheeze. Áigin raised his fist but Bávvál stopped him.

"Leave him with his humor," he said with a knowing sneer.

~

The sun's harsh outline softened with a passing cloud. Bávvál lowered his hand which shaded his eyes from the midday heat and glare. He was pleased to see the villagers pushing against the backs of his soldiers, their eager faces peering over shoulders and heads. Whispers grew in anticipation as the solemn procession of counselors and clergy entered the circle. Their flaxen robes had been replaced by red vestments, which set them apart from the muted yellow of soldiers' uniforms and the dull browns and greys of villagers. When the crimson pageant reached open ground it stopped, then parted. A herald raised a short length of polished goat horn. The resounding tone commanded attention, even in its distant echoes.

With his head raised just enough so that he could gaze down his nose, Bávvál advanced to accept a hasty flourish of homage. He then paused in the center of the circle with his hand raised. The whispers died away. Bávvál heard the banners snap above his head as a wind picked up, freshening the stale air that reeked of unwashed bodies and fermented fish.

The herald stepped forward. He drew himself up to his full height with his horn by his side.

"Those gathered here will stand witness to the just punishment of the Brethren of Hunters," the herald called out. He walked the circle's boundary as he continued, "By sheltering those they have been sworn to kill, the Piijkij, these Immortal Hunters, have brought upon themselves the gods' wrath. Be it the deed of one or many, justice holds all accountable."

The herald paused. Bávvál nodded his head.

"Guards, bring forth those whom the gods have chosen for judgment," the herald cried out, stepping back.

Onlookers to the right parted. Their jostling caused a flurry of disgruntled abuse. But they fell silent when the guards dragged forward a man. His bare torso was bruised and caked with blood. His head hung forward under its own weight and the tops of his feet dragged across the ground as the guards carried the man by his arms. Stopping beside the herald, the guards lifted the man's slack head by the hair.

Bávvál stepped forward. "Dávgon, Avr of the Brethren of Hunters, brother among the Piijkij. With full knowledge and free will, you harbored a Jápmea among the Brethren. You trained the creature with the intention of using him to extend the control of the Brethren and to deepen the power of the Avr. You have given your soul to darkness. You stand before the gods charged with betraying your own people."

Bávvál paused to survey the crowd. He could tell that his words were having the desired impact. His pleasure, however, was cut short by a strangled voice.

"I see no gods before me. Only a weasel, pretending to be a man."

Those closest to Bávvál gasped, but the rest of the crowd stood too far away to hear the doomed man's insult.

Bávvál signaled to the herald.

The man's booming voice rose up again. "Bring forward the Brethren."

The crowd pressed in tighter.

Bávvál leaned in closer to the prisoner. "You think yourself unbroken. But, Dávgon, before this day is over, you will beg me for death."

The High Priest stepped back, his attention on the soldiers who led forward a group of what appeared to be walking corpses. The crowd drew back at their sight, then edged closer when the tattered prisoners, mostly boys and old men, were arranged in front of the High Priest. Bávvál again gestured to the herald.

"You, who call yourselves Piijkij, who are the Brethren of Hunters, are brought before the High Priest of the Order of Believers to atone for the crimes you have committed against the gods and their people. Step forward and meet your fate." The pronouncement complete, the herald stepped back. Shouts from the crowd were met by nervous laughter and jeering.

Bávvál raised his hand, calling for silence. "The deeds cannot be undone. Yet, the gods teach that mercy and atonement can be partnered with punishment when justice is served." Bávvál paused to gauge his listeners, prisoners and gathered villagers alike. Assured he had their full attention, he continued, "I say to those of you in chains, foreswear the Brethren's Oath. Pledge soulful obedience as a true Believer and you will find mercy."

Some in the crowd clapped to show their approval. Others taunted the prisoners.

"But," Bávvál said, then waited for the crowd to settle. "Cling to your calling as a Piijkij and you will meet judgment's blade."

A cheer rose up through the crowd. Bávvál felt their bloodlust and it fed his soul.

"Come forth, each of you, and choose!" he called out, letting his words crescendo.

Sweat trickled down the High Priest's spine. The guards holding the Avr brought Dávgon forward, then forced him to his knees.

"Dávgon, I want you to see this," Bávvál said casually, as if he spoke to a friend. To the other prisoners he commanded, "Stand before your gods and choose!"

A giant soldier pushed forward the first hollow-eyed Brethren. The sagging, aged man looked to his leader.

"No. Bihto," Dávgon said, shaking his head.

"I am a Piijkij," Bihto said.

The crowd booed. The giant soldier unsheathed his dagger, then drove it through the man's ribs and into his heart.

Bihto arched, his mouth wide as if to scream. Only a gasp escaped before the light left his eyes. He fell forward onto his knees, then onto his belly. The crowd erupted with a roar. The soldier leaned over, grabbed the body by its feet, and dragged it to one side. Villagers shoved their way forward to spit upon the corpse.

"That is one for you, Dávgon," Bávvál said, as if they played a game of stones.

The High Priest waved impatiently to another soldier who pushed the next man forward.

"Choose," Bávvál said. His command reverberated.

"I am sorry, my Avr," the man whispered to Dávgon. Then he raised his voice and said, "I foreswear my Oath. I renounce the Brethren." The crowd cheered, and the soldier shoved the man to the other side, away from his former brothers-in-arms.

"And that is one for me," Bávvál said. "Can you see how this game is played, Dávgon?" He paused to wait for an answer. When none came, he continued, "I wonder who of us will win?"

Bávvál snapped his fingers. A thin and reedy prisoner stumbled forward, pushed by a guard. Tears streaked his dirty face. He looked more a boy than a man.

"What do you choose?" Bávvál asked loud enough for all to hear.

The youth froze, his eyes upon some lost horizon.

"What do you choose?" Bávvál repeated.

The youth swallowed. "I am Piijkij," he said quietly.

The soldier moved up.

"No!" Dávgon screamed.

For an instant, a spasm of terror passed across the youth's face, then blood burbled over his full lips, and he collapsed. The soldier tossed the limp body with the other in front of the Avr of the Brethren of Hunters.

Dávgon doubled over, his head straining to reach the ground where the bodies lay.

"Oh no, Dávgon, you must watch," Bávvál said, then motioned to the guards to lift the prisoner's head. "We have so many more of your loyal Piijkij to speak with."

Dávgon's body jerked, his head held up against his will.

"You dishonor your men," Bávvál tsked.

Before another prisoner could be called forward, the crowd closest to the gates parted as they exclaimed crude epithets. The soldiers in the inner circle drew their weapons. A mounted soldier rode up to their ranks and dismounted, then faltered, alarmed to find himself face to face with the High Priest. The head of the guards stepped through his men, taking the hapless soldier aside to speak with him in hushed tones.

Voices that had been whispers became boisterous as the crowd grew restless. Those that were already rude became strident. Bávvál himself grew angry at the interruption in the spectacle he had devised. Finally, the head of the guards escorted the newly arrived soldier to where the High Priest waited.

The soldier bowed deeply. "I bring word from our scouting party."

"And?" Bávvál prodded, his ire exacerbated by the heat of the sun.

The soldier looked uncomfortable but stepped closer to the High Priest. Lowering his voice he said, "The boy and the Jápmea have eluded our men."

"Eluded your men," Bávvál's voice rose. "They are but children."

The soldier glanced warily at the scene around him. "They are Jápmean and one is a Piijkij."

Dávgon chuckled softly. A guard kicked him in the gut. He grunted, but his rasping laugh resumed, as he said, "I believe I have won, Bávvál."

The High Priest's head snapped around. His hatred of the man before him clouded out any other thought. His words came out in a shrill shriek. "Cut off his head!"

Startled, the guard holding Dávgon pushed him to the ground, pinning him beneath the weight of his foot. Another guard drew his sword, then kneeled. He brought his blade down on the prisoner's neck. The laughing stopped but Dávgon's head remained attached.

"Off!" screamed Bávvál. "I said *off*. Cut it off!"

The blade came down again. And again. The tip of the sword broke off in the ground. Still, the soldier hacked at the slack body until the head rolled free.

Bávvál lunged forward. He grabbed the head and held it up to the crowd to see. Blood streamed down his arms and onto the white sleeves of his robe.

"The gods' will has been done!" he shouted, then dropped the head on the ground and walked away.

CHAPTER SEVEN

WHEN THE WHITE LIGHT of pain cleared from Marnej's eyes, he looked up to where the roots had broken. The belts once secured to them were now wrapped around his aching wrist. He shifted and felt the stabbing outline of each branch he'd brought down in his fall.

He swore to himself, then called out, "Dárja." When no immediate response came, he thought to add, "Are you there?" But after the protest his ribs made at uttering her name, it seemed a waste of breath. She was there. She was injured. She couldn't walk.

One long moment passed into another. Dárja didn't appear, nor did she respond.

Marnej's certainty turned to doubt. Had she crawled away and left him? She'd said she would, had she been left on her own.

"Dárja." He called out louder though it hurt him to do so. He heard the edge of alarm in his voice.

Marnej rose onto his elbow, then sat up gingerly, but he still couldn't see above the rim. He uncoiled the belts encircling his wrist. The two lengths of leather weren't long enough to wrap around the closest tree trunk, even if he could somehow reach it. The sinking realization that he might be stuck in this hole crashed down on him. Then a dark crown of hair inched forward until Dárja's entire dirt-stained face appeared above him. She looked down at him, as if she were silently judging his worth.

Finally, she extended her hand, her braid dangling like an untrustworthy root.

"Hand me the belts," she said. "I'll secure myself to the tree and then help pull you up."

Marnej was about to object that she wasn't strong enough to pull him up. He stopped himself. Who knew what she could do? *I need to stop thinking like an Olmmoš*, he told himself.

Marnej stood and handed Dárja the belts, careful to keep his movement smooth as doubt crept into his thoughts. Dárja disappeared from view. The small distrustful part of his brain called him a fool. *She can just take the belts and leave.* She'd thought him capable of the same treachery. He tried to slow his breathing as he waited for her to reappear. When she stretched over the precipice to reach down her arm, unfamiliar relief washed over him.

Dárja's hard-calloused hand grasped Marnej's wrist. He pulled against her, at first cautiously, then with surety. He dug his toes into the sluffing dirt, struggling against a landslide of soil and rock. Dárja grunted, straining to draw him up. Then his free hand latched onto a sturdy root and he scrambled up and over the lip of the pit, his cheek in the scruff of a crowberry bush. Catching his breath, Marnej sat up. His left hand was stained red with unripe berries where he had clawed through the undergrowth.

Dárja leaned against the tree trunk, rubbing her wrist. Her brow furrowed. "What?"

Marnej realized he'd been staring, trying to reconcile his misgivings with the fact that she'd once again helped him escape.

"You're covered in blood," he said, voicing the first thing that came to mind.

"Instead of gaping," she said pointedly, "cut a branch so I can bind my ankle."

Dárja's rebuke stung more than Marnej cared to admit. It reminded him that they were allies by circumstance, not by choice.

He bit back his retort, telling himself he could just walk away and leave her. He had no need for her sullen company. Yes, he owed his life to her, but he could discharge that debt. He would find a horse, put her on it, and point her north to her kind. But even as he thought it, he knew it wasn't that simple. Dárja was more than a way for him to escape. She was the only link to his father—and, more importantly, to the truth about himself.

Marnej picked up his sword from where it had landed in the crowberry bushes. He stalked off to the closest sapling, hacked at its trunk until it fell, and tossed it to Dárja.

In turn, she tossed him his belt.

Marnej caught the belt, noting the ugly smirk on Dárja's face as she tore her tunic's hem into strips. He fastened his belt about his waist, tucking his sword into its scabbard.

"I'd like to be near water," she said.

Marnej glanced up. Dárja had braced both sides of her ankle with the bent sapling and had bound it with the cloth strips she'd torn from her tunic.

"In case you're gone for a long time," she said, looping her belt around herself while seated. "I'd like to be near water."

Marnej bristled at the command in her voice. He turned on his heel, determined this time to walk away. He tromped through the crowberry bushes and made it as far as a tight clump of birch saplings before logic overtook his resolve. She was right. He could be gone for hours, perhaps days. It was also possible he could be caught by soldiers and never return. The slow-dawning appreciation of what that meant felt like a rock in the pit of his stomach.

"What's he like?" Marnej asked, his heart pounding with the sudden need to know. "My father, I mean."

A long silence stretched after his question in which only the wind and the birds answered him. When he could no longer bear the insult of being ignored, Marnej looked over at Dárja. He'd expected to see her smug expression staring back at him. Instead, she sat, looking lost, blinking, tears in her eyes. He froze, unsure of what to do. If she'd attacked him with a sword or a knife it would have been more welcome than her tears. He took a step forward. Dárja's hands flew to her face and she roughly brushed them across her eyes.

"He's driven by his love for you," she said, her voice thick and broken.

Her words drove the breath from him like a punch to the gut. He'd been told Irjan was a traitor to the Brethren—a traitor to himself and his dead mother. All the dark stories and furtive whispers came rushing back to him, threatening to push him down to his knees. He hated Irjan. He'd always hated him.

Marnej's turmoil turned to anger. "How can you say that? He killed my mother. He left me. He turned his back on his duty!" Marnej paced in a circle, finding his way through the feelings that clouded his mind and choked his breath. "He spent his life . . ."

"He spent his life trying to get you back," Dárja cut him off, her dark eyes narrow and hate-filled. "And when he failed, he spent the rest of his life in prison, punishing himself for how he had lost you. He didn't turn his back on his duty." She spat in disgust. "He sacrificed everything. For you! He sacrificed himself. Kalek. Me. We all paid a price for his duty to you—his precious son."

Marnej whirled, ready to unleash every injury and injustice he'd kept inside of him all his life. "Don't you . . ."

Dárja sat up straight. "Shut up!"

Marnej sputtered. "Don't tell me . . ."

"There's something moving," she hissed. "Out beyond my sight."

Hooves crashed through the forest undergrowth. Marnej spun in time to face a mounted soldier, charging at him. He rolled to one side, coming up on to his feet, aware that the rider was alone. At least for the moment.

Marnej hoped the rider's momentum would carry man and mount into the pit, but the soldier stalled his horse, bringing it sharply around to bear down on him once again.

Marnej drew his sword, but was distracted by Dárja, who labored to get to her feet. She was drawing her weapon. *She can't stand and fight*, he thought. The soldier charged again, his blade raised to strike. Marnej ducked in time as the clang of metal on metal reverberated through his arm. He ran around the horse, placing himself between Dárja and the soldier. The horse reared up. Its hooves clawed the air before coming down with such violence that the earth shook beneath Marnej's feet. He readied himself. Both hands grabbed his hilt, his legs bent, poised to defend. The soldier sneered and wagged his sword tip. Then the sneer morphed into an ugly grin as the man's attention shifted past him.

Marnej glanced over his shoulder. Dárja leaned against the trunk of a white birch with her sword drawn, her expression wooden. He couldn't tell whether fear or determination ruled her, and he didn't have time to think on it when the soldier spurred his horse, cutting around him, riding directly at Dárja.

～

The moment the horse skirted around Marnej, Dárja had an instant to decide how best to defend herself. With one hand she held her sword. With her free hand she drew the knife from her belt. Taking the short blade by its tip, she whipped her arm forward, sending the knife hurtling at the advancing soldier. The blade flew wide. The momentum pitched her to the ground, and pain shot up her leg, radiating through her whole body. Aware of her vulnerable position, Dárja rolled onto her back as she sliced the air with her sword. Angry sounds of rider and horse filled her head. She swung again, attempting to cut the horse's legs out from under it. The animal reared, its hooves looming over her head, black and menacing. She rolled again, coming up against a tree.

Time seemed to slow as Dárja waited for the hooves to crash down upon her. Then the horse screamed, and the animal stumbled sideways away from her. Its head arched unnaturally. Its eyes were wild. She scrambled to her knees as the soldier fell from his saddle, a bone-handled knife jutting from his neck.

Marnej dove for the horse's reins, barely catching them. The horse shrieked and reared again, then back-stepped, dragging Marnej across the ground. Then, in one swift motion, he pulled himself to standing and heaved himself into the saddle. The horse dropped its head and kicked wildly, wanting to shake him free. But Marnej held on until the animal surrendered with one last obdurate shake of its shaggy head.

Dárja stood, leaning against a tree, as the animal snorted and pawed the ground. She smelled the sweaty tang of the horse's ebbing fear and wondered about its song, what it might sound like. But Marnej cut short her musing when he leaned down and stretched out his arm.

Dárja sheathed her sword, then scanned the area for the knife she'd thrown. She hated the idea of leaving a weapon behind, but there was no time to look for it. With one hand she took hold of Marnej's arm and gracelessly pulled herself up behind the saddle rise. She'd just swung her good leg over the back of the horse's rump when the animal started at the sound of far-off shouting. Dárja cried out in pain as her tender ankle banged into the horse's flank.

Marnej twisted around to look at her.

She looped her arms around his waist. "Go! Just go!" she said.

He nudged the horse's sides and the animal bolted into the rangy woods ahead.

Looking back over her shoulder, the forest was a green blur behind them.

"I think he was a scout," she called out.

"We need to put as much distance between us and them as we can," he said, his voice just audible above the horse's hoof beats and the wind whipping past them.

Marnej leaned forward, pulling Dárja with him as he urged the animal to go faster. With her injured ankle bouncing, she cursed out loud the horse beneath her as she clenched her teeth to hold back a howl of pain.

Behind them, the sounds of trailing soldiers grew louder. Marnej tucked himself lower, wedging Dárja's hands in the fold of his body. The saddle rise battered her ribs, crushing the breath she held. A faint whirring passed her ear, followed by a solid thump on a receding tree, and then another thump.

"They're in bow shot range," she managed to yell.

Marnej veered the horse sharply to the left and then right as arrows flew past them. Pine branches slashed them on both sides. Dárja thought she heard hooves behind her, but she didn't dare look to see if the sounds were real or imagined.

Suddenly, Marnej sat up, bringing Dárja with him. His head shot back over his shoulder one way and then the other.

"Hold on tight," he said and ducked down again.

"I am!" she yelled, her strength beginning to fail as her body drifted away from Marnej and the horse.

For one glorious moment, Dárja registered a reprieve from agony. Then she saw the earth fall away as the three of them flew over a ravine. Dárja screamed and was still screaming when she collided on the ground with Marnej and the horse.

~

It was twilight when Dárja awoke, lying beside a fire. Every part of her body ached. Even a shallow breath hurt. She eased herself up to sit, but her head spun like a spindle, and she immediately laid back down.

"What happened?" she croaked, her tongue thick and dry.

"You fell off the horse when we jumped over the gulley," Marnej said, not meeting her eyes.

Then she remembered. *The soldiers.*

He raised his hand to calm her. "We're safe," he said, adding a branch to the fire.

A moment passed where Marnej disappeared in a pine-scented haze, then from behind the smoky veil hc casually said, "I picked you up, and we rode on."

Dárja closed her eyes. "The fire? How?"

"The soldier had supplies," he said.

As Marnej spoke, Dárja became aware of the saddle blanket beneath her. Her hand brushed against the coarse wool. She nodded her head, thankful, but unable to say the words before darkness reclaimed her.

CHAPTER EIGHT

M ARNEJ POKED THE FIRE, listing the reasons why he should stay and why he should just go. Go and he would be free. Free of it all. His father. The Brethren. The lies, and the truth. Stay and he might be reunited with his father. *Pathetic*, he thought. He'd lived his whole life without his father. Why did he need him now? Indeed, why did he need him at all?

Marnej looked at Dárja, who slept. The flames of their fire lit her face. There was a softness in her features that was not evident when she was awake. He wondered what it had been like for her to grow up with his father. Had Irjan watched her sleep like this? Had he held her close and soothed her nightmares when she was little? No one had done that for him. His childhood fears and nightmares were his own to conquer or risk a beating.

He poked the fire again, sending embers flying into the air. Whatever Dárja believed, his father was a traitor. He'd left his people to live with the Jápmea. He had chosen sides. If Irjan had truly wanted Marnej, he would've come back to the Brethren. Dárja had lauded his father's sacrifice. But what had Irjan sacrificed? *A father who loves his son should be with his son, not living among the Immortals.*

Marnej leaned back to look at the sky, as though the faint stars could give him direction. But the rosy dusk offered him nothing but time to think. He rested his head on the crook of his arm and took a deep breath, closing his eyes, willing himself to sleep. The scent of crushed pine needles and decaying leaves, at once fresh and sour, held his awareness at the surface. He listened to the fire pop and sputter. Dárja shifted, the sound of her deep, even breathing momentarily interrupted.

Marnej opened his eyes. He couldn't sleep. *Not with this light sky*, he thought. And not with soldiers lurking somewhere out there. But it was the growing sense that he'd made the wrong decision that caused him to sit up. *I have no business being with an Immortal*, he told himself. The Jápmea were his enemy. Maybe he couldn't go back to the Brethren, and maybe he couldn't change the fact some part of him was like her, but he was Olmmoš. He was human. That meant he wasn't like her. He didn't have to be like her. He didn't need those voices and the Song to hide. He could take care of himself without them—without her.

Besides, she's better off without me, he reasoned.

Without him around, Dárja could hide in the voices. She could travel north to her people on her own. Then she would be where she needed to be, and he would be where he needed to be. On his own. *It's for the best*, he decided, rolling onto his feet. A trail of pine needles and leaves scattered as he walked to where he'd ground tied the foraging horse.

The horse raised its head at his approach, its ears twitching. Marnej reached out his hand and stroked the animal's neck. The beast snuffled appreciatively. He looked over to where Dárja slept. He would leave her everything. He would just take the horse and ride west. His tracks would draw off the pursuing soldiers, and she would be safe. It was better this way. It was better for all of them this way.

～

The fire was out when Dárja woke. She rose slowly, mindful of what had happened the last time she sat up too quickly. This time, her head seemed steady. She turned to look for Marnej. He was gone. So was the horse. A sinking feeling pulled on her limbs. This time it had nothing to do with dizziness.

Dárja stared at the saddle resting on the ground. She told herself that Marnej wouldn't have left her. Not after all they'd been through together. But doubt's cruel and insidious voice began chipping away at her faith in him. What did she really know about him, other than he was Irjan's son and a Piijkij?

But they'd escaped together. She hadn't forced him to leave the Brethren behind. The Brethren had betrayed him. He'd chosen to flee with her. So why would he leave her now? He could've left her in the woods as they ran, or in the pit as she rested. But he didn't. *The horse*, she thought accusingly. *He wanted the horse*. He'd been adamant that they needed a horse to have a real chance of escaping. But really, if Marnej were to have a real chance of escaping, he needed to be free of her. She was injured. Dead weight. *I might've done the same*, she told herself.

But that last part was a lie. Dárja knew she wouldn't have left him behind because she hadn't. She'd fought alongside him and helped him escape. Together, they'd run into the forest, where she'd helped him find his way into the Song of All.

"Coward," Dárja swore out loud, but she also blamed her own foolishness. *How could I've been so blind as to trust an Olmmoš?*

"Coward," she said one more time, bitterly. But haranguing the absent Olmmoš wasn't going to change her predicament. She was alone and she had to face that truth. To spend more time wondering why wouldn't serve her. She needed to do for herself what needed to be done. Cautiously, Dárja shifted onto her knees. Her whole body ached with the effort. Searing pain shot up her leg and was almost too much for her to bear. With trembling arms, she forced herself to crawl to the spreading branches of a young spruce. Rising shakily to her knees, she cut a long, sturdy branch, then dropped back to the ground, exhausted. As she caught her breath, Dárja whittled the branch's jagged top with the edge of her sword blade, wishing she still had her knife. It was an ugly job, but at least no splinters would dig into her palm. When she finished, she used her sword and new staff to get herself to standing.

Placing all her weight on her good leg, Dárja used the branch as a crutch and limped back to the saddle blanket. Just beyond the blanket's edge, beside the cold embers, lay a leather pouch and a carved wooden cup. She sat down carefully, aware of each throbbing limb, then picked up the pouch. It was heavier than she'd expected. She dumped the contents on the ground: cordage, a whetstone, a poultice and bone comb, and two smaller pouches. One contained tinder-makings. The other had a needle and thread. It was not much, but it was all useful.

Then her eye caught something reddish-brown in the dirt. It was flat and no bigger than her palm. Dárja picked it up and dusted off the dirt. She sniffed it, then held it to her tongue. *Meat.* She tore off a piece between her teeth and chewed, groaning with pleasure. It had been days since she'd eaten, though it felt longer. Her teeth and jaw protested with the effort, but she eagerly tore off another piece, savoring the flavor. Eventually, she would need to find water, but at the moment she didn't care.

When she'd finished the last morsel, Dárja looked around for more. There was nothing but dirt, soot, and trampled weeds. Her disappointment was cut short by the sound of snapping twigs. She froze, listening. For one brief moment, she thought it was Marnej returning, then she heard the grunts and squeals of a bierdna and her cubs coming closer. The crunching sound of crowberry shrubs and saplings came from behind the stand of thick pine to the east. She squinted, looking for any movement, any glimpse of brown among the green. If the bears came through the trees they'd be directly upon her.

Dárja stuffed her supplies in the larger pouch and tied it to her belt. She slung the saddle blanket over her shoulder, then, using both her sword and walking stick, struggled to her feet. Pain flared in her ankle, and she almost crumpled. *Stand and hold your ground,* she told herself, her eyes trained on the eastern forest. The grunts grew louder, then she saw the rustling of the undergrowth. Sweat coated her face and back, cold and slick like eels. Dárja gritted her teeth against the pain as she raised the sword's tip from the steadying ground. The high note of a cub's cry sounded in the distance, then the deep grunts of the mother bear faded away to the south.

Dárja let the tip of her blade hit the ground. She swayed forward, leaning onto the pommel. Her vision swam, and sounds seemed to be filtered through thick wool. She drew a long, shuddering breath. When her eyes finally focused again, she found herself staring at the ash of the cold fire-pit and the forgotten saddle. There was truth undeniable.

Marnej was gone. She couldn't count on his returning, and she couldn't just stay where she was, waiting to be discovered or set upon by wolves or bears.

Dárja pushed herself up straight. She shifted the saddle blanket which had fallen across both her shoulders like a shroud. Using her sword and walking stick to support her, she took a tentative step. A vision of the long journey ahead rose, daunting and depressing. And then questions, sharper than any blade, cut her to the quick. What if she made it back? Could Irjan forgive her? Would he? Wasn't it better to wait here for her end, listening to the sounds of the birds, the trees, and the wind?

Dárja stilled her mind and concentrated. The tendrils of the Song of All began to wrap around her. Longing to be within it, she sent out her own song, each word rising from her heart.

I am daughter of the gods.
I am sister among the Jápmemeahttun.
I started my life at my Origin, with sadness and joy as my companions.
I braved dangers and met enemies, and can see the truth of friendship.
I go into the world to meet my destiny, knowing that the stars watch over me.

A jumble of voices swelled, then rushed across her internal world. They filled her mind, quelling hollow doubts. The voices wound together into the most beautiful chorus, more uplifting than any music. Her soul reached out, wanting to join with everything around her.

Then she heard a song of longing and sadness. It spoke of once running free across the plains. It lamented the weight it now carried. It yearned for freedom. The song was so strong and yet so foreign that Dárja's own song faltered as she listened. *A horse*, she realized, suddenly aware of her body and the pain in her ankle. She fell forward as unbearable heaviness claimed her limbs again.

"No," she cried out, keeping her eyes shut tight, trying to call back the Song.

Sitting on hands and knees, Dárja finally opened her eyes.

Marnej towered above her, seated on the soldier's horse.

CHAPTER NINE

THE NINE BRETHREN SAT in front of the sputtering fire, covered in grime. They leaned in to take turns cooking rabbit meat skewered to their knife points. They grumbled, but exchanged few words.

Those who had eaten stared off into the distance, swatting at the bloodsucking chuoika. A couple of the men stretched out on the ground with their eyes closed, either impervious to the tenacious insects or too exhausted to care.

In the distance a branch snapped.

The nine men sprang to their feet, their weapons at the ready. They scanned the twilight forest surrounding them.

"South. Twenty paces. Behind the fallen larch," one of the men whispered.

"Circle and surround," said another.

The men scattered into the forest. Their footfalls disappeared into the startled rustling of birds. They moved from tree to tree, listening for each other and what else lurked in the shadows.

The yellow of a soldier's tunic appeared from behind a stand of larches. His easy movements were like a deer that had not caught danger's scent. The soldier took two cautious steps before a Brethren grabbed him from behind and cut his throat. The soldier gurgled and fell to the ground. A fleeting spasm contorted his body.

"Ivvár," a voice called out, then more yellow tunics emerged from the surrounding forest.

"Here!" cried one of them.

The soldiers drew together. Too late, they recognized their mistake. Before any could make use of their brandished weapons, they were set upon. In an instant, it was over. They were dead beside their comrade, their yellow tunics soaked red with blood.

Without posture or comment, the Brethren disappeared back into the forest cover to await another attack. When none materialized, the cawing of the crow brought them forth, one by one. As they circled the bodies, one man prodded the dead with his scuffed boot. Another squatted to rummage through a soldier's pouch.

"Beartu, take the pouches. Feles, Válde, their weapons," a sharp voice commanded.

"Gáral, you give orders without a backing," the squatting man said as he rifled through the soldiers' clothing.

Signing to the others to do as he said, Gáral confronted his challenger. "Herko, you have too easily become a scavenger."

The squatting man grunted without looking up. "I take what I need. Nothing more."

"What of the rest of us?" Gáral asked, coming to stand directly behind the man.

"If you did the work of killing, then take what you need," Herko said.

Edo, the youngest in the group, reddened. "You shame the Brethren."

Herko's head shot up. "We're all that remain." He gestured in a circle. "We're not the Brethren of Hunters. We're a scrabbling lot of men, more dead than alive. The sooner you understand that, Edo, the better off you'll be."

Edo sprang forward, his sword leading, but an arm held him back.

"He's right, Edo. We're not the Brethren of Hunters any longer. We're the hunted."

"My oath still stands," said Edo, shaking himself free. "So does yours, Redde, and yours, Herko!"

"Oath," Herko hooted. "We took an oath to protect the Olmmoš from the Jápmea. Which we did. And when we finally succeed in driving those creatures from this world, the weaseling dirt-turners turn against us. There's no honor! There's no oath! There's only this day and the next, until we all are hunted down and killed by the same soldiers we led into battle. That's our reward."

A couple of heads nodded in agreement.

"You may be right, Herko," another voice broke in. "The oath we took to protect the Olmmoš may no longer bind us. But honor does. How many of your friends did you see die the day the soldiers attacked our fortress?"

"Too many!" Herko shouted.

"Did they fight with courage and with honor?" the other asked.

"Válde, you're using pretty words to ennoble a slaughter," Herko said.

"I am asking you to honor your friends, your brothers who have died," Válde said. "Do not dishonor them. Avenge them."

"Enough!" Gáral shouted. "If we stand here arguing like sheep herders over the price of wool, then we will find ourselves facing an army."

Válde did not move. Instead, he examined the haggard faces of each man in the circle.

"Let us take their weapons and turn them against the soldiers, against the Believers. Let us be avenged!"

The last word hung in the air, holding the men in place, even as Gáral encouraged them to move.

There were murmurings of assent.

"If we take this course," Herko spoke up, "then I trust you'll not stay my hand to spare the life of every dirt-turner."

"Herko, do not think so low," Válde said.

The man puffed himself up ready to answer, but Válde cut him off. "Is the farmer tilling his field the one who brought down

Mikko and Lasse and Oaván?" he asked, naming off men close to Herko who had died defending the Brethren fortress. "Let us avenge our comrades on those who acted against us. On those who betrayed us. The Believers are our rightful enemy. They and their soldiers. Let us raze the temples, and let the gods claim their messengers."

The chorus of agreement grew excited.

Gáral endeavored to intercede but was shouted down.

Válde gathered the dead soldiers' weapons.

"Listen," he said, raising his voice above the others. "We may be hunted, but we are still Piijkij. Let us use our talents and skill to strike fear in the hearts of those who chose to turn against us." He handed out the weapons he had gathered. The men fitted the extra blades alongside their own sacred miehkki. The new weapons lacked the beauty and history that Piijkij blades possessed. But, in a fight, they would cleave flesh just as well.

Beartu, who had gathered the soldiers' pouches, shared them out among the Brethren. Herko did not object. It seemed that Válde had found the one thing that could stem the tide of his dissent—revenge.

"We should return to the campfire and douse its flames," Válde said. "We do not have much time to put distance between ourselves and those who track us."

The others agreed, returning to their campsite to gather what few items remained to them.

Standing at the clearing's edge, Válde called out, "Gáral, douse the fire."

Gáral scowled. "So we are to take orders from you now?"

"Leave it be," Herko said, picking up a fallen branch. "You'll get your turn as soon as Válde's honor gets him killed."

The men looked to Válde.

"We travel west," he said.

"Bastards will feel the cut of my blade," Herko murmured with certainty as he swept away their tracks with the bristles of the pine branch.

~

One of the foot soldiers stood at attention. "Sir?"

The chuoði olmmái looked down his helmet's nose guard.

"Your order, sir?" the soldier asked.

The mounted commander removed his helmet, revealing a face dotted with angry red splotches. He wiped his sweat-plastered brow with the back of his hand.

"Take two groups of ten. Fan out. Search for the scouts."

"Sir." The foot soldier hesitated. "The mounted men have speed. They can reach greater distances than those of us on foot."

The commander swatted the midges that buzzed his freshly shorn head. "We'll not waste horses on this search, Niilán. Besides, foot soldiers are closer to the ground and able to see their tracks."

Niilán disagreed but he kept his tongue. Little was ever gained by challenging those above him.

"Yes, sir," he said.

With Niilán at the fore, the two groups of men fanned out into the woods. Some of these twenty-odd men had experience, but most were young and green. They had probably joined the Believers' army in the flush of excitement after the victory over the Jápmea. They were farmers' sons with no prospects or the third, fourth, and fifth sons of families with some land and wealth, but not enough to share. They were young and brash, but their swords wavered in their hands, and they jumped at the sound of every mouse that scampered out from under a bilberry bush. Older than most of the foot soldiers in his squad, Niilán had fought in the battle against the Jápmea and had survived to return to a family and farm already lost to him.

When the woods thinned enough to sight the sun, Niilán paused to look west. He estimated they had covered at least a league, maybe more. The light had changed since they had made their way through the dense forest, and the growing shadows made him wish his men had more training.

"Over here," a panicked shout echoed through the trees.

Niilán made his way over the soft mounds of moss, lichen, and berry bushes. Urgency pushed him to see what the soldier had discovered, but he did not want to risk twisting his ankle on a hidden rock and wind up lame. *A sure way to end up dead.*

His men stood in a stunned circle. By the expression they wore, Niilán suspected death was an unfamiliar sight.

"Do not stand there like sheep in the rain," Niilán yelled. "Set up a four-man sentry. The rest of you look for tracks."

He pushed his way through the new recruits who continued to gawk at a pile of dead bodies.

"All right," he said, breathing through his mouth to keep the foul stench of blood and shit at bay. "You have seen them. Now go back to looking for tracks."

As the men scattered, Niilán knelt to examine the fallen scouts. It seemed to him that death had become predictable in its shape and forms. Like so many on the battlefield, these dead men lay with limbs in awkward positions, their eyes open, staring and lifeless. The blood-smeared cuts and gashes were no longer red and vibrant, but brownish. *This is what we will all look like*, he thought glumly. He reached out and touched the flesh. No longer warm. Then he tried to shut the staring eyes. The lids were stiff, unmoving.

Niilán stood up, drawing the attention of those closest.

"They have a half-day on us," he said with the certainty of a weary soldier.

"What are we to do with the bodies?" one of the sentry asked.

Niilán wiped his hands together as if to clean them.

"We can either carry them back to the rearguard or we can leave them here for the wolves and ravens to pick over."

He let the new recruits' shock play out without comment. Glorious battles were the stuff of legends and joiken sung by drunken men seated before a fire. Dead bodies left to elements and scavengers were the reality behind the tales of high deeds and heroism. It was a hard lesson to learn. But once mastered, never forgotten.

"We need the horsemen," Niilán said.

"We'll lose more time as we regroup," answered the sentry.

Niilán respected Osku's opinion. They had served together before. He knew the man did not waste his words needlessly.

"You are right. But I have no desire to come upon the Brethren with these unseasoned recruits."

"But that's cowardly," one rosy-cheeked youth objected.

Niilán looked him over. Arrogance swelled the boy's broad chest and stubbornness squared his jaw. Niilán wondered if he had ever been that young.

"Do you believe your fate would have been different had you been with these men?" he asked, his tone measured. "Cowardly is looking at the truth and calling it a lie."

With his comrades staring at him, the youth puffed himself up to argue.

Osku cut him off. "From the time they take their first step, the Brethren begin training to kill. None of us stand a chance against that. No freshly weaned pup. No veteran of battle. Without the strength of numbers we will be killed like these men. And you? You'll be just another body for us to drop at your mother's threshold."

The men grew restless.

"What are we to do then?" a voice rang out.

"We send the fastest back to bring the rearguard forward," Niilán said without hesitation. "When we have our army behind us, we go after these killers and hope that we are not the ones caught by surprise."

The general murmur of assent heartened Niilán, who silently wondered whether reason or fear drove these men around him. Aloud he asked, "Who among you consider yourselves fastest?"

A few hands rose.

"Go," he said. "Bring up the rearguard. Explain the condition of these scouts, and impress upon the commander a need for haste."

The three men who had raised their hands turned and swiftly wove their way through the white birches until they disappeared into the deep shadows of sloping pines.

"Who has the sharpest eye?" Niilán asked. "And who have been called the keenest hunters?"

More hands rose. Coarse mocking caused some to withdraw their upstretched arms.

"Spread out in pairs," Niilán said. "Look for signs that might tell us something of the Piijkij and the direction they went."

The volunteers scattered.

Those left behind waited for Niilán's instruction.

"You two," he pointed at the youth who had protested earlier and another standing next to him, "lay the bodies out as best you can. Let us give them what small respect there is to give."

Niilán divided the rest of the duties among the remaining men. "If fortune smiles upon us," he said, "the rearguard will be quick." Then with a lingering look to the dead, he added, "But we may also be here longer than we might like."

With the men set into motion, Niilán had a moment to consider both what he surmised and what it implied. The Brethren had been routed at their fortress. Those Piijkij who survived had not hesitated to kill these soldiers—soldiers they might have once led into battle. Niilán had served under their command. He had witnessed their deadly skills. They were unmatched. He knew he had been right to call for support before continuing on, and only the untried would fault him. The problem was, he now belonged to an army filled with fledglings and upstarts where rank ruled over knowledge.

CHAPTER TEN

D ÁRJA SHIELDED HER EYES to look up at Marnej, seated on the shaggy horse. Relief flooded through her, followed by bitterness.

"You were going to leave?" he asked, eyeing her newly hewn staff.

His incredulous expression proved too much for Dárja. "I thought *you* had left," she said, her rancor rising to the fore.

Marnej jumped off the horse to land in front of her. She took an uncertain step back, and readied herself for a fight, as she had with the bear.

Marnej stood his ground but did not advance. His neck flushed red beneath the layer of grime. "That's the second time you have dishonored me." His voice rose. "You were asleep. I went to scout the area, to see if we were still followed. Which we're not—being followed, that is. We're two leagues from farms to the east and there are hunter's tracks to the west of us."

Dárja opened her mouth but couldn't trust herself to speak. She wanted to scream. She wanted to wipe away the arrogant set to his features. Instead, she limped around him toward the horse.

"I wouldn't have left you," he said to her back.

Dárja snorted but kept moving forward one painful step at a time.

"Are all your kind so filled with suspicion that you can't believe what you have been told?"

Marnej's derisive tone stopped her in her tracks.

"You expect me to believe the word of a Piijkij?" she jeered, struggling to turn around.

"I'm not a Piijkij!" he shouted.

"You will always be a Piijkij." She spat out his title as though it was a nasty taste in her mouth.

"Is that what you think of my father too?" he pressed.

Dárja's reply died on her tongue. Marnej's breath came and went in a quick succession that made his nostrils flare.

"We're wasting time arguing," she said, turning with a hopping half-step to face the horse again.

"You didn't answer me," Marnej said, repeating his question. "Is that what you believed of my father?"

"No," she said without facing him.

"I thought not."

The contempt in Marnej's sharp laugh set Dárja's teeth on edge.

"You hold him in high regard and you condemn me when we're both Piijkij," Marnej continued to harangue her. "I didn't choose to be a Hunter. You can lay that at my father's feet. But here I am, turning my back on everything I've ever known to help you escape. You. A Jápmea."

Dárja spun, nearly stumbling. "Call yourself that ugly name too!" She leaned heavily on her staff. "I didn't ask you to help me escape."

"No. But without me, you'd still be trussed up like a pig on a spit," he said.

"And without me, those Olmmoš that you call family would have torn you limb from limb," she snapped.

Marnej took a step forward to stand over her. "Well, neither one of us would be here if you hadn't been on the battlefield, pretending to be a warrior."

Dárja's eyes narrowed. "Pretending to be a warrior? You ask those Olmmoš soldiers I killed if I was pretending. I only wish I'd had a chance to kill you. I would've, you know. I still might."

Marnej didn't doubt Dárja for a moment. But her threat rankled, and her eyes continued to follow him as if she were the wolf and he the prey.

"What have I done to you?" he demanded, his voice rising. "Is it because I'm Olmmoš and you're Jápmea?"

Dárja's mouth pressed into a thin line. "I'm Jápmemeahttun. Or can't your ill-formed Olmmoš mouth say it properly."

Marnej inwardly damned the crisis of conscience that had made him return to her side. He should've kept on riding west. There'd been nothing craven about leaving her.

"I know you would've as happily gutted me as talked to me," he spat. "But you and I are strangers. We're nothing to each other."

"I am nothing to *you*," Dárja said, her emphasis thick with disdain. "That's right. I've always been nothing, compared to *you*."

Marnej wanted to shake her. He wanted to wipe away the injustice of her scorn and hatred. "I don't understand."

Dárja reared back, as if she thought he might strike her. "It doesn't matter."

Marnej stood his ground. "Yes! It does. You blame me for something I know nothing about."

Dárja leaned forward within inches of Marnej's face. "There's nothing you can do."

"Then take the horse," he snapped, stepping back from her. "Go back to your Immortals."

"Immortals," she scoffed. "Is that what you think? What you Olmmoš believe?" Her laugh came out harsh and ugly. "Haven't your kind killed enough of us to know that we're not immortal?"

Marnej started to argue, but Dárja spoke right over him. "We're not immortal. Our lives are just different than yours."

"Then help me understand!" Marnej shouted, his frustration fueled by the sense of loss he'd kept locked away inside of him.

She shook her head. Her long braid shivered down her back. "Even if you could understand, there's nothing you can do," she repeated, shifting her weight with effort. Her shoulders rolled forward and she swayed.

Marnej reached out to grab her arm, but Dárja straightened. She tightened her grip on her staff, her knuckles turning white with the strain.

"We should go," she said.

Marnej stood rooted, stinging from the bite in her tone. *If spiteful determination is all that's needed*, he thought, then left off the rest as he watched her halting progress toward the horse. Each labored step drew out more of his own shame.

He stepped forward and slid a hand under her elbow. He'd expected her to wrench her arm away. Instead, she wordlessly accepted his help as he shifted the saddle blanket from her shoulder to his.

Marnej snuck a glance at Dárja as he helped her lean against the horse's neck. Her eyes were squeezed tight, her expression pinched. He tossed the wool blanket onto the horse's back, recalling how she'd laid upon on it, sleeping as he'd ridden away. His guilt settled into disgust in the pit of his stomach. *It doesn't matter if she can find the voices if she can't walk*, he admonished himself.

Marnej straightened and smoothed the blanket's folds. When the horse shifted, Dárja rebalanced herself with her wooden staff to stand apart. The silence between them became unbearable. It felt like an accusation. One that he couldn't deny. He briefly thought to ask her what she'd meant when she'd said there was nothing that could be done. But now that they stood so close together it seemed impossible to speak of it. Everything was complicated. Nothing was clear. He almost missed the days of his boyhood when the rules were set and he had only to worry about his training. But even as he thought it, he knew it wasn't true. His boyhood had been anything but simple.

"It will be easier for us to ride together without the saddle," he began, looking to her for an objection. When none came, he continued. "We should avoid the cartways, but it would be best if we found the voices."

Dárja's shoulders rose and fell with a long sigh. "It won't work. Neither of us is skilled enough to bring the horse into the Song with us."

The animal, which had begun to graze upon the low shrubs, raised its head. Marnej patted the animal's neck to soothe it, but his own irritation with a new and unfamiliar world made him want to ride into whatever awaited them, and be done with it.

"But, I saw you and my father and the other Jápmemeahttun," Marnej argued, his voice controlled as he carefully pronounced Jápmemeahttun. "You appeared out of nowhere astride your reindeer."

Dárja turned her head enough for Marnej to see her profile. "The binna we ride have a free spirit. They've spent their lives with us. We know their song and they know ours." She turned to fully face him. "I can't really explain it beyond that. I know this horse has a part in the Song of All but I don't understand it. It would take the skill and strength of someone far older than me, an almai or a Taistelijan, to bring it in against its will. It's complicated."

∽

Marnej's confused expression made Dárja aware that her explanation had only raised more questions. She tried to remember how she'd brought herself and her binna in and out of the Song of All when they'd migrated north to escape the Olmmoš. The recollection immediately brought Irjan to mind, and her heart skipped a beat, reliving her panic when Irjan had suddenly spurred his reindeer into the snowy forest, before disappearing. She'd followed, fearing she'd never see him again. But she couldn't recall exactly how it had happened. It felt as if it was by instinct that both she and her binna acted as one. One moment she was riding after Irjan with the voices around her, and the next she was in the silence of the Olmmoš realm.

She hadn't the time then to think about how strange it had felt because she'd no sooner crossed over than she was fighting off Olmmoš soldiers. The hurt she'd felt realizing that Irjan had not been escaping from the Jápmemeahttun, but rather seeking out his son threatened to crush her once again. Only this time she couldn't draw her blade on Marnej as an enemy Olmmoš and the one who could take her beloved bieba from her because he was helping her return home. And, there was no Irjan here to intercede between them, to command Dárja to return to the Song, even as Marnej pushed him to fight. Irjan was in the Pohjola, waiting. Perhaps not for her, but at least for his son.

Dárja's regret escaped her in a long shaky sigh. "Besides," she continued, "we're so far from the Pohjola and there are so few voices left that it's been hard for even the two of us to move into the Song."

Marnej drew his hand across his forehead, as if he were wiping away the furrows. But the tension in his shoulders told Dárja her answer still didn't sit well with him.

She didn't want to argue anymore. And she didn't want to admit she'd never really given the matter much thought. She'd never had to.

"I don't understand," Marnej said, more a confession than an affront. "You talk about the Song as if I should understand. But I don't understand. I hear voices. Yours. Mine. Others that I don't recognize."

Dárja could see that his agitation was building, and she cut him off, but this time gently. "The Song of All is everything. It's all the voices. Everything has a song." She put her hand up to forestall his interrupting her. "Those voices you hear, the one's you don't recognize, those are the rocks, the trees, the streams. They are the birds and animals. The Jápmemeahttun. They are everything around us."

He gave her a sharp look. "You didn't say Olmmoš."

Off-guard, Dárja hesitated. "No. I suppose not." She paused again. "I've never heard an Olmmoš within the Song of All. I don't know why the Olmmoš don't have a part. But if they did, we wouldn't be safe."

What she didn't say was that this was why the Elders had kept Irjan a prisoner, and why they would also fear Marnej. Irjan and Marnej were both Jápmemeahttun, but they were both also Olmmoš, Marnej even more so.

"Could we just try?" he asked.

It took Dárja a moment to realize that Marnej had returned to his earlier question about the horse. And his earnest expression reassured her that he didn't seek to provoke her. Rather, he held a glimmer of hope. She didn't share his optimism, but it made her willing to consider his request.

"All right," she said, keeping her reluctance well-hidden. "Help me onto the horse, then climb up behind me." Dárja didn't know if being seated on the horse would make it easier to bring the animal into the Song of All, but she dared to sound confident.

"Close your eyes," she said. "Focus on the voices. Center yourself on them and follow them."

Dárja closed her eyes, desperate to hear the soothing sounds of the Song, and to feel a part of something again, instead of feeling alone and besieged. She tried to ignore Marnej's physical presence behind her, the twitch of his leg muscles as he attempted to get comfortable, and the heat of his breath as he finally relaxed. Dárja pushed herself to go deeper within and shut herself off from the Outside. Then, as if emerging from the cool depths of a lake, voices came rushing into her, one overlaid upon another. She added her own to them. She felt the energy of the horse beneath her, the vibrancy of the trees surrounding them, and then, like unsettling intrusion, she felt Marnej. She didn't have to turn around to know that he was within the Song.

She felt as much as she heard his question. "Now what?"

Rather than answering Marnej, Dárja focused on the horse's throbbing pulse just beneath its skin, trying to reach out to it with her own life force. Recalling the animal's sad chorus, and the longing it contained, she pushed her own song into the background, hoping the horse's song would come to the fore and give her the answer she needed. When it broke through it was a low murmur. A muttering.

I was once free.
I ran with the herd.
I was once free.
I ran with the herd.

Then the song swelled, so forceful and so foreign, more feelings than words. But gradually Dárja made sense of it.

We ran with the sun.
We ran with the stars.
Wind rushed.
Grasses bent.
Snow fell.

We are now tied.
We are now bound.
Back swayed.
Flesh cut.
Our path is not our own.

In answer, Dárja cast into the Song of All an image of the horse, running across the tundra, master of its life.

Be with us now.
Be free once again.

The horse shook its head with an agitated whinny. Muttering replaced the powerful images.

I was once free.
I ran with the herd.
I was once free.
I ran with the herd.

Dárja encouraged the horse once more, but was again disappointed. She allowed herself another moment in the Song to bask in the connection of everything around her, even the stubborn horse, even Marnej, his song as much a part of the All as hers. Then Marnej moved behind her and she sensed that he was urging the horse forward. The horse, however, stood still, eating berries and leaves.

"It won't move," Marnej said.

Dárja almost pointed out it was a horse, and what did he expect. But she thought better of it.

"It's not in the Song. I can't make it enter and I can't bring it in," she said. "If we're to travel by horse, then we'll need to travel outside of the Song."

Marnej shifted behind her. She imagined he'd squared his shoulders. She'd seen him do it on several occasions in their short time together. She was coming to understand it was as much a gesture of acquiescence as resolve.

"We have a great distance to travel," he said.

He was right. Even if they could ride the length of the long day, they were still many days from the Pohjola.

Dárja listened one more time for Irjan's song. *Please*. Her wistful plea echoed in her mind. When he didn't answer, she let her own internal voice go quiet. The other voices grew distant and faint. Cut off again, the vibrant thrum of her world collapsed into the oppressive silence of the Olmmoš realm. But this time her stomach held and her limbs recovered more readily than they had previously. She wondered if it became easier with each shift. The prospect unnerved her. Did it mean she was becoming less Jápmemeahttun? She didn't want to be Outside. She didn't want it to be easy. She wanted to be home. She wanted to be back with Kalek and Okta, and most of all, with Irjan. She swallowed back the lump that had formed in her throat.

"Are you ready?" Marnej asked.

"Yes," Dárja said. Her voice held steady.

Marnej flicked the reins, guiding the horse through the trees, heading north.

CHAPTER ELEVEN

FROM WHERE NIILÁN SAT he could see most of the gathered men. The trackers had long since returned to join the watch rotation. The rearguard, however, had not yet arrived. Niilán rubbed his hands together over the fire as he silently dismissed the possibility that the runners had met the same fate as the scouts. He doubted the Brethren would have doubled back. They were seasoned fighters. They would expect an army to follow the scouts.

Through the fire's smoke, Niilán observed his men as they went about their routines. The experienced soldiers not on watch closed their eyes, taking rest while they could. They knew that once the rearguard arrived they would likely be marching through the night. The new recruits sat with their knees hugged to their chests. They searched the shadows with nervous eyes, waiting for something to happen. Niilán had seen a lot of these fresh faces on the way north to fight the Jápmea. Most of them had not come back.

In hindsight, he had no more business being on a battlefield than any of these boys. He had been a farmer, a bad one at that. Niilán and his family had survived because of his wife's family. But even with their charity it had not been enough. Each summer brought a new mouth to feed. Every other winter, the season of snow would lay claim to a life. His wife would mourn the child, then her sorrow would turn to hate that she would direct at him. In turn, he would go in search of a friendly face and cup of juhka at the travelers' hut.

Niilán did not begrudge his wife her feelings. He was, by his own admission, a man singularly blighted when it came to crops and livestock. Barley died in the field under his care. Goats' milk soured at his touch. Still, he had ignored the first call for soldiers, telling himself he was needed to tend to his crops and livestock, however poorly. All the same, one night he had been dragged from his bed by rough men who had informed him he was no longer a farmer but a soldier in the Believers' army. Niilán had struggled briefly and received a lashing for his effort. One sharp taste of the whip had been all he needed to know that his life had taken an unimaginable turn for the worse.

That night, Niilán joined a long line of tired farmers and herders headed to fight the Immortals. Had the gods appeared and prophesized that before the next season of snow he would have fought in and survived the greatest of all battles, Niilán would have dismissed it as a drunken vision of a wind-pissing farmer. But here he was, no longer a wind-pissing farmer, but a seasoned soldier with no farm to return to.

Again, Niilán did not fault his wife. She had believed him dead. In her place, he would have thought the same. He had been pitiable as a farmer. There was nothing in his character to indicate he would be any different as a soldier. But it had been a revelation to him to discover that he was actually glad about how matters had turned out. He no longer had to worry about mouths to feed or whether the barley would survive too much late rain. Plus, he no longer had to grovel before his wife's family for their handouts. He was now a soldier, and surprisingly adept at his new calling. But victorious armies were different than armies at war. In war, it only mattered what you could do with your sword, knife, and shield on the battlefield. Now, he had to contend with men who liked to give orders while standing far removed from danger. *The*

Brethren might be traitors, but at least they had led from the ranks and fought in the battle, he thought with a certain nostalgia.

"Sir," a sentry called out. "The rearguard approaches."

Niilán stood. The fire warmed his back as he regarded the approaching foot soldiers and the mounted guard behind them.

"Niilán!" the commander shouted, riding forward. The man's florid face was even more red than it had been the last time Niilán had seen him, and he briefly considered the possibility that a blight still plagued him. All eyes turned to him when the commander shouted his name again.

Niilán's urge to stay rooted made for a long, awkward pause before he finally stepped forward to help his superior dismount.

Feet on the ground, the commander tossed his cloak back over his shoulder with a flourish. The braided colors of his rank were wrapped around the waist of his yellow tunic. "Give me your report," he ordered.

The setting sun cast an orange hue upon the commander's sanguine face, reminding Niilán of a ripe duordni—a berry he had never liked.

"The advanced scouts are dead," he said without emotion. "Their weapons have been taken. Their supplies as well. Tracks heading northwest from here suggest the Piijkij are on foot."

"The men?" the commander asked, craning his neck to look around Niilán.

Niilán moved out of the man's way. He pointed to where the dead lay side by side. The commander walked around the bodies but did not bend down to examine them, then his eyes darted around the gathered soldiers. Lowering his voice, he said, "There's no need for this tale to spread. It weakens us. Sends the wrong message."

"What is the wrong message?" Niilán asked before he could stop himself.

"Weakness," the commander said with irritation. "The gods have no love for weakness. Nor does the Vijns. Nor do I." His attention shifted back to the bodies. "The Vijns and his people will hear how this army found and killed the escaped Piijkij."

Drawing close to Niilán, the commander said, "Cut off their heads. Choose four of your men to ride. Have them spread word of our victory over the last of the Brethren. But I want the heads lying in front of the Vijns before my regiment returns to the Stronghold."

Disbelief made Niilán careless. "You want the men to lie? To claim their dead comrades are the escaped Piijkij we seek?"

The commander glowered. "There is no lie."

"And their bodies?" Niilán asked, barely able to swallow his disgust.

"Without the head, the bones of a man are no different than any other," the commander said, turning to swagger back to the milling rearguard. Over his shoulder he added, "Bury them if you must. Or leave them for the scavengers."

The man's retreating figure gave Niilán a target for his silent outrage. He had not felt this sick since his first moments upon the battlefield. In fact, he wished he were back in that chaotic mêlée. He might have saved them all this man's leadership by running him through with his sword. But wishing the past changed was as useless as wishing his crops had not failed. Niilán was one soldier, a good one, but not one with power.

At least I can choose my men, he thought. *Though they will not thank me for it.*

"Find Matti and Joret," Niilán called out to Osku and Jonsá. "Meet me back here."

The two shared a look but said nothing. They left without asking their purpose.

Niilán stood over the fallen scouts. He studied the faces of each dead man. One had a hawkish nose. Another had ears that stuck out. Yet another had a wide brow. These details made the men individuals. They had died heroes but their commander would turn them into traitors.

Niilán glanced back at the man encircled by several fawning subordinates. He would never have led them into battle. He would have hung back, shouting orders and berating soldiers who feared to advance. Likely, he would have been the first to abandon his men to their fate. Niilán thanked the gods he had been spared this man's authority in battle. He thanked the gods for the Piijkij who had fought at his side until the very end.

Looking back to the dead men, Niilán reasoned with himself as he came to terms with what he'd been tasked to do. He knew they would feel nothing. *Even so*. To cut off a man's head condemned his soul to wander the forest, forsaken by the gods who could not recognize him. Of all his actions—his failure as a farmer, his bloodlust in the battle, his relief at losing his family— this one, the one he had just been charged with, was the one that he feared would damn his soul.

When the four soldiers appeared at his side, Niilán gave up worrying about what might happen to concentrate on what must happen.

"We will take them to the Piijkij encampment," he said, then bent and hefted one of the dead scouts onto his shoulder. The body sagged against him, releasing a vile stench. Niilán took the lead without comment, avoiding his men's questioning looks. He had orders to follow. But, if this ruse went awry, he had no doubt his commander would denounce him.

At the abandoned camp, Niilán laid down the body he carried, then waited for all the others to be gathered before him.

"The commander has ordered that you each ride to share the news of the Piijkij defeat at the hands of our soldiers," he said to his men. To avoid discussing the obvious fact that the Piijkij had not been defeated, he added, "You will carry their heads as proof."

"But they're our scouts," Osku said. "Our men."

"The commander says they are Piijkij," Niilán said, keeping his voice even and hating himself for it. "These Brethren were slain by our men. They have felt the Believers' power."

Osku stared at him, his disbelief evident. Niilán met his gaze, steadfast. "Go requisition your horses and prepare to ride. It will be done by the time you return."

The four riders departed, grumbling among themselves. Niilán noted that none of them dared ask him his part.

When their yellow uniforms disappeared into the green forest, Niilán grabbed a body under the arms. He dragged it toward a thick, fallen pine tree beside the cold fire ring. With a rough heave, he rolled the heavy body onto its stomach across the tree's trunk, then pulled off the soldier's cloak, and peeled back the tunic collar. Dried lines of sweat and dirt ringed the pale neck. Niilán laid his blade upon the taut flesh.

His stomach revolted as his mind hastened to find a way forward. He remembered how, as a small boy, his mother had once put a hatchet in his hand. The chicken's head was caught between two nails on a tree stump with its neck stretched out. "Do it," his mother had said. The wings had flapped and the screams echoed. His hand had shook. "Do it," she had said, "or I won't feed you ever again."

Niilán raised his sword. With more strength of will than physical effort, he severed the dead man's head from its body. The head rolled off into a patch of bearberries. The body lay across the log as if in repose. Niilán swallowed. His tongue was thick and dry. He grabbed the scout's legs, careful to make sure the gruesome wound faced away from him as he pulled the body aside. Then, with grim precision, he severed the heads of the remaining bodies.

With the last one done, Niilán slumped to the ground. His strength drained from him. He sat back against the log. The scent of warm pine mixed with his dizziness. He leaned forward to rest his head in his hands, but recoiled at the sight of them.

When Osku and the others returned, they each gave him a lingering look before their attention furtively slid away. Niilán got to his feet. He took the dead scouts' cloaks and wrapped each head in the fabric, tying the ends together. He recalled his wife carefully sewing a shroud around each of their dead babes. She would hand him the small bundles to bury. His eyes were always downcast. As were they, now.

From atop his horse, Jonsá hesitated then held out his hand. His mount shied, avoiding contact with the crude satchel. Unwilling to hold on to it, Jonsá wrestled with what to do with the heads. In the end, he dismounted and attached the bundles to his bedroll.

As if in solemn ritual, each man bowed his head before taking hold of what Niilán proffered. But he doubted that this simple, heartfelt gesture would be enough to stave off the misgivings they all shared.

"The burden weighs more than what you actually carry," Niilán said, wanting to acknowledge their sacrifice. Osku persisted in his indifference. While Jonsá's normally amiable nature had turned morose with this duty. Niilán hesitated, aware that these men might never be the same again. "You know the truth. You have been asked to spread lies. I cannot tell you how this will play out in your days and nights, but I do know that it is a duty shared by us all."

The men nodded, their expressions grim. Matti sat in his saddle, looking like he would rather be behind a horse and plow. And Joret's restless hands fiddled with his reins.

"The news must be shared," Niilán said, confirming his own resolve as he shored up that of his men before he doled out their directions.

"Jonsá, go west. Osku, north. Matti, east. Joret, south. Travel to as many farms and villages as you can before returning to the Stronghold by the new moon." He paused, then added, "Do not add yourself to the Brethren's tally."

These last words were an afterthought, but a salient one. Whatever falsehoods they were about to tell, the Brethren remained a threat. Still, Niilán could not shake the feeling that the real danger ranged much closer to home.

CHAPTER TWELVE

MARNEJ BUMPED AWAKE. HE sat in front of Dárja, who held the reins. They'd traveled unnoticed through the forest for three days. Dárja had been anxious to quicken their pace, but he had been careful not to tax the animal. They would not be gifted another horse if they ran this one to ground. So far, they'd been fortunate, but he knew that fortune was fickle, often choosing the most inopportune moments to shift.

"We should stop soon," Marnej said. "The horse needs rest and we need to eat." They'd had little chance to forage or hunt for food, and Dárja had long ago consumed what few rations they'd taken from the dead scout.

"I'm fine," she said. "We should keep going."

Tired and lightheaded from hunger, Marnej didn't want to argue with her. They'd finally reached an uneasy truce where she afforded him a cautious level of respect that had made their time together, if not agreeable, at least bearable. But the horse needed rest and food and so did he.

"Maybe your reindeer can run all day on nothing but air and the Song, but this is a horse and it needs to rest and forage." Without waiting for her to object, he pointed to a grove of birch saplings and lichen covered rocks. "That looks like good forage there."

Marnej couldn't see Dárja's expression but he observed how her hands gripped the reins. Her injury had made her no less willful. After a long moment, however, she eased the horse in the direction he had pointed. At a patch of bright green club moss, she let the reins fall. The animal dropped its head to eagerly feed on tender shoots.

Marnej swung his stiff leg back around the horse's rump. With an unceremonious groan, he jumped to the ground, jolting his spine and his limbs. When the painful tingling faded finally, he stretched his tight muscles, yawning.

Dárja waited for him to help her off the horse.

He was gentle, but she still winced when her foot brushed the ground.

"How's your ankle?" he asked.

"Better," she said.

Marnej didn't call her on the lie.

The horse raised its head and nudged Dárja's shoulder.

"I'm glad you like it," she said, as if she and the animal had shared a private thought.

The horse went back to grazing, and Dárja limped over to a large boulder. She leaned against its rough surface. The yellow lichen blooms sloughed off as she slid down to the ground.

"I'll see what else there is to forage," Marnej said, waiting to see if Dárja would argue.

She didn't. In fact, she'd closed her eyes, resting her head at an odd angle.

That'll hurt, Marnej thought. He moved to right her, then stopped himself. Instead, he walked around the rock to where their horse now feasted on seed-heavy grasses. He had hoped to find bilberry bushes full of nearly ripe berries. But those closest had been picked clean. *No animal is this thorough*. The thought made him wary. He scanned the distance for a long moment before moving farther afield.

Marnej was out of sight of the boulder when he finally found the ripe, almost black bilberries. He dropped to his knees and pulled off a handful of plump berries, stuffing them into his mouth. They burst, sweet and tart all at once. He began to strip the bush of its fruit, mounding the berries in his palm. Bright blue juice dripped between his fingers. Then beneath the leaves of the bilberries, he spied the yellow crown of a guobbâr. Marnej cut the fleshy mushroom off at its base and nested it upon the berries he held, imagining what it would taste like with onions and browned butter. His mouth watered as he swept his free hand through the undergrowth, determined to find more mushrooms.

Dárja's voice broke the afternoon's stillness. Marnej froze, cradling the small cache of food he'd accumulated, as he perceived the distress in her muffled words. He jumped up, dumping the forage on the ground. He ran to where he had left Dárja, his miehkki drawn. Prepared for a fight, he almost tripped over Dárja's still sleeping body.

Relief washed over Marnej as he slumped against the rock. Dárja moaned, her legs twitching as she continued to sleep. The boulder's warmth against his back felt comforting as he slid down to sit beside her.

"Dárja. Wake up." He shook her shoulder.

Dárja's eyes popped open. She sat up. Her hand sought the blade on her belt. She looked wild, as if she'd seen some horror that she could not escape.

"Are you ill?" he asked, his hand still upon her shoulder.

Dárja's eyes fixed on him. She shook free of his hand.

"I'm fine," she said, but her voice wavered.

～

Marnej drew back. "I thought the soldiers had . . ." He trailed off.

"I'm fine," Dárja said again with more force than she had intended. Her stomach knotted, then gurgled with emptiness.

"I managed to find some berries and a mushroom," he said. "But I dropped them when I heard you call out." He stood up not meeting her eye. "I'll go get them."

Dárja wrapped her arms around her mid-section. She nodded but said nothing, worried her voice might crack.

Marnej disappeared behind the rock. She listened as his footfalls faded away through the undergrowth. Her heart still hammered thinking about what might have happened if the soldiers had come upon her. *I would've been helpless*, she thought and began to shake.

A warm breath at her ear made Dárja start. Her hand instinctively went to her knife, but the leather loop was empty. Her panic gave way to annoyance when she noticed it was only the horse.

"Go back to your forage," she said, her tone brusque and sullen. But the animal didn't listen. The horse hung its head close to hers, even after she repeatedly pushed it away.

"Go back to your forage," Dárja said again, this time softer and chiding.

"What did you say?" Marnej asked, leaning around the rock. His outstretched hand held a golden mushroom nestled among fat, dark berries.

"We can roast some fiddleheads," he added, crouching down beside her. "When we come to a stream, I can try to catch us some fish."

The sound of the horse snuffling made Dárja aware of the quiet that had grown around them. Conscious of Marnej resting beside her, she said, "Or we can go to a farm." Then she corrected herself. "I mean, you can go to a farm. Maybe you can get us enough food to make it to the north."

Marnej's expression brightened, and she realized that, for the first time, she was witnessing his smile. It was a lopsided grin that made him look more like a fox than a human.

"Yes," he said eagerly. "We've been so careful. But we need food. I can go to a farm and steal what we need." He popped a berry into his mouth, then held out his trove to her.

Dárja's unease returned as she scooped up a handful of berries. "Couldn't you just ask for some food? Are your kind not generous to each other?"

Marnej shook his head. "Asking leads to questions."

Sunlight cut through the trees, forcing Dárja to squint, but she could still make out Marnej's sly grin as he carved the mushroom. He held out half to her on the tip of his knife. Dárja took it gratefully but couldn't help thinking it would have tasted better cooked with butter and onions.

"What if you get caught?" she asked. The spongy mushroom squeaked as she chewed it.

"I won't," Marnej said.

The smugness in his voice turned the fresh mushroom sour in her mouth.

"But what if you do?"

Try as she might, Dárja couldn't keep the doubt from her voice.

Marnej waggled his eyebrows at her. "I'll sneak in undetected. I'll use the Song."

Without intending to, Dárja let out a bark of a laugh that caught both her and Marnej off-guard. His gaping stare reminded her of a giant perch. She broke down into a fit of coughing laughter at the idea of Marnej as an enormous, wide-mouthed fish.

"Well, that was odd," he said.

Catching her breath, Dárja glared at him.

"There!" he exclaimed. "There's the scowl I know."

Dárja leaned over and took more berries, leaving a few for Marnej. She dropped a couple in her mouth, crushing the juice out of them with her tongue before swallowing them. She shook her head.

"What?" he asked. His eyes narrowed. "Don't tell me I'm not skilled enough to carry food with me into the Song."

"No. That's not what I was thinking," she began to protest.

Marnej crossed his arms in front of him. "Then what?"

"Well." Dárja faltered, her attention momentarily fixed on dark blue stains that peaked out between his splayed fingers.

She looked up. His smile was gone. His features hardened.

"I don't know what you can do?" she said, frustrated that the easy moment they'd shared was now gone. "I've lived my whole life in the Song, but I can't tell you exactly how it works. Or, how it might work for you."

"But you knew we couldn't bring the horse in," Marnej pointed out, his chin leading and defiant.

She wanted to knock it back into place.

"I knew that we couldn't bring the horse into the Song because I'd asked Irjan about it," she said.

Marnej leaned forward. "And what did he say?"

What came to her mind was a vision of Irjan from her recent dream. She shuddered. The taste of berries and dirt welled up as her stomach began to churn. Dárja covered her mouth and turned aside.

"Can't even tell me that, can you?" Marnej snorted, scrambling to his feet. "I'm not asking you to reveal your darkest secrets. I'm just trying to figure out how to survive long enough to get us to Northlands."

"I know," Dárja said, aware that both her anger and the contents of her stomach were about to erupt. She swallowed, breathing in and out through her nose. Finally, she said, "I'm just trying to remember."

Marnej waited for her to continue, his arms still crossed and his arrogance palpable.

"I remember Irjan saying that there were limits to what he could do," she said, then paused, unsure if she could continue. The image of Irjan's dark, pleading eyes hung over her. "I was small, a mánná. I was always asking him questions. I must have asked him about what he could and couldn't do. I remember him saying that he couldn't bring some animals into the Song—like a horse. I remember because I didn't know what a horse was. All I had ever seen were binna. I'd never seen a horse until we'd encountered you and your men. But now I know that they have their own limitation."

"Limitation?"

"Their spirit is broken," Dárja said, keeping her tone matter-of-fact as she recalled the horse's song with sadness. "They can act wild, but they have no free will."

Marnej cocked his head, disbelief written across his wrinkled brow.

"What joy is there in bending another's will to your own?" she asked, her disgust bubbling to the surface even as she endeavored to keep it contained. "Working together. Moving together. Being joined in purpose. That's joy. That is . . ." Dárja struggled to find the right words. "That's how we are supposed to act."

Marnej's frown changed into a smirk. "Do I need to ask permission of the food I intend to steal?"

Dárja labored to get to her feet, her face flushing with the effort and her aggravation.

"You say you want to know, to understand. And I try to explain, but you choose to mock. I don't know why I bother. You've got a wooden stump for a head, just like every other Olmmoš."

"I'm sorry," Marnej said, with surprising sincerity.

Dárja leaned heavily against the rock, letting it take her weight as her anger cooled.

"I don't know what you'll encounter," she said, tired of arguing. "Maybe it'll be easy for you to take what you need. Maybe it'll be like the horse. But if you're not prepared . . ." Her thoughts trailed off.

"It'll be fine," Marnej said.

His confidence was at once impressive and infuriating.

"I won't let you do this alone," Dárja said, hoping she sounded as sure of herself as Marnej seemed to be about himself.

Marnej laughed. He held out his hand to her. "I'd expect nothing less."

Dárja took Marnej's hand, eyeing him to see if the gesture held any scorn. She saw only a genuine smile that, this time, looked more human than fox. As he helped her shuffle over to the horse, she wondered if all Olmmoš were as changeable as Marnej. He was like a frog, leaping from the shore to the lily pad and back again, trying to catch flies. The only problem was that she seemed to be the one exhausted by his antics.

Marnej took hold of the reins and pulled himself up onto the horse. He smoothed the saddle blanket he'd managed to twist, then held out his hand to her once again. The horse shifted as he drew her up in front of him, but Dárja held on tighter to his hand, managing to settle herself in a series of awkward adjustments. With a gentle flick of the reins, Marnej guided the horse west toward the arcing sun.

As the day progressed, the smooth, almost gliding motion of the horse's trot might have lulled Dárja to sleep were it not for the fact that she felt unsettled. She told herself it was because she disliked relying on Marnej. But it was more than that. If she was honest, she would have to admit that she was conflicted.

On the one hand, she couldn't put aside her resentment toward Marnej. His presence acted as a constant reminder of the sacrifice she'd had to make in order for him to be alive. He'd received the life force meant for her when Irjan had interfered in her birth. Dárja thought about the old Jápmemeahttun stories of how the gods had given them the power to transform. Sitting on the horse, with Marnej behind her, she now bitterly wished that power had been enough for three souls. Perhaps then her oktoeadni would have survived. And she herself might have lived a life free of secrecy—free of the fearful knowledge that she would never give birth. Never become an almai.

Still, Dárja had to acknowledge that Marnej was helping her return north—return home. And what of his own home? What little she knew about Marnej had been pieced together from what she'd seen of the Brethren and what she'd overheard from Kalek and Okta. But their knowledge of Marnej was as an infant. He was now, in Olmmoš terms, a grown man and a stranger to her.

"Did you want to be a Piijkij?" Dárja asked, interrupting the rhythm of hooves and terrain.

Marnej shifted behind her, but said nothing. She briefly wondered if he had taken her question as another challenge. Dárja braced herself for what would likely be a biting answer.

"It's all I know," he said cautiously.

Relieved and curious, she asked, "But, did you like it?"

Marnej pulled back on the reins, slowing the horse's pace as they entered a dense, shady grove of pines. "I liked being good at something."

Dárja shivered. She told herself it was her cooling sweat and not Marnej's disembodied voice drifting past her ear that disturbed her.

"I never killed a Jápmemeahttun outside of battle, if that's what you're wondering?" he said.

The vehemence of his response felt like a jab to her back. "Not even the day Irjan came at you, with the rest of us behind him?" she asked, defiance lurking in her tone.

"No," he said.

The finality of his denial stretched out into silence until a crow squawked above them. Dárja took the bird's harsh cawing as censure. *Caw. See what you get for asking questions. Caw.* The crow broke through the branches, spreading its wings, then disappeared somewhere behind them.

"I struck some blows," Marnej said harshly. "Then you were in front of me. And then Irjan came between us."

Dárja watched Marnej's fingers curl around the reins. The blue veins on the back of his hands rippled.

"He wouldn't fight," he said with a snort.

Dárja told herself to ignore the slight. *Let him believe what he wants.* But she couldn't ignore the accusation of cowardice.

"He wouldn't fight *you*," she said. Her emphasis on the last word.

"Because he's my father?"

"Yes. You were—you are everything to him," she said, her jealousy stinging like a fresh cut.

～

Marnej was grateful Dárja faced forward, unable to see his face. All he'd ever wanted was to belong. To have a father who loved him and longed for him . . . that was too much for him to accept.

He swallowed the howl swelling in his chest. He knew he should hate the Brethren—those who'd trained him and those who'd taunted him. But he couldn't. They were all he had.

"I knew I wasn't like the others," Marnej said, to the back of Dárja's head. "Being Irjan's son was a curse I didn't understand as a boy. But as I grew up, I understood and I grew to hate him."

Dárja's back stiffened. Marnej tensed, preparing himself for another unwavering defense of his father. But it didn't come. Dárja said nothing. But whatever gratification Marnej felt was fleeting as he relived the whispers, the suspicion that had slowly eaten away at him. He wanted someone to understand. He wanted *her* to understand.

"Every day I was judged by his actions," he said in a rush. "I had to be better, stronger, and more loyal, just to be considered an equal to the others. But I wasn't like the others. I heard the voices. I didn't know what it meant, other than it made me different. Later, I worried the voices were a sign I was like my father. I thought it was the voices that had made him betray the Brethren." He paused, knowing that he couldn't turn his back on the truth now.

"But I still listened," he said.

"What did the voices say?" Dárja asked, her profile coming into view.

"I used to think they were my mother," Marnej said, his voice as soft as the feeling of Dárja's hair brushing against his face. "A memory of her singing me to sleep."

He cleared his throat. "When I got older, I convinced myself it was the gods talking to me. I told myself that they'd chosen me to remove my father's stain upon the Brethren's noble history." He snorted. "I thought if I was loyal, beyond doubt, then I would be seen as myself and not the shadow of my father."

"But they knew," Dárja said, as if she'd always known this to be the truth.

Marnej shook his head as the betrayal sank into the deepest parts of him. "They knew," he repeated, adding in a whisper, "the Avr knew and he let me believe."

"He let you believe a lie," Dárja said pointedly.

"He let me believe a lie," Marnej agreed, lost in the enormity of what it all meant.

The wind picked up, bringing with it the rustle of birch leaves and the faint scent of smoke.

"I fought for them," Marnej said, then stopped, unable to go on.

"It's not fair," Dárja said gently, her words almost disappearing with the wind.

A long interval followed before Marnej added, "I killed for them."

CHAPTER THIRTEEN

"WE NEED HORSES," HERKO grumbled.

The Brethren had been traveling west on foot for five days. As individuals, they were exhausted. As a group, they were demoralized. For a time, Válde had been able to raise their spirits by appealing to their need for vengeance. He had taken their discord and directed it toward a worthy recipient—the Believers. But each step they took further eroded their eagerness for justice. They were hungry, tired, and besieged by the likelihood that they were the last of the Piijkij, the last of the Brethren of Hunters.

"We need horses," Herko repeated.

"We heard you the first time," Edo said. "But, as you might have noticed, Herko, we are in the middle of a forest and there are no horses around. So, if you feel the need to list the things we need but do not have, please keep it to yourself."

"Prancing upstart," Herko muttered.

Mures smirked at the comment but added nothing as he stepped over the gnarled roots of the rocky path they followed.

"Herko has a point," Gáral piped up, slowing to stop. "It's all well and good to cast us against the Believers, but there are needs that must be met before we can begin to act."

Válde knew Gáral's observation was directed at him. The man's unflagging anger at not being accepted as their group's leader made Válde want to cede the position and be done with the pettiness. But to do so would doom them to ruin. Of all the men in their group, Gáral was the most erratic. His emotions swayed like the grasses. At least with Herko, his motives were clear and consistent. Herko wanted comfort and ease, which for their calling seemed odd. But it was a dependable ambition.

Válde stopped walking. He surveyed the boulder-strewn section of forest they now traversed. He heard the sound of flowing water nearby. It sounded strong enough that he thought it might be a river and not some trickle of a jogaš.

"We should stop and rest here," he said, looking directly at Gáral to see if he would object. "It sounds as if there is a river near where we might have water to drink and a cool place to soak our feet."

A murmur of approval rippled through the group. Válde led the way, listening to the sound of moving water with growing thirst. When they reached the river, it was bigger than he anticipated, and he moved them upstream to where the water widened into a pool around a rocky outcropping.

Some of the men dropped to the ground to lie upon their backs. Others went to the river's edge to drink. Válde knelt on the bank and drew several handfuls of water to his mouth. He pushed past the warm water at the surface to the cool depths, then dribbled water on the nape of his neck, enjoying the refreshing feeling as the droplets slid down the length of his sweaty back.

Pointing into the eddy that fed the pool, Beartu said, "There are fish."

Without hesitating, he cut a slim birch branch, then split its end and whittled a point with deft flicks of his sharp knife. Válde sat down upon the bank, joining the others to watch as Beartu tore off a length of his tunic, weaving it around the four prongs of his spear to widen the gap. Then the man stripped naked and slowly slipped into the pool.

"Careful, Beartu," Mures called out. "The fish might think your dangling bit is a worm."

The others chuckled, but Beartu ignored them. He bent over, peered into the swirling current, and raised his spear.

Válde saw a flash in the water. But Beartu stood frozen, stone-like, his spear poised. The jeers died down. Then the spear flew from Beartu's hand, startling everyone. The fisherman pulled a trout from the water. Its brown-spotted flank twisted on the spear's end.

"Catch us another," someone called out as Beartu tossed the fish onto the riverbank where a round of cheers greeted it.

Beartu, however, was already engrossed in the task.

Válde scanned the stream's edge, then reached down, and pulled up a handful of green stocks with their roots. He held them to his nose.

"There is wild onion here," he said, holding up his find. "What else is there that we can eat?"

A few of the men got to their feet and began to look. Válde noticed Gáral was not among them. Nor Herko.

"Herko," Válde said, getting to his feet and brushing off the pine needles, "You are supposed to have the best nose for finding mushrooms. Do you think you could find us some to go with Beartu's fish?"

Herko complained a little, but did not ignore the appeal to his pride.

Válde looked to Gáral. He suspected the man would eventually get up and try to find forage for their meal, if only to keep the good will of the others.

"I got another one," Beartu called from the water, tossing it to shore.

Válde picked up the two fish. "Get all that you can, Beartu. We could use some full stomachs to stop the bellyaching."

Beartu waved his spear in a salute.

Herko returned, his hands filled with mushrooms. His normally surly face looked pleased. The others noted this with good-natured ribbing.

"Gods spit on the lot of you," he swore back at them as he dropped the mushrooms alongside the other foraged food

Next to a pile of growing foodstuffs, Daigu gutted and cleaned the fish.

Beartu, who had been so still that the others had forgotten about him, threw his spear into the water in a flash of energy. This time the spear came up empty.

"They've grown cautious and wise," he said coming out of the stream, his legs bluish from the cold. His wrinkled feet stumbled on the rocks by the shore.

"Come stand by the fire," Válde urged. "Warm yourself."

Beartu trotted over on tender feet to stand naked near the fire. The water dripping off him disappeared with a hiss as it hit the heated rocks.

Feles brought the man's clothes and boots to him. "Don't stay too long like that or the midges will make quick work of that flesh of yours."

On the other side of the fire ring, Daigu splayed the fish on a makeshift stone hearth. A pleasing sizzle caught everyone's attention. Edo and Mures brought the mushrooms, wild onion, sorrel, and pine sprouts to the fire. Beartu, now dressed, took charge. He lifted up one of the fish, poked at its pinkish flesh, and then placed it back down.

"Come on Beartu," Herko groused. "How much longer must we wait?!"

"If you want to eat your fish raw, Herko, I'm not stopping you," Beartu said over his shoulder.

Herko fell silent. Beartu lifted the fish again. "There's half for each and a handful of mushroom and greens," he said, standing aside to let the others crowd in.

"Skunk-assed-bearshit, that's hot," Redde said, shaking his hand and blowing on his fingers.

Válde clapped Beartu on the shoulder in appreciation, then waited for his portion.

Moments later the sound of a crackling fire dominated the

makeshift camp. The tender fish gave the men something to occupy themselves with other than their old rivalries and recent arguments. The first to finish slaked their thirst at the river, then returned to sit and enjoy a full belly. Herko used one of the bones to pick his teeth. Beartu hummed a low, melancholy tune.

"That was a worthy meal," Válde said.

When the murmurs of agreement died down, Gáral said, "One meal is only one meal."

Daigu complained, "Leave it be, Gáral. Let us enjoy this before you bring us back to all that we lack."

"It's surprising you survived, Daigu," Gáral said, undeterred. "You can't see much in front of your face. Nor do you care to."

The insulted man leapt up, heading for Gáral. Válde blocked his path with a hand to his chest.

Daigu pushed against him, then stood down, returning to where he sat with a rude sucking of his teeth.

"Gáral is right," Válde said, surprising the others. "This is only one meal. Tomorrow it will either be forgotten as we eat another meal or remembered as we go without." He paused, aware that he had everyone's attention. "But each meal builds our strength. Each day we elude capture builds our reputation. Herko was also right to say we need horses. We do. Our safety and ability to strike back depends on speed. Without horses we will only ever be fleeing."

"The question is then, how do we get horses?"

Válde had scarcely enough time to take in Gáral's smug expression before suggestions came from all sides.

"Farms."

"Traveler huts."

"Village stables."

Herko shook his head. "We are nine. We'll need at least five horses but more would be better. Farms, at best, will have a pair. To be sure, the bigger farms, or the wealthier ones, may have more horses, but they also have more people to stand in our way. That's a problem, unless Válde, you've given up your convictions."

"No, Herko. I stand firm that killing farmers does nothing but turn potential allies into enemies," Válde said.

Herko shrugged.

"But, you are right to say that most farms will not have the number of horses we need. One or two horses will not help us," Válde continued.

"A travelers' hut or a blacksmith's stable would get us what we need," Beartu said.

"Preferably a travelers' hut," Redde added. "I've no desire to run the risk of getting caught by being in a village."

"Your aversion to risk sounds more like a measure of weakness," Herko said.

"Herko!" Válde snapped.

"Redde's right," Daigu said. "Getting caught in a village isn't something any of us are willing to risk. At least with a travelers' hut there's a chance of escape back into the forest."

"Feles, where do you place us?" Válde asked.

The quiet man stroked his long red beard before answering. "About ten leagues west of the Order of Believers."

"That's a single day's hard ride," Gáral pointed out.

"Yes, but the soldiers are coming from the south, like us. Not from the east," Feles countered.

"Still," Redde hesitated.

"We must be close to villages and farms," Daigu said.

"The farther west we go, the fewer opportunities we'll have to get horses," Herko said, adding, "And, unlike the Jápmea, I am not keen to ride on the back of a smelly reindeer."

"Don't worry, Herko, you're ugly enough to scare off a whole herd of reindeer," Redde said.

Herko's hands balled into meaty fists. "You're the one that'll run scared."

"Stop it!" Válde shouted. "We have a decision to make. We can continue west and hope to come upon an outlying settlement or traveler's path. Or, we can head east, where we are sure to come upon the northbound trade route."

"The route will be patrolled," Daigu pointed out.

"Then we will need to be careful," Válde said.

"It's decided then," Herko clapped his hands, sounding impatient.

When no one contradicted him, Válde said, "We will have a few hours of rest. Set two watches. We will take advantage of this twilight." He turned to Gáral, "You organize the first watch and I will take the second."

The almost imperceptible twitch of Gáral's mouth served to confirm Válde's concern about his would-be challenger. He and Gáral had never been friends but neither had they been enemies. They had trained together but had been in different regiments. Gáral had distinguished himself in the battle, but also blamed himself for not being able to protect the Avr upon their return. Válde wondered if guilt continued to motivate him. But whatever the origin, the man's need to prove himself would work against them.

Gáral strode toward the perimeter of their camp. "Mures. Herko. Edo. Take the north, west, and east perimeters. I will take the south."

Válde watched their silhouettes fade into the forest. He hoped he had done the right thing by trusting Gáral. If not, then not even horses would be able to save the Brethren of Hunters.

CHAPTER FOURTEEN

As Dárja rode in front of Marnej, she noticed that something unforeseen yet fundamental had shifted within her. When Marnej spoke of his time with the Brethren, she'd not only recognized his struggle, but she'd also identified similar conflicts within herself. She'd experienced betrayal, and she'd fought and killed to prove herself. Despite a childish wish that it was otherwise, she had to admit they were not so different.

Still, he doesn't need to know that, she thought. *He's already overbearing.*

"We're getting close," Marnej said.

Dárja gladly turned her attention back to the present. She heard far-off voices carried on the wind. From their distant tones, she assumed they were an Olmmoš man and woman, but she couldn't tell what they were saying.

Marnej drew back on the reins, stopping the horse.

"I'm going to see if they have anything we can use," he said, placing the reins in Dárja's hand before jumping down to the ground.

"I'm counting on you to not disappear into the Song while I'm gone," he said, patting the animal's wither. His tone was both mocking and veiled.

"I can't bring the horse into the Song," Dárja said. "Even if I could, I don't desert my comrades."

Marnej's grin faded. "I didn't mean it like that," he said, not meeting her gaze. He ran his hand along the horse's neck. "If I don't come back . . . ride north."

Though his insult still stung, Dárja found it difficult to maintain her annoyance. She rolled her eyes at Marnej. "You'll come back. Now, go find us some food. I'll be waiting."

Marnej patted the horse again, then gave her a determined nod.

Dárja snapped the reins lightly, leading the horse back into the green cover of the woods. Sensing that she was being watched, Dárja looked over her shoulder. Marnej stood among saplings, facing her, rooted like the other trees. His smirk was gone. She waved her hand, urging him on.

~

Walking away from Dárja, Marnej's shame hung over him. He'd jested about her leaving, yet he'd been the one who'd left her while she slept. He'd been the one to twist weak excuses into justification so his honor would remain intact. And, he'd been the one to get on the horse and ride west two leagues before his guilt made him turn around.

Dárja had called him her comrade. He felt worse for it. He couldn't call her the same. She wasn't a comrade, nor a friend, nor a sister. She was his link to another world, his savior. But even as he thought it, it felt wrong. A savior brought forth gratitude. With Dárja, he always felt frustrated, as if he were constantly swimming against the current, yet making no headway. Besides, he didn't need saving. He was the one going to get *them* food.

Marnej came upon the edge of a farm. Still mulling over the puzzle that was Dárja, he crouched low to the ground and surveyed the terrain ahead. Green rows covered the tilled field between him and the squat, turf hut in the distance. *At least there will be turnips to eat*, he thought.

Darting forward, Marnej snatched from the ground the closest bunch. Pale white turnips hung below their leafy tops. He tossed the harvest to the nearest tree behind him, then moved forward to grab another bunch, and the one after, pitching them with the others.

From where he knelt, Marnej saw no one in the field, nor could he hear any voices, but smoke rose from the tiny structure ahead. He weighed his options. He could skirt the forest's edge to get within range of the hut, but at some point, he would have to risk being seen to get a better view of their stores. A flash of movement caught his eye. He tensed. His fingers curled around his knife's hilt, then he saw it was only the fluttering of wash hung out to dry.

Marnej considered entering the Song. Even now, he found it hard to believe this other realm existed. He'd thought his earlier experiences, all those voices and sensations, had been visions. Now he knew the Song of All was real. What he didn't know was what he could do within this other realm. And Dárja had been of little help. Marnej reasoned that he was better off relying on skills he'd developed in his own world—the world of the Brethren.

The wind shifted. Marnej smelled meat and vegetables cooking in fat. His mouth watered and his head swam for a moment. He shook off the temptation to run forward and chase after the enticing aroma, reminding himself that Dárja was counting on him. She needed him. And he needed to make amends for his conduct.

Voices drew his attention. A man with greying hair emerged from the hut. He took long, purposeful strides, heading toward a lean-to shed. At the outbuilding, he spun on his heel to face the direction he'd come. A woman's voice issued from within the earthen walls. The man's posture stiffened, then with a brusque wave he dismissed whatever had been said and entered the outbuilding.

Marnej waited to see what the man would do. He didn't like having two unknown points of action. When he felt he could no longer hesitate, he raced across the rye pasture between the forest and the eastern side of the grass-sloped hut. Crouching below the hut's lone window, Marnej looked back across the pasture and winced. Bent and broken stalks marked the way he'd run. His trail was clear to any who cared to look, and his decision to forego the Song now felt reckless.

Marnej closed his eyes and willed the voices to come to him. *Come on*, he silently urged whatever gods had power over the Song of All. What he heard was the sound of a crackling fire and the swift scratch of broom bristles along the floor. A woman's light and absent-minded humming floated out above his head. Marnej forgot about the Song and flattened himself against the wall.

Unable to discern a pattern to the sounds coming from the hut, Marnej took a chance. He popped up to peek through the window, then dropped back down again with his heart pounding in his ears. He held his breath, expecting the woman to come to the window to investigate.

When time passed and the woman hadn't shown herself, Marnej's pulse slowed. He felt foolish for worrying about being discovered when he could just enter the hut, kill the woman, and take what he needed. *It would be so easy*, he thought. He edged closer to the doorway. The scratching broom continued as a counter-point to the woman's low humming. *So easy and simple*, he told himself. If the man returned, Marnej could kill him as well. He and Dárja could then rest in the hut.

Only these two people stood in his way. Marnej's hand hovered above his blade. He was so tired and hungry. An image of Dárja flashed in his mind. Would she think him a monster if he killed these two Olmmoš? Or even care? She hated the Olmmoš. Besides, she thought the worst of him already.

But he wasn't a monster. Whatever else the Brethren thought him capable of, he'd taken an oath. He wouldn't kill the unarmed or the innocent.

Marnej sheathed his blade. Sensing his opportunity was slipping through his fingers, he eased around to the doorway. Beyond it, a wooden cover lay across the ground at an angle to the grassy slope. *A root cellar!* Marnej's initial excitement instantly faded when it registered that he would need to pass by the door to the north side of the hut where he would be clearly visible to the man in the shed.

Hunger won over circumspection. Marnej dashed past the open door, then pressed himself tight to the turf wall, feeling the tickle of grass blades against his sweaty neck. Wasting no time, he bent down and pulled open the root cellar's door. The leather hinges squeaked with a mouse-like protest. Marnej froze, listening. But the humming inside the hut continued as before.

He quickly descended the few steps into the underground gloom. Without waiting for his eyes to adjust, he began to rummage through familiar shapes of vegetables: carrots, onions, turnips. His head bumped into something weighty that swung away from him. Catching it on its return arc, Marnej held the smoky hunk to his nose. *Meat*. It took all his fortitude to not sink his teeth into the curing ham right then and there.

As his eyes adjusted to the darkness, Marnej saw that the cellar contained more than he had expected. Smoked dried fish hung in a neat row. He grabbed the closest one and tore off a piece, shoving it into his mouth. He chewed with earnest focus as he pulled his tunic over his head. The frayed fabric caught on his belt, but he tugged savagely until it pulled free. His hands reached out in all directions, grabbing what he could, to pile food in the middle of his discarded tunic. Speed made him sloppy, and he realized a moment too late that the woman's humming had stopped.

Marnej rushed to tie the corners of his tunic around the bounty. With a curse upon his lips, he emerged from the cellar into the bright sunlight to see the outline of the man walking in his direction, a scythe in hand. Abandoning all pretense of stealth, Marnej sprinted past the startled woman. The farmer chased after him. Rage coursed through the man's shouted abuse. Marnej leaped over the furrowed rows, his feet crushing the growing plants as his heart raced ahead of his pounding footfalls.

"Take this," he wheezed, coming upon Dárja at the edge of the woods.

Dárja caught the bundled tunic just as Marnej pulled himself up behind her. The startled horse side-stepped. Dárja drew back on the reins, but the animal had a mind of its own. It took off at a jolting pace that momentarily threw her backward into him. The heat of her sun-warmed leather vest pressed against his bare, sweaty chest. Marnej's mind swam with her heady scent, his own hunger, and the excitement that rushed through him. Encircling her waist with his arm, he let out a hoot of exhilaration. Then he felt the thrill of Dárja's laughter ripple through her as the two of them flew like the wind.

~

Dárja sat on a rock, watching the horse graze.

"Ready?" Marnej asked.

She popped the last piece of carrot into her mouth, mumbling a yes as she continued to chew.

Marnej grabbed hold of her long braid. He held it out from the nape of her neck, taut. She felt the blunt edge of the cool niibi blade on her skin. Then her head jerked back as Marnej cut upward in one quick motion. Her thick braid, however, resisted his effort.

"Do all your kind have hair like cordage?" he asked.

Dárja ignored the question. Instead she picked up where their earlier conversation had left off.

"Even if the scouts have made it this far," she said, "they'll be looking for a Jápmemeahttun nieddaš and a Piijkij. No one will be looking for two Olmmoš boys riding north."

"The northern trade route isn't safe," he grumbled as he continued to saw at her braid.

Marnej had been erring on the side of caution, keeping them to forested paths. He stole only what they needed, and only when he was certain there was no risk. But her impatience grew daily.

"Oh," Dárja gasped as Marnej severed the last stubborn tendrils of her braid. Her hands went to where her hair had once been. She felt suddenly naked and vulnerable.

Marnej held out her braid in front of her. For a moment, she regarded the long dark coil, then took hold of it, feeling its weight. She picked out a twig from between the plaits.

"Go on," she said. "Finish it."

Marnej took small hanks of her remaining hair and cut them off with his knife. When the soft rasping sound stopped, he came around to stand in front of her. He frowned with hands on his hips as he surveyed his handiwork.

"Well, at least your hair will pass for a boy," he said, "and, if we move fast enough, hopefully no one will take notice of us."

Dárja stood up from the rock upon which she sat. She took a leather tie from her pouch and cinched the cut end of her braid.

"It'll grow back," Marnej said.

Dárja pursed her lips, nodding. Her vision blurred as she thought of Irjan, weaving her hair into plaits for her until she was old enough to do it herself. "So like her mother," Kalek had often commented. But Dárja saw herself in Irjan's likeness, her dark hair like his.

She limped over to the supply sack. Her ankle had nearly healed. Even so, she relied on a walking stick to steady herself on the uneven ground. Tucking her braid into the sack, she felt a nudge at her side.

Dárja reached out her hand and stroked the curious horse. In a low murmur she said, "There are no more carrots." To Marnej, she called out, "Ready?"

Marnej sheathed his knife but made no move toward the horse. "I want to make it to the Pohjola as much as you do. But I don't think it's safe to travel out in the open."

They were back to their old argument. Dárja was convinced the soldiers who tracked them hadn't made it this far north. Marnej was not so sure.

"How much farther, do you think?" he asked.

His exhausted tone gave Dárja hope that he was finally ready to agree with her plan.

"The voices feel stronger," she said.

"You've been in the Song?" he asked, his expression darkening.

"Whenever we make camp," she said, realizing too late Marnej's irritation.

He stood up. A mask had fallen across his face. He came forward, held out his hand for her walking stick, beginning the ritual they reenacted whenever they readied to leave. Dárja handed him the stick, wondering if she should say something else.

He drew himself up onto the horse, then held out his hand to her.

"I am not going to walk away and leave you," she said, the renewed tension between them making her defensive. "I wouldn't do that."

Marnej pulled her up to sit behind him. "This is neither the time nor the place for another argument." He nudged the horse into a walk, threading their way through the dense pine trees onto the trade route. "Besides," he said. "I could've found you. It's what I'm trained to do—find Immortals."

Dárja gaped at the back of Marnej's head.

Before she could retort, he added, "And would it harm you to offer thanks on occasion?"

"Thanks?" she sputtered. Her incredulity nearly left her speechless. "I should thank you?"

Marnej tensed. He craned his neck in all directions.

"What is it?" she asked, looking over his shoulder to scan the road ahead of them.

"Smoke," Marnej said, letting her draw her own conclusions. "We should leave the trade route."

Before either of them could say anything else, they heard the fast clip of horses approaching from behind.

Dárja looked back. The dusty yellow of soldiers' uniforms drew closer.

Marnej swore under his breath.

~

"Stay or run?" Dárja asked.

Marnej's mind rebounded between the two options. Neither gave him what he needed. *Run and they chase. Stay and they catch up.*

Gods be damned they were caught either way. He took another look over his shoulder. The outlines of half a dozen men filled his vision.

"Move to the side," Dárja said, finally. "Maybe if we look like humble Olmmoš, the soldiers will pass.

"And if they stop?" Marnej hissed.

"If they stop, you tell them we're returning to our farm from the market," she said in a tight whisper.

"If I say that they'll search us for coin and kind," he said, knowing too well what Believers' soldiers were like. "I'll tell them we're headed north to look for work as herders."

"And if they don't believe you?" she asked, her voice trailing off.

"Then we'll head into the woods," he said, silently adding, *and hope we can hold them off in a fight.*

Marnej slowed the horse to a walk. He eased the animal to the side, as if he were expecting to give way to those going much faster.

The riders came upon them four astride in the lead and two following. Marnej willed them to pass, but his training made him keen to observe the threat they posed. The four soldiers in the front were older, their faces hardened by many seasons of snow. The two in the rear were young, nearer to his age.

Of the two closest soldiers, one wore his blade on the right and the other on the left. It was this second soldier that concerned Marnej. In one motion, the man could swing around to slash both he and Dárja.

"How far to the travelers' hut?" one of the men called out.

Marnej turned, noticing Dárja's sidelong glance. The soldier who'd asked the question had a scar across the lower part of his face that looked fresh.

"I don't know," Marnej said. "We are ourselves traveling north."

The soldier with the scar eyed him. Marnej was relieved that Dárja did not meet the man's gaze.

"Our farm lies far to the east," Marnej said.

One of the seasoned soldiers sniffed. "Návrrás farmer."

"Turnips," the youngest soldier said wistfully.

"I wouldn't mind some turnips," said one of the older men, his eyes appraising both Marnej and Dárja.

Marnej hunched his shoulders. He furrowed his brows, hoping he looked sufficiently cowed. "I'm sorry, honored soldiers. My brother and I have no food."

"That's a big sword for such a young lad," the scarred one said, edging his horse closer.

"It's our father's," Marnej said, sensing Dárja stiffen behind him. "He died in the battle. It's all we have left of him. I let my brother carry it so he feels better about traveling so far away from our farm." Marnej felt that he rambled but he could think of no other way to diffuse the situation. "We've got a mother and younger brothers and sisters to care for. We're hoping to get taken on as herders."

The soldier glanced at the blade again and then at Dárja. He flicked his horse's reins. The animal started, jumping ahead of the others. Over his shoulder the scarred one said, "Take comfort that your father rests with the gods."

He may have said more, but his words were lost in the sound of the soldiers setting off at a trot.

Marnej slumped back into Dárja, releasing the breath he'd been holding.

"What was that 'honored soldiers'?" Dárja mimicked him. "I would've shoved my knife into his belly and given him another scar. One to remember the Jápmemeahttun."

Marnej straightened. He guided their horse toward the woods to their right.

"What are you doing?" she asked. Her mocking had turned into alarm.

"We need to get off the trade route."

"No. We're close," she insisted. "We fooled them."

"For now."

"We can do it again."

"Why are you suddenly in such a hurry that you're willing to risk ending up back where we started?" Marnej demanded.

"Why can't you just go along with me instead of always questioning me?" Dárja spat back.

Marnej led the horse into the pines.

"Can't you feel the pull?" Dárja's question trembled with desperation. "Can't you sense we're near?"

"You're giving me too much credit," Marnej said evenly. "I don't spend my time in the Song like you do."

"Stop," Dárja ordered. "Get off the horse."

"Why?" Marnej hedged.

"Because I'm tired of reasoning with the back of your head."

"I'm not getting off the horse" Marnej said.

"Why? Because you think I'm going to race off with it?"

"Maybe."

Dárja shifted. "Maybe I will."

Marnej turned around to look at her. "What are you doing?"

"I'm getting off the horse."

"But the soldiers could come back."

"If they do, they'll find two brothers having an argument because one of them is so sow-headed he won't listen."

Marnej watched Dárja as she slid off the horse. "Give me one reason why we need to risk our lives on the trade route, when we could go through the forest and be safe."

Dárja's short, uneven mop of hair momentarily blocked her hateful glare. But hostile eyes had watched Marnej his entire life. They had peered out of the Brethren faces of boys and men alike, making hallways feel dark and crowded and food taste like sand even when he was hungry. The constant scrutiny had made him quick to anger, merciless in fights, and resentful of his wounds. And all because he was Irjan's son.

If only his father hadn't betrayed the Brethren's oath.

If only. If only. If only.

Marnej had lived his whole life wishing for another one. And now that there was one waiting for him, with the Immortals, with his father, all he could think was, *What if?*

What if Irjan's not to blame?

What if I'm not worthy of his love?

Dárja brushed the hair from her eyes. Their dark intensity bore through him, condemning him, confirming his worst fears.

"You can come with me," she said. "But you can't stop me."

CHAPTER FIFTEEN

IN THE FIVE DAYS since Dárja's outburst, she and Marnej had not spoken about what had happened. In fact, they rarely spoke, keeping to topics of food and shelter, of which they'd found far less than they'd hoped. Neither of them considered sleeping rough under the twilight sky a hardship, but food, particularly meat, had been scarce. Still, Marnej was surprised when Dárja agreed he should try and get them food at a travelers' hut. He wondered if her new affability was the result of hunger or a heavy conscience.

Probably hunger, he thought.

"I'm just going to see if they have any food to spare," he said, handing her the reins. Dárja took them without comment. Her gaze remained fixed on a point beyond the travelers' hut. Taking a chance, Marnej asked, "Will you wait here?"

Dárja's attention snapped back to him. Her dark eyes were guarded, as if she'd suddenly been backed into a corner. Then, with a sullen shrug of her shoulders, she said, "Yes."

Dárja claimed to steadfast and true, but Marnej wondered if she'd come upon a moment of doubt as he had. Perhaps she'd succumb to the pull of the Song she'd spoken of, the one he couldn't feel. He left her to her conscience and crossed beyond the stable to a door cut into the sloping sod roof. He didn't look back. He didn't want her to know the depth of his concern.

Marnej pushed aside the thin linen curtain meant to keep out flies. He ducked under the doorframe. It took a moment for his eyes to adjust to the gloom. Then another to get accustomed to the smoke. The cramped room had a bright fire going, over which hung a pot of some kind of soup.

A round woman with an equally round face came toward him. She wiped her hands on her apron, streaking its rough surface with blood.

"Here for food?" she asked, hands on her wide hips, "or something to drink?"

Aware of the woman's frank appraisal of him, Marnej decided against asking for food right away.

"News, if you have it," he said, noting they were alone.

The hutkeeper raised an eyebrow. She took hold of a wooden spoon and began stirring the soup. The weak aroma hinted at a thin, watery broth with little to recommend it. Still, to Marnej's starved body, it was enough to make his stomach growl.

To hide the tell-tale sounds of his hunger he said, "I heard thieves have been seen nearby."

The woman stopped stirring. "Likely. We don't take much notice up here in the north.

"Soldiers passed my brother and me several days back."

She laughed, more disgusted than amused. "Several days back and many leagues south. We've no soldiers in these parts. We're left to sort things out for ourselves." She paused. "But, if you've heard word of thieves, then keep your wits about you."

Marnej sensed a softening in her demeanor. He hoped it was an opening for his real need.

"Would you happen to have any food to spare?" he asked, then, seeing the woman's cagey expression, promptly added, "Not for myself. It's for my younger brother, waiting outside. We've had no food for days, and I'm worried he'll starve before we make the Pohjola."

"I doubt that," she sniffed. "You can pitch a pinecone from here and hit the Northlands."

"But," Marnej began.

"Either you've got coin or kind to pay for food, or you don't. Here in the north we don't dole out charity to strong men who can work."

Marnej was about to object, but the woman raised a finger, warning him, "Not even if they have a starving little brother waiting outside. If you've got nothing, you get nothing. Now I've given you valuable advice. Use it wisely."

With her hands back on her hips, Marnej knew he stood a better chance of milking a bull than changing this woman's mind. He ducked back through the curtained door, squinting into the light that streamed through the trees. He looked to where Dárja sat upon the horse, and couldn't help but notice that even with her mop of cropped, dark hair, there was no way to mistake her for an Olmmoš, let alone his little brother. The curve of her waist and hips was apparent even with her shapeless tunic. And the muscle of her arms and shoulders rivaled his. Marnej mumbled his thanks to the gods who, so far, had kept fortune on their side.

"No food," he said. "No soldiers either." He signaled to her to scoot forward so he could get onto the horse.

"You ride in front," she said, shifting back. "I'm sore from sitting on the shoulders."

"Withers," Marnej corrected her.

"Withers," she repeated, holding out the reins.

Marnej patted the stalwart animal, offering the horse praise before saying to Dárja, "You ride. I'll walk. The hutkeeper said we're very close to the Pohjola." He said the last part as if in passing, then waited to see her reaction, knowing that getting to the Northlands was all Dárja cared about.

Still, it stunned him to hear her state matter-of-factly, "I know."

∿

Marnej removed the saddle blanket from the horse's back, then slipped off the bridle as Dárja stroked the animal's neck. She leaned in close to whisper something he couldn't hear, then she patted the horse's flank. It didn't move. Instead, it turned its eye to Dárja and circled around her.

"Go on," she said aloud, shooing the animal off.

The horse shook its head, its forelock coming to rest across one eye.

Dárja stroked the animal's long arched back. "There are none of your kind here," she said softly. "You're free. Go. Find them."

The horse nickered, then started off at a trot.

"I hope you're right about this," Marnej said, watching their mount disappear into the distance.

"We won't need him," Dárja said. "We're close."

Marnej regarded the green rolling hills, spare of trees, but dotted with red and yellow, where berries peeked out in the scrub-covered landscape.

Dárja held out her hand to him. "Close your eyes. Find the Song."

Marnej did so, but was uncomfortably aware of Dárja's hand in his, remembering when she had first held it like this. She had said, "Listen to the voices. Call to them. They'll guide us back to our kind." *Our kind*, he repeated to himself.

Dárja had called the Pohjola home. She'd said *they* were going *home*. And they were almost there. And yet, Marnej couldn't believe he had a home, not when so many doubts scurried about in his mind like mice in an autumn field.

Dárja's hand suddenly felt hot in his. When sweat made their grip slick, Marnej thought she would slip out of his grasp and disappear, leaving him alone. He tightened his hold on her hand, crushing the bones, then loosened his grip, fearing he'd hurt her in his panic. Marnej took a deep shuddering breath and tried to release it slowly. He felt her fingers intertwine with his. His heart raced. It seemed a lifetime since he'd entered the Song of All.

Marnej pulled his attention inwards. But it was as if he was tethered to a stubborn beast. Gradually his heart slowed as he listened to the sounds that were both a part of him and outside of him. When his shallow panting eased, he began to feel light, full of air. A peaceful stillness beckoned him to lie down and surrender to visions just beyond his reach.

In an instant, the stillness shattered into a thousand different voices. The cacophony drove Marnej to press his hands to his ears in a futile attempt to block out all the competing fragments. The abrupt knowledge of what the earth feels, what the wind hears, and what the air believes stirred within him. He gasped, begging the gods for mercy. All those voices, vying for attention. It was too much.

Marnej opened his eyes, ready to run, and staggered forward. Dizziness pulled him down. He shook his head to focus, but his vision blurred. He took another step, and stumbled. Still the voices surrounded him, filling his head. He searched for his own thoughts in the maelstrom that had taken over his mind. But the other voices were stronger than his own. Then with devastating clarity he heard:

We are the Jápmemeahttun.
We are the guardians of the world.
Our memory stretches back to the start of days.
Our vision reaches beyond all tomorrows.
We sing together as one so that our one may always survive.

The refrain repeated over and over, mixing with his own thoughts and memories. The Avr. The Immortal army descending through the valley. Green fields. Flashing swords. Then a refrain that had been murmuring in the background came to the fore. He heard the new voices in his head, but felt their power in his heart.

We are the Taistelijan.
We are the warriors of the Jápmemeahttun.
Our swords serve our kind in death.
Our knowledge our continued life.
We walk into battle to end what was long ago begun.

Then he heard Dárja's voice, as if she was within him. So strong. So full of purpose.

~

"Marnej?" Dárja said, shaking his arm as he swayed with his eyes open. "Marnej."

He blinked, unhearing.

"Are you all right?"

He blinked again. The dark centers of his eyes narrowed. "It just takes getting used to," he said.

He shook his head. His hair was a straw-colored halo.

It occurred to Dárja that, up until this moment, she hadn't thought to inquire about what Marnej had experienced within the Song.

"What does it feel like?" she asked, masking her curiosity by picking up their supply bag.

Marnej looked around him, as if he were seeing the world for the first time. "Didn't you ask my father that?"

"No. Why would I?" Dárja replied, bewildered by the question.

Marnej held out his hand for the supply bag, but she put it over her shoulder.

"Because we're the same," he said, his tone suggesting that he'd just stated something obvious.

Dárja was about to say that they weren't the same at all but stopped herself. "I suppose I think of Irjan as Jápmemeahttun. He's been with me my whole life."

"It's strange," Marnej said, rubbing his face with both hands. "Everything's slightly blurred. I feel dizzy, like when you spin in a circle too long." He furrowed his brows as he took a step forward. "And it's hard to walk. It's like the ground is shifting under my feet. I can't find myself in all the voices." Marnej massaged his temples. "I want to shout at them to be silent. They make my head hurt."

"I miss them when I'm Outside," Dárja said. "I feel alone. Cut-off."

Marnej's confusion deepened. "Outside?"

"In your world," she said, then clarified. "Not in the Song."

"Well, inside or outside, it all looks the same. But it feels," he hesitated, then gave her a rueful smile. "This is the first time I've had to think about it."

"But you've been in the Song before," Dárja said."

Marnej nodded slowly. "But this is the first time I've talked about it."

He took a wobbling step, then another more assured one. "At first, when we were escaping. I didn't have time to think about how I felt," he said. "I just knew we had to run. But now you're asking me to look at what I see and feel." He paused again. "It's not easy."

Marnej's discomfort made Dárja self-conscious, as if she were causing him pain.

Changing the subject, she said, "Well, if you can walk, we still have a bit ahead of us."

"I can walk," Marnej said.

His prickly tone put Dárja immediately on guard.

Then he raised an eyebrow and gave a lop-sided grin. "You're the one who's hobbled."

She laughed. "I'll make it there before you."

His grin widened. "That's because you know where we're going and I don't."

"Home," she said. "We are going *home*."

Squinting at the distant tree-line, Dárja began walking east. She wanted to run. She thought of Irjan and Kalek and Okta. They would all be there. Her friends, too. A twinge of conscience made her look over her shoulder at Marnej. He gave her a smile which she returned, even as doubt began to creep in around her. She'd been so focused on getting back to the Pohjola she'd pushed aside concerns. She'd told herself she'd think them when the time came. Now she had to face the fact the time had come. She had no idea how Marnej would be received.

"Alive," Marnej said from behind her.

Dárja stopped. "What?"

"Everything feels more alive," he said.

~

Marnej fell into step behind Dárja. There was something different in the way she held herself, as if the strain that had made
Dárja so rigid had been replaced by something resembling ease.
She was still impatient, but there was a quality of anticipation
rather than agitation. For this reason, he'd allowed her comment about going *home* to pass without correction. He'd wanted
to point out that it was *her* home, not his. But perhaps it would
become his home as well, a place where he might belong, a place
where he could begin to know his father. This idea filled him
with wonder. He thought of Irjan, the father he'd never imagined wanting. The sudden need he felt unnerved him. Marnej
shook the thought of Irjan from his mind, focusing on his own
song while the words rose within him.

I am the vessel of a father's soul.
I have journeyed into the realm of the dreams of the dark sky,
And traveled back in a blaze of light.
I enter into the world to meet my destiny,
Knowing that I have been touched by the gods.

As the rhythm of the chant rose and fell, some part of Marnej,
perhaps the Olmmoš part, began to question how this song came
to be a part of him. He'd never heard the refrain until he encountered his father that first time. Yet, he knew that this was his
song. It was his soul made into music.

Marnej listened intently, as if he were hearing his song for the
first time. And, in some ways, he was. His song sounded much
stronger now, like a shout instead of a whisper. Each refrain
came to him layered with meanings, all of which clamored for his
attention.

"You're singing," Dárja said.

It took Marnej a moment to realize that she had spoken to him out loud.

"What?" he asked.

"You're singing."

"You said everything sings."

"I mean . . . you're singing out loud."

Marnej felt a flush rise up his neck toward his ears.

"Not that it was bad," Dárja added quickly. "You have a nice voice."

Now Marnej's skin burned with humiliation. Eager to shift her attention he said, "Where does your song come from?"

"It was given to me by my oktoeadni," she said, her voice trailing away with the wind as she walked ahead of him.

"Oktoeadni?" he repeated, unsure of what she meant.

"The one who gave birth to me," she said.

"Your mother."

"Yes," Dárja said after a slight pause, "but Irjan is the one who sang it to me. He is my biebmoeadni."

"Your guardian," Marnej said.

"Mmm," she agreed, still ahead of him.

"Where did mine come from?" he asked, cringing at how pathetic he sounded.

Dárja stopped, then turned, waiting for him to fall into step with her. The Dárja he'd known before they'd crossed into the Northlands would've looked smug, every bit an Immortal. But this was a different Dárja, more human somehow.

"I don't know," she said. "Your mother?"

She said "mother" slowly, taking care to match his tone and inflection.

"What was your mother like?" he asked.

Dárja grimaced. Marnej glanced down at her ankle, thinking she had stepped wrong.

"I didn't know my oktoeadni," she said, picking up her pace. "She died."

With his longer stride, Marnej caught up to her easily.

When it became clear that Dárja would say nothing more, he said, "I didn't know my mother either." This confession made Marnej feel instantly weak and vulnerable. The truth was, he had learned the words for *knife* and *sword* before he had learned what a mother and father were. His father, Irjan, had killed his mother and left Marnej to die. This was the explanation offered by the Brethren when he was old enough to ask about his parents.

"I know," Dárja said, bringing Marnej back to the present.

Startled, he stammered, "Do you know . . . how she died?"

Dárja shook her head but didn't meet his eye. "Irjan rarely spoke of your mother."

Marnej's anger flared without warning, clouding his judgment. He reached out to make her stop and face him, but drew his hand back just as fast. He'd learned that forcing Dárja to do anything never worked in his favor.

As they descended a small stony ridge side-by-side, the sharp click of Dárja's walking stick on rocky ground was the only sound, now that the harassing wind had died down.

"He rarely spoke of her because it was painful for him," she said, breaking the silence.

Even though she'd spoken softly, Dárja's pronouncement hit Marnej like a rebuke. And yet, desperation pushed him to ask her what she knew about his mother. What did she look like? Did Irjan truly love her? Did she love me? The questions within him cried out for answers, but the words would not come out.

Instead, fear of the very answers he sought made him ask, "How did your mother die?"

When Dárja didn't answer right away, Marnej glanced at her. To an untrained eye, she appeared to be concentrating on where to step as they descended the hillock through juniper and birch scrub. However, he had spent a full moon cycle observing her. To him it seemed she struggled with something inside herself.

"You don't have to answer," he said, wanting to recapture the ease they'd finally found with each other.

Dárja nodded her head and walked on, her mouth pressed into a grim line.

As they trudged up the long slope of the next ridge, Marnej found it hard to settle into a comfortable stride. The voices bombarded him. They pushed against one another, competing for his attention. If he attempted to follow just one voice, he would become overwhelmed. But if he just let the sounds pass through him, without fighting for control, then he could almost discern the hypnotic melody of the All.

When they crested the hill, Marnej was so engrossed by new sensations that he hardly noticed the changing vista. Dárja, however, let out a gasp that brought him back to himself in time to see her break into a limping run across the plateau ahead of them. Off in the distance, the broad, dark outlines of a structure cut across the blue sky. His heart skipped a beat. He recognized the outlines of the wooden spires and the rounded cornice crenellation. He had seen them in one of his visions. Yet he couldn't find the right name for what he now saw. The structure was neither fortress, nor temple, and it was clearly not a hut, nor a farmhouse. But it *was* the home to the Immortals. This much he knew.

Marnej ran after Dárja. He told himself he ran to protect her from falling. But really he ran, just as she did, to reach those far-off walls which he hoped would be a sanctuary. As they drew closer, he slowed, letting Dárja gain a long lead. When she reached a low stone wall with a carved gate in its center, she stopped. Though still some distance back, he watched her struggle to open the gate. Finally, she gave up and climbed over the stones.

Marnej slowed further, taking in all the details. A yellow lichen bloom on the dark wood of the edifice drew his attention. He recalled a verse he'd memorized as a boy.

The yellow-eyed raven god
dove down from skies with open claw,
to wrest the helpless soul from flesh
and make the journey into endlessness.

Marnej also recalled the resounding clout to the head he'd received for asking why a Piijkij needed to learn the verse. The old brother who'd taken pleasure in hitting him took equal pleasure in informing him that death claimed all, but rewarded few.

Reaching out, Marnej touched the wall before him. It was no trick or fancy he'd invented. Splintered and deeply grooved, the wood looked as if it had been charred by fire. The yellow lichen, by contrast, blazed like the sun. *The yellow-eyed raven god.*

Across a garden of herbs, Dárja banged on a door. Marnej stepped to the stone wall just as the door opened. A pale Immortal with long blond hair and broad shoulders appeared, then stooped through the low door frame.

Dárja collapsed to the ground. Her words lost in sobs. The pale Immortal dropped to his knees and embraced her in his arms, rocking her back and forth, his face tucked into her neck. Marnej felt he should turn away, but the part of him that longed for this kind of greeting made him stare, until he noticed that he also was being observed.

Part Two

BEYOND ALL TOMORROWS

CHAPTER SIXTEEN

KALEK WRAPPED HIS ARM around Dárja's shaking body, cradling her as she rested her head against his shoulder. He touched his forehead to hers and breathed her in. She smelled of forest, dirt, and sweat, but she was alive.

Movement beyond the garden caught Kalek's eye. A tall, sinewy Olmmoš boy stood behind the stone wall. His grime-smeared face peered out below a thick crop of straw-colored hair. Kalek had not seen him before, but he knew this was Marnej. The boy possessed the same arrogant stance as his father. But for the color of the hair, it was like looking upon a young Irjan.

He and Irjan had been such unlikely allies. Irjan had saved Dárja's life, and Kalek had saved his. Together they had risked both their lives for the boy. On the coldest days, he still felt a dull ache where he had been wounded. Kalek did not want to be reminded of Irjan sitting alone in his cell, blaming himself for the fact Marnej would grow up, as he had, to be a Piijkij. He wanted to remember Irjan as he was in their last moments—whole and honor-bound.

The boy stood still, watchful. He was likely as dangerous as his father had once been. If Kalek had learned anything in his time with Irjan, it was that the Brethren trained their Hunters to be ruthless. But the boy was with Dárja. If she had been his captive, then circumstances had changed. Still, Kalek could not shake the feeling of foreboding that almost overshadowed his joy in seeing Dárja once again.

"Come, let us get you inside," he whispered in Dárja's ear, pulling her to her feet.

"Both of you," he added, beckoning Marnej with a curt wave.

Once inside the apothecary, Kalek sat Dárja down before the fire. He stoked the embers to life, glancing back to see if Marnej would enter. When the doorway filled with shadow, a small, petty hope died. Kalek secretly wished the boy would return to his kind. But, like his father, Marnej was as much Jápmemeahttun as he was Olmmoš. He was a part of their future, whatever that might look like.

"Come, sit and rest." he gestured.

Still, the boy hung back.

"There is a stool here for you."

The boy cautiously stepped forward. When he neared, Kalek saw that Marnej was taller than his father, with pale grey eyes instead of Irjan's dark ones. Tightness squeezed Kalek's chest.

He cleared the lump from his throat. "I am Kalek," he said, stepping away from the fire to make room for the boy to sit.

"I am Marnej," said the young Piijkij as he sat down warily.

Kalek busied himself with putting water to boil on the fire. "We have no food here in the apothecary, but I can make some tea to warm you."

Dárja rewarded him with a weary, wordless smile.

Marnej said nothing.

Kalek noted that he kept his eyes on Dárja. She, by her expression, tried to reassure him.

Looking directly at the boy, Kalek said, "You are welcome here."

Doubt narrowed his Olmmoš eyes.

With more force than relief, Kalek said, "The war is over."

Dárja and Marnej shared another look that made him believe they both had been a part of the battle, but had no desire to recount events.

Dread washed over Kalek as he walked to the clay pots lining a shelf. He brought down one and then another, fighting the urge to look back at Dárja. He scooped out herbs into two wooden cups, then ladled boiling water into them. The smell of warm uulo and muorji acted as a balm to his nerves. Kalek handed one cup to Dárja and the other to Marnej, then observed them with a healer's critical eye.

Sharp angles carved Dárja's tan face. Her arms, once roped with muscle, stuck out like twigs from her tunic sleeves. She was not the mánáid he had watched grow or even the fiery nieddaš who had defied them all. She looked as if only part of her walked in this world.

Marnej, on the other hand, twitched like an oarri whose cache of nuts was threatened. He sat with his spine straight, his eyes darting from side to side, poised to either fight or flee. The two of them, sitting in front of the fire, were like the sun and the moon. Yet, there was something between them.

I cannot tell them about Irjan now, Kalek thought, then promised himself he would, once they had rested.

"I will go and fetch food for you," Kalek said, easing toward the door. "Drink the tea. When I return, I will look at your ankle."

Dárja jumped to her feet, knocking over her stool. "Irjan," she said, ignoring the scalding tea she had spilled down the front of her tunic.

Panic gripped Kalek as the two of them looked at him with hope in their careworn faces. He could not speak the truth. Yet. So he lied.

∾

"Are you sure I'm welcome?" Marnej asked, pacing.

"Yes," Dárja said, her eyes on the door. "You're safer here than you were with your own kind."

Marnej snorted.

"I've known Kalek my whole life. He would not lie."

Marnej fiddled with the knife on his belt. "I can't believe that a Piijkij would be a welcome sight here."

"Irjan was a Piijkij and Kalek trusted him. You should trust Kalek," Dárja said, impatient. Her stomach was in knots and no amount of tea would soothe it.

"But you said Irjan was in prison," Marnej argued, "Why would I be treated differently?"

Dárja wanted to tell him to sit and drink his tea. She opened her mouth, then shut it, as her sense caught up with her. Her own feelings toward Marnej a might've changed, but she couldn't be sure what the others would say or do were they to know about him.

Her hesitation put Marnej on his guard. He strode toward the door that led to the herb garden.

"They won't put you in prison," she called after him, projecting confidence she actually lacked. "Kalek's right. The war's over."

Marnej circled back. "Then where's my father?"

Dárja didn't know where Irjan was. But she wasn't about to admit that. Nor could she admit that she wondered what was taking Kalek so long to get him. "Irjan will be here," she said. "He will be here soon."

Marnej took up his pacing again. "Just as likely, he'll return with guards to haul me off."

Before Dárja could argue, Marnej's words tumbled out of him, his stride acting as a counterpoint.

"I didn't travel to the ends of these lands to find myself in a cell next to my father."

Dárja leapt to her feet to stand a breath away from Marnej's face. "What will it take? Do you want me to go the prison and prove Irjan isn't there? Or do you want me to promise that I'll go in there with you? Because I've been in a cell. I've been a prisoner. Have you?"

"I don't need to be here," Marnej said, heading to the garden door again.

"Fine!" Dárja shouted. "You go out that door. I'll go out this one."

Dárja stood in the door frame, one foot in the apothecary and one in the torch-lit passageway. Marnej's scraggly jaw tightened, as ugly as it was obstinate. *Let him rot with the rest of his kind*, she thought. *He's not my responsibility. I saved him once. That's enough.*

Marnej glared at her. His distrust was as plain as any feature on his dull Olmmoš face. Dárja slammed the door to the apothecary shut, cutting off the view, then turned and ran, a fresh wave of pain adding to her anger and her doubt. She was finally home, finally safe. *Why couldn't he just hold his tongue?*

In truth, she didn't know where Irjan was. Being part Jápme-meahttun had afforded him some privileges. However, he was part Olmmoš and a Piijkij. Perhaps even after all these seasons of snow—after the war—they still considered him a threat. Dárja hurried along the corridor toward the gathering hall. She heard her name being called, like a fly buzzing her head. Rather than stop, Dárja ran. She focused on how much farther she still had to go to reach Irjan's quarters. *Cell*, she reminded herself.

Arriving at the prison corridor, she saw that no torches burned and no guards stood sentry. Winded and flustered, Dárja waited until her eyes adjusted to the gloom. Then she edged along the familiar passage stalked by a growing sense of apprehension. Throughout the journey home, she'd prayed to the gods. She'd made bargains with them. She'd promised anything and everything, if she could only make amends. Now, standing mere steps away from what she professed to want, she faltered. Dárja rested her palm on the door and felt the solid grain beneath her hand. She'd believed her anger justified, but she'd been a coward.

Dárja held her breath as she banged her fist on the stout wood. The door opened with a creak. She pushed harder and the door swung wide. The cell was empty. Her heart skipped a beat. Was Irjan free? Was he somewhere in the sanctuary? Maybe he was eating or with the binna. Happy memories of gangly-legged reindeer calves, with their soft ears and noses pressed into her hands, came flooding back.

Wherever he was, her bieba walked free. Dárja chided herself for letting Marnej plant doubt in her mind. Gods, he was able to bring her to madness faster than anyone she'd ever met. Still, she had to agree that he'd been right to question his safety. She wouldn't have walked into the Brethren's embrace upon his word of welcome alone. But she'd expected that kind of faith from him. Dárja retraced her steps with a new wave of anxiety. She needed to make sure that Marnej was, in fact, truly safe and welcome.

～

Marnej crossed the apothecary. He followed Dárja out into the passageway, cursing her the whole way for being so stubborn. *She's worse than an ox stuck in mud*, he mumbled under his breath, then stomped down the corridor, rehearsing what he would say when he caught up with her.

She couldn't have gotten this far ahead, he thought as he jogged around another corner. His next thought vanished when he came to an abrupt stop in a large, open hall. Marnej gaped at the scale. Based on the apothecary, he'd expected all the rooms to be small and cozy. A ridiculous assumption. Why would Immortals limit themselves in any way? Still, the wide expanse stretched the bounds of his imagination. The ceiling appeared to be supported by immense trees. Staring at them, he realized they weren't actual trees but towering, lifelike carvings. And among the carved trees stood the Immortals.

Marnej looked from one face to another, unable to do anything but blink. Women and children stared back at him. The women varied in age, but none were grey-haired. Marnej momentarily wondered if the Immortals aged at all. Then he saw several white-haired men standing off at the far side of the hall. Wizened and stooped, they appeared ancient beyond all measurable time. Then it struck him there were no younger men, like himself, or like Kalek, nor boys for that matter.

The women whispered among themselves. Some began to retreat, drawing the younger ones to them. He scared them, even though they greatly outnumbered him. Still, they might see their advantage and come at him as an angry mob. Marnej took a step back, then felt a hand on his shoulder. He whirled to face Kalek.

"Let us return to the apothecary," Kalek said with more concern than his demeanor belied. Guiding Marnej away from the hall, he added, "I have brought you and Dárja food."

Marnej accepted Kalek's counsel gladly, but he also made sure they weren't being followed by the others.

"They're afraid of me," he said, peering back over his shoulder.

"Yes," Kalek said without turning or stopping.

At the apothecary, the healer stood aside and waited for Marnej to enter first. Suspicious, Marnej rested his hand lightly on his miehkki. The weapon's heft comforted him. He cast an eye about the room. Empty, as he'd left it. Kalek closed the door, and Marnej spun on his heel, still on the defensive.

"You should eat," Kalek said, placing a platter of food upon the long work table.

If Kalek had noticed Marnej's hand upon his sword, he didn't mention it. Instead, he motioned for Marnej to sit. "Where is Dárja?"

Marnej eyed the dark bread and pungent cheese. Hunger gnawed at him as he noted with particular interest a roasted leg of some small fowl.

"Dárja left to find Irjan," Marnej said. "I tried to follow but ..." He left off unable to explain. What should he say? He couldn't tell Kalek that he and Dárja had fought because he didn't trust the healer. Marnej sat down on a stool and stared at the food. His fingers eased over to the platter. He picked up the fowl by the bone. It was still warm. Marnej's mouth watered and his mind swam with want, with weakness. His stomach, however, churned. He slowly placed the meat back on the platter.

"I'm only one man. Yet, they're afraid of me," he said finally.

"You are like your father," Kalek said, his tone not unkind.

Marnej rubbed the smooth wood of the table. "Because I'm a Piijkij?"

"Yes, that." Kalek said.

The grim set to the Immortal's features told Marnej there was more to it.

Then it came to him, and he felt himself redden. "It's because I'm here. Because I am within the Song of All," he said. And it occurred to him that, at some point he'd begun to think of himself as Jápmemeahttun.

Kalek's broad brow furrowed. "I thought the Elder's visions concerned your father. Now, I believe they spoke of you."

Marnej's throat tightened. "What did they say?"

Kalek exhaled, his eyes downcast. "They said that our undoing walks among us."

Marnej reeled back as if he'd been hit. He slumped against the table, the food forgotten. He searched for the conviction to defend himself, to tell Kalek it wasn't his choice. But he'd heard the voices. He'd used his skills to seek out the Immortals.

"I'm no threat to you," he said, as much to assure himself as to convince Kalek who sat as still as stone, observing him.

"I hope that is true," the healer said, taking another deep breath. "But then . . . perhaps the worst has been done."

Marnej flinched, truth cutting deep. "I did what I was trained to do," he said. "But that's over now."

Kalek pursed his lips and nodded.

"Am I truly welcome here?" Marnej wondered out loud.

The Immortal met his gaze directly. "I say you are welcome. What others might say remains to be seen." Kalek paused, his features softening. "We have all lost so much."

"Then I'm not welcome," Marnej said, getting to his feet.

"I didn't stand beside your father all these seasons of snow to cast you out now." Kalek said. "Sit."

Marnej sat back down, aware of the weariness in the healer's eyes.

"You and my father are friends?" Marnej asked hesitantly.

The Immortal shook his head. "No. We are something beyond friends. A friend you make by choice. Your father and I are joined by something much stronger than a choice."

Kalek's broad shoulders seemed to sag, as if he'd been fighting some unseen battle and had finally lost.

"How did you meet?" Marnej asked, breaking the silence that had stretched out between them.

"I killed one of your kind, before he could kill your father," Kalek answered dully.

This made no sense to Marnej. "A man was going to kill my father? An Olmmoš?"

"No, a Piijkij," Kalek corrected him. "Irjan tried to stop the Brethren from taking you, but he was too late. They had laid a trap. Your father was fighting one of your Hunters and he lost his balance. He looked to be finished. I stabbed the Piijkij through the back with my sword."

Kalek's pale eyes dared Marnej to comment.

Marnej glanced away. A moment passed. "Vannes. You killed Vannes," he said, remembering the story from his boyhood. "It was further proof of my father's treachery."

"Your father might have been a traitor to the Brethren, but he never betrayed what he valued most."

Marnej did not need Kalek's pointed look to know what he meant. He'd already heard Dárja argue the matter more than once. Still, he couldn't believe he'd always been his father's sole concern. His heart might wish it to be true, but his mind dismissed it as impossible. A man who cared so much for his son didn't leave him alone.

"You should eat," Kalek said, pushing the platter closer to Marnej. "You have had a long journey."

Under the healer's watchful insistence, Marnej took a tentative bite. He didn't think he would have the stomach for food, but the taste of the fowl with its thick layer of vuodja and dill reawakened his hunger. The butter had cooled, coating his tongue in delicious fat and bright herbs. Marnej tore off a piece of rye bread to sop up the juices that had pooled. His hand was halfway to his platter when the door opened.

Marnej dropped the bread, and jumped to his feet, grabbing

hold of the knife at his belt. A stout, old man stopped abruptly. His bushy eyebrows arched like an angry marten.

"Put that away," the old one glowered, shuffling into the apothecary. "I have not lived this long and made the mistakes I have to feel the blade of an Olmmoš whelp. Even if he is one of us."

Taken aback, Marnej did as he was told but didn't sit. Kalek got up to close the door behind the old one, who walked to the fire and seated himself with an audible sigh. Marnej waited for one of them to say something. Kalek, however, wordlessly prepared a cup of hot water and herbs. The ancient one took the cup with a nod of gratitude, then sipped cautiously, watchful. Marnej fidgeted with his belt, growing increasingly resentful of the scrutiny as a thick silence descended upon the room.

Marnej was about to burst at his seams with restlessness when Kalek saved him by saying, "Okta, this is Marnej. He has returned with Dárja."

The old one said nothing.

Marnej wondered if his ponderous pace was a sign of dotage or something innate to the Jápmemeahttun elders.

"Dárja is with us?" Okta asked, his voice as slow and even as melting snow.

"Yes," Kalek said.

"Where is she?"

"She went to find my father," Marnej blurted, unable to control his impatience.

Both Immortals favored him with a hard look, then seemed to share a silent understanding.

Marnej sat taller in his seat. "I brought Dárja back," he said. "I've proved my goodwill."

Okta kept his eyes on Kalek. "How long has she been gone?"

"Not long," Marnej said, his indignation wavering in the face of the old one's intensity.

"If it were only a matter of time," Okta said.

"What do you mean?" Marnej demanded, his voice rising.

Okta regarded the cup in his hands, but did not take a drink.

"I will inform Einár," he said finally.

Kalek inclined his head. His long hair hid his expression.

Once again Marnej's hand drifted to his blade. "Who is Einár? And, what must you tell him?"

"Gods intent be known!" Okta snapped. "Stay your hand! Do not think I am so old I cannot see what you are doing. I have seen more battles than you can imagine in that young head of yours."

Marnej moved his hand from his waist, chastened.

Okta stood up, followed by Kalek.

Marnej sprang to his feet. "Why are you both uneasy? And don't tell me that you aren't. I know you are. Is it my presence?"

"You are like your father," Okta said, his tone sharp.

Before Marnej could opened his mouth to object, Dárja exploded through the door.

Her smile slipped, but promptly returned. "Irjan's not in prison," she said triumphantly, addressing Marnej directly.

Then she saw Okta, and her smile became radiant. She ran to the ancient healer and embraced him tightly about his waist. Okta hugged her to him, his eyes closed and his brows furrowed.

Kalek's expression darkened, causing a chill to pass through Marnej's body. All at once, he wanted to leap forward to face the specter that had entered the room. Then some part of him shrank from it, as if he lacked the strength to withstand it. Marnej stood still, waiting for his world to be turned on its head once again.

Dárja released her grip on the old Immortal. She stood back, smiling. "Where's Irjan?"

Okta took hold of Dárja's hand. "Irjan is dead," he said quietly.

CHAPTER SEVENTEEN

"WHERE IS HE?" DÁRJA repeated.

"Irjan is dead," Kalek said.

Dárja's focus slipped past Okta, who still held her hand in his.

Pity tugged at Kalek's noble features, turning his face into a grotesque mask.

Behind him, Marnej held her gaze, transfixed. His eyes were wide like a hare caught in a trap. She watched with fascination as he swayed. *He's going to fall*, she thought in some far-off part of her mind.

Kalek reached out to brace him, but Marnej staggered back against the table, breaking the spell.

Dárja snatched her hand from Okta's. "How did he die?" she asked, her voice overriding an internal scream.

"He died on the battlefield," Okta said with cool acceptance.

Dárja glanced at Kalek for confirmation.

Kalek sat with his head in his hands, his long fingers snaked up into his hair.

As Dárja looked back at Okta, a sequence of events took shape in her mind, making terrible sense.

"It's my fault," she heard herself say calmly.

Three sets of pale, ghostly eyes fixed on her, boring into her.

Irjan's dead, she silently repeated, the reality of it sinking in. She would never have to face the possibility that he wouldn't forgive her for the terrible things she'd said to him.

"Irjan chose his destiny," Okta said. "He chose to fight and die among us. He believed a debt was owed and wished to repay that debt as a free man. If you need to place blame, then blame us for giving Irjan that which he asked."

She would never have to watch Irjan choose Marnej over her.

"I said many things I regret," Okta continued, "Your young heart should not take on the burden that those older and wiser should carry. I am the one that bears the responsibility. Not you. Not Kalek."

She would never have to share Irjan with Marnej.

Okta turned from her, easing himself onto a stool. "Events were set in motion when you were born," he began, then paused before adding, "Irjan acted as he thought best. As did I."

Kalek stood, then stepped to Okta's side, placing a hand on the old healer's shoulder.

"I cannot say I would have acted differently knowing what has become of us all," Okta said. "But I can say I regret the pain it has caused."

Irjan would always be hers.

A surge of relief coursed through Dárja followed by immediate guilt. She glanced over at Marnej. He had watched her day after day on their journey home. He'd learned to read her as well as he could read the tracks of men and animals. *He knew.* She was certain of it. He knew that she took comfort in the thought Irjan would always be hers and never his.

Blood pounded in her ears. A dull ached had settled behind her eye.

She began to shake.

Stop it, she told herself. But the trembling continued, moving from her knees to her chest. She fixed her mind on the scent of bitter herbs.

"It is time to rest," Kalek said, but his voice seemed far off and weak compared to her own, which continued to shame her with craven satisfaction.

～

Kalek guided Dárja to Okta's pallet. He helped her down onto the furs, resting her head upon a brushed, woolen pillow. He sat beside her, shaken by how much she had changed. It was more than her close-cropped hair and Olmmoš clothing, or the fact she was dangerously thin. Hair grew, clothes could be replaced, and bodies could be restored with food and rest. Kalek could address these outward signs of Dárja's trials and hardship. It was the change in her spirit, however, that frightened him. Spirit could not be mended easily, especially if she did not wish it.

Kalek took up the bowl of herbs and steaming water that Okta had given him. He wrung out the soaking cloth, then gently wiped Dárja's brow and temple. Her unblinking gaze pained him. He dipped and squeezed the cloth, repeating his ministrations until the warm water turned muddy. He refreshed the water and turned his attention to her hands, pouring his heart into his task. When Kalek finished, he bowed his forehead to meet their entwined fingers. He closed his eyes, listening to Dárja breathe, praying to the gods that exhaustion would soon claim her and she would sleep.

"What was my oktoeadni like?" Dárja's voice cut the silence.

Kalek raised his head. Dárja stared upward into the deep shadows of the roughhewn rafters.

"Why do you wish to know?" he asked, wincing at the defensiveness in his voice. Then he let out a long, slow breath, hoping to push back the dread closing in on him.

"Aillun was gentle," he said finally. "She trained as a healer with Okta." And as an afterthought, he said. "As did I."

Kalek picked his way through memories, both suppressed and cherished.

"She was quiet, and well suited for working with herbs. She

liked to work with her hands." He smiled in spite of himself. "She had an open heart," he said. "Like you."

Dárja turned her unseeing gaze to him.

"We fought before she left for her Origin," he said. "She did not trust me well enough to tell me her time to change had come. I was angry. I said things I now wish I had not. But I said them because I was hurt ... Those angry words were the last we shared."

Dárja's lip quivered.

Kalek feared she would draw the wrong conclusion from his sudden candor. There were too many seasons of snow ahead of her. He did not want atonement to turn into something cruel and twisted.

"But you went after her," she said. Her brimming eyes betrayed her dulled voice.

Kalek, brushed the hair from Dárja's damp forehead. He smiled to reassure her. "I went to find you."

"Irjan killed her," Dárja said, "and I killed Irjan." The strange lightness and far-off quality of her voice worried him.

Kalek cradled her face in his hands, willing her to see him. "Irjan did not kill Aillun. You did not kill Irjan."

Dárja shook her head fiercely, denying this truth.

Determined to get through to her, Kalek continued, "Irjan was trying to save Marnej. He did not know there would be consequences to his actions."

She grabbed hold of his wrists. The jagged edges of her fingernails dug into his skin. "I knew what I was doing when I went to his cell."

"Listen to me, Dárja. Okta was right. Blame us. Blame me." Kalek fought to keep her eyes on him. He fought to keep her from despair. "Do you believe he would have stayed in his cell as we marched off to fight?" Without waiting for her reply he continued, "You know as well as I, Irjan would not stand by to let others fight without him. He chose his destiny. You must let him have that. You must."

Kalek paused, feeling the loss as he honored the truth. "Just as we could not stop you from going off to battle," he said.

Dárja released her hold on him. She rolled onto her back, hiding her face in the crook of her arm.

Kalek leaned forward, resting his elbows on his knees.

"When Okta found him, a part of me left this world to join his spirit." Kalek's voice cracked. He went on in a whisper, "But that was not the worst of it. Because what I dreaded most was coming home to tell you, knowing it would break your heart." He shut his eyes. Still, he could not stop seeing the battlefield. The bodies. Irjan. "When we returned and discovered you were gone . . . it was my heart that broke."

Dárja hiccupped. Kalek raised his head to see her gaunt body shaking.

"But you are home," he said, aware of both his pain and joy.

Dárja sat up in an awkward rush, burying her face in his shoulder. Kalek held her tight to him, rocking her back and forth. He thought of Irjan. He could hear Irjan talking to him as he had so often done when Dárja was small. Kalek kissed the top of her head. Her short curls filled his nostrils with the scent of smoke and he breathed her in, understanding now what Irjan had tried so often to explain to him about the bond between a father and a child.

∼

Eerie quiet pressed in all around Marnej as he sat the table. He wanted to say something, to do something, anything but sit there. But he couldn't move. He couldn't think other than to count the loss. They'd all lost something: Kalek and Okta a friend, Dárja a guardian, and he . . . he'd lost a father, one that he'd never known. Dárja'd had his father, while he'd had a lifetime of lies.

This new jealousy irritated Marnej. He was a grown man who had no need of a father. But as he cast envy aside, alarm took its place. He began to obsess on the possibility he might have killed his own father on the battlefield and not even realized. It had been chaos that day, and he'd been swept up in the frenzy. *If it was my blade* . . . But he would not let himself finish the thought. The slow descent into paralyzing guilt awaited him if he persisted. He needed to concentrate on something he could be sure of. Clear reasoning brought him back to the fact he would never meet his father, never be free of doubt. Dárja and Kalek might speak of his father's love for him, but he would he would always wonder.

"What's to become of me?" he asked, his question like a shout in the quiet room.

"We will go to the Council of Elders," Okta said, without directly answering Marnej.

The ancient healer rose to stand like a disapproving monolith. "They may already know you are here, but it is better to seek them out than to wait and be found."

Marnej tensed at the inferred threat. "Will they imprison me like my father?"

"We are beyond that," Okta said.

Marnej marked the hasty response and doubted its truth. "So . . . no one will stop me if I try to leave?"

Okta threw up his hands as he walked toward the door. "Who among us can stop you? We are all the young and the old and the weak."

"You have no warriors?" Marnej asked, still seated at the table, undecided if he should follow.

"There are a few. If called upon, they will fight."

Marnej stood up, though not necessarily to join Okta. "Won't they attack me if they see me?"

"If you are worried for your safety, then stay here," Okta said, his exasperation evident in his rising pitch. "But it is your destiny we are to discuss and you may have interest in that." The old healer pulled open the door and waited for Marnej to walk through.

Marnej hesitated.

"No harm will come to you in my presence," Okta said. He gestured to Marnej's sword, adding tartly, "but if you need reassurance then keep your hand upon that hilt."

Marnej did not move. His reticence came more from obstinacy than concern for his safety. He'd had enough of others deciding his fate. He would leave. He would make a life for himself the way his father had—on his own. But he wasn't like his father, or at least he assumed he wasn't. But what did he really know?

Marnej grudgingly took a step toward the door, then another. Without intending to, he caught up to Okta. Just before the old healer entered the great hall, Marnej faltered.

Okta looked back over his shoulder, then motioned for him to come forward. Marnej walked out into the hall under the watchful gaze of the gathered Immortals. They whispered. The air became hot and stale around him. Marnej felt himself flush. He ventured to mimic Okta's authority, then felt foolish. They were women and children. They were no threat to him. He let slide his hand, embarrassed that he'd rested it on the knife in his belt. As he continued walking, he was careful to not make eye-contact with anyone. Then without warning, a woman, red-faced with rage, ran at him. Before he could react, she spat in his face.

Marnej wiped the spittle off his cheek, staring at the glowering woman as other women ran forward to pull her back.

"I am not afraid of this Olmmoš," she snarled as they tugged at her arms.

"Enough," Okta said, stepping in front of Marnej.

"No! It is not enough!" she shouted back, trying to push Okta out of her way. "It is too much to bear. Our warriors lie dead upon some field and *he* walks through us with impunity!"

"When you know enough of life, then you can speak," Okta said. "Until then, Úlla, step back and join the other nieddaš."

Unbowed, the woman named Úlla shook off the grip of the other women. She stepped back from Okta but did not turn away. Her mouth twisted into a sneer. Unnerved, Marnej followed Okta across the hall, wondering if all of the Immortal women were as fierce as Dárja and this last one.

As if reading his mind, Okta said, "Úlla feels the pressure of the changes wrought upon us."

The pressures of the changes wrought upon us, Marnej repeated to himself. The healer had not added, "By your kind." But it had been implied. They walked on in silence. To Marnej's great relief no one else accosted them. Still, he couldn't rid himself of the image of Úlla's face as she swooped down on him like a hawk with her talons out, ready to rip him apart.

Okta stopped at what looked like a dead end, catching Marnej mid-stride. The healer reached forward to push aside the barrier, beyond which lay a torch-lit room. Marnej followed Okta, his head tilted back, amazed to see the night sky with its stars above him. *Impossible*, he thought. They were still in the season of light where true night sky was cast in twilight hues. He glanced down to gain his bearings and found himself facing a line of six ancient Immortals. They wore plain linen robes the color of harvest wheat. Their indifferent expressions offered little to distinguish one from the other.

From the center of their ranks, one of the ancients moved forward. He appeared to glide, his robe hardly rustling. Marnej grew increasingly uneasy. He considered the likelihood there had been some poison in his tea or food which altered his senses. He stepped back, and a hand grasped his. It was Okta, but the ancient healer's firm grip was not reassuring.

"Einár," Okta said in greeting, with a discreet nod of his head.

The one called Einár stood directly in front of them. Like Okta, he was bearded, and his brow was furrowed. Unlike Okta, however, his eyes were bright, deeply set, and filled with distrust but tempered by something Marnej couldn't quite place.

"Marnej, son of Irjan," Einár said.

Marnej was unsure if this acknowledgment served to honor or condemn him. Then he recognized what he'd just seen, what he'd just heard. It was resignation. This moment had long been expected, though not desired.

"I have witnessed Guovassonásti's rebirth countless times. I have contemplated our Life Star in the heavens, seeking to discern the will of the gods. I believed that I knew their intent." The

Immortal paused. A crescent smile appeared for an instant, then vanished behind the curtain of his white beard.

"When your father stood before me, I still held that belief. Now, with everything that has come to pass, I understand it was an illusion."

Marnej didn't know how to respond or even if he should. He was sure his prolonged indecision would earn him a prodding, but it went unnoticed.

"When your father stood before me," Einár said, "I asked him if he understood his destiny. In my arrogance, I believed I knew his fate and could therefore control it."

Einár turned to Okta. Something unspoken passed between them before he continued. "Like you, he was Olmmoš and a Piijkij. We could not release him once he was with us. But he was also Jápmemeahttun, and we could not kill one of our own. So, we imprisoned him. But destiny does not respect walls, nor locked doors, nor the idea of a prison. Irjan escaped time and again until his true calling was fulfilled."

Marnej stole a brief glance at Okta, hoping to grasp the meaning of what was being said and what was about to happen. Okta's face revealed nothing.

"To have you here, was his true calling," the ancient Immortal finished.

Marnej shifted, clasping his hands behind him, discomfited by the fact that they felt moist. He wanted to wipe them on his pants, but the solemn atmosphere stifled his further movement.

"You have a choice, Marnej," Einár said.

Marnej's heart skipped a beat.

"You, like your father, are one of us," said Einár, with the nodding approval of the other five Immortals.

"We will not imprison you to protect ourselves from our fate. But you are feared. If you stay among us, you must reconcile that. We have lost more than you can imagine. Some will hold you accountable. However, the choice is yours. Stay and claim your place among your kind, or go and take with you the responsibility of our lives."

Marnej stood speechless, aware that this time he could not remain silent. He thought of his father and wondered what Irjan would have done given this choice.

He met the ancient Immortal's penetrating gaze. "I choose to stay among you," he said.

CHAPTER EIGHTEEN

VÁLDE SWEPT HIS HANDS to the right, signaling the others to keep low. He kept watch on the travelers' hut for signs of possible trouble. If there was any chance for them to act, they needed horses. Five of them at least, as Herko had belabored, to carry the nine of them. Nine Brethren to stand against the Believers with only their skill and their swords.

Válde removed his cloak, trusting that his soiled tunic would help him blend with the birch trees around him. He glanced from the travelers' hut entrance to the stables, just beyond the northeastern corner of the low-slung log shelter. Smoke rose from the roof, telling him the fire was centrally placed. What the faint wisps could not tell him was whether or not any of those gathered around the fire included soldiers. Movement along the patchy eastern tree-line caught his eye. The others were in place.

Observing the comings and goings at the hut, Válde had discerned there were at least four horses, possibly more, stabled within. While no soldiers had arrived thus far, he still worried there might be a stable boy or a smith who could raise the alarm. Herko had been quick to point out that while Válde directed their moves, it was the others who assumed the risk. Válde had not disagreed but reminded the others he would be the one left behind if the plan failed.

Herko's distrust had not offended Válde. The men had lost everything, save their lives, and he had persuaded them to gamble even that on vengeance. But he could think of no other way forward. They were not farmers or potters or wool merchants. They were the Piijkij of the Brethren of Hunters. They had lived with structure and training, with an oath and honor that had been codified and passed down for generations. They had a sacred calling without which they each risked going mad or ending up dissolute. But Válde had to admit that lurking so close to the Believers' Stronghold hinted at folly.

He scanned the trade route where the cart path curved behind a young larch thicket. There had been no signs of movement on the road for some time. Still, Válde wavered between taking it as a sign for action or an omen to stay hidden. He had been taught to hunt Jápmea and to lead men into open battle. He had not been trained to skulk behind trees like a brigand. But that was what they were now. Brigands. Perhaps Herko had been right that honor and oaths were a thing of the past. Maybe the sooner he came to terms with that the better it would be for him, and all the men.

Enough, Válde decided.

He signaled the others. They emerged from cover at a run, low to the ground like a pack of wolves. Once they reached the outbuilding they were hidden from his sight. Válde's attention roved between the road, the hut, and the stables. Movement caught his eye. Redde had eased himself around the stable's western side, headed to the opening in the south wall, where he disappeared within. Válde strained to hear any sounds from the stable. For an instant, he thought he heard someone gasp, then felt foolish for mistaking a hitch in his own breath.

Válde scanned the road again. When he looked back to the stable, Gáral, Feles, and Daigu traced Redde's earlier path, followed by Beartu and Herko. That left Edo and Mures as rear guard.

Sweat ran down the small of Válde's back as Gáral and Feles emerged from the stable, leading two horses. The excitement that surged through him turned cold with alarm when a pair of swaying soldiers stumbled out of the travelers' hut. They were drunk on juhka, but still capable of raising the alarm or worse.

Válde grabbed his cloak, fastening it around his neck as he moved to the edge of the trees. He broke through the undergrowth of pine saplings with a stagger, slurring as he sang a well-known joik, "The gods rejoice at their warriors' return . . ." He trailed off into humming as he brushed clean his cloak with broad, clumsy strokes.

He raised his hands in greeting, beaming. "My friends! Why are you leaving? I said I would buy the next round!"

Válde used his unsteady weight to turn the two soldiers back toward the travelers' hut.

"Went to piss and got myself lost," he exclaimed with a loud laugh. "Trees all looked the same! Ha!"

The two soldiers slowed as if searching their memories.

The three took a few ungainly steps back to the hut door.

"Did I ever tell you the story of the farmer whose goat got up on the roof?" Válde blustered, placing his arms around the soldiers as if they were lifelong friends. "Well, you see the goat . . ." And that was as far as Válde got before the soldiers shrugged off his chummy grip.

"Friend," the shorter of the two said, trying to get Válde's attention. "You mistake us for someone else."

"No. No. No," Válde pretended to argue happily. "We were by the fire, drinking juhka, and I said I needed to unburden myself, but said I would buy another round and finish my story when I returned."

The taller soldier, the one with a clearer eye, pushed Válde back lightly. "Friend, your story's finished."

Válde allowed himself to sway backward onto his heels, keeping a grin on his face.

"But the goat is on the roof of the farmer's house and the wife comes out," Válde began to tell the story, pulling at the sleeves of the two soldiers with good-natured humor.

Together, the soldiers wrested their hands from Válde's hold, then turned toward the stable. Over their shoulders, Válde saw Redde and Daigu leading two horses into the forest.

"That's my horse!" the taller soldier cried out. "Stop!"

Redde and Daigu glanced back, surprise registering briefly as they swiftly mounted the horses to ride off. Before the two soldiers could find their footing, Válde lunged forward, his long knife in hand. He skewered the short one with a single thrust through the man's back. The man screamed. His tall friend, just a pace ahead, spun to see his compatriot fall. Then, Válde's blade slid through him. The tall soldier crumpled, his hands pressed against his middle as blood pulsed through his fingers. With a sickening crack, Válde wrenched the tall man's head, letting the body fall forward as he headed for the stable.

"Get the horses and get out," he called into the stable's dark interior, pushing past Beartu on his way in.

"Grab the other one," Herko cried, as he passed by.

Válde reached for the reins, moving to follow Herko. The horse whinnied. The white of its eye was visible in the sliver of light that cut through the gloom. Válde reached out again, and this time his fingers wrapped around a long leather lead. *A cart horse*, Válde thought bitterly as he pulled the reluctant animal out of its pen.

Hurling abuse at the gods who plagued his every step, Válde encouraged the horse to match his stride as he began to run. The horse, however, stood its ground, unmoving.

"I do not have time for your cart," Válde told the stubborn beast as he looked toward the hut. He grabbed hold of the horse's mane at the base of its neck, then hopped, and sprang up onto the its back. The horse shook its head but Válde held on, kicking his heels into the animal's sides. The obdurate beast began to lumber toward the road.

"Not the road," Válde swore under his breath, pulling on the reins. "Head toward the forest." In an agonizingly slow arc, the animal finally changed its course.

"Hurry up," he hissed through clenched teeth, but his exhortations did nothing.

Válde kicked his heels into the horse's side even harder and was rewarded by a jerking trot straight into the thickest part of the forest. Small branches snapped in his face and large ones threatened to brain him, but he encouraged the horse to run. Gripping the animal's girth with his thighs, he leaned low, his eyes watering from the lashing they received. The horse's back was already slippery with sweat even though they were barely above a trot. Válde tucked himself closer to the animal. The horse hair stuck to his neck, itching, as he muttered oaths and invectives against any and all.

When the forest thinned, Válde sat up to peer over the horse's head. He caught a glimpse of movement. *Herko*, he thought. Then he saw a flash of color and Feles's red head popped into view before disappearing into the cover of trees. Válde hoped all his men were ahead of him. A good leader should have made sure none were left behind. But in the rush to escape, he had become just a man. If any were lost, he would carry the shame.

Válde hazarded another glance up, relieved to see that Herko rode directly ahead of him. In the distance, more men came into view. Válde gently slowed his horse. He had no desire to jerk the animal to a stop and land on his backside or worse. They'd had a rough enough beginning.

"Well done, cart horse," he said, patting its shaggy side where the heat of the animal rose like steam.

Válde came alongside Herko, who had also slowed.

"What happened back there?" Herko asked, nodding his head in the direction they had just come.

"Soldiers," Válde said. "I tried to get them back in the travelers' hut, but they were the only soldiers I have ever met not interested in having a drink paid for by someone else."

Herko let out a gruff laugh. "It's all that praying they do now."

"I don't think we were seen," Válde said.

Herko shrugged. "I don't think it matters."

"Because we have horses?" Válde asked.

"No. Because we're brigands and rogues, and it doesn't matter who knows it," Herko corrected him. "That's all we are to those fish-bellied Believers. Why shouldn't we act as charged?"

"Brigands and rogues," Válde repeated, Herko's reasoning sinking in.

Válde clapped the man on the back. "Well, at least you look the part," he said, adding a teasing smile to the jibe.

"I may look like one," Herko said, running a meaty hand across his bald head, "but you—you smell like one. Did you ride that horse or mate with it?"

Válde let out a laugh, savoring the release of tension as they made their way to rejoin the others

"Where is Daigu?" Válde asked, his laughter cut short by sudden dread.

"He's gone off to bring up his food," Redde answered.

Confused, Válde turned his horse in a circle looking for the missing man.

"He hit a low branch and knocked himself off his horse," Redde said. "When he got his breath back, he crawled into the bushes."

"Daigu," Válde called out, as he gingerly slid off his horse, tossing the reins to Herko. Behind to the left he heard a muffled voice. He followed the sound until he found Daigu, kneeling on all fours.

"Should I leave you be?" he asked.

Daigu nodded his head, his stringy hair covering his face.

"If you do not stand up and walk out of there soon, I will come back for you," Válde told him.

The prone man nodded again, then arched in sickness.

Válde retreated, satisfied.

There were eight men, plus himself, and seven horses. It was enough for them to put much needed distance between themselves and the Believers' army. And hopefully, they could get two more horses along the way.

"I've seen better acting from a bellyaching bear," Gáral said, coming to stand by Válde.

Still flushed with the effort of the escape, Válde gave him a sharp look, but was surprised to see Gáral smiling. The lopsided grin sat awkwardly upon the man's face. Even so, he was heartened to see it.

"What I lack in artifice, I make up for with a sharp knife!" Válde said, bowing in Gáral's direction.

"Almost as sharp as Gáral's tongue," Mures muttered loud enough for the laughing Redde to hear him.

"One could only wish, Mures, that your wit was half as sharp," Feles said dryly, though his broken nose twitched, betraying his good humor.

Mures's mouth hung open in shock. "The Red Rock speaks," he mocked.

"The Red Rock made a joke," Redde chimed in.

"If we left it to you two, it would be all gas and belching," Edo said.

Mures and Redde turned to each other, feigning dismay. Then with a shrug, Mures said, "I've never encountered a fart that I didn't find funny."

Laughing, Válde sat down on a fallen tree. Though dirty and ragged, he was pleased the men still had their spirit. Perhaps it would be enough to see them through to the future.

Daigu staggered out of the woods, one hand pressing branches out of his way and the other wiping his mouth. Redde and Mures where the first to upbraid him.

"Was it your plan to ride into trees so no one would ride with you?" Redde asked.

"The horse doesn't even want to ride with him," Mures corrected.

Daigu grimaced in their direction, now holding his hands to his gut.

"Next time, Daigu, rely on the horse's eyes, not your own," Redde said, to the amusement of his friend Mures.

"Can you ride?" Válde asked.

"I should think the answer to that is obvious." Mures continued to laugh.

Válde ignored him in favor of Daigu, "Can you?"

Daigu nodded.

Válde took the man at his word. "We have seven mounts, but one is a cart horse," he said.

"We should get moving," Gáral opined, his habitual impatience serving a purpose.

"Four to share and the rest on their own," Válde said. The corners of his mouth then crept up into a smile. "Daigu, you should consider riding with someone."

Beartu stepped forth to pat the beleaguered man on the back. "I'll take him."

Daigu grimaced but followed Beartu.

Without comment, both Gáral and Herko mounted their own horses.

Válde was not surprised by this. There was no love between Herko and Edo or Feles.

"Come, Redde," Mures said, "I'd like to ride with someone who's not a bore." He squinted mockingly at Edo.

Válde would once again have to ride the cart nag. Gods help him if the horse could not keep up with the others.

"We will switch whenever you wish," Feles said to Válde, giving both Gáral and Herko a long withering look.

"Which direction do we travel?" Redde asked.

"North, and then east," Válde said, flicking the reins.

CHAPTER NINTEEN

Bávvál's fur-edged sleeve caught the lip of the plate before him, catapulting food into the air. The soft cheeses and ripe fruit landed with a wet thud upon the dais, the chair, and his lap. Three acolytes hurried to assist the High Priest, but their rushed and clumsy efforts only created more of a mess.

"Áigin," Bávvál shouted above the clucking of concerned priests and servants. "Áigin."

The man materialized beside Bávvál like a wraith. He was too thin, too tall, and too quiet—a scarecrow masquerading as a man.

Bávvál shoved the steward who wiped the red stain from his robe. The hapless man toppled backward, knocking over a bishop who had strayed too close in his fawning efforts.

"Too many hands and not enough thought," Áigin said.

The acerbic comment infuriated Bávvál with its astuteness. "Bring the rider to me," he commanded, fending off the ministrations of those around him.

"Yes, my Vijns," Áigin answered, bowing, before disappearing into the buzzing crowd.

Bávvál batted away the last probing hand. "Leave me alone," he barked as he shrugged off his soiled garment.

The milling crowd parted, and Áigin took a direct path to the

High Priest, his boney arm supporting a soldier covered in filth from head to foot.

The shambling man in Áigin's care held a stained burlap satchel. Hands flew up to cover nose and mouth. Some in the gathered cortege turned away in disgust as the pair crossed the hall.

"The gods thank you," Bávvál offered the formal greeting.

"As I thank the gods," the bedraggled soldier said, his voice shaking. The pitiful man attempted to kneel, teetering forward dangerously. Áigin grabbed hold of the soldier to act as a counterbalance.

"Stand . . ." Bávvál motioned, encountering as he did the wafting onslaught of rotting flesh. He instantly covered his nose and mouth with one hand, indicating with the other for the soldier to hurry.

"My Vijns, I am Jonsá. Soldier in the western regiment," the rider said.

Breathing through his mouth, so as not to have the putrid odor invade his nose again, Bávvál said, "Give me your news."

"Those Brethren too craven to fight, who sought to escape, have been slain by our army," Jonsá recited, unwrapping the bundle he carried. "They've been punished by the gods through the righteous order of the High Priest who commands the army of Believers."

Jonsá held two severed heads aloft. Bávvál drew back. The stench was even more overpowering now that the decaying flesh twisted in the air.

"I have traveled west with this news and return now to honor you, my Vijns," the soldier said, placing the heads at the High Priest's feet.

Bávvál flapped his hand at the closest man in his retinue. "Take the heads, Rikkar!"

The startled counselor flinched as if he had been hit.

"Put them on the pikes outside, beside Dávgon's skull," Bávvál said with muffled gusto. "A leader should not be without his disciples. Even in death."

Rikkar took an uncertain step forward, his normally proud face filled with loathing as he bent over. Carefully he picked up the gruesome tribute by the hair, holding the heads far away from his pristine robes. As he turned sharply on his heels, the vile relics slipped from his fingers, landing on the floor with a gut-turning splat.

Áigin tossed the soiled burlap from the soldier's hands to Rikkar's feet. The counselor glared at him, then lifted the hem of his robe and prodded the heads onto the cloth with a reluctant toe. He raised the burlap corners, tied them together, and, this time, mindfully carried the rotting heads away.

"The people and the gods know their will has been done," Bávvál said, endeavoring to restore some decorum as he settled back in his chair.

"And what of the Piijkij who fled with the Jápmea female?" he asked.

Jonsá cast a worried glance to Áigin. "I do not know, my Vijns."

~

Weariness hung upon Niilán like a second skin. They had covered more than ten leagues a day in less than half as many days. And, while the foot soldiers, like himself, looked like dirt-covered beggars, Niilán could not help but notice with resentment that his commander and the mounted soldiers appeared fresh and ready for action. He glanced back over his shoulder, checking that his group of men remained intact, then turned to face the looming gates of the Believers' Stronghold.

On the palisade, where banners had once flown, the pikes were crowned by rounded shapes. Even at this distance, they could not be mistaken for anything other than human heads. Niilán's stomach knotted as the ranks of soldiers carried him forward toward the gruesome sentinels. He felt their unseeing eyes staring, judging him for his part. Niilán lowered his own eyes to watch the dusty footfalls of the soldier in front of him until the whispers and pointing of the advanced ranks drew his reluctant gaze upward.

"The Vijns put the last of the Brethren's heads on pikes." The men on either side of Niilán passed on the news with unwarranted satisfaction. But he could not do the same, not when the voices in his head condemned him.

Those marching in front came to an abrupt halt, followed by a ripple of disgruntled shouts and invectives. Niilán shifted back to avoid the scuffle, and felt a soft squish beneath his heel. He lifted up his dung-smeared boot to confirm what he already knew. Shit coated the cracks and tears of the old worn hide. Niilán cursed the mounted phalanx, their privilege, their rank, and their tender feet in kid-leather boots.

Pushing continued on all sides as soldiers raised their voices.

"Get off my foot you fat moose."

"Why have we stopped?"

"I just want to sit down."

Niilán disregarded the comments and questions, intent on staring daggers into the straight backs of the mounted soldiers with the Ten Stars of the Bear emblazoned on their cloaks. If he'd had enough saliva to spit, he would have.

Then, far up in the ranks, Niilán heard a voice shouting for quiet.

"It's the High Priest," someone said, repeating what someone else had said, heedless of merit or truth.

From where he stood, just inside the wooden palisades, Niilán could see nothing that gave him any useful information. Just horses' asses and the backs of men's heads. Then the mounted soldiers broke ranks, allowing a small figure dressed in deep blue to come into view. Halfway up the bridge to the defense tower, the figure held up his hands, his words lost in the din.

A few men dared to shush the others. Niilán left them to their futile task.

When quiet finally descended, whatever opening remarks had been made were lost forever and they were none the wiser. Then, like the rush of fire come to life, voices from the front reached Niilán.

Those around him rushed to join in at the tail end, saying, "As we thank the gods." *Like good soldiers*, Niilán thought, failing to make the same effort himself. Instead, he focused on the High Priest ahead, willing his ears to catch some part of what was said. He thought he heard praise for their actions as soldiers and true Believers.

The crowd surrounding Niilán shouted their support of whatever had been declared but unheard this far back. The soldiers began chanting, "Juhka. Juhka." Their faces were alive with anticipation. Then the chant turned physical as men jostled their way forward. Niilán's attention, however, was drawn to a tall, gaunt man with greying hair to his shoulders and a soldier's yellow tunic. The man stood out like a scarecrow among the clergy who were clustered like bright, plump berries.

~

As Áigin wove through the restless foot soldiers, the bright yellow of his new tunic stood out among their dirty, faded uniforms, an oversight he now regretted. He had but a moment to consider his error when the pushing and shoving of unruly men sent him sprawling to the ground. Áigin swore loudly as shuffling feet surrounded him. The swirling dust coated and choked him. Then as quickly as he had fallen, helping hands brought him back to his feet again.

Now almost as filthy as the other soldiers, Áigin reprised the role he had intended to play. "Many thanks, friends," he said to the men who steadied him. "My legs won't carry me much farther."

"We're glad to see the end of ten leagues a day," two of the soldiers commiserated. The agent murmured his agreement, all the while observing the other men around him and their conversations. Grousing and complaints echoed everywhere, but nothing spoke of sedition or unrest. However, the juhka had yet to flow. Strong drink made the weak bold and the wary honest.

As the sun dipped to the horizon and silhouettes lengthened across the Stronghold's palisades, Áigin moved about, ducking in and out of groups of men. Sometimes he poured the juhka, listening to bawdy jokes. More often than not, good-natured ribbing mixed with complaints about worn feet, aching backs, and lack of food. But that was nothing new in a soldier's life or outlook.

By deep twilight, the fires dotting the encampment were surrounded by drunken merriment and gap-toothed grins. But around one fire, five men sat huddled together, their expressions brooding as they drained their cups. The hair on the back of Áigin's neck stood up and a tingle of anticipation spread through his body. For a man like him, who had spent the majority of his life rooting out coveted secrets, the chance of discovering a new one was headier than the spirit in his cup.

Áigin dipped down into the thick band of smoke that blanketed the gathered troops. He skirted the fringes, rather than approaching the five men directly. From where he sat at a neighboring fire, he was able to observe them as they leaned in close to speak. Their secretive postures beckoned him to creep within range to hear their hushed conversation. Edging closer, he pretended to lay back and rest where he sat. Still, he watched and listened.

Of the five, Áigin could see the faces of three, and those three looked as if something sat poorly with them. By the way the others deferred to him, it was the soldier with the shorn head and close-cropped beard who held authority in the small gathering. The grey in the man's beard made him appear older than his compatriots and there was definitely something about him that suggested hard-earned experience.

One of the two men with his back to Áigin spoke in a rush of mumbled words. The weathered leader looked around at each of the men, as if he searched their faces for something. Reassurance? Compliance? The man leaned forward, his voice too low to understand. Straining to inch closer, Áigin heard, "I didn't choose the lie, and I didn't relish the task. But, it was an order, and I followed it, just as you all did."

The other soldier with his back to Áigin nervously glanced around, his face visible in the firelight. *Jonsá*. The shock of recognition momentarily stunned the spy. Then he heard their leader say, "Our safety is in our silence."

Wise, but a little too late, Áigin thought, his mind racing to piece together the puzzle. *Deceit is to be expected when ambitions ran high*, he mused. And, the Vijns had made it well known that he would reward any who brought an end to the Brethren. Áigin was certain these five were not instigators. They were pawns. Still, like all pawns, they served a purpose, and he had the rest of the evening to think upon that purpose.

～

Niilán sipped his juhka with Jonsá, Joret, Osku, and Matti. None of them shared the good cheer of their comrades.

"They were ours," Jonsá said softly, looking nervous as he shifted. "Are we supposed to ignore that?"

"Surely some family member has recognized one of them." said Matti.

In Matti's wild eyes, Niilán saw his own fears materializing and harshly pushed them aside. "If they have not yet been recognized, it is safe to say they will not be."

"How can you be sure, Niilán?" Matti demanded.

"Because I cut off their heads and even I do not recognize them," Niilán said, passion raising the tenor of his voice.

Osku's hands fidgeted with a stone, picking it up, then putting it down, before picking it up again. "Let's forget it and be done with it."

"But the Piijkij remain at large," Joret argued.

"True, but their numbers are not known. So none can take a tally of their dead and come up short," Niilán said.

"The heads began to rot as I rode with them from farm to farm," Jonsá whispered in disgust. "The flies followed me everywhere I went." He paused to drink from his cup. "I can still smell it."

"It was no different for the rest of us," Joret complained bitterly.

A grim quiet descended upon the group. Joret leaned forward and poked at the fire with his knife.

Niilán felt the pressure to say something more, something that would give heart to men who felt a black mark upon their souls. But he had very little left in him that spoke to hope. The best he could offer was to strengthen their resolve.

"The commander crafted the lie and the order," he said. "But if it comes to light we will deny everything."

Jonsá looked as if he wished to argue. Niilán cut him off. "I take no comfort in this, other than knowing it will protect us. If we do not break, then none can break us."

When the others tired and drew out their bedrolls, Niilán left them to their dreams. His own mind would not quiet long enough to allow sleep to descend. Doubt about the others ranked foremost in his thoughts. They had agreed, for the moment, to remain quiet. But the gods only knew how long it would last. At least the five of them were all in the same regiment where he could keep a watchful eye on them. In time, perhaps they would be able to forget. Or maybe some greater problem would take its place. Regardless, he would need to remain vigilant. Too many men now held his fate in their hands.

Niilán stood apart from the crowds of drunk and slumbering men. He looked up into the sky's deep twilight, regretting his decision to stay with the army. A cool breeze swept up smoke to choke him. He coughed, reality replacing his regret. He snorted to himself. *There's no farm waiting. It's the soldier's life or the binna.*

CHAPTER TWENTY

ÚLLA SAT WITH THE other nieddaš, eating the morning's warm porridge, a meal she normally enjoyed. But her dark thoughts made even the honey and cream taste bitter.

"He doesn't belong here," she said.

Birtá put down her spoon. "Why do you bring him up when we're trying to enjoy our meal?"

The other three nieddaš agreed.

Úlla reddened, but she did not back down. "I mention him because you are all like rabbits, too scared to poke your heads out to see the world as it is."

Ravna snorted. "When did you become an Elder, Úlla?"

"When I took over the forge," Úlla snapped. "Melting metals burns away one's silliness."

"Please, Úlla, do not pretend you are the only one among us to work hard," Ravna turned up her already upturned nose. "We all work hard. Ello is tilling the fields. Tuá butchers the animals, and I am tanning hides. None of us are cowering in our holes like rabbits."

Momentarily chastened by her friend's sharp words, Úlla joined the others as they quietly resumed eating.

"Well, I think he's fine-looking," Ello said abruptly, scraping the porridge from the side of her bowl with concentrated effort.

When heads snapped up to look at her, Ello blushed clear to the crown of her red hair. "I mean, for an Olmmoš."

The others sat aghast while Úlla gathered up the remnants of her earlier righteous indignation.

"You see!" she said, pushing her food aside. "He should not be here. He is a danger."

"A danger to Ello," Tuá snickered and received a pinch in return. "Ow!"

All but Úlla joined in the laughter. "You make jokes," she reprimanded her friends. "He is a Piijkij. He killed our kind."

"Well, I heard his own kind were going to kill him after they found out he was one of us," Ello said, arching her brows.

"One of us? One of *us*?" Úlla's eyes widened in disbelief. "He is not one of us." Her voice rose in frustration. "He is an Olmmoš! A Piijkij!"

"The war is over," Ravna said. "He is an extra pair of hands to help with the work. Besides, Irjan fought for us. The Elders have made a wise decision. Can you not let it be?"

Úlla hit the wooden table with the flat of her palm, nearly spilling everyone's tea.

"The war is not over! We are still dying. You see Lejá over there? The time has come for her to return to her Origin and she is terrified. She does not want to go. But she knows if she does not there will be one less Jápmemeahttun in this world. The war is not over. It is with us each day we live."

Emboldened by the pitying glances the others made in Lejá's direction, Úlla pressed on.

"Marnej is worthless!" she said. "He does nothing that serves us. He just runs about in the woods swinging his sword. Perhaps come spring we will have need of someone to kill the biting flies. Then he might serve a purpose."

Úlla's heart raced, and her breath had turned ragged. "As far as I am concerned, he is just another mouth to feed."

"Úlla," Ello's soft pleading voice escaped her half smile.

Úlla flushed with anger and disbelief. "No, Ello. If you want to grow his grain and Tuá to butcher his meat and Birtá to cook for him, that is your own folly. He gets nothing from me, except what he deserves."

She stood, disgusted with the silly nieddaš she called friends— sisters even. They knew how she had suffered, and still they sided with that human. She could not bring herself to even think his name.

Úlla grabbed her bowl and, in her haste, finally spilt tea across the surface of the table. She hesitated for an instant, feeling that she ought to clean the mess, not wanting to burden another. They were all too burdened as it was. Then she noticed Dárja standing off to Birtá's side. Her resentment crystalized, putting a decisive end to whatever doubts that lingered.

"I should go," she said. "I have work to do."

~

Dárja felt Úlla's thick golden braid lash her as if it were a whip. She shrank back, feeling the loss of her own beautiful braid keenly. Then she recalled Úlla's thin-lipped smirk as she'd turned on her heels. Pulsing anger built in Dárja's chest, threatening to charge like some wounded bear. But before she could do anything, she felt the soft touch of a hand upon her own.

"Do not pay attention to her, Dárja."

At the sound of her name, Dárja glanced down and saw sweet Tuá, looking up at her.

"When Kálle did not return . . ." Tuá began. "Well, Úlla has not been the same."

"She's miserable and wants the rest of us to join her," Ello said. "Have you noticed that she's wearing Kálle's tunic and belt?"

Tuá frowned at the young nieddaš, then tugged on Dárja's hand with an apologetic smile. "Come, sit with us. We have not seen much of you since your return."

The others chimed in quick succession.

"Sit with us."

"We have missed you."

"It hasn't been the same since you left."

The entreaties ended with a red-faced Birtá.

Dárja's gaze followed Úlla's broad shoulders and swinging braid. Úlla had always been so quick to judge, so ready to find fault in others. Nothing, it seemed, had changed. Then Dárja felt the cold prick of her own conscience as she sat down with a heavy thud.

I'm no better than her, she silently admitted, shame clouding her thoughts. She'd condemned Irjan without looking beyond her own broken heart. She'd blamed Marnej without ever knowing the truth of his life.

"Dárja," Tuá's gentle voice roused her.

Dárja blinked, suddenly aware of four pairs of eyes staring at her intently. What was she to say? Should she confess her guilt over Irjan or share her horror of the battle? Panic gripped her as she realized that she had nothing in common with these nieddaš.

Dárja's distress must have been evident because Tuá said in a rush, "We know you have suffered so much and experienced things we have not."

Then Ello's bright voice interrupted, "I think you're the bravest among us and I'm happy to see you."

"You do not have to speak of the past," Ravna added.

The lump in Dárja's throat swelled. Her hand rose on its own to rub the exposed nape of her neck.

"That's right!" Birtá added, clapping Dárja vigorously on the back.

Dárja rocked forward, a tiny cough escaping her.

Birtá blushed, and they all began to laugh, including Dárja.

"So, tell me about Marnej," Ello encouraged, a sly smile twisting her full lips.

"Ello!" the others chorused.

"What?" she asked, her eyes wide with mocking innocence. "I'm merely curious about him." Ello leaned in toward Dárja. "Does he snore?"

The other nieddaš groaned, but Dárja laughed.

"Yes! And he smells!" she confided.

Ello grimaced, causing a round of giggling.

When the laughter died down, Dárja wondered how long it had been since she'd truly felt light at heart. Before the battle. Before she learned the truth. But that was the past. In this moment, she just wished the lightness could continue.

"Have you decided what trade you'll take, now that you're back?" Birtá asked, her plump cheeks still rosy atop her smile. "I'd love some company in the kitchen!"

"Or in the fields," Ello added hopefully. "Or maybe on the looms. Ávrá needs a good quick hand, one with a sharp eye."

"No one wants to work with hides," Ravna said, her lament half-hearted.

"Or the messy work of butchering the animals," Tuá said.

Dárja looked at their expectant faces, feeling heartened. *It is good to be home*, she thought. But some part of her was reluctant to answer their question. In truth, she didn't have an answer. She'd trained to be a warrior. But their kind had no need for fighters now, nor would she be accepted among the remaining Taistelijan, even though she'd fought in the last battle. She was a nieddaš and would remain so for the rest of her long life. None of her friends would understand. None of them would share her experience. With or without Irjan, she was alone. The weight of this ill-timed insight pressed in on her, crushing her, body and spirit. In a panic to free herself and regain the carefree moment that had passed, she said without thinking, "I guess I'll be a healer."

Dárja managed to affix a smile as a barrage of appreciative responses overwhelmed her. She imagined herself a healer, like Kalek, like her oktoeadni, Aillun. Dárja tried to dredge up the word Marnej had used. Then she remembered. *Mother*. Dárja repeated the word silently, sounding out its parts, telling herself, *I will be a healer like my mother.*

"Oh, I'd like to be a healer too," Ello spoke up. "Especially if I got to work with Kalek." Ello's grin widened, waiting for the other nieddaš to respond.

"I thought you liked the look of Marnej," Ravna said.

"My eye finds many pleasing," Ello said, looking down her freckled nose and feigning an air of dignity.

~

Marnej had counted the days leading up to the full moon and then had counted those of its waning. He'd endured the sidelong glances of the Immortals and had ignored their disapproving whispers when he'd passed. Dárja had been withdrawn, rarely venturing from her sleep chamber. At a loss, Marnej had spent most of his time in the apothecary where at least the two healers welcomed him. But when both Okta and Kalek were working, his presence became too much. The healers endeavored to be kind and patient, but he had sensed their frustration, and had begun to make it his habit to go out into the surrounding forest.

On these forays, Marnej encountered nature not as a force to be reckoned with or terrain that needed to be crossed quickly, but as a rich landscape of sight and sound that sometimes bewildered him with its beauty. Trees that had only been a forest to him became unique in their kind and their song. Birdsong that had merely heralded the arrival of morning or evening was transformed into a trilling of each moment in between, a reminder that everything was alive.

At times, the Immortal world was too much for him. Too much to take in. Too much to feel. Too much to share. The profound discomfort he often felt drove him to action. But without guidance or a role among the Immortals, he fell back on the routine of practice and exercise from his days among the Brethren. Lately, however, he found himself creating an imaginary opponent to practice against until exhaustion claimed him. As a boy, he'd fought and killed his father in these made-up battles. But Irjan was now dead. That battle was over, if not resolved.

Frost-outlined footsteps trailed behind Marnej as he crossed into the clearing where he usually practiced. In the golden hush of falling leaves, he drew his sword and cut the air before him. He wished he could've heard what his father thought of his form and style; whether his skill would've matched that of Irjan's. On rare occasions, Marnej had heard whispered praise among the Brethren of Irjan's expertise. But now he knew why Irjan had been so skilled at hunting the Immortals.

He was one himself. Like me, he thought.

Both of them had used their hidden connection to do the impossible, and both had ended up traitors to their own kind. But Irjan had chosen to betray his oath. Marnej had not. He'd been forced to renounce his identity or lose his life. Then again, perhaps his father's blood, his Immortal blood, ran so strong in him that he would've chosen this path eventually.

Marnej swung his sword, slicing the crisp morning air, wanting to dispel the questions for which he had no answers.

"Have care that you do not end up cutting yourself," Kalek's warm voice carried across the chilly clearing.

Marnej spun, at once startled and embarrassed. In all the mornings he'd come here, he'd never seen another in this part of the woods. He'd begun to think of this glade as his own, which he knew to a real Immortal would've been preposterous because there was only ever the All. But then he wasn't a real Immortal. Only part of him was. The bigger part was Olmmoš, and a Piijkij, as he'd been reminded on any number of occasions recently.

Kalek knelt down on the edge of the clearing. Marnej retraced his steps through the melted frost. The bent grasses squelched under his weight. When he got close enough, he saw Kalek was studying the small, tear-shaped leaves of a low-lying plant. Marnej stood to the healer's side, expecting Kalek to acknowledge his presence. But Kalek continued to observe the plant as if he were alone.

Marnej became impatient. "Kalek," he whispered.

In the quiet forest, however, the whisper sounded like a shout.

Kalek, if he did hear Marnej, ignored him and brushed the leaves of the plant, almost like a caress.

Marnej shifted his weight and bent forward, interested to

see what the healer was doing. But he was doing nothing. He was once again still.

"I am listening to the plant," Kalek said finally, as if he'd read Marnej's thoughts. "Do not distract me further. Go sit somewhere until I am done."

Marnej let himself be offended, but then his better judgment came to the fore. He walked over to a thick-trunked birch and slid down it to sit at its base. He laid his sword down beside him, then brought up his knees and rested his arms upon them. He leaned his head back against the trunk but continued to watch Kalek, who brooded over the plant, unmoving. Finally, Marnej grew bored and closed his eyes.

"For one who could not wait for my attention, you found rest easily enough," Kalek said.

Marnej came awake with the healer standing over him. Kalek's mouth twitched to one side in amused annoyance.

Marnej jumped to his feet, snatching up his sword. The cold hilt stung his hand as he rushed to put it in his scabbard.

"What were you doing with that plant?" he asked, breaking into a loping run to catch up with Kalek's long stride.

"I was listening to the plant's song. I wanted to know the best time to harvest the leaves and roots," Kalek replied without looking at him.

"But it's a plant," Marnej said.

Kalek arched his brows. "And you are Olmmoš, but I do not judge you harshly."

Marnej let the rebuff stand, knowing that he'd offended the healer. The two walked in silence for some time, their breath fogging the air between them.

"Kalek," Marnej said finally, weighed down by his need for answers.

"Mmm," said the other, as if lost in his own thoughts.

"When I first met Einár, he spoke about the gods and knowing destiny," Marnej said, unsure of how to begin. "Do you believe the gods have mapped out our destinies, the way our songs say?"

The wind picked up, bring down cascade of bright yellow birch leaves upon them.

"That is a question for Einár and for the Elders, not a healer like me," Kalek said.

Marnej swept the leaves from his shoulders. "I just thought you'd have an opinion."

Kalek stopped. "Why?"

"Because . . ." Marnej hesitated.

Kalek's eyes flashed a warning. But Marnej's need to know prevailed.

"Because your actions brought my father here."

"Are you asking me if I believe it was my destiny to bring your father here and intertwine our lives together?" Kalek asked, his voice hardening.

Marnej squared his shoulders. "Yes," he said, then faltered. "I mean no. I mean: do you believe the gods have made this life for us or have we?"

When Kalek didn't immediately reply, Marnej went on in a forlorn ramble, "Was I always meant to end up here? Or did circumstance and my own action bring me here?"

The hard set to Kalek's features relaxed. He nodded his head as though he understood Marnej's intent.

"These are matters I have asked myself in the darkest of times," he said. He raised his hands and gestured to the surrounding forest. "What do you see and hear?"

"The forest. The trees. The plants," Marnej replied in quick succession, then paused, uncomfortably aware of the deeper qualities around him, yet unwilling to speak of them. Haltingly he finally added, "I hear the wind and the birds. I hear the Song."

Kalek's gentle smile radiated a weary appreciation.

"We have lived within the Song of All for so long that we believe we see and understand how the world around us works," he said. "Maybe this has led us to believe that we understand the gods, and perhaps we even act in their stead." He stopped and looked around the forest. "But I think there is a mystery that cannot be heard or fathomed no matter how hard we listen to the Song."

Marnej waited for what Kalek would say next, but the healer began to walk again.

"Wait," Marnej called after him. "You can't say that and walk away. What is it? What's this mystery you believe exists?"

"What does your Song say?" Kalek asked, stopping beside a narrow stream that flowed down into the eastern glade.

Marnej balked, suddenly conscious of his own reticence.

Kalek waited with arms crossed. "Come. It is not a secret you must keep. It is something I and all others can hear in the Song of All if we choose to listen."

Marnej gave Kalek a sidelong glance which he hoped spoke volumes about his reluctance.

Then he said tentatively:

I am the vessel of a father's soul.
I have journeyed into the realm of the dreams of the dark sky,
And traveled back in a blaze of light.
I enter into the world to meet my destiny,
Knowing that I have been touched by the gods.

"Do you believe what you say?" Kalek asked.

Marnej shrugged. He didn't want to admit that he considered his song just some magical incantation that allowed him to disappear from the Olmmoš soldiers who hunted him. But he also didn't want to admit that he'd never given the meaning much thought.

"Where does it come from?" he asked.

"Your father," Kalek said.

Marnej thought again about each line, but he found himself no closer to understanding.

"I don't know, Kalek" he said, his voice crisp with irritation. "I don't know what it's telling me. What it's saying about me."

The healer hung his head. He swore an oath under his breath, then looked up through furrowed brows in a way that made Marnej suddenly wary.

"Your father gave you that song after Aillun gave him Dárja's to sing. He said the words came from him, as if they had always existed in his heart."

Marnej shook his head. "But Dárja said her mother was dead."

"Dárja's oktoeadni died in Irjan's arms," Kalek said, "Before Aillun died, she gave him Dárja's song, to make him her guide mother."

By Kalek's expression, it was clear that he expected Marnej to make a connection he couldn't readily see.

"Please, tell me plainly," Marnej begged. "I hear your words, but I'm missing what you want me to understand."

The pity that welled in Kalek's eyes pushed Marnej to the edge.

"Just tell me!" he demanded, sounding more like a petulant boy than a man.

Kalek fixed his pale eyes on Marnej. His voice came out low and measured.

"The priest in the village where your family lived had some-how learned Irjan had once been a Piijkij," he said. "Irjan never found out how the man knew, but the priest desired your father to hunt us once more."

Disgust played across Kalek's face before he was able to go on. "Irjan tried to deny what he was. When that failed, he refused the service. Then, when there were no immediate reprisals from the Brethren, Irjan believed he had succeeded in escaping his past." Kalek paused. His eyes narrowed, as if judging Marnej ready or not for what he next had to say. "He went to the last market before the season of snow, and returned to find his wife in death's embrace. You had already gone onto the gods."

Marnej's mind went blank, even as he knew he was finally hearing the truth.

"Irjan held your mother until she passed. The following morn-ing, as he prepared the grave, he said he heard a voice that gave him hope. He heard Aillun."

A chill passed through Marnej that had nothing to do with the cold morning.

"Irjan remembered the old Brethren tales of our kind," Kalek went on as relentless as he was compassionate, "Legend said our birthing could bring life back to the dead. Irjan tracked Aillun like he had all the others of our kind and he found her with Djorn, Aillun's birthmate."

Marnej shook his head to disavow what was about to happen next.

Kalek rebuffed Marnej's unspoken plea with maddening calm. "You are shaking your head, but you have asked. You cannot have it both said and unsaid."

The reproach stung Marnej, as if he had been slapped.

"Go on," he whispered.

"Aillun and Djorn fought your father, believing he had come to kill them. Aillun wounded Irjan just as Djorn began to ascend."

"Ascend," Marnej repeated. "What does that mean?" His voice sounded shrill, but he could do nothing about it. His pulse throbbed in his temples.

Kalek grabbed him by the shoulders. "Djorn's life was meant to give birth to Dárja and to help Aillun become almai like me. But Irjan thrust your body into the spirit stream."

Marnej blinked. There was only silence and the throbbing behind his eyes.

"No," he said, shaking his head vehemently. "No."

But as he protested, Marnej recognized the truth—the source of the sadness he saw in Kalek's eyes and the reason behind Dárja's hatred and resentment.

Marnej swallowed. The pounding in his temples faded into the background.

"I am alive because of what my father did," Marnej said, voicing what he should have comprehended long before now.

Kalek sighed. His tall frame sagged.

"I am alive and Aillun is dead and Dárja will never transform,"

Marnej said, a new lightheadedness making his words seem distant and not his own.

Kalek jerked to attention. "She told you that?"

"She blames me. All this time." Marnej began to pace, needing to move as his anger came to life. "But it's not my fault!"

Marnej rushed Kalek, stopping a hand's width from the Immortal. "I didn't choose to live. My father did that! But she blames me. She should blame him!"

"She blames herself most of all!" Kalek bellowed.

Marnej staggered back, momentarily silenced.

"She blames herself," Kalek repeated, his voice softening. "She blames herself for Irjan's death. We all kept the truth from her. Even so, she learned what had happened. She confronted Irjan, and they argued."

"But he's the one to blame," Marnej interrupted.

"And what would you have done?" Kalek argued. "Would you have let your child die if you believed there was a chance he would live?"

Marnej began to pace again, beads of sweat prickling his skin. "I would have . . ." He started to defend himself then discovered he had no answer other than his dismal anger.

"Precisely," Kalek said as the gap in Marnej's argument lengthened into silence. "What would any of us have done in that situation? I do not believe the gods choose our actions. They may set the course of events, but it is *we* who decide what direction to go in."

CHAPTER TWENTY-ONE

A LIGHT DUSTING OF SNOW fell on the tight circle of men. The soft flakes hissed as they hit the fire. Válde crouched before them, a short stick in hand.

"The outpost has the one gate, here." He marked the ground with an X. "They have sentries posted at the four directions. But the southern sentry is rarely posted on the palisade. Instead, he is by the gate."

"He can still raise the alarm," Gáral pointed out.

"If we intercept the messengers on the forest path, he'll be none the wiser," Beartu said, rubbing his hands together. "The trees and the shadows of these darkening days will hide us."

"Let's make sure it's not Daigu waiting to pounce," Redde warned. "In these conditions, with his eyesight, he's bound to jump too late."

Mures snorted.

Daigu shot the two a murderous glance.

"This is not the time for high spirits," Feles said.

"You wouldn't know high spirits if they kicked you in your stony backside," Mures retorted, garnering a snicker from Redde.

"And you two are like fox kits, yipping to hear their own voices," the normally stoic man answered.

"Enough," Herko grumbled.

"Beartu is right," Válde said, seeking to bring the men back to the plan at hand. "Our best chance to take the messengers is within the woods." He weighed the skills of those gathered. "Feles will shoot the men from their horses. Gáral, Herko, and I will dispatch any who remain alive. Edo, you and Daigu and Beartu, secure the horses. Mures and Redde, keep a watch on the path."

"And their valuables?" Herko asked, his mouth breaking into a crooked grin.

"Take what you can," Válde said.

Edo sniffed. "Is it not enough that we slay men who have done us no harm? Must we scavenge their bodies for whatever shiny trinket catches our eye?"

Herko scowled at the man.

Válde jumped to his feet, ready to interpose himself, but the fool Redde beat him to it.

"Edo, you should have become a priest rather than a Piijkij," he said.

Edo's narrow chin quivered. "The Piijkij are Hunters, not rats feeding on a diseased carcass to survive."

Herko rose to this challenge. His bulk blocked Edo's wiry frame from view. "Don't you get it? That's what we're doing. Surviving. We're rats, stealing what we can to live. Let go your pride, Edo. Decency won't feed you."

"This is not what I pledged to do," Edo said, his voice tight and menacing.

"Stop!" Válde shouted, stepping forward. "Edo, Herko is right. This is about survival." He took in the ragged faces of the men. "Our nobility is behind us. It was lost the day the High Priest betrayed the Avr. But we can make them pay for what they have done to our Brethren. To do this, we must live. You have a choice, Edo. You can stay among us and carry on, or you can leave and live by whatever ideals you choose."

Válde avoided Edo's simmering stare, not wanting to push the man to act from wounded pride. Instead, he addressed the others. "The same goes for all gathered here. You have a choice. If you stay, you acknowledge that this is the truth of our lives." He looked directly at Gáral, expecting to see defiance, but instead saw a nod of approval.

"Well, I can't leave while I share a horse with Redde," Mures said.

Nervous laughter passed through the former Brethren. Even Edo smirked and then shrugged.

Válde took the gesture to be his pledge to stay. "Does everyone understand their part?" he asked, then waited to see if there would be any further dissent. "Right, douse the fire and let us take our positions. Redde, keep watch for our messengers. Beartu, you will be his relief. We wait for your signal."

～

In the dark hours of early morning, Niilán stood sentry along the western side of the Believers' Stronghold. The wind had picked up. He shivered, noting the change in the weather and the shortening days. The season of snow approached. He could smell it. This is why he hated standing sentry. Not because of the harsh elements or the loss of sleep, but because it gave his mind too much time to think, too much time to dwell on matters beyond his control.

Niilán stomped his feet and rubbed his hands.

"Gods keep me from this," he muttered, his breath a trail of mist through which he saw a figure approaching. Alert now, Niilán drew his sword, taking note of the fact the man wore no uniform. He broadened his stance.

"State your purpose," he said in a loud, clear voice when the man was within earshot.

"I have come to speak with you, Niilán," the man said, stopping just beyond reach.

Beneath the warm woolen cap he wore, Niilán's scalp tingled. "You use my name, but you are not known to me."

"I am known to few, but those who know me find value in my acquaintance." The man opened his arms in a benevolent greeting, the kind that Niilán associated with those who had power to wield over others.

The man took a step forward. The thin sliver of a moon shed no light on his features. There was, however, something naggingly familiar in his lanky bearing.

"I approach you undisguised. I am armed, but I will not draw my weapon unless your actions force me to do so. My purpose is to make you an offer I believe you will find to be of interest."

"Never trust the words of gods or beautiful women, and never accept something easily given," Niilán said, repeating his father's warning to him and his brothers.

The man laughed. "Wise, but I am neither."

"Then who makes this offer?" Niilán asked, loosening his shoulders and preparing himself for a fight. "You? Or someone else?"

"I am Áigin." The man inclined a bare head. His shoulder-length hair swung forward then fell back into place as he straightened. "I make the offer, but I act in the service of the High Priest."

Niilán stepped back, reluctant to sheath his sword, but also conscious of giving offense.

"What interest can you or the High Priest have in a common foot soldier?"

"Your modesty is a shrewd defense, but it's not necessary with me," the man said, leaning in toward Niilán. "I know your secret," he whispered, the smell of anise on his breath. "As does the Vijns."

Niilán felt a tremor pass through his limbs. He said nothing, not wanting to give indication one way or another.

"I understand your reticence," the man called Áigin said. "It gladdens me to see someone who can keep his tongue. But, as I said, it is not necessary." Áigin pushed back his cloak to pull something small and rolled from his belt.

Niilán instinctively shrank back, bumping against the palisade's uneven stakes, his hand poised above his weapon.

"You will not need your sword to fend off what is written," Áigin said, waving the roll in front of him.

Niilán shook his head as he extended his hand. "I cannot read."

In the grey of dawn's light, Niilán saw the man's toothy smile overtake his sharp features. "Then let me tell you what it contains."

Niilán took the scroll.

"By order of the High Priest, you, Niilán, will be given command of a chuoði. Your regiment will be tasked with hunting down and killing the remaining Piijkij."

"But, I am already part of that regiment," Niilán began to protest.

Áigin drew close, his dark eyes narrowed. "Are you willing to remain under the command of someone who asks you to commit treason? Or are you willing to truly answer to just one master? Naturally, the choice is yours. But, between beheading for acts against the Believers and taking the power of command, I would choose the latter."

Though the man's raven eyes held him in their sway, Niilán gathered together enough presence of mind to ask, "How do I know you speak the truth?"

Áigin stepped aside, clearing the path in front of Niilán. "Come with me now. Hear these same words from the High Priest himself."

～

Bávvál leaned back in his chair, pulling his furs tight around his shoulders. The previous night's fire had died down to embers and he had banished the servant who had brought more wood.

"You acted without orders," he said to Áigin.

"I often act without orders," the wiry spy admitted, "but always with my Vijns in mind."

From any other, this kind of fawning would have been irritating, but coming from Áigin the flattery was amusing. Almost.

Bávvál sprung from his chair to stand directly in front of his spy. "This altruism is a fine show for an audience, but I know you prize secrets above all else." He circled the man. "What have you kept from me? What angle do you see that I do not?"

Áigin stood impassive. Neither interest nor offense registered on his face.

"Niilán is a seasoned soldier who fought in the battle, and has the allegiance of those closest to him. He will not underestimate the Piijkij," Áigin calmly rephrased his earlier reasoning.

Bávvál sniffed. "Misguided as his actions were, they showed initiative." He tapped his fingernail lightly on the carved edge of the desk. "And the regiment's commander?"

One corner of Áigin's thin lips curled. "He has joined the council as their military advisor."

"Lies and deceit are the domain of the Court of Counselors," Bávvál agreed. "Not my army."

"I took liberties in what I offered him, but felt they were appropriate for your needs," Áigin said, his tone blithe.

"Quite," Bávvál said. He walked backed to his chair, dragging his finger along the length of the desk. "In the future, act with more care. I value you, Áigin. I would hate to lose you."

Bávvál sat back down, certain that his point had been made. "I am encouraged to hear that you have confidence in your new man." He wiped the beeswax polish from his fingertip. "Because I have just received word that the messengers from the Skaina outpost were attacked and killed."

"Skaina? That's on the western side of the far northern border of the Pohjola," Áigin said. A furrow creased his wide forehead. "There's proof that it is the work of the Piijkij and not banditry?"

"They left one rider alive to deliver their message," Bávvál said, keeping his tone mild.

Áigin's leathery skin blanched.

Bávvál took pleasure from the fact that he had caught his spy unaware. It was a rare occurrence. At any other time he might have enjoyed gloating, but this was not the moment.

"The first of many to come," Bávvál said. "Their words."

"The temple outposts must be strengthened," Áigin said promptly.

"But not at the expense of the Stronghold," Bávvál warned. "I have no wish to find myself at the end of their blade because we rushed off to protect the borderlands."

"We can use Niilán," Áigin said. "His regiment can escort reinforcements to the temple garrisons as he roots out the remaining resistance. The soldiers stationed at each temple need only a few experienced men to lead," Áigin added, engrossed in problems and possibilities. "The new soldiers who have joined will have no direct knowledge of the Brethren, but they will learn by experience or example."

Satisfied with the overall plan, but not wanting to inspire his spy to further liberties, Bávvál said in his most imperious tone, "Send another regiment south. I do not want Niilán's chuoði to wander there when the attack was in the north."

"Of course, my Vijns," Áigin said, without a trace of wit, then bowed. "I will see to it at once."

"And the Jápmea female and that halfling Piijkij," Bávvál said in passing. "You will see to them. Won't you?"

Áigin's lips twitched. "Assuredly, my Vijns."

"The gods thank you," Bávvál said.

Áigin bowed. "As I thank the gods."

CHAPTER TWENTY-TWO

THE PLEASANT SMELL OF simmering herbs permeated the air of the apothecary as the healers worked in companionable silence. Okta paused with the pestle in his hand to observe his apprentice, who in truth had long ago become a master healer. Kalek's devotion, however, made it all too easy for Okta to forget that in favor of old and comfortable habits.

In his long life, Okta had trained many healers, but he had decided that Kalek would be the one to replace him. He acknowledged the almai's reluctance to step forward, and he accepted the role loss and heartache played in his hesitancy. But there would come a time, very soon, when he would no longer be there for his assistant, and he needed to prepare Kalek for that eventuality. For the time being, however, he was willing to let Kalek be.

Okta resumed grinding dried berries into powder, his thoughts upon the work at hand. Then a sharp pain, like a knife to his side, ripped the breath from him. He let drop the pestle into the mortar's bowl to steady himself with both hands on the work table. Okta had counseled enough patients in his long life to know what was happening to him. His end time drew near. It would be useless and foolhardy to believe otherwise. When the pain released its grip on him, he slumped against the table's edge, weak and dizzy.

Through his haze, he heard Kalek call his name. Then Okta felt two hands guiding him to sit. When he could focus once again, Kalek knelt before him. His pale face was as white as the snow falling outside.

"Are you unwell?" Kalek asked, his care at once touching and worrisome.

Okta patted the almai's shoulder, feeling the sharp angle of bone. "I am fine. Just a meal that is not sitting well with me. And, in that vein, when did you last eat?"

Kalek shrugged off the question.

"You could do with a little something," Okta said.

Kalek stood. "What do you mean?"

"You are too thin, Kalek."

The young healer shrugged again. "I find that I am not hungry," he said, then added, "Do you want me to make you some salmonberry tea?" And without waiting for the old healer to answer, Kalek went to the work table and began to shift jars around until he found what he wanted.

We are both hiding the truth, Okta thought, then softened his judgment. They were both at the beginning of a long and difficult journey, and a little tea never hurt. He smiled, "Yes, some salmonberry tea would do me a world of good."

"Has Dárja spoken to you?" Okta asked, rubbing his gnarled hands together, trying to rid himself of their unnerving tingle.

"Mmm. We talk every day," Kalek answered, dipping the wooden ladle into the warming water.

"What does she say?"

Kalek sighed, turning to hand Okta a small steaming bowl. "Mostly we talk about Irjan."

Okta accepted the bowl with a nod, blowing across its surface to cool it before taking a sip. As he did this, he considered the best way to proceed.

"Does she still blame herself?" he asked.

"She knows she is not to blame," Kalek said, sitting down opposite Okta. He picked up a basket of unfinished poultices. He rooted around until he pulled out a needle and spindle of thread. "But knowing and feeling are very different. I believe she still feels responsible."

"Has she mentioned what she plans to do?" Okta inquired, sipping his tea.

"I do not understand," Kalek mumbled, the thread now stretched between his teeth to cut. When the string broke he continued, "What do you mean by plans?"

"Kalek, she cannot continue as she has been," Okta said.

"I agree," Kalek said, his eye squinting to thread the needle. "That is why I think she should take up her sword practice. She could train with Marnej."

Okta brought the bowl to his lips and sipped the tea before he suggested, "Perhaps her skills would be better served under your tutelage."

Kalek tied off the knot. "I am hardly equipped to oversee her fighting skills," he said, beginning to stitch a poultice closed. "At best, I was adequate with the sword."

Okta shook his head. "Hardly true."

Kalek was about to protest, but Okta raised his hand, his stamina waning. "I am not suggesting you instruct Dárja in her sword work. I am asking you to guide her in the art of healing."

Kalek looked up, his sewing forgotten.

"The time for fighting is at an end," Okta explained. "There is nothing left for us to fight over. We are defeated, but we must continue on." He paused, knowing Kalek would rather avoid this topic, just as he had avoided counseling the nieddaš who were preparing to birth. For too long now, Okta had allowed his apprentice to shirk that responsibility out of compassion, but this duty could not be dismissed.

"Dárja needs to have some part to play because there are no more battles for her to fight," he said.

Kalek's fingers played with the edge of the poultice. "Do you believe she will accept the role of a healer?"

"I believe she will if she is led in that direction," Okta said.

Kalek stiffened, dropping the poultice into the basket at his side. "You are asking me to meddle in affairs that are not mine."

"It is your affair," Okta said sternly. "It is my affair. It is yours. It is all of ours. Dárja needs a purpose. We all do. She has made herself into a warrior, but that cannot sustain her here with us. Unless we can give her something that will fully engage her, she will fall victim to discontent."

"And you think that being a healer will forestall that?" Kalek asked, his doubt verging on disdain.

"I believe that learning to heal others will help Dárja to heal herself," Okta said, softening. "But I do not believe she will come to this understanding on her own. The darkness surrounding her clouds all other possibilities."

"Why must I be the one to lead her in this direction?" Kalek objected. "Why not you? You are the teacher. I am your apprentice."

"Because I am in need of her forgiveness and therefore cannot be heard," Okta said. "Besides, more than any of us, you have shared her life, and you are ready to be a teacher."

Kalek's expression drifted from denial to defeat. When the almai exhaled a long slow breath, Okta knew that he had managed to convince his apprentice of his point, but worried that he had pushed him too far. He was not proud of what he had done, but it had been the right thing to do.

Okta had always tried to do what was right. Viewed from the present, some of their kind would say he had been wrong. They would judge him for bringing Irjan to them and would even blame him for the war. In his darkest hour, Okta had blamed himself as well. But when he surveyed his actions, he saw life emerging from death. He saw the very spirit of the Jápmemeahttun.

Once, when he was young and rash, he had believed victory was possible and noble. Now he knew that even if they had won the battle against the Olmmoš, it would have been no victory. A victory is an end. And as Okta saw life before him, there was no end. There was only the cycle of life and death, where one gives way to the other endlessly.

Okta studied the serious face of this fine, honorable almai he had called for so long student and friend. Soon, Okta would head out for his Origin like countless old ones before him to offer the service of life bringer, and Kalek would carry on the art of healing, gaining knowledge and imparting wisdom until his own time came to return to his Origin. The beautiful simplicity of their lives had worked for as long as Guovassonásti had shone upon their lives. Okta then thought of Dárja and Marnej. They were a wondrous unknown. He regretted that he would not witness their lives unfold.

Okta finished his tea, then placed the bowl upon the work table. "I am in need of a rest," he said, his heart at once sad and grateful.

~

When a low rumbling snore came from the adjoining room, Kalek let himself consider Okta's suggestion. The idea of Dárja training as a healer had much to recommend it, provided she wanted to.

But what will she do when the other nieddaš become guide mothers? he wondered. He supposed that there was nothing to prevent her from becoming a biebmoeadni. After all, Irjan had been Dárja's bieba. But for their kind, the role of guide mother was meant to prepare a nieddaš to give birth. It was a way of lessening the sorrow of giving one's birth child to the care of another to become almai. At least that was how it had been for him.

Kalek's guide child, Kearte, was a mature nieddaš when he returned from his Origin with his birth child. Irjan had once asked if Kalek had found it hard to give Ravna over to her guide mother. Kalek had truly searched his heart before he answered. He'd had no misgivings. Still, Irjan's question had made him aware of his own assumptions. From a distance, he had watched Ravna grow up. She had a devoted guide mother and a loving world of friends. As far as Kalek could see, she had no need for him.

Whatever loss Kalek had felt giving over his birth child had been short-lived compared to the physical changes that followed the birth. He had endeavored to explain this to Irjan but the gap in their experience had been too great. Irjan had been born a male and had grown up to be an Olmmoš man. He had never been a female, nor given birth, nor endured the change. Irjan had accepted the role of guide mother, but Kalek doubted he appreciated the true meaning of being a biebmoeadni. In his most truthful accounting of this man he had loved, Kalek knew that Irjan had never relinquished his role as a father to the son he had lost.

In some ways, Dárja was more like Irjan than her birth mother, Aillun. Dárja would likely never give birth, nor go through the change. The thought that she would never sing her child's song pained Kalek. As did his recollections of Aillun, who had been very young when her time came. *Too young*, he thought. She had only been a guide mother for a short while, and he had been too blind with love for her to see what was happening until it was too late. He would not make the same mistake with Dárja. He had seen her potential for bitterness in the way she watched the other nieddaš, and without something to fully engage her, Dárja's discontent would grow and fester.

Kalek knew he had to do something. He had to figure out some way to talk to Dárja, without manipulation, and without touching on subjects he would rather have left unmentioned. Kalek put the finished poultices on the table. He turned his attention to the fire where the herb tincture had reduced greatly in his absence. Stirring the remaining liquid, his mind was absorbed with the problem of how best to deal with Dárja.

"I think you're burning that," a voice said.

Kalek reeled around. His resolve drained away like the tincture dripping from his spoon at the sight of Dárja.

"I did not hear you enter the apothecary," he said, his pulse quick and guilty.

"Clearly," Dárja said, inspecting the pot over the fire.

Kalek strained out the softened root.

"Are you making an urtas remedy?" she asked, sniffing. "Because this smells more like boiled frog than angelica root." She screwed up her face in disgust.

Kalek pulled the pot off the fire. He waved his hand over the boiling mixture, as if the little breeze he created might actually cool the tincture before it was ruined.

"What are you doing here?"

"Where else should I go?" she asked.

Her petulant inflection felt accusatory to Kalek's sensitive ears.

He wrestled with what to say, and his renewed discomfort made him anxious for any available answer. "Go . . . go practice in the woods with Marnej," he said more sharply than he had intended.

CHAPTER TWENTY-THREE

D ÁRJA TRUDGED ALONG THE overgrown forest path. Her skin burned with humiliation after her banishment from the apothecary. All she'd done was point out the tincture was scorching. Kalek should have offered her thanks instead of treating her like a misbehaving mánná—she was no child.

I should've returned to my room, she thought. Marnej could be anywhere out here and the longer she walked, the more she wished she hadn't stormed outside without her hat and gloves. Dárja blew on her hands, then stuck them into her armpits. Without her arms out to balance her, the boggy path became more treacherous, adding to her ill humor.

I'm only going as far as that pine growing out of the rock, she told herself. If she couldn't see Marnej from there, then she would turn back. Dárja felt a prick of guilt. She hadn't seen much of Marnej since they'd arrived in the Pohjola. She'd left him on his own to figure out how to be among their kind. She knew it could not have been easy, not when most of them would blame him for what they'd lost in the battle. But she'd had her own struggles. Not only was Marnej a reminder that Irjan was gone, but his presence would not let her forget that she had taken comfort in the fact she would never have to share Irjan with him. If Marnej knew this, he'd hate her. Likely, he already hated her because she'd had his father's love when he hadn't and never would.

Dárja reached the tree in the rock, then turned on her heels without looking up.

"Hey!" Marnej's Olmmoš voice called to her.

Dárja twisted around. In the distance, she made out his figure sitting by a large snow-dusted spruce.

Dárja stood still, her feet sinking into the mud. *I should never have turned around*, she thought. Now she couldn't go back, at least not without Marnej knowing she'd seen him and had chosen to ignore him. She took a step out of the mire toward Marnej.

"Your limp is gone," he said when she got close enough that he didn't need to shout. Dárja tensed, hearing censure for her absence. He didn't move from where he sat, and from his expression, she couldn't tell whether he was pleased or annoyed to see her.

"What are you doing sitting under a tree?" she asked, deflecting her thoughts from her failings.

Marnej squinted up through the branches. "Just listening to it. It takes me a while to sort out all the songs, to focus on just one."

He looked back at her, his face was streaked with shadows. "What are you doing out here?"

"Kalek sent me," she said, avoiding his scrutiny by looking up at the passing clouds.

"Why?"

"To get me out of his way," she said, shaking her head, the indignity returning. "He told me to go practice with you."

Marnej frowned. "To what end?"

Dárja heard an unwelcome note of suspicion in this question. "I'm going to go back. This was a bad idea."

Marnej jumped to his feet. "No. Don't go. We should practice."

He walked out into the clearing, then turned to face her. "Although you look a little weak, and you are a girl."

"I have fought and killed bigger Olmmoš than you," Dárja scoffed before realizing he'd been teasing her. "And I'm not a girl." She sounded out the word in Marnej's deep Olmmoš accent. "I'm a nieddaš, or haven't you learned anything yet?"

"Are you always like a burr in the boot?" he asked. "Or is this some special gift you're intent on sharing just with me?"

Dárja pretended to give the question some thought before saying, "I believe you bring it out in me."

He bowed. "A natural talent I'll need to rid myself of."

She bowed in turn. "Don't be so hasty. You don't have that many talents to begin with."

At this, Marnej drew a short sword, momentarily catching Dárja off guard. Then he skipped away from her to goad her with a wave of his hand.

Dárja tossed aside her bow and quiver to unsheathe her own sword.

"You look so pale," he said, beaming with amusement. "I promise not to draw blood. I don't think you could afford to lose even a drop."

"I make you no such promise," Dárja said, lunging in a flash of motion.

Marnej parried. He cross-stepped to come at her weak side. Dárja feinted, then swiftly withdrew, letting Marnej's blade swing far short of her. He closed the gap with a thrust. Dárja met his blade. The clang of metal upon metal briefly numbed her arms, revealing how weak she'd become since returning home. She stepped back, losing her footing in a deep, muddy patch to fall onto her backside.

Marnej came forward, dropping the point of his blade. "Are you hurt?"

Dárja rolled over her shoulder, coming up into a squat with her weapon ready. Marnej batted the blade, then bounded away when she leapt forward. She laughed, missing him completely. The two traded blows until Marnej stepped back and broke off the engagement.

He wiped his face with his sleeve. "Not bad." He grinned. "Not bad for a nieddaš who has been lying in bed since the harvest moon."

Bent over the pommel of her sword, Dárja rose to the taunt.

"I take it back!" he said laughing, holding up his hands. "That's not bad for a Taistelijan who has been lying in bed since the harvest moon."

Dárja narrowed her eyes into an icy stare. The smirk dropped from Marnej's lips and his forehead wrinkled. She held her penetrating stare just a moment longer, enjoying her victory, then broke out into a fit of giggles that turned into a wheeze. Dárja coughed, trying to catch her breath. Marnej sat down on the ground in front of her. She followed suit, heedless of the frost and the mud. She leaned back to look up at the sky.

"See, there you are, lying down once again," he said with a note of triumph. "Is that how they train you Taistelijan warriors?"

Dárja sat up, her pulse quickening. "Irjan trained me."

"I knew from the moment I saw you fight that my father had trained you," Marnej said, still lying down but alive with new tension. "You move like a Piijkij."

Dárja exhaled, telling herself to relax. Marnej's observation hadn't been a slight. "He didn't want to," she said. "I begged him. I begged him until he relented."

For a moment, the memory spun her in its lonely web. She'd been so little and so determined. *Poor Irjan.*

Dárja stirred, aware Marnej watched her through lowered lashes, as if he didn't want her to know that he was paying close attention.

It was a ploy she had often used around Kalek and Irjan.

"At first, Irjan just pretended to teach me about the sword," she said, surprised to find that she wanted to talk about him. "His lesson seemed to be more like dancing than fighting. Later on, something changed and he began to take our practices seriously." Dárja reflected on how the shift had come about, then shrugged. "I'm not sure what prompted it. I was just excited to learn and to practice with him."

Marnej rolled to face her, feigning interest in the dried stalks of grass they had trampled in their mock battle.

"I miss him," she said, then steeled herself for what needed to be said next. "And I'm sorry that you'll never know him."

Marnej's hands stilled.

Dárja cleared her throat, praying her voice would not fail. "It's my fault. No matter what Kalek says. Irjan would've stayed here if I hadn't said that I hated him and never wanted to see him again." She sniffed back the cold tears that stung her eyes. She'd cried enough.

Marnej just lay there, staring at her. Dárja wanted him to yell and scream at her, because then she'd be able to accept her responsibility. But he just lay there, not moving, not speaking, his pale grey eyes like a distant storm.

~

It took Marnej a moment to realize that Dárja had stopped talking because all he heard was her saying that she was sorry that he would never meet his father. And she looked as if she truly believed she was to blame—the one who'd struck the blow that had killed his father.

Marnej scrambled to his feet, leaving a startled Dárja in his wake. He needed to move. If he didn't, he felt he would rip wide open, unable to contain his anger at Dárja, at the gods, or fate or whatever had cursed him. He took a step in one direction, but it felt like running away. He turned back only to confront Dárja. The sympathy in her eyes burned right through him. He wouldn't suffer pity. Pity was for the weak—for the powerless. He'd been a Piijkij. He'd been trained to kill. Marnej swung around in a circle, overwhelmed by his need to regain what had just been stripped from him with one tearful look.

Out of the corner of his eye, beyond Dárja's profile, a trio of deer emerged at the clearing's edge. Their heads bent to graze on the thawing ground.

"Where's your bow?" he hissed.

Dárja shrank from him, pointing behind her.

Marnej dropped low and ran as quietly as possible. He picked up the bow and quiver as he moved forward, intent on the deer. He judged the wind direction, then shifted to stay downwind of the trio.

Behind him, he heard Dárja's breath catch.

He took pleasure in ignoring her whispered protests. He had no need for someone to always remind him that he was something less than his father. He crouched as he glided forward, nocking an arrow into place as he'd done hundreds of times to make perfect his technique. *Thank the Brethren for their thoroughness.*

"Marnej, don't," Dárja said somewhere far behind him, her alarm just another sound.

The deer tensed, their ears up, alert.

Marnej straightened, adjusting his aim.

The trio leapt away, the larger two bolting into the forest, and the smallest skirting the far side of the clearing.

"Stay out of this Dárja," he warned, racing forward, sighting along the arrow's shaft as he chased after the lone deer.

Dárja's shouts to stop made him all the more determined. Every step he took it seemed that someone, or something, stood in his way. But not here. Nothing stood between him and his quarry. He was a skilled hunter. Maybe not as renowned as his father, but he'd prove Irjan's equal in the end. He released the arrow.

The arrow flew true. The bow's twang echoed in his ear.

In the instant before the arrow hit its target, he heard Dárja's plaintive cry, "What have you done?"

Marnej's triumphant response fell away like a hewn tree as pain exploded in his mind and then in his body. He cradled his head, pleading for the cries within to stop. Time stretched out in an endless, agonizing screech, as he shrank further into himself, praying for the torment to cease, promising anything if only it would. And then it did. As suddenly as it began, it stopped.

Marnej fell forward onto the ground, too weak to do anything but thank the gods that the pain had stopped. When he finally regained his strength, he pushed himself up to his knees. As he straightened he saw Dárja, lying on the ground, curled into a ball, her body trembling. He scooted forward, every muscle straining in the effort.

When he laid a hand on her shivering body, she whimpered. "Why did you do that?"

Marnej sat back on his heels. "I didn't do anything."

"You killed it," she cried, rocking back and forth, keening. "You killed it."

"Yes," he said. "I killed it."

"But it was too young," she sobbed. "Didn't you hear its song?"

"What do you mean?" Marnej demanded, his insides sick and his thoughts confused. "I killed a deer for food."

Dárja sat up, her red-rimmed eyes full of loathing. "You can't kill the young in the Song," she shouted at him, pounding her fists on the ground.

It was too much for Marnej. "Damn the lot of you," he shouted her down. "You blame me for things that I don't know and despise me for things that're beyond my control." He pushed himself to standing. "I didn't choose to live, or kill your mother, or ruin your life."

CHAPTER TWENTY-FOUR

Dárja burst through the garden door into the apothecary. Her face was streaked with dirt, her furs coated in mud.

"Kalek, we need your help," she cried out.

The panic in her voice acted like a lightning strike to the healer's quiet contemplation.

Kalek knocked over a stool in his haste to make it to her side. "Are you hurt? What is wrong? What has happened?" His questions flew out, chased by dread.

Dárja shook her head, her eyes wide. "No one's hurt."

She looked back toward the garden, then took hold of Kalek's hand, pulling him down the short, dark hall and out into the frost-covered garden.

Marnej stood just beyond the stone wall, as he had the first time Kalek had seen him. His expression today was no less uncertain.

Still holding his hand, Dárja breathlessly rambled. But Kalek did not need to hear what she said to understand what had happened. The deer draped across Marnej's shoulders told him all he needed to know—it was too young. Sadness washed over Kalek, relieving his heart of fear but not the sense of foreboding.

Marnej would not meet his eye.

Dárja ran after Kalek. "He didn't mean to. I thought he knew . . . I tried to stop him but he just didn't know. It's not his fault."

Kalek put his hand on Dárja's shoulder to calm her. "I know it is not his fault. Marnej has only been with us a short time. He has not been taught all that he needs to know. That is not his burden to bear, but rather ours. Mine and Okta's and the Elders'."

Kalek turned to Marnej, who still would not meet his gaze, but he did not need to see the boy's eyes to know that he was troubled. Marnej's jaw was squared and clenched, and the ropy muscles of his neck were taut. He rocked ever so slightly as if readying himself for some action.

In an instant, Kalek understood the mistake he had made, the mistake they all had made. Marnej, like Irjan, had been trained for action, but none among their kind had given that fact the weight it deserved. They were all too tired, too disheartened to do anything other than pretend their lives had not changed. They had just let Marnej wander, aimless, and that had proved dangerous.

Marnej needed a calling to suit his soul, because unlike Irjan, who had a prison to bind him, Marnej had chosen to stay among them of his own accord. Kalek neither wanted the boy to regret his decision to stay, nor end up in prison if he decided he wanted to leave.

"Dárja, go inside and clean up," Kalek said. "I will accompany Marnej to the carver and tanner. The damage has been done, and we have learned something that will not soon be forgotten."

Kalek approached Marnej, cautiously reaching out a hand as if he were gaining the trust of a wary animal.

"Come," he gestured, adding, "It will be fine."

Marnej stood frozen, looking at Kalek's outstretched hand. Then he nodded, his hair falling into his eyes to hide them from view.

"I want to come with you," Dárja said.

Kalek turned back to her, shaking his head.

"I need you to go into the apothecary and finish what I have started at the fire. Strain the liquid and place it in a large wooden bowl, then remove the bark, and leave it dry on the table. When you have done that, let the pot cool before you wash and dry it. We should be back by then."

"Wait," she called after them. "Marnej, wait!"

Marnej kept walking beside Kalek. The deer's head lolled against the boy's shoulder. Its dark eye stared up a Kalek, holding him responsible for Marnej's recklessness.

Dárja caught up to them, planting herself in front of Marnej, forcing him to look up or run her over.

"I'm sorry," she said, winded. "I think you know things I know because . . . because you're Jápmemeahttun. But you don't."

Marnej sagged a little as he exhaled.

Kalek started to remind Dárja that she was needed back in the apothecary, but she interrupted him.

"Yes, I blamed you for what happened to my oktoeadni and accused you of ruining my life," she said, a hint of challenge in her voice.

Marnej stiffened.

"Dárja, this is a matter to discuss later," Kalek said.

"No, Kalek. That's the problem. Too little's been said or too much has been held back." She put up her hand to prevent Marnej's advance.

"I know that it wasn't your choice," she said. "Maybe it's time for us to stop blaming others for what can't be changed and learn how to live as we are."

Kalek, touched by the hope he saw in Dárja's fragile smile, waited to hear what Marnej would say.

"I have a lot to learn," the boy said, meeting her eye as he stepped around her.

Dárja attempted to follow, but Kalek held her back. "I trust you to take care of the apothecary for me, just as you must trust me to take care of Marnej." Then to ease not only her conscience but his own, he added. "This is not the first time this has happened. We have all learned in our own way and in our own time."

Kalek watched Dárja's retreating back just long enough to

be sure she would follow his direction, then he closed the gap to keep in step with Marnej.

"She tried to stop me," the boy said. "I didn't listen."

Kalek let silence fill in the space between them until Marnej was ready to say more.

"I was so frustrated," he began, then abruptly stopped. After a long pause he said, "We were talking about Irjan. Dárja was blaming herself for what happened and then she said she was sorry that I would never know him and the look in her eyes . . . I just wanted to scream."

"But not at her," he added with a sidelong glance.

"I wanted to scream and yell at whoever was really responsible. The Brethren. Your warriors. The gods. Somebody. Anybody." Marnej's tone grew more anxious. "But there was no one, and I felt like if I didn't do something, if I didn't take action, then I would rip myself apart from the inside out.

"And then I saw the deer. I knew it was something I could do," he said. "I can hunt. It's what I was trained to do. And I just wanted to prove that there was something within my power that I could control."

Marnej grabbed Kalek's arm. "You must believe me. If I'd known what would happen, I'd have never done it."

Kalek took hold of the boy's cold hand and squeezed it. He looked into his troubled eyes to make sure that he would be heard. "I believe you, Marnej. I know you would not have killed the animal if you had known the consequences."

"Does everybody know what I've done?" he asked, shame creeping into his face.

"No." Kalek shook his head. "Perhaps the Elders and the old ones who spend all their time listening to the Song, but you will not be singled out."

They began to walk again.

This time it was Kalek who struggled with what to say as a new fraught silence surrounded them.

"I think it is time that we help you learn what we all take

for granted," he said finally, waiting for the boy's reaction, and relieved to see him nod.

"Was it like this for my father?" Marnej asked.

The tentative inflection of his words, reminded Kalek that Marnej was still very much a boy—one who longed for his father.

"No. It was easier for Irjan. He had no choice in the matter. His movements were tightly controlled for many seasons of snow. What you are doing is much harder."

Kalek went on, ignoring the fact Marnej had stopped walking. "I think you may find it easier if you can choose a purpose that suits you."

When Marnej caught up to him, Kalek added, "Okta and I are happy to have you in the apothecary, but we are aware you are not inclined to listen to plants or wait for the right time to harvest."

Kalek felt certain Marnej would not challenge this blunt assessment. He might, in fact, even find relief in it. Still, he explained himself, "You have been trained for action. Plants and medicine are an art requiring patience and stillness. I do not know if your heart speaks to you about its true desires. If it does, then you should listen. If it does not, then you should ask."

Marnej said nothing until they approached the stables. "What happens if I don't find something?"

"I think it is rare for a heart to be without desire," Kalek said, moving to lift the deer from Marnej's shoulders.

Marnej drew back. It was a gesture some would have read as defiance. But Kalek took it to be a sign of his remorse, not just for the death of the deer, but also for the hate he had harbored toward Irjan.

"The deer is dead. It will not be wasted," Kalek said gently, coaxing the boy to give up the burden he carried.

Easing the animal into his arms, Kalek briefly bowed his head, honoring the animal's spirit and sacrifice. Then he passed through the stable doors, the boy at his heels.

Marnej shrank back toward the doors, rubbing his neck where the animal had rested, waiting patiently for the butcher to finish sharpening the tools at hand.

When axe and cleavers were finally set down, Kalek cleared his throat. "Tuá."

At her name, the nieddaš turned around. She glanced from Kalek to the deer and then to the doors where Marnej stood, his arms folded in front of him.

She stepped forward, placing her hand on the arrow in the deer's side. She closed her eyes and mumbled something which Marnej couldn't make out.

"It is unfortunate," Kalek said when the nieddaš opened her eyes, "But it is done."

"Indeed," Tuá said, her voice surprisingly gentle, Marnej thought, for one who butchered animals.

The nieddaš peered around Kalek's broad shoulders. Despite his desire to stay hidden, Marnej came forward to stand beside the healer. He'd never been a coward. He wouldn't start now. If this nieddaš wished to condemn him, then so be it. He would withstand the judgment and all others to come.

"A pity," she said, caressing the deer's long, slender neck. "Still. As you say, it is done."

"I will handle the matter," Kalek said with authority.

"And I will handle this matter," Tuá said with equal authority.

At a loss, Marnej hesitated when Kalek turned on his heels to leave. He stood in front of the nieddaš, wanting to say something—to explain. But he couldn't find the words, other than to say he was sorry. Tuá, looked at him, her axe in her hand. She acknowledged his apology, then motioned for him to leave. Marnej walked back out into the paddock, but glanced back to where Tuá worked, rendering the animal with focused intensity. He had hunted and killed animals for food and had never given it any thought. Now he worried that he would never be able to hunt again. How was he supposed to know which animals he could hunt? Kalek had pointed out he didn't have the patience to listen to plants. But maybe he didn't have the ability to listen to the animals either. As they entered the main sanctuary near the kitchens, Marnej offered up a silent apology to the animal, and to the gods if they listened.

"Marnej," Kalek said, startling him.

"I think, for the moment, it would be best if you returned to the apothecary. At least until I have spoken with the Noaidi."

"I should explain myself," Marnej said, feeling he was too old and had lived too long without a father to have someone protect him from his own actions.

"In time," Kalek said. "But for now, let me do what should have been done for you much earlier. In return, you can make sure that Dárja followed my instructions, because I sense you are gaining her respect."

Marnej snorted, then realized the healer had been trying to raise his spirits.

"I'll go and check on her," he said. "But I won't be telling her that."

"I don't think there is much any of us can tell Dárja," Kalek said, and Marnej detected an undercurrent of concern beneath the casual statement.

Before he could turn in the general direction of the apothecary, Kalek added, "And, Marnej, give some thought to what I said earlier. You deserve a path of your own."

Marnej watched the healer disappear around a corner, unease descending upon him once again.

He had railed against the gods and everyone else who stood in his way. But now that Kalek said he deserved his own path, he began to wonder if he truly merited it. He wasn't blameless in his actions, and he'd carried hatred in his heart for so long that he doubted he would find desire there. Still, walking along the corridor, Marnej reflected on Kalek's instruction.

What is my heart's desire? he quietly mused.

A muffled grunt of disgust escaped his lips.

I have no idea what that means, he admitted to himself.

He'd been trained to be a Piijkij, and he'd done what was expected of him. But now Kalek wanted him to come up with a calling of his own. *Well, I won't be a hunter*, he thought grimly, then shuddered, reliving the scream he'd heard in his mind.

"Have you no other purpose than to wander like the witless?" A sharp voice rang out ahead of him.

Marnej looked up to see with sinking recognition, the imposing nieddaš who'd spat at him his first day among the Immortals. Okta called her Úlla, and he'd seen her on occasion, but she hadn't come near him since that first day. The expression she presently wore wasn't much friendlier than their first encounter. Marnej wished he could avoid her, but he couldn't turn around without seeming weak. Determined to ignore her, he started walking again, prepared to take whatever she offered in stride.

As she neared, Marnej kept his gaze forward, but he couldn't help but see her scowl. The dark smudges on her cheeks made her look like a wild creature. When he passed her without incident he exhaled, relieved.

"Witless and spineless," Úlla laughed.

Marnej continued walking.

"You are no better than your father," she called after him.

Without thinking, Marnej turned and took a lunging step toward the nieddaš.

"Say what you will about me, but don't compare me to him. You know nothing of the matter!" Marnej's voice boomed in the empty passageway.

Úlla stood her ground, her broad shoulders rolled back, her fists at her side.

"You are just another mouth to feed," she hissed.

Marnej stood eye-to-eye with the nieddaš. "What would you have me do? You, who has opinions on everything. Tell me. What should I do?"

Úlla drew her head back, opening the space between them. "You can leave. Crawl back into the darkness that spawned your kind."

Marnej came in close again, taking in the hard curves around her mouth, the etched line between her brows. He laughed at her. "And give you satisfaction? No. I think not."

He stepped back, his pulse racing, but feeling in control finally. "I'm happy to live here peacefully. In fact, I believe I'll become a smith like you. After all, I'm skilled with weapons. Who better to craft them?"

Úlla glowered at him, but said nothing. Then she turned and strode away. Marnej chuckled, first at himself for being worried to cross paths with that spiteful nieddaš and then at the idea of taking on the trade of a smith. But the longer he considered it, the more it made sense. He had some experience with the forge, and being skilled with weapons made him a good judge of quality. Plus, it would give him great pleasure to make Úlla squirm. Marnej's step lightened as he continued on his way down the corridor to the apothecary. Maybe it wasn't his heart's desire, but it was a path.

CHAPTER TWENTY-FIVE

"I WILL LEAVE YOU TWO so you may work," Okta said, reaching for his thick brown cloak that hung on the peg.

Kalek looked up, stricken. "Where are you going? I thought you would help us with today's lessons."

The ancient healer smiled broadly. "I am going to gather the last of the herbs before the hard frost comes. You are more than capable of conducting the lessons, Kalek."

Kalek glanced furtively at Dárja, certain he had seen doubt in her eyes.

"Perhaps, I should gather the herbs and you conduct the lesson," he said, beginning to untie his apron.

Okta waved the suggestion off and put on his cloak. "It is time for you to take on an apprentice, and who better than Dárja?"

Kalek stared at Okta, willing him to return. But his mentor did not even look back before slipping out into the garden.

"We should begin with simple mixtures," Kalek finally said through the lump in his throat. His voice sounded like a croak, but he pressed on determined to regain his dignity.

"If we start with a simple mixture, then you can be of assistance as your training progresses." Coming to stand beside Dárja, he asked. "What will we need for the coming dark season?"

"Mixtures to soothe fevers, coughs, and chills," she readily supplied.

For one brief moment, Kalek gaped at her, then recovered himself enough to close his mouth.

Dárja shrugged off her readiness. "I grew up here, or don't you remember?"

Try as he might, Kalek could not keep a serious face. He crossed his arms, then leaned back, opting for levity over the rote droning of a master to a pupil. "What else did you observe?"

Dárja's ears reddened, their tips like bright toadstools peeking through her dark mop of hair.

"Well, I remember you can use honey to sooth a raw throat," she said, drawing out her response. "And it can be used to keep a wound clean," she added, picking up speed. "You can also mix honey and uulo and heal a cough." Dárja paused, casting her eyes upward, as if to recall far-off memories.

Kalek waited patiently. When it became clear she was at a loss, he said. "Good. You picked an excellent place to start. Let us look at uulo. Could you recognize the plant if you needed to?"

Dárja shook her head.

"In spring we will examine the plant, listen to its song, and watch it change through the seasons," he said, reaching up to untie a bundle of dried branches. "For now, you should know it can grow to waist height and spread in a wide patch. The leaves are deep green and oval, about the length of your small finger." He plucked a dried leaf from the bunch, holding it out to Dárja, who placed it in her palm.

Kalek went on, "One side is smooth and the other has a wooly coat. Even dried you can feel the difference."

Dárja ran the tip of her finger carefully over one side of the leaf and then the other.

"The flowers begin opening in Geassemánnu, when the days grow long. They bear five petals." Kalek put the bundle of herbs on the work bench in front of Dárja. "Tell me what you remember about uulo."

Dárja repeated Kalek's description with only a trace of youthful haste.

"Good," he said. "What parts would you use?"

"The leaves," she fired back.

"Yes. For what purpose?"

"You made a tea for me when I had a cough!"

Kalek nodded. "Excellent. You are right. But the beauty of this plant, like so many that support our lives, is that it has many roles."

He listed the three main uses, then finished with a rhyme apprentices learned when they began. "Root, leaf, and flower. All share their power."

Dárja nodded, repeating, "Root. Leaf. Flower. All share their power."

Kalek hid his smile by turning to a row of baskets behind him. He pulled two down, placing them in front of Dárja. Then he laid out the smooth weight stones he carried in his pocket.

"Measure two stone's worth of each. One is uulo. The other is bearberry. Grind them together and place them to simmer in the pot above the fire. I want you to note the changes at each stage. Smell the scent as they join together."

Kalek stepped back to watch Dárja as she began her tasks. He was reminded of Aillun. He marveled at Dárja's easy movements. One motion flowed into the next, without fumbling, without hesitation, until she stood before the fire stirring the herbs into the simmering water. *So like Aillun*, he thought, his heart aching at the resemblance.

"Kalek, how long have you studied with Okta?" Dárja asked, inhaling the rising steam.

"Half my life it seems," he said.

"Did you always want to be a healer?"

"No. When I returned from my Origin, I thought I wanted to train with the Taistelijan."

Dárja looked over her shoulder at him.

"Do not look so surprised," he laughed. "It was not that strange an idea, you know."

"Sorry. It's not that you aren't suited to be a Taistelijan," she said. "It's just, I never thought you were interested in it." Dárja trailed off, a blush blooming on her cheeks.

As Kalek watched her resume stirring, he silently marked the strange ways of the gods. He had been the one to train with the Taistelijan, but Dárja had been the one to fight. Images of the battle sprang back to life. And not for the first time, Kalek acknowledged that had he fought, it was likely he would not have survived. But Dárja had survived. He regarded her. It was as if Kalek saw her broad shoulders and well-defined muscles for the first time. Yet, he did not want to let go of the sweet mánná who had run behind his legs, giggling, believing she was hidden from both him and Irjan.

"You know, you were incredibly brave," he said, the enormity of Dárja's deeds sinking in. "I don't think I ever told you that when you returned to us. I was too concerned, too willing to see you as our mánná."

Dárja continued to face the simmer pot, stirring and breathing in the aromas.

With her back to him, it made it easier for Kalek to continue.

"Earlier, you reminded me of your oktoeadni. Your movements are so like Aillun's," he said unable to restrain his astonishment.

"And also like Irjan's," he added in a rush. "But, you are unique unto yourself. You have a gift."

Dárja bobbed her head once, as she continued to stir in slow even loops.

"I think you should continue to train with Marnej," Kalek said finally.

This time Dárja whirled around. Concern clouded her dark eyes. "You don't want me to work with you?"

Kalek could not help but let out a deep resonating laugh. "Oh no," he said. "Your work here is required. But, in addition to your studies with me, I wish you to practice your sword work and archery with Marnej."

Dárja's expression darkened.

Kalek felt the pressing weight of yet another misstep. "What?"

She shook her head.

Kalek stepped back, equal parts his own hesitancy and a need to appraise his student. "If you do not share what troubles you, I cannot help you find a way forward."

Guessing what might be troubling her, he said with great care, "I know it is not the same as practicing with the Taistelijan, but of the few who remain, none now train."

"Even if they did train, they wouldn't accept me," Dárja finished his words.

"No," Kalek said. "I believe they would accept you. But there is so much loss in their hearts they cannot see a future."

"That's not what concerns me," Dárja said, her attention on the herbs as she stirred.

"Irjan." The name escaped Kalek's lips before he could stop, and he wanted to kick himself for his blindness.

Dárja nodded, turning to face him. Her expression was drawn but her mouth trembled with emotion.

Kalek stepped forward and gathered her into his arms. "I know your heart hurts. I cannot say when or if the pain will recede. But I do know that your bieba would want you to continue—to show us all your depth of spirit. You honor Irjan by honoring what he taught you. And, you can give Marnej a piece of his father he has never had."

Kalek held Dárja at arm's length to look at her. "You are the best of us all."

He leaned in, then kissed the top of her head. "Now, go back to your herbs and tell me what you observe."

Dárja wiped her eyes and roughly ran her sleeve under her nose. She smile shyly as she picked up the ladle. "They smell sweet," she said, "like when fresh flowers are thrown on the bonfire of Longest Day."

"Good," Kalek said, taking down a pair of jars. He retrieved one of the weight stones and measured out the two different herbs. "You want to remove the simmer-pot from the fire just as the scent of fresh flowers turns bitter."

Kalek stole a glance at his young apprentice. *My apprentice*, he repeated to himself, feeling a twinge of misgiving. To be a good mentor, Kalek knew he had to rise above his feelings: his feelings for Aillun, for Irjan, for Dárja. But he was not sure he could do that. As he leaned against the work table and watched Dárja. He saw no part of him in her. Yet, he could not shake Irjan's insistence that Kalek was Dárja's father, in the way Irjan had been Marnej's father. Kalek repeated the word silently. It was a simple sounding Olmmoš word, but it had taken Kalek seventeen seasons of snow to say it.

I am her father, he thought, overcome by conflicting emotions and a daunting sense of responsibility.

~

The door to the apothecary swung open, banging against the wall. Both Dárja and Kalek jumped.

"She is insufferable!" Marnej groused, slamming closed the door as though it offered offense.

Marnej then proceeded to stomp through the quiet of the room as if he meant to crush everything in his wake. "Insufferable," he repeated, throwing himself into a chair.

The chair creaked under his weight.

"Who?" Dárja asked, her attention drawn back to the fire.

"Úlla!" Marnej said, his head in his hands.

Kalek laughed, as he sat down beside Marnej.

"In-suff-er-able," Marnej dragged out the word in exasperation, then leaned back in the chair, splaying his legs out in front of him. He looked at Kalek. "Would you believe, my task today was to chop wood for the fire?"

When Kalek shrugged, Marnej sat bolt upright. "All day. Any time I asked a question, she pointed to the axe. Any time I rested, she called for more wood. I chopped and carried and stacked wood. There is enough wood for the furnace now to last until she's old and grey, but she always wanted more."

"*She* won't get old and grey," Dárja pointed out, stopping her stirring.

Marnej glanced over, annoyed. "You get my point. She thinks she can order me about because her hair is golden and her eyes are green and rare. Well, I've seen that before."

"She can order you about because she's the metalsmith," Dárja said.

Before Marnej could register his outrage, Kalek interrupted, "Dárja, take the herbs off the fire now or they will be ruined."

Dárja twisted back to the fire. She reached for the handle on the simmering pot of herbs, then shrieked, holding her hand to her body. Kalek jumped from his seat, pulling her to the water barrel. He plunged her hand into its cold depths, then looked up at Marnej.

"Make yourself useful!" he shouted. "Take the pot from the fire, but use the leather gauntlet."

Marnej sprang to his feet, following instructions. The room smelled bitter and sour.

"I'm sorry Kalek," Dárja began to apologize.

Kalek held up his hand. "The healing arts require patience and attention. I will remind us both of this in the future." He left Dárja's side, then unrolled a length of linen, giving Marnej a withering glare.

"And I will remind you that the apothecary is not the bunk quarters of heavy-footed warriors. If you are weary, go to your bed. It will save us all your bellyaching. If you require assistance with a problem then please act with restraint and decorum."

"I'm sorry Kalek," Marnej apologized. "I'm tired and I'm frustrated. I want to do my part and contribute, but Úlla seems determined to punish me when I've done nothing to her."

Kalek rounded on him. "Úlla lost her beloved in the battle. For all she knows, you were the one who dealt the last blow."

Chastened and unable to think of anything else to say, Marnej mumbled contritely, "I'm sorry, Kalek. I didn't know."

"I do not require your apology," Kalek said. "Nor do I think Úlla will accept one. Your greatest hurdle, Marnej, is to be humble." The healer paused, then sighed. "Please try to understand that any task you do, even the most mundane chores, serves the lives of us all. So I say, thank you for chopping wood today. It should be Úlla's place to say it, but until she can, I will."

CHAPTER TWENTY-SIX

"Y OU HOLD THAT MIEHKKI like an Olmmoš," Dárja said, trudging out into the snowy clearing.

Marnej's slashing sword jerked to a stop.

"I'm sure the snow thanks you for showing mercy," she added, quite enjoying the opportunity to make Marnej flush red in the face.

"So your hand has healed," he said, raising his blade.

Dárja revealed the vibrant pink flesh of her palm which had recently been an angry cluster of blisters.

"It's not my fighting hand," she said, lifting the blade she carried.

"Seems a little thin," he said.

"Like your skill?" she suggested.

Marnej swung low, forcing Dárja to jump back or lose the tops of her reindeer skin boots.

Without thinking, Dárja sliced the air with her blade, the tip finding something solid.

Marnej winced, his breath a sharp inhale.

"I'm sorry," she said, sheathing her sword to move forward.

Márnej lashed out, catching Dárja's shoulder through her furs. She grabbed her arm and held it tight, the sting overshadowed by her surprise.

"Shouldn't you care for that?" Marnej asked, his grey eyes as icy as the snow around her.

"It's just a small cut," she said as she dropped her hand. "I've had worse. Move back and I'll show you."

Marnej dug in his heels, making a great pretense of holding his ground.

Dárja feinted left, then slashed right. Her thin blade cut the air with a lethal swipe.

Marnej leaped back just in time to avoid its bite.

"Running from a nieddaš?" Dárja asked, making light of her attack.

Marnej tightened his grip on his sword. "No, just avoiding a Taistelijan."

Dárja heard the mockery in his words and rushed him, but Marnej deflected the attack while stepping backward.

"You intend to back your way out of the Pohjola?" she asked, her attention on Marnej's footwork.

Marnej ducked under her high swing, then scooped up a handful of snow and threw it into her face.

Dárja swung blindly as she cleared the snow from her eyes, then froze, feeling the cold point of iron on her neck.

"Surrender and accept my terms," Marnej said.

"Never," she said, still wiping away the snow.

Marnej stood tall, his face serious, proud even. "Accept my terms."

Dárja flinched as the point dug deeper. "Name your terms, and I'll consider them."

"Return to the apothecary, treat your wound, and admit defeat," he said.

A reasonable enough request in other circumstances, but Marnej's imperious tone and condescending smile made it impossible for Dárja to consider it. She needed some way to escape, to deny him his smug authority. Unfortunately, his long reach kept his body safe from her kicks, and the blade against her neck made any advance to close the gap unwise. *But if I can knock aside the blade as I kick*, she thought. *I might have a chance.*

"By agreeing to your terms, what do I get in return?" Dárja asked cautiously, alert to any changes in Marnej's stance.

He began to laugh. With his head leaned back and his focus distracted, Dárja saw her opportunity. She swung both her sword and her leg around at the same time. Her blade pushed aside Marnej's weapon and her foot landed in the crook of his arm. Off balance, he stumbled to the side, and Dárja sprinted into the open ground.

Behind her, she heard Marnej's mumbled swearing, but she kept running, looking to the stone wall of the herb garden. She planned to use its height to her advantage.

Dárja was within sight of the herb garden's border when Marnej's great weight pushed her to the ground, burying her face in the snow. Dárja kicked and bucked to free herself until hands spun her around, dropping her on her back. She punched upwards with her sword hilt. Pain spiraled up her arm as the bones of her hand met even harder bone. Then, before she could move, Marnej sat astride her, pinning her arms to her side. Blood oozed from a cut above his left eye.

"Accept my terms and admit defeat," he said, panting.

Dárja arched up to push him off, grunting. "Never."

Marnej's eyes narrowed, and his mouth tightened into an ugly grimace. Then, to her amazement, he pushed himself off of her to stand.

"You are singularly incapable of accepting defeat," he said, his disgust writ large as he wiped the blood streaming into his eye.

Dárja rolled to her feet, her heart pounding. "The same can be said of you," she shouted at Marnej's back as he stormed off through the dormant winter garden.

"You can't accept being bested by me," she taunted venomously. Marnej opened the apothecary door, then slammed it closed, loosening the snow on the long, sloping eaves. Dárja bounded after him. Ready with more cutting insults, she pulled open the door that just moments before had closed on his swaggering backside, then ran ahead into the apothecary's work room.

Marnej was nowhere in sight. Dárja doubted he would disrespect the healers by hiding in their sleeping quarters. More than likely he had gone toward the forge. It was the only other place that his oversized opinion of himself had room enough to exist. *Cheating son of a mud-covered boar!*

With her indignation insisting on the last word, Dárja crossed the apothecary. She yanked open the door to the interior corridor, wincing. The cut to her shoulder began to throb in earnest, rapidly draining her interest in proving her point. The fire's warmth behind her beckoned. She closed the door with a resounding thud, then stomped back to the fire where she threw herself into a chair.

"Cheating Olmmoš," Dárja mumbled as the fire's warmth seeped into her, making her aware of all the places in her body that ached.

When the door to the apothecary opened, Dárja jumped to her feet, ready with a fresh litany of outrage against Marnej. Her words died on her lips seeing Kalek enter the room.

"You are wet," he commented, walking directly to the work table.

"It was Marnej!" Dárja all but shouted. "We were sparring. He got me at blade point, then demanded that I admit defeat. When I escaped, he chased me into the snow."

Dárja slumped back down into the chair before the fire. "And I'm the one who can't accept defeat," she muttered to no one. "He's the one who can't accept defeat."

"You are bleeding," Kalek said, taking hold of her shoulder.

Dárja twisted to look down at her arm. "It's a small cut. I didn't want to stop." She shrugged out of the healer's grasp. "Besides, you told me to practice with him."

She resettled herself, a slight smile curling up. "Well, I showed him something of Irjan."

"Take off your furs and shirt," Kalek said, sitting down beside her. "You have earned another opportunity to learn something about healing."

Dárja sighed heavily, then dutifully removed her outer layers and finally her tunic.

Tossing the clothing upon the work table, she stood with her hands on her hips. "Well, what will I need?"

"Let us see what you have learned so far," Kalek said, leaning back. "Take what you believe you need and begin. I will correct you if you need correction."

Dárja stared at Kalek, gauging his mood.

Comfortably ensconced in his chair, he gestured for her to begin.

Gods, Dárja hung her head, then resolved herself to gather what she needed. *Clean linen, honey, wild garlic, and salt.* As she made this mental list, she walked about the apothecary loudly protesting Marnej's cowardly tactics and his loutish behavior.

Kalek sat with arms folded, his head cocked to the side like a curious bird.

Dárja drew water from the barrel, then stalked over to where the braided garlic hung.

"All he can ever do is argue," she said, pulling off a head of garlic with a rough snap. The braided bunch swung into other drying herbs. Delicate leaves fell like a small flurry of snow. Dárja noted Kalek's disapproval, but ignored the mess she'd made. She pulled free several garlic cloves, then crushed them on the work table under her palm with a satisfying crunch.

"In the time we've known each other, Marnej hasn't changed at all. He's arrogant and rude and insufferable." Dárja banged her hand down again on the cloves as if to emphasize her point.

Kalek remained impassive, neither defending Marnej nor admonishing her. Dárja began to feel silly. She'd just called Marnej insufferable, but she was the one who had tromped around the apothecary like a mánná having a tantrum.

Dárja scooped out some boiling water and ladled some into the crushed garlic to make a paste. To the remaining water she added salt, stirring until the salt dissolved. Still she could not escape her fury. Marnej made her mad with frustration like no one else. Even her petty squabbles with Úlla were nothing compared to Marnej. Úlla had always judged Dárja harshly. That hadn't changed since her return. And Dárja certainly didn't envy Úlla having Marnej underfoot every day. A few moments was enough to make her want to scream. It was as if he deliberately wished to upset her.

Dárja blew across the salted water, then tested it with her elbow. Finding the liquid cool enough to apply, she placed her arm over a basin, then poured the hot, salty water down her shoulder. The sting made her draw in her breath through her clenched teeth. Dárja rinsed the fresh blood that seeped from the cut. The wound was deeper than she first thought, but she didn't want to admit that Marnej had been right to be concerned. She scooped up the garlic paste and rubbed it across the wound. Besides, he'd pushed her into the snow. Dárja's irritation flared, sparked in part by the bite of the garlic in her cut.

"Do you know, that clumsy Olmmoš sat on me like a moose about to calve," she said, looking over to Kalek for some support. He merely raised his eyebrows.

Annoyed with his lack of response, Dárja went on, pleading her case. "I couldn't get him off me. And when I refused to admit defeat, he stormed off."

She went to the basin, rinsed the paste off, and then dried the cut. Pleased to see the wound no longer oozed, she spread a swath of amber honey across the cut, then took a strip of clean linen and went over to Kalek.

Handing the healer the strip of cloth, she held out her arm for her shoulder to be wrapped.

"He said I was incapable of accepting defeat," she snorted in disgust.

Kalek worked quietly, intent on his task of tightly binding her shoulder. But Dárja perceived a reproof in his continued silence.

"What do you think, Kalek?" she asked, wanting to be vindicated.

The healer looked up, giving her a vague smile. "I think you should ask yourself why you are really angry."

He stood and patted her arm, then reached for the broom. "Your work just now was quite good."

Dárja looked over her wrapped shoulder to her mentor. Kalek was absorbed in sweeping up her earlier mess. She wanted to ask him what he'd meant, but that would just prove her querulousness. She knew why she was angry, but admitting it to herself was proving harder than she'd imagined.

~

Marnej stormed down the hall toward the forge. One moment Dárja acted the friend and then without warning she turned into a spitting badger. It made him think she still held him responsible for all her troubles, even though she now claimed it to be no one's fault.

Marnej passed the dining hall. It was early for the midday meal, plus he'd no stomach for food. But he didn't want to go to the forge just yet and endure the smug stares of the other smiths as he submitted to Úlla's pecking scrutiny. *She is worse than a barnacle goose on a nest.* He backtracked to enter the dining hall, happy to find it sparsely occupied. Even though the Immortals no longer avoided him, no one welcomed him to sit with them either.

Just as well, he thought. Isolation suited his mood today. He just needed a moment's peace to calm down and to collect himself.

Marnej sat down at one of the long tables, away from the fire. He rested his arms on the welcoming surface, then lowered his head, releasing the breath that he'd been holding.

"Didn't they give you a place of your own to rest," a voice behind him said.

A little peace. Is that too much to ask for? Marnej thought, raising his head.

Twisting to see who spoke, Marnej recognized Dárja's friend, Birtá. The nieddaš stood with her arms crossed in front of her.

"I needed a quiet moment," he said, his cheeks flushing as he met Birtá's frank gaze. He turned quickly, hoping the she hadn't noticed. *What's wrong with me?* he inwardly cringed.

"Well, I've been friends with Úlla my whole life and she is nothing if not demanding," Birtá said, drawing her own conclusions about what Marnej had shared. "Let me get you some stew. It'll help."

Marnej turned back in time to watch Birtá's round face soften into a knowing smile.

"You stay here," she said.

Birtá left him, a sigh escaping her which Marnej couldn't decipher. Perhaps he irritated her as well. *And why not?* he thought. It seemed to be a skill he'd perfected since coming to the Pohjola.

Birtá returned to his side sooner than he'd anticipated. Her plump curves had fooled him into believing her more measured than the others. It was another mistake in his judgment.

"Thank you," Marnej said, taking the bowl of stew she offered, not wanting to give offense.

"You should eat while it's hot." Birtá motioned to him not to dawdle.

Under her watchful gaze, he took his first bite of the stew still convinced he had no appetite.

The wonderful meaty broth filled his mouth. "Mmm," he mumbled as his body changed its mind and decided it was, in fact, hungry. Marnej took a couple of spoonfuls in quick succession.

Seemingly pleased, Birtá left him to return to the kitchen.

Marnej ate what remained, then used his finger to wipe down the sides of the bowl. He licked his finger with a wet smack of contentment.

"That good?" a voice said.

Marnej looked up from the empty bowl to see another of Dárja's friends, and nearly groaned, managing a cough instead.

"Can I sit with you?" she asked, and before Marnej could answer, the red-headed nieddaš with freckles bridging her nose sat down across from him.

"I'm Ello," she offered.

"I'm Marnej," he answered slowly.

She giggled, revealing small white teeth, perfectly lined up like soldiers. "I know who you are. We all do."

Marnej put his bowl down. "I suppose that's true."

Ello leaned in over the table to whisper conspiratorially, "We talk about you all the time."

Marnej's alarm must have been evident because Ello immediately added, "Nothing bad. I mean mostly. Is it true Dárja saved you?"

The nieddaš took a bite of her stew while watching him. Marnej wanted to be annoyed with her but her sweet open face showed only inquisitiveness.

"We saved each other," he said.

Ello blew a red curl out of her face, then took another spoonful of her food. "Úlla told me you're her apprentice. I work in the fields."

This time Marnej could not stop himself. "She calls me her apprentice?"

"When she's feeling kindly," Ello snickered, then began choking.

Marnej stood to help, but the nieddaš waved him down. She cleared her throat.

"Are you all right?" he asked.

Ello nodded.

"I'm more her lackey than her apprentice," he said, sitting down.

"Well, Úlla doesn't like you. You're a Piijkij, and you fought in the battle," Ello paused. Seeming to sense she was headed into a dangerous subject, she promptly changed topics. "But, Úlla probably treats everyone who works with her as a lackey. She treats me like I'm still a mánná, just because she's so much older than me. But she hasn't had a guide child yet. Well, she refused it when she found out Kálle had died." Ello's lively chatter ended abruptly. She shoved a spoonful of the stew into her mouth, looking embarrassed.

"How old are you?" Marnej asked, curious now that the subject of age had come up.

"I'm between my third and fourth mihttu," she said, still chewing on her stew.

"Is that old?" he asked, not really understanding what she meant.

Ello wiped her mouth, then grinned. "No. I'm quite young. Dárja's younger than me though. She's between her second and third measure."

Marnej interrupted, "But how old is that? How many seasons of snow?"

Ello snorted, "We don't measure those. I mean, we do, but . . . they aren't important." She paused, frowning in concentration. Then her smile returned like the sun from behind the clouds. "I think I'm between twenty-four and thirty-two seasons of snow, which makes Dárja close to eighteen seasons of snow. But I'm not certain of that. She always seemed older to me. Perhaps because she spent so much of her time apart from us."

Marnej toyed with the empty bowl in front of him. "You mean with my father?"

Ello's face scrunched. The freckles on her nose briefly over-lapped.

"I mean, Irjan," Marnej said.

Ello's features smoothed. "Yes. Dárja was mostly with her bieba when we were children and then later too," she said. "Although, I do remember playing with her occasionally."

"And Úlla?" Marnej asked.

Ello snorted again. "I don't think Úlla ever played with Dárja or anyone."

"No, I mean how old is Úlla?"

"Oh. She'll be in her fifth measure this Guovassonásti return."

"That doesn't seem so much older than you," he said, unsure of how many seasons of snow that was.

"Well, no. Not like Birtá and Tuá and Ravna." Ello pushed her bowl away to the center of the table. "They are all beyond their sixth measure." Then Ello paused as if something had just occurred to her. "How old are you?"

"Eighteen seasons of snow," Marnej said proudly.

"Oh," Ello said with an uptick of surprise.

"What?" Marnej asked, instantly wary.

"I thought you were much older. But you're so young. Like Dárja," Ello said, her disbelief evident in her appraising look. "I just assumed that because you're Olmmoš . . ." she didn't finish her thought.

"So in Immortal time," he began.

Ello burst out laughing. "Immortal? Is that what your kind think?" She gaped at him, her mouth open, stunned. Then she recovered herself with a knowing look. "Well, we certainly don't live forever. We're not like the gods. Only they are eternal. We just live longer than your kind."

"My kind," Marnej repeated, realizing he still thought very much like an Olmmoš.

"Oh, I'm sorry," she said, blushing red to the roots of her auburn hair. "I didn't mean it like that. It's just. It's just. Well, I don't know. I'm sorry. I didn't mean to give offense."

Ello's abject expression made it impossible for Marnej to stay irritated. He smiled to reassure her. "You didn't give offense. I'm just trying to understand."

"I'm sorry," she said. "It must not be easy for you."

Marnej shrugged. "I just want to understand."

Ello stood, then leaned across the table to pick up her bowl.

"Why did you sit down with me?" he asked, again curious about this nieddaš in front of him.

"Because I think you're handsome," Ello answered without hesitation.

Marnej felt the tips of his ears burning.

Ello let out another hearty, carefree belly laugh. "And because I was hoping you'd sharpen my tools." She wiggled her thin, arched brows at him then laughed even harder at his astonishment.

"That was far too easy," she said, when she regained her composure.

"What was too easy?" a sharp voice asked.

Marnej and Ello both turned at the same time to see Úlla standing at the end of the long table.

Ello's face fell, and Marnej muttered under his breath.

"There is more firewood to chop," Úlla said.

Marnej bit back the harsh words waiting to fly from his tongue, remembering Kalek's admonition.

"You're right," he said, standing up. He smiled at Ello, noting that she was really quite striking. "Thank you for my lesson today. I look forward to the next."

Marnej started to walk away to return his bowl, when he heard Ello behind him. "And don't forget, you agreed to sharpen my tools."

CHAPTER TWENTY-SEVEN

Gáral and Válde approached the travelers' hut out-side of Hassa from the north. Twice now Gáral had reminded Válde that stealth was not required. Rather, they needed to appear as forthright as possible.

"Like two binna herders looking for work," he had said.

But Válde felt stripped bare without his miehkki.

"Short knives are good enough for gutting farmers," Herko had said.

"But not enough for soldiers," Válde grumbled, laying his sword in Feles's hands.

"Well, you can't go strolling in there with a pair of swords claiming to be dung-reeking reindeer herders," Herko had pointed out, ever the pragmatist.

It had been a strange reversal of roles, but Herko had been right. Irritatingly so.

Other than their swords, not much remained to distinguish them from any other Olmmoš. They had long ago surrendered the emblems of the Piijkij, and their escape from the Believer sol-diers had coated them with enough grime and evidence of hard living to challenge their mothers to recognize them.

Not that any of them had seen their mothers since they had learned to walk. Most had been sold or given to the Brethren by their families who had one too many mouths to feed. After twenty seasons of snow with the Brethren, Válde had only a vague recollection of what his mother looked like. She was only a halo of wispy golden hair and a yeasty smell.

Gáral thumped Válde on the shoulder before opening the squat door. He folded back the reindeer pelt and entered the travelers' hut. Válde followed Gáral's impatient lead and was greeted by a wall of smoke and the stench of the fetid room. Válde swallowed his disgust as he scanned the clothing and faces lit by fire and torch. Assured that the hut contained no soldiers, he wound his way to a pair of low stools near the hutkeeper's barrels where Gáral had positioned himself.

The two of them rubbed their hands together, coaxing blood to flow.

"Food or drink?" the hutkeeper asked. Her pendulous bosom almost touched her thighs as she leaned forward to cup a hand to her ear.

"Food," Válde said.

"Drink," Gáral grunted.

The keeper nodded, then pushed herself straight to shuffle the short distance to the barrels.

"Keep a clear head," Válde warned.

Gáral snorted. "Keep your own counsel."

The woman returned, handing a cup of juhka to Gáral and a greasy bowl of stew to Válde. A lump of congealed fat rose to its surface, threatening to change any idea Válde had about eating. Hunger, however, won over his better judgment. He slurped from the bowl, watching Gáral tip back his cup. *At least the juhka is palatable*, he thought, envious.

Válde lifted his bowl to his lips, listening to the muffled conversations around him. Over the bowl's rim he regarded the huddled folk scattered in pairs about the hazy room. But it was the group of five nestled at the far end of a long communal table that drew his attention. Their loud garrulous voices rose above the other murmurings. *They must think the juhka palatable as well,*

Válde thought. He nudged Gáral lightly to guide his attention to the table.

"I tell you we were better off with them Immortals running around and us none the wiser of it," one of the five lamented, his vowels long and slurred.

"Shhh," another warned.

The first waved off his friend. "A man can speak his mind."

"Keep it down. You don't want soldiers hearing you talk," the friend said with a furtive glance around.

"I hear there's a regiment headed this way," a third man added, draining his battered wooden cup. "My brother's a farrier. He got called to the Stronghold. Sixty horses needed shoeing before they left." He held his cup forward and waited for it to be refilled.

"And?" one of them prodded.

"And what?" the man with his cup out said.

"And, what about the regiment?"

The man banged his cup on the table. The cautious friend shushed him.

"My brother said they're going to fortify the temple garrisons against them Hunters."

The hutkeeper shuffled over and filled the cups.

"I served with them in the battle," the first man tapped his chest, spilling some of his juhka.

"We all did," another pointed out.

"They were a tough lot," someone deep in the corner said. "I'd never thought they'd be the sort to be killing women and children."

"Cowardly, if you ask me," the one with the farrier brother shook his head.

Gáral paused with his second round of juhka halfway to his mouth. His eyes flashed over the cup to Válde, who scratched the side of his beard and nodded imperceptibly for Gáral to keep drinking, worried that the man's temper would flare at the offense. Gáral, however, kept his gaze loosely scanning the room. Válde was grateful for his comrade's forbearance because even he was sorely tempted to beat these drunkards for the answers he wanted and be done with them.

The five in the corner fell silent, some drinking, others perhaps too far gone to make the effort to talk.

Then like a bell on a clear and crisp morning, the one hidden in the corner said, "Well, a regiment headed here isn't good news. Even if they do hunt down and kill those rogue Hunters. Horse riders and foot soldiers require food and shelter and we've had poor harvests. We can barely feed ourselves, let alone a regiment of hungry mouths."

"I tell you it was better when them Immortals were living hidden away," the first man reprised his original lament. "At least there was no army making you fight or forcing you to feed them."

His friend filled the man's cup, speaking over him, "Did you hear that Árvet's sow escaped the pen and walked into the house? Árvet's wife was inside and when she heard snoring behind her, she turned to scold Árvet and found the sow laying before the hearth and Árvet asleep in his chair!"

The five men broke out into roars of laughter, then continued to speak about Árvet's bad fortune.

Gáral raised his eyebrows and hinted at leaving. Válde waved over the hutkeeper and gave her payment, which she held close to one eye to examine before dropping it into her apron pocket. The two Piijkij stood, pulling their cloaks tightly about them, then walked slowly through the room like two men who were not looking forward to the cold and dark world. Once outside, the pair picked up their pace, winding their way north into the trees where they met the rest of the Brethren.

"They spread lies," Gáral barked, before Válde could think of how best to share the news.

Beartu's expectant face fell. "What do you mean?"

"They accuse us of killing women and children," Gáral spat.

"But we did not," Edo sputtered, his anger flaring. "Nor would we ever!"

"No, Edo, we would not," Válde said to calm his indignant friend as he gauged the impact of the news. The expressions varied but the mood of the group was dark.

"There's got to be a better way," Dáigu said.

"There is," Herko said. "We live up to their lies. Let's give them something to fear and gossip about that'll at least be true!"

Muttering, like an unsettling wind, rippled through the group. Gáral's eyes honed in on Válde. "We have been too mild."

"And what would you have us do?" Válde asked, concentrating not on the insult given but where they might actually succeed.

"Burn the temples," Gáral exploded. "Let's see if the gods will answer their prayers when their temples are in ashes."

"Yes." The others chorused.

Dáigu and Edo, however, shifted, one uneasy and the other sullen.

"All men should be heard before we decide our future," Válde said, his belief in this absolute.

"Protect us from Edo's honor," Redde mocked.

The others smirked, even the normally stern Feles.

Edo's small features pinched into an even tighter cluster. "Laugh if you must. Once we begin down this path, we will not have a moment's peace until our end."

"Is peace what you want, Edo?" Gáral challenged, his vulnerable pride giving him stature. "Because, if it is, you can leave now and try to find a peaceful corner where you can keep your honor warm."

"Gáral! Enough," Válde said, his own patience balanced on an edge. "Edo has a right to speak. His voice is as strong as yours."

Válde turned to the seething Edo. "What you say is true. There will be no peace. A regiment has been dispatched to hunt us down and end us. They are to fortify the garrisons as they travel. If we are to strike, as Gáral has suggested, we cannot wait. We must strike before the outposts receive reinforcements, while they are still unaware."

Válde stepped in front of Dáigu, who had yet to speak. "And you? What is your say?"

Dáigu's normally comic features were harshly set. He dipped his head with the air of resignation.

"So, we are in agreement," Gáral stated, receiving enthusiastic support.

Válde noted the arrogant twist of Gáral's mouth.

"Hassa has a temple," Válde said, meeting the challenge.

Herko grinned. "Not for long."

~

Darkness hid the Brethren as they crept to the edge of the snow-dusted forest. The Believers' temple lay in the middle of crudely built log and turf huts. From the southeast, thick smoke rose from the garrison, weaving its way up through the low-lying mist.

"Starting the fire in these wet conditions will be difficult," Feles said.

"Not if we get inside," Herko corrected him, his restlessness evident.

"Separate fires will make quick work of it," Redde added, for once serious in his suggestion.

"Best to cut between those two huts," Gáral said, pointing. "The large one there and the small to the left."

"Gáral and I will go first," said Válde. "We will signal for the rest to follow. Dáigu, you stay behind with the horses. If we are caught you owe us no loyalty."

Dáigu did not protest.

Válde followed Gáral across the open ground, keeping low as he ran. When they reached the long hut, they hugged tight to its straight lines and deep overhangs. As they moved, Válde strained to hear if any soul stirred in the dismal gloom. But to his ears, he and Gáral were the only two about on this dark, freezing night.

At the corner of the long hut, Gáral stopped. Válde peered around him. They had another long stretch of open ground to cover before reaching the temple.

"Let's hope no one is about," Gáral said, echoing Válde's own thoughts.

Before Válde could acknowledge the comment, Gáral sprinted across the grey expanse of snow. Válde ran after him, his eyes sweeping the open ground until he reached the temple's low, sloping wall where icicles as thick as sapling branches menaced from above.

Gáral crept along the uneven wall, his lead hand searching for an entrance. He swore under his breath. "We will have to try the front."

Válde inched around Gáral to take a look for himself. If they pressed close to the roughhewn wall, they would only be visible when they reached for the front door. Voices on the path startled them. He and Gáral flung themselves onto their stomachs. This time it was Válde who cursed under his breath.

"Shh. The sentry will hear you," a loud voice slurred.

"We are the sentries," the other chuckled.

The two soldiers crumbled into hysterics, falling into each other as they laughed.

"Shush," one said, recovering himself enough to stand.

"Shh," said the other, with an exaggerated gesture.

The two bodies staggered past the temple, their renewed laughter fading into the haze.

Válde and Gáral jumped up and darted forward. Gáral pressed against the door. It creaked, but did not move.

"It's barred from the inside," he said.

Válde scooted forward to the next corner, then craned his neck around the edge.

"There is a stable," he said, looking back to Gáral. "If there is livestock . . ."

"There's a kitchen," Gáral finished the thought and slipped around the corner of mounded snow. With four long strides, he reached the lean-to stable that jutted out from the temple's southern wall.

Gáral lifted up the latch, grinning as the door swung open.

Válde could not help but grin back. "Go signal to the others. I will scout the kitchen and get torches ready.

Gáral disappeared around the corner as Válde entered the stable's dark interior. The pungent smell of animals and their dung replaced the fresh, cold air. Válde's mind raced ahead to anticipate obstacles and possibilities. Chief among his concerns was the chance that a cook resided beyond, or worse, armed men. The stable livestock rustled, aware their quiet evening was about to be disturbed. The roosting chickens awoke to protest with a rolling cluck, and the goats, contributed a few mournful bleats. Válde crossed the stable toward the sliver of light that winked beyond the pens.

At the door, he pressed his ear against the rough planks. No sounds from beyond alerted him to danger, but a cautious internal voice halted his advance. It would be better to have the strength of men behind him if they were to face armed guards.

Válde crossed back to the edge of the stables, careful not to bump into the dozing sheep and curious goats. Moments passed as an eternity as he waited impatiently for the others.

Greeting their arrival, he whispered, "There is light beyond the far door there. No sounds. But I cannot be sure if there is anyone beyond."

"Kill any that you meet quickly and quietly," Gáral said to those behind him.

At Válde's signal, the first of them rushed through the kitchen door, weapons at the ready to discover an empty kitchen with embers glowing in the hearth. Emboldened, the men pushed out into the hall, their desire for a fight growing. Gáral stalked back across to the kitchen, returning with four lit torches.

Válde spoke up as Gáral dispensed the torches. "One man sets the fire, the other keeps guard. The first out, release the animals and head for the woods."

Without comment, the men moved off, their need for vengeance filling the shadowed passageways. Swords drawn, Válde and Gáral reached a pair of matched doors. Gáral handed Válde the torch. A memory of their Avr flashed before his eyes. His recounting of the old story of "The Farmer and the Three Doors" came to mind.

"Be bold," Válde said, repeating the Avr's words now. "Death awaits us, whatever door we choose."

Gáral looked up, surprised. A slow grin split his brooding face. He pushed open the door, and Válde entered, fending off the room's inky darkness with the light of his torch.

The smooth edges of a table came into view. In its center sat a wooden box filigreed with bone. Gáral picked it up, and hearing the sound of clinking coinage, he said mockingly, "The gods thank you."

"As I thank the gods," Válde replied, bowing. With a sweep of his arm, he cast the stacked books and vellum into a corner, then drove his torch into the nest of papers, enjoying the crackle of the dry parchment.

Gáral broke open the box with the pommel of his sword, scattering coin and crude jewelry. He scooped the contents, then tossed the box onto the growing fire that had begun to lick up the fissured walls.

"What are you doing?" a panicked voice cried out.

Gáral swung around, the point of his sword aimed at the gaping man's throat. The figure, dressed in a sleep tunic with a fur about his shoulders, trembled in the doorway, despite the heat of the growing fire.

Gáral's blade dug into the man's flesh as he pushed him out into the hall.

"Are you the temple priest?" he snarled.

Válde brought the torch near the man's face. His eyes were wide with fright.

"Are you the only one in the temple?" Válde pressed.

The man made a sound somewhere between a whimper and a sneeze that made Válde think the man had said, "Yes."

"Move," Gáral motioned. The priest shuffled, his tunic held unflatteringly above his boney knees. "Run and I will kill you," Gáral added menacingly.

Válde set his torch to the straw mattress in the next room.

"I will have nothing. Nothing at all," the man whined, shielding his face from the flash of intense heat.

"You will still have your gods," Válde said, rejoining the pair in the hall.

Gáral nudged the priest, keeping the sharp point of his blade at the man's back to remind him of what would happen should he run. "Let's go," he said.

The sound of approaching footfalls met the trio as they neared the kitchen. Válde turned ready to engage but relaxed when Edo turned the corner with Herko on his heels, wearing a grin on his face and a bulging pouch at his belt.

Válde eyed the pouch wordlessly.

"Nothing that the gods can't spare," Herko answered without being asked.

"You should have seen the tapestry light up," Mures laughed, bringing up the rear.

"No!" the priest moaned, his knees giving way before the blade at his back made him straighten with a sharp intake of air.

"Save your laments for the Vijns," Gáral said, pushing him through the kitchen and into the stables beyond.

"You are not going to kill me?" the priest stammered in disbelief as they emerged into the snow-blanketed night.

"If I killed you, how would the Vijns learn that the Brethren of Hunters send their regards?" Gáral smirked, then turned serious. "But I also can't have you running to the soldiers until we are long clear of here."

The priest crumpled to the ground, crying out in agony, blood spurting from the back of his unshod heel where Gáral had cut him to the bone.

CHAPTER TWENTY-EIGHT

NIILÁN RODE WITH THE vanguard of his chuoði, leaving Jonsá and Joret to mind the regiment's rearguard. He reasoned that if he were first to hear the news, then he would likely be hearing the truth and not some version meant to garner favor or hide culpability. However, he also kept Matti and Osku with him, to ensure his orders would reach the rearguard intact.

Niilán pulled his cloak tighter about himself as they rode north into the day's increasing darkness. He wished he had full furs to keep warm, but no one had full furs. It seemed the Believers' army did not need furs when they had the gods to protect against frostbite. Niilán believed in the gods just as much as any man, but he also believed he would have been warmer in furs. *Who cares if they hide the army's emblems and rank?* he silently complained. Still, he could not deny that there were advantages to promotion. He was thoroughly grateful to be astride a horse instead of on foot. But there were drawbacks which the Vijns's agent, Áigin, had neglected to mention. The reality of the simple assignment was proving to be far more complicated.

Niilán was at pains to simultaneously track down the last of the rogue Piijkij as he traveled between temple outposts, bolstering their ranks and warning them against desperate acts. The two tasks were not necessarily at odds, but the slow, circuitous route hampered his chance for success in the first directive. Niilán wished he could have a fully mounted unit, but there were not enough horses to spare for the entire regiment. He knew that he could set a much more demanding pace, but he took pity on the foot soldiers, having once been in their place. It would not serve him to devastate his forces in the initial push. They would make it north when they made it north, and he would track down the rogue Piijkij eventually. Time and superior forces were ultimately on his side. If fortune favored him, then Niilán would soon capture the remaining Brethren. If fortune merely turned a blind eye to him, then he had to hope the Vijns might find a little patience. Niilán doubted either outcome. But for the moment, at least, he had one master, which was better than the three he'd had as a foot soldier.

A scout rode toward him, bringing his horse around, steam rising from the rider's mount.

"We have reached the next village," he reported.

"What is this one called?" Niilán asked, resignation taking hold of him.

"Ullmea."

"Small or large?"

The scout snorted. "Small enough to have only one travelers' hut, but large enough to have a temple."

Niilán acknowledged the soldier's scorn with a quick nod and a crooked smile. He knew he should reprimand the man for his slight to the Order of Believers. However, as a new commander he was more interested in garnering his regiment's loyalty. The Believers would not be here to defend him in an attack. This man would be.

Niilán resumed his reserve. "How far?"

"A league at most," said the scout.

"Excellent," Niilán said, truly glad for the news. "Ride by my side for a moment."

"Osku," he called out.

The stout soldier on a sturdy light bay horse appeared beside him.

"Sir?"

"Gather the men to be stationed at this garrison. We will ride ahead and perhaps avoid a lengthy stay. Have Matti ride to the rearguard and prepare them to travel through Ullmea without stopping."

With a silent nod, Osku and his horse broke to the right.

Niilán heard the roll call of men's names, recognizing a couple. Both were seasoned men and a loss to their dwindling force.

Osku circled back to his side, trailing a half-dozen men.

Niilán looked at the scout, "Lead on."

~

Approaching the outskirts of Ullmea, Niilán was dismayed to discover his scout had described the village accurately. He had held out hope it would be better than a cow stop in the middle of a cart path. It wasn't. Fortunately, they need only go to the garrison, deposit the men, and share their news. With the grace of the gods, they would be done before the foot soldiers broke through the woods, providing the scribe was readily available and the outpost commander was not drunk.

The lack of village fortifications suggested that Ullmea had few, if any, resources to protect. Still, they had managed to erect some semblance of a gate. Rough-cut logs were guarded by a pair of dirt-smattered sentries. Above their heads hung the Vijns's ten-star shield next to a crudely carved symbol of the local temple, which was either a crescent moon or a bull's horns. Niilán could not tell. The angle made it hard to know. *At least we have a greeting party*, he thought.

At the makeshift gate, Niilán's horse shied, filling the air with black wings and a crow's accusatory chorus. His men waved off the crows, looking like ungainly birds themselves. In place of the scavengers was a woman's head, impaled upon a pike. Her flesh, mottled by violence and the cold, had been pecked down to the bone in places. Niilán had seen enough death that it should have held no fascination and yet he gawked. A slow-dawning awareness took hold of him as he stared at her broad brow and the one eye that remained.

A skinny soldier with mud up to his knees grinned ear to ear.

"We got another one of them," he said. His crooked teeth whistled mockingly.

"What is this?" Niilán demanded, guiding his mount forward to tower over the sentries.

"They won't come here again when they see her," the other sentry said.

Not even old enough to have been there, Niilán thought. These guards were pups—runts. He swallowed down his distaste. It was one thing to kill Jápmea warriors on a battlefield, but to kill their women when the Immortals were already defeated was an insult to all those who had died. Niilán wanted to wipe the grins from their idiot faces, but there was nothing to be gained by it. The sooner he could dispatch his duty in this wretched village, the better it would be for all of them.

"Your bravery was truly missed in the Great Valley," he said, then asked, "where is your garrison?"

While his companion tried to parse Niilán's meaning, Crooked Teeth pointed to the east.

⌇

Garrison is too grand a name for this outpost, Niilán thought as the icy snow mixed with rain to make him more miserable. The palisade, such that it was, would not keep out a determined moose. And the moat was hardly more than a shallow ditch. But that was the commander's problem, not his. Once he presented the Vijns's orders and deposited the needed men, he would leave without a moment's regret. Niilán dismounted, noting the warped planks across what was a natural bog and not any man's effort at a defensive ditch.

He handed his reins to the scout. "Stay with the horses. Make sure they are fed and watered, but do not unsaddle them. I want to leave as soon as we have conducted business."

The scout took the reins without comment. His bedraggled horse pawed the mud that stuck to everything.

"Bring the men," Niilán said to Osku.

Osku dismounted, motioning to the others to follow. The men tethered their horses together with curious regard for their new circumstance. Niilán marked their disappointment, but their morale was no longer his concern. Leading his party across the sagging planks, he hoped there would be at least a warm fire inside.

"I bring word from the High Priest and men for your camp," he called to the hunched sentries.

The guards shifted. They eyed Niilán and his men before opening the gate. The outpost, because Niilán refused to think of it as anything else, was hardly more than a few huts arranged within a wooden palisade. The defense tower sat on a hillock that was little more than a sloping mound. Saddle-sore, Niilán limped up the incline with a pessimistic, plodding step, his mood only slightly improved at the sight of rising smoke. At the top, he stopped before a pair of puffed-up guards.

"Niilán of the Vijns's personal regiment. Orders from the High Priest and men to bolster these ranks," he said, waiting for these soft-bellied louts to step aside. Their slow recognition fueled his foul temper.

"I will speak to your commander," he said. "Now."

The men stepped aside. Niilán strode up to the defense tower, determined to be done with this task. At that door he repeated himself. This time the guard acted with haste to usher him along.

Scarred and balding, the outpost commander scowled when Niilán entered.

"Orders and men from the Vijn," Niilán stated without pleasantries, walking directly toward the fire. He was damned if he would stand in the drafts.

"About time," the commander said, then appeared to reconsider his smugness by holding out his arm in the accepted greeting of equals. Niilán grasped the man's arm, relaying his information.

"I have farm boys and failed acolytes," the commander said, pulling a ewer out from under his chair. "I could use some men."

Niilán held up his hand to stave off the pouring of whatever festered in the pitcher. "The men I bring are experienced. They are not many, but they are driven and all that we can spare. We are heading north on reports there have been Brethren attacks."

The commander gulped down his drink. "Brethren? I thought they'd been routed."

Niilán shrugged. "The survivors have begun a . . ." And here he faltered, unsure of what to say. He settled on the weakest response, "They have begun a resistance."

The commander swallowed the contents of his cup with a grimace. "They always were a brazen bunch," he said.

"The Vijns's orders are to stay alert for danger and protect the temple and village," Niilán replied, intent again on his purpose.

"Not much to protect," the commander sniffed.

Niilán did not waste time agreeing. "Your scribe?" he asked. "I want to put these orders in writing and enlist these men in your roll."

The commander poured from the ewer and shouted, "Selen!"

A soldier appeared.

"Get the scribe."

The soldier turned and left.

"Experienced men you say?" the commander asked, picking up on their earlier exchange as he eyed Niilán. "You look experienced yourself. Were you in the Great Valley?"

Niilán nodded. "I was fortunate to make it out."

"We all were," the commander said.

Niilán considered the man. *Just a soldier caught up in saving himself*, he thought, then wondered how many more were like him.

The outpost commander held out his cup to Niilán in a salute.

Niilán held up his hand once again to decline the offer, adding silently, *Far too many men.*

CHAPTER TWENTY-NINE

THE NOAIDI STOOD BEFORE all those who remained to honor Darkest Day. Once their kind had gathered outside in the hushed snow because no walls could contain their numbers. Now they all sat within the confines of the gathering hall. Einár bowed his head in remembrance. A weary sadness had taken root within him.

In the past, the ritual centered on faith, on hope, on the sun which would choose the Jápmemeahttun over the gods and return to shine upon them once again. Even now, when so much had been lost, Einár believed the sun would eventually return, as it always had, season upon season. But he feared that the same could not be said for their kind.

One by one, the Elders came forward to join him. Candles cast a soft glow across their faces, and Einár prayed that his own misery would remain hidden. He held up the ancient, deerskin drum in his hand, then closed his eyes and began to chant, drumming in a rhythm that matched the beat of his heart.

We are the Jápmemeahttun.
We are the guardians of the world.
Our memory stretches back to the start of days.
Our vision reaches beyond all tomorrows.
We sing together as one, so that our one may always survive.

Einár listened to the swelling sound in the room, his drumming like the binna sweeping across the land. Then he sought the voices within him. The shifting melodies of the Song of All greeted him with a comforting familiarity. Einár wanted to lose himself within their splendor, but his duty to those who relied upon him for guidance remained forefront in his mind.

The chanting fell away to a hum as the drum beat grew in strength.

On cue, Einár began the story of their kind. "We entered this world creatures of the gods. We embraced the world and were grateful for its beauty and its bounty. And we flourished."

Guovassonásti had shined upon Einár longer than any. *More than two hundred seasons of snow*. Yet, these opening lines still held meaning because the very essence of the Jápmemeahttun was woven into them.

He changed the drum's tempo, the timbre softening.

"We flourished and our wellbeing blinded us to action and consequence until we stood upon the dark abyss." Einár instinctively inhaled, readying himself to repeat their history, their faults, their travails, then found himself questioning the need. They were facing their end. *Why not embrace hope?* he thought. *As the first to witness the miracle had*.

Those gathered became restive as Einár made his decision to reprise the story close to its end, his drumming the soft patter of spring rain.

"We are reminded of our past in these dark days," he said, "But, in darkness there is light. We yearn for the return of the sun just as we once begged the gods for the chance to live. Let us remember that tomorrow and each day beyond is part of our journey into the light. Let us offer thanks for the gift of darkness."

The candles in the room flickered out until only one remained aglow. Einár laid down his drum. He took the last lit candle and walked slowly through those gathered. For the first time in his long life, the Noaidi was glad the deep shadows veiled the faces turned toward him. He could neither bear witness to their hope nor could he endure seeing their despair. As he walked out of the gathering hall, Einár kept his gaze forward, intent on the flame.

~

Okta followed the Noaidi at a courteous distance. He did not wish to intrude on the last moments of Darkest Day, but the Elder's deviation in the story fed his uncertainty. As Okta wrestled with his doubt, Einár opened the door to his chamber, then closed it with a soft thump.

Okta hesitated before the door. He placed his ear to its polished surface like a curious mánná, listening for some sound that would tell him whether his visit would be welcomed. Then he chided himself for his silliness and knocked loudly.

"Come," the Elder called from within.

Okta entered, at once relieved he did not need to suffer the doubt of a second knock and distressed about the nature of his visit.

"Okta," the Elder beckoned the healer in. "You are a welcome sight."

Okta's heart sank even further, but he let the warm greeting between two old friends prevail.

"You spoke to my spirit tonight, Einár," Okta said, embracing the Elder.

"Sit, Okta. Let us enjoy the fire."

Healer and Elder fell into companionable silence, each staring at the flames as if they offered answers to whatever matter occupied their thoughts.

"We are facing our end," Einár said finally, as if a force outside him had required a reckoning.

Okta met his gaze. He wished he had the conviction of an earlier time to argue this point, to believe in a better path. But there was no better path. There was only the one they were on now.

"I believe you are right," Okta said and then, because his heart would not let him doom those he loved, he amended his thoughts.

"Perhaps not tomorrow or in a hundred tomorrows, but there will come a time when the sun will not rise for us."

Einár leaned forward to prod the embers.

"I will not be here to see it," Okta added.

There, I have said it. It is done, he thought, savoring his first deep breath in days.

Einár's eyes caught the firelight. Their watery borders wavered. "Your time has come?"

"I feel it in my body," Okta said, slowly unwinding into the truth. "I have counseled too many not to know."

Einár frowned. "Can you tell . . ." he began, then let the question drop away.

Okta offered his old friend a sad smile. "I doubt I will enjoy the bonfire of Longest Day with you."

Einár nodded. "Does Kalek know?"

Okta shook his head. "No. I have not wanted to burden him with this knowledge. He still lives with the darkness of war and Irjan's death. He is too observant to not recognize what is becoming of us, but his heart is also too fragile to meet it head on."

"Will he be ready to take on your duties?" Einár asked bluntly.

Okta considered the question before answering. "He is a fine and gifted healer. What he needs is something to bring hope back into his life."

Einár leaned back in his chair, his shoulders hunched. "What of Dárja?"

"She is his apprentice now. Their bond is strong and tender. But Irjan's spirit haunts them both."

Einár's brows furrowed. "When will you tell them?"

"I do not know," Okta admitted. "I have promised myself I will tell Kalek when I feel he is ready, but in truth that may never be the case."

"At some point he will suspect. You yourself just said he is observant."

Okta acknowledged Einár's concern with a shrug. "We watch the nieddaš leave, trusting they will return to bring us life. But fewer return. We see what is happening, but we wish for a different outcome each time. We are all observant, but we choose not to see."

Einár leaned forward and put his hand upon Okta's. The reassuring pressure offered comfort.

Okta stared at their hands. Their fingers were crooked after so many seasons of snow. *Knuckles like knots upon a tree*, he thought, recalling how these hands had comforted mánná, wielded swords, caressed loved ones, healed bodies, and guided souls. There was a lifetime of experiences in them both.

"Einár, tell me what I should do," Okta pleaded.

The Elder tilted his head back and chuckled. "After all these seasons of snow, only now do you ask my guidance."

Okta took the gentle mocking, deserving of it. "Better to see the wisdom now than never," he said.

Einár's laughter trailed off into a burdened sigh. "My old friend, I find I cannot advise you on when to tell Kalek because my own heart aches when I think of the loss I must also endure."

Now it was Okta's turn to offer solace both to a friend and a revered Elder. He struggled to find the right words, the right gesture. He came to the crushing realization that his long life, with all its experience, had not prepared him to meet the broken spirit of the Noaidi. Okta took Einár's hand in his and held it as they sat quietly listening to the Song of All within, wondering how much longer the melody would continue.

∾

Kalek hummed to himself, pulling down jars and examining their contents.

"You seem in fine spirits," Okta said, glancing up from the vellum before him. "Having an apprentice agrees with you."

"It is a blessing to have Dárja back with us," Kalek said brightly. "I think she has a skill for herbs and healing."

Okta sniffed. "Well, I should hope she picked up a thing or two. She did grow up running around under our feet."

Kalek shifted his consideration from the jars to Okta. "It is more than that. She is thorough and precise without my admonishment."

"I imagine that would be Irjan's doing," Okta said, cutting a sharper edge to his quill.

Kalek returned to his measures and Okta scratched out lists and ingredients and instructions, listening to the wind whistle through chinks in the walls. *I will need to see to repairs come the melt*, Okta noted to himself. *Or rather, Kalek will.*

"Do we have more dried alder bark?" he asked, running out of ink just as his gloomy thoughts took hold.

Kalek scanned the fading birch-skin labels. "We should darken these," he said, opening one to sniff. "You and I know what each is, but Dárja does not."

"You are right," Okta said, distracted briefly by the idea. "How is Dárja with her script? If I remember correctly, our long-ago lessons did not go well."

The corner of Kalek's mouth curled up into a half-smile but his brows remained dubious. "She was small and you were impatient."

When did those lines become so deeply etched? Okta thought, studying his apprentice. Kalek was still young, barely into his tenth measure, with many a Life Star return to anticipate. He should not have lines like that.

"You have ink on your cheek," Kalek said.

Okta raised his sleeve to wipe away the unseen ink. "You did not answer me, Kalek."

"She is proficient," he said.

"Then have her retrace the labels," said Okta. "She can familiarize herself with the contents and location in addition to the naming."

"How much of the alder bark do you need?" Kalek asked, waiting to measure out some from the jar.

Okta rose. "Leave it to me. But, I would like you to go to the forge to see if there is a nail I can use. I can finish gathering and grinding the ingredients for the ink while you are gone."

Kalek placed the jar on the table. His eyes narrowed, but his voice remained playful. "Do you desire to be rid of me?"

"Mercy of the gods, cannot a boaris ask a favor of his young apprentice without his motives being questioned?" Okta began to admonish, then changed his mind. He let go of his counterfeit scowl and smiled at his apprentice. "There is no one I would rather spend my time with."

"That's because no one else will put up with you," Kalek snorted. "And you are not nearly as old as you pretend to be. Boaris! Indeed. When did you start calling yourself that?"

"The moment I had apprentices, like you, who caused the hair in my beard to turn white while waiting for them to do as I asked!"

Kalek waved off the rebuke as he walked to the door. "Can I bring you something besides the nail?"

Okta shook his head. "No. Just the nail."

When Kalek closed the door behind him, Okta sank into his chair as a wave of pain took hold of him. He had felt it building as he and Kalek talked. He had been praying for privacy because he feared he could not disguise it. Sweat dripped from his brow as heat suffused his chest, making his skin prickle as if on fire. He grasped hold of the edge of the table, waiting for it to pass. When it did, his consolation was that he had sent Kalek on the errand. He could not have hidden his discomfort, and Kalek would have worried. Then Okta would have had to face questions he could neither answer truthfully nor lie about.

Okta rose slowly to his feet. He steadied himself, then turned and looked at the jars, scanning their familiar but faded labels. Kalek was right. They needed to be refreshed. Okta ran a fingertip across the faint marking on the jar before him. Vuodjarássi. He measured out, then crushed the dried dandelion before adding the water he had set to boil upon the fire. He hoped the tea would ease the ache in his limbs.

When did we last inscribe the jars? Okta wondered as his tea steeped. He could not remember. *Perhaps when Aillun was first apprenticed.* He shivered, expecting another spasm. But this time Okta's discomfort was not physical. Rather, his unease came from a sense that the past promised to repeat itself.

No. Okta shook his head to banish the idea. *Dárja is different than Aillun.* Then to offer proof to himself, he made a mental list of all their differences until the worrisome feeling passed. Just as his last seizure had. Okta busied himself with the ingredients he needed to replenish his ink as his mind wandered back to thoughts of Kalek.

Two sides of an argument pulled at him. Okta knew he should tell his apprentice, and yet how could he when Kalek's mood had finally brightened? He wanted the almai to live in lightness, for a while at least. Kalek had already experienced too much of the dark. *And besides, what good will it serve either of us to have a long drawn out ending?* he asked himself. Kalek would only fall back into desolation, and Okta would be helpless to change it. The old healer looked over his shoulder to his forgotten tea. He ladled out a cup and strained it. *No. It is better to leave it to the very end*, he thought as he absentmindedly blew across the already-cooling surface.

CHAPTER THIRTY

KALEK COULD NOT STOP thinking about Okta's odd manner as he walked toward the forge. There was something veiled in his words but Kalek could not be sure what it was. Perhaps Okta was concerned about Dárja. Perhaps he thought her not up to the task. If that was the case, Kalek trusted he had changed his mind. Dárja had proved herself more than capable. She was actually quite talented. But he would not tell her that. He did not wish to give her reason to ease off in her efforts. Still, he counted himself blessed to have Dárja in his life. Although, she often drove him mad with frustration. Kalek smiled to himself, thinking it odd how even her fits of temper were becoming precious to him.

Dárja will make a fine healer, he thought. And before he could stop himself he added, *Like Aillun*. Not for the first time, Kalek observed that the passing seasons of snow had not wiped away his regrets. Rather, his memories seemed to be covered in a fine layer of dust which blurred their sharp contours.

Walking into something solid, rudely brought Kalek out of his musings. He stumbled back a step, then recovered himself, saying. "Ello, forgive me."

He held out his hand to the nieddaš who sprawled before him on the ground. "I was lost in my thoughts."

Ello wiped her hands off, then took Kalek's, "Well, as long as you were thinking of me," she said, her flash of pique turning to brashness.

Kalek pulled her to her feet, then attempted to release her hand, but the nieddaš held on.

"You were thinking of me, weren't you?" She smiled brightly with a wink.

Kalek hesitated, taken aback by her wolfish grin. "I was thinking of Dárja," he said vaguely, prising his hand free to take a stiff step back.

"Well, if it were anyone else, I'd be jealous," she teased him, tossing her red braid over her shoulder before darting off in the opposite direction.

Unnerved by the encounter, Kalek looked back toward Ello, only to be further perplexed by her playful wave as she brazenly stared back at him. Kalek resumed his walk to the forge, watchful now of those around him because, clearly, he was the victim of some kind of jest.

When he reached the forge without further incident, Kalek dismissed his suspicions as ridiculous and unwarranted. Likely, his misgivings were the product of his uneasiness about Okta's strange behavior. Ahead of him, the forge resonated with a cacophony of grinding millstones, pounding hammers on anvils, and the roar of fire. Through the din, Kalek heard Úlla shouting at Marnej who worked the furnace baffles.

"More air!" she ordered.

Marnej's arms flapped furiously like a goose getting ready to fly. His sooty face was streaked with sweat.

The shimmering heat of the coals pulled Kalek's eye to where Úlla drew out a glowing hunk of ore with a pair of tongs. With a practiced and confident hand, the powerful nieddaš placed the ore upon a hewn piece of wood. Marnej rushed over, placing another piece of wood on top. As the wood took to flame, Úlla brought her hammer down again and again. Kalek watched small rosy chunks fall off, until Úlla laid her hammer down. Grasping the rapidly cooling ore with the tongs, she placed it back into the shimmering coals. Marnej began to work the baffles again. Flight still eluded him.

Kalek remained rooted, watching the two repeat the process, before deciding it best to return later. Before he could leave, a loud, lingering hiss replaced the hammering as Úlla doused the ore in water. Through the rising steam she hailed Kalek with a perfunctory nod.

"Okta has sent me for a nail," he said. His voice competed with the ringing in his ears.

Marnej stood, releasing the bellow. "That's an odd request," he said, stretching.

"He is making ink," Kalek said. "Can you spare one?"

"Get one," Úlla ordered Marnej.

Kalek expected the young Piijkij to grumble. Instead, he reached back into a crudely carved wooden bowl and brought forth a square nail which he ceremoniously presented to Kalek.

The healer took it, thanking him.

"You look out of sorts, Kalek," Marnej said.

Kalek shrugged and turned to leave, then spun back around to Marnej and Úlla. "I ran into Ello on my way here." He paused, ordering his thoughts. "Her manner was so odd . . . as if she meant to confound me."

Úlla wiped her hands on a cloth. "That is not unusual for Ello. She rarely makes sense."

"What did she say?" Marnej asked, leaning back against an anvil, his arms crossed in front of him.

"She asked me if I was thinking of her," Kalek said, perplexed.

"She fancies you!" Marnej laughed.

"That is not possible," Kalek said, his face growing hot as he blustered. "She is a child, only just out of her guide mother's care."

"You have been hiding with your herbs for too long," Úlla said, her voice unusually mild. She pushed back a strand of hair that fell across her face. "There are few almai left, and you are much discussed among the nieddaš."

Kalek's embarrassment reached new levels. Still, he could not avoid Úlla's probing green eyes, their glint unmistakable.

"You know it is not that easy," he said, his tone sharp.

Úlla's head dropped.

Kalek instantly regretted his anger, his pride, his cruelty.

Úlla needed no reminding of her loss. As he stepped forward to apologize, Úlla's head shot up.

"That is true," she said, "You and I both know what we lost. But we will all lose more unless you open your eyes."

Kalek stood stunned. His apology withered on his tongue as Marnej stared, wide-eyed at Úlla.

Úlla grabbed a gauntlet and her tongs. "The bellows need work, Marnej, or would you rather stand there like a gasping salmon?"

Marnej looked to Kalek who absolved him with a wave.

"Thank you for the nail," he said to no one in particular, then left the forge more disturbed than when he had arrived.

Kalek reached the refectory unresolved as to his duty. He stood at a loss. It was long past the meal hour, but Birtá sat on a low stool peeling vegetables.

"Is there anything in the kitchen I might bring to Okta?" he asked, coming to stand alongside the cook.

"Oh, Kalek," Birtá jumped, surprised, but evidently pleased to see him. "Yes. Sit down and I'll put together something for him. Is he feeling ill?"

"No. Just working," Kalek said, reflecting on the fact that recently Okta had left his food untouched.

Birtá put aside her vegetables, lifting the corners of her apron to keep the peels from falling to the floor. "I'll be right back."

Kalek slumped down on a bench, eyeing the freshly skinned turnips and carrots, as if they held some wisdom. He picked a piece of peel from the floor that had escaped Birtá's notice. He wished he could just ignore Úlla, and discount her words as those of a naïve nieddaš. But he could not. Once the peel was off, there was no way to put it back on again. Úlla's wisdom had been self-evident, even if it was profoundly distressing to him. He was one of the few remaining almai, but had not wanted to consider the implication. Now that Úlla had chastised him, he could think of nothing else.

Kalek had been heart-pledged to Aillun. The passing of time had not changed that bond. Still, as a nieddaš, he had loved others. And after Aillun there had been Irjan. The very thought of him suddenly made Kalek feel as if he could not breathe. His love for Irjan had been slow to grow and made all the more profound by their uncanny friendship.

But love was not needed to bring new life, Kalek reminded himself. It was a physical experience, enhanced by love, no doubt, but not necessary. He had not been in love with Háral, the almai who helped seed life in him. Kalek had enjoyed their time together, but they were not heart-pledged. The idea of experiencing that connection again felt foreign to Kalek. But his duty did not require a heart-pledge.

Birtá came back to the bench where Kalek sat. She placed a tray of stewed meat and roasted nuts in front of him.

"Did Lejá come by?" she asked.

"I have not seen her," Kalek said, standing to take the tray.

"Oh. Well, she said that Ávrá was feeling ill. I told her to go find Okta. Perhaps she did." Birtá's words trailed off as she sat down to resume her peeling.

"Birtá, am I needed?" Kalek asked, marveling at her ability to create delicious meals, when her mind wandered.

"What? Oh. I don't know." She blushed. "I suppose so, if neither you nor Okta have seen Ávrá."

Kalek, concerned that he was remiss in his duties, thanked Birtá, then hurriedly retreated, balancing the tray of food she had given him.

When he pushed open the apothecary door, he found Okta dozing by the fire. Kalek unburdened himself of the tray, then shook his mentor's shoulder.

Okta blinked below bushy brows. "I was enjoying my nap," he groused.

"Has Lejá come to see you?" Kalek asked.

"Yes," the old healer yawned.

"Then I do not need to attend to Ávrá," Kalek said, conscious of a strange relief.

"What does Ávrá have to do with Lejá's quickening?" Okta asked.

"Birtá told me Lejá was looking for me on Ávrá's behalf," Kalek explained. "Has Ávrá been to visit you?"

"No one has been here since you left," Okta said, sitting up in his chair. "Did you bring me the nail?"

Kalek reached into his pocket, pulling out the nail which he dropped in Okta's outstretched palm. "I also brought you food from the kitchen."

Okta stood and stretched, then walked to the work bench. He inspected the food with vague interest.

"Should I go?" Kalek asked.

"Go where?" Okta mumbled, moving beyond the food to where the mortar and pestle sat.

"To see Ávrá."

Okta picked up the pestle. "If she is need of a healer, then, yes."

Kalek hesitated. "I thought you might like to go."

The old healer shook his head, grinding the alder bark in the mortar's deep bowl. "I wish to work on my ink supply," he said. "I have many notations to make and I am out of ink."

On his way out the door, Kalek reminded Okta to eat.

When he did not respond, Kalek stopped and turned. "Did you hear me?"

Okta looked up. "Yes. Yes. You brought me some food. It was not necessary. But thank you, Kalek." The old healer smiled, then busied himself with the remaining ingredients before him.

Kalek left Okta to his work, a seed of resentment taking root in him. He did not mind caring for Ávrá, but he did not want to see Lejá. Not now. Now when he knew that she would be returning to her Origin to give birth. He did not trust himself to keep the pity from his eyes. Another reason why Úlla's reprimand had battered his conscience. He knew that his heart-pledge to Aillun was not the real reason he had kept his solitary ways after Irjan's death. It was because he could not face sending a nieddaš to her death. Because that was what birthing had become.

Kalek rounded the corner leading to the kitchens, mulling over his conversation with Úlla. He wished to have the final word. But it was a callous and empty desire. He would not give voice to his true fears. Not to Úlla. Not when she likely shared them.

Just then, Kalek saw Lejá coming toward him from the other side of the latnja. Even at this distance he could not miss her flustered bearing.

"Kalek." Lejá breathed out his name as if relieved to see him.

"Birtá said you were looking for me," he said, aware that a fog of guilt continued to cloud his ability to think.

"Yes. Ávrá is unwell and bade me find you. But I missed you at the forge and then Birtá mentioned you were returning to the apothecary." Lejá drew a long breath, her swelling belly rising to Kalek's attention.

"I was on my way to see Ávrá," Kalek said, looking everywhere but at the nieddaš before him. "Did she say what ailed her?"

Lejá shook her head. "She is resting in the weavers' quarters. She began to work early, but felt ill. I had her lie down."

Kalek nodded, then gestured for Lejá to lead the way. He realized too late that, by walking behind her, he would be forced to witness the sway of her body, unable to avoid the thought of what awaited her. Anxious to escape this, Kalek plunged ahead, passing Lejá in a couple of strides, saying, "I will go ahead so you may be at ease."

With each step, Kalek widened the gap. Yet, he could not outrun Lejá's future with this kind of cowardice. He stopped, his heart racing, to wait for Lejá to draw beside him, then with an abashed smile he resumed walking at her steady, slower gait.

"Ávrá is blessed to have friends who care for her," he said, trying to find something to fill the space between them.

"She is usually the one who cares for us," Lejá said, unaware of Kalek's struggle. "I think she misses being a guide mother. As I do."

Lejá paused. Kalek listened to the other sounds around them. Conversations. Laughter. The squeak of a handcart. The clack of someone playing stones. He listened to everything else other than Lejá's labored breath.

"But all things change," she said. "Do they not?"

Kalek winced, briefly questioning if he should return to the apothecary for his herb pouch. But that was weakness masquerading as prudence.

Lejá and Kalek climbed the stairs to the weavers' level, their steps in time. The boards creaked with the strain. Kalek found himself alert to Lejá's wheeze and slowed. She, however, continued ahead, as sure of herself as he was unsure of himself.

Kalek followed Lejá into the weavers' quarters. The looms stopped their shifting staccato. Nieddaš and boaris peeked around the wooden looms to exchange glances before resuming their warp and weft.

"She is lying down in the back," Lejá said, sitting down at a silent loom where the dark shades of what she wove deepened from blue to purple to black in the dim corner.

Kalek thanked her with an overly formal bow of his head, then walked to where Ávrá lay, covered in furs, her eyes closed.

Kalek knelt beside the nieddaš and gently placed a hand on her shoulder. "Ávrá."

The nieddaš's eyes fluttered open.

In spite of his discomfort, Kalek made himself smile. Ávrá turned to him. He smoothed back the hair plastered to her forehead. He was reminded of rye pushed to the earth after a hard rain.

"You have a fever," he said.

"I felt weak, as if I could not stand," she croaked, pushing off her furs as if they would soon suffocate her.

"Let me see your tongue," he said, as he felt along both sides of her jaw.

Ávrá stuck out her tongue. A thick white coating covered its pink surface. Kalek leaned back. The nieddaš's eyes avoided his.

"Nothing serious ails you, Ávrá. You just need some rest. Some uulo tea should help." Kalek placed a hand to her arm. The warmth of her skin made him unexpectedly aware of his gesture.

Ávrá seemed to sag into her bed with relief. "I was afraid that . . ." Her words dropped off.

As he waited for her to go on, Kalek observed her hands tightly clutched before her.

"I was afraid that my time had come," she said in a rush. "I am one of the oldest of the nieddaš." She paused, looking down at her hands. "I know there are some beyond my age, but few. My time cannot be far off and I thought . . ."

"And you thought this was it," Kalek said. He shifted uneasily where he sat. His mounting distress made him anxious to find any excuse to flee Ávrá's side.

Ávrá nodded. The lank strands of her hair stuck to her feverish cheeks and long neck. A neck he had just touched. Kalek moved to get to his feet, overwhelmed by a sense of hypocrisy.

Ávrá's hand shot out to him, then withdrew to her lap.

"Please do not misunderstand. I wish to be an oktoeadni and become almai. It is just that . . ."

Kalek made himself look into Ávrá's wide, shining eyes where he saw everything he did not wish to confront.

"You are frightened you will not return," he said finally, his voice a whisper.

Ávrá nodded, her eyes now shut, even as her fingers twisted the edge of her shawl.

Kalek shut his own eyes, fending off the images: Aillun, the dead upon the battlefield, Irjan, the despondent boaris he saw every day.

The lump in Kalek's throat felt like a stone. He swallowed and opened his eyes.

"Ávrá, there is no shame in your fear," he said, placing his hands upon hers, stilling them. "It is just and right. I share your fear. We all do."

Kalek noticed that Ávrá had bitten her nails to the quick. Tender, swollen skin pushed against the dried blood at the corners.

He knew he could no longer hide and let Okta carry this burden.

"I wish with all my heart the world Outside were safe. But it is not." Kalek broke off, hating to say what needed to be said. He inhaled and tried again. "The journey to your Origin will be more than a test of your ability to stay within the Song. It will be a test of survival."

Kalek looked up in time to see Ávrá's face drain of all its color, and he berated himself for his clumsy effort as he endeavored to go forward. "It is true, we need the mánáid returned to us if our kind is to continue, but none of us wish it at the price that is asked."

Ávrá nodded, a tear escaping her brimming eyes.

Kalek pulled the nieddaš into a hasty embrace, unable to bear further witness to his hapless counsel.

Gods help me, he thought, praying for guidance. Kalek shifted Ávrá to rest his chin on her head, his arms tightening around her, as much for his comfort as hers.

"It is not wrong to wish to have as much time as possible," he said, listening to the looms' clatter and shush weave regret into both the fabric and the Song of All.

CHAPTER THIRTY-ONE

AGAINST HER BETTER JUDGMENT, Dárja had let Okta shoo her out of the apothecary. He said he needed to be alone to concentrate on his writing and that she should be with her friends. Now, she perched self-consciously beside Ravna and Tuá who were nestled together on woolen cushions in a corner of the gathering hall.

"There are a dozen rabbit pelts and four deer skins waiting for you by my table," Tuá said.

Ravna sighed, then smiled. "That should be enough work to keep my mind off these dark hours."

Úlla rubbed at the long, black smudges on her palms. "I never lack for work," she said pointedly without looking up.

Birtá waved from across the latnja, and Dárja rose expectantly to greet her, doubting even Birtá's kindness could sweeten Úlla's presence. Still, she teased out a clean linen cloth from her pocket.

"Here," Dárja said, handing it to Úlla.

Úlla faltered, then reached out to take the cloth. "Your Olmmoš is turning out to be a hard worker," she said, wiping her sooty hands.

"He's not my Olmmoš," Dárja said, regretting now that she'd offered the nieddaš the cloth.

Úlla looked up through her lashes. "Oh, that is right. He is just the offspring of your bieba."

Dárja sprang to her feet, her clenched fists at her side ready to wipe the smirk from Úlla's face. A tug on her tunic drew Dárja's attention to Tuá's pleading eyes. She sat back down, but continued to glare at the spiteful Úlla, who had always taken pleasure in tormenting her.

"I have never harmed you," Dárja said, her frustration getting the better of her, "but you act as if I have."

Úlla tossed the now-dirty cloth onto the floor at Dárja's feet. "Blind as always," she sniffed.

Dárja opened her mouth to protest, but Ravna spoke instead. "We are here for Lejá, not your petty squabbles." Her normally soft voice had an edge to it that invited no argument.

Chastened, Dárja apologized.

Úlla said nothing.

Birtá rushed up to the now-quiet group, beaming, "She's coming," she said in a sing-song voice.

The nieddaš all looked over to see Lejá accompanied by Ello. Linked arm in arm with Lejá, Ello appeared to be sharing a good story because Lejá was smiling and laughing.

"She's telling one of her bawdy jokes," Birtá said with a laugh.

"It comes from being around all those rutting animals in the field," Úlla said, either unable or unwilling to find a kind word to say.

Ravna shushed her as the two nieddaš reached the group.

"Come and sit between us," Tuá said, motioning to the low cushion wedged between herself and Ravna. Lejá, already far into her quickening, looked doubtful. But with Ello and Birtá's assistance, she plopped down between Ravna and Tuá, flushed by the effort.

With everyone settled, an uncomfortable silence descended on their group. Dárja searched for something to say, then blurted out the first thing that came to mind.

"That's a lovely shawl, Lejá."

Lejá brushed the contour of her shoulder. "Ávrá wove it for me."

"Where's Ávrá?" Úlla asked, her earlier sullenness seemingly forgotten.

"She is not feeling well," Lejá said.

An uncharacteristic reticence once again took hold of the group. This time Dárja had nothing to offer.

"Here," Ravna said, retrieving a fur bunting from the floor. "For the baby."

"And Birtá and I made you dried reindeer meat," Tuá spoke up.

"That's not fair," Ello said, dismayed. "I can give her nothing from the farm. Unless you want garlic or an onion."

Lejá blushed. "Your story was quite enough."

"Will you be sharing that story?" Birtá asked.

Lejá shook her head. Her dark springy curls bounced merrily.

Dárja kneeled before Lejá, holding out a leather pouch. "I made you tinctures for strength and healing. There's also a balm for your belly," she said. Then, feeling suddenly shy, she withdrew to sit across from Úlla.

"Well, fine gifts indeed," Úlla said. She placed a dagger in a sturdy, leather sheath on top of the bunting. "To them, I add mine."

The animated talk died as the nieddaš all looked down at the dagger.

"Úlla!" Tuá hissed.

Lejá raised her hand. "No, Tuá. It is all right. It is a beautiful gift." Lejá smiled tentatively at her companions. "We all know there is danger Outside." She picked up the dagger and unsheathed the blade. The sharp edge shone briefly in the candle light before Lejá put it back in its cover. "I pray I will not have to use it, but I will be grateful to have it if I must."

Lejá bowed her head. Ravna and Tuá put their arms around her, and for the third time since they'd gathered, this group of once-cheerful nieddaš slipped back into silence. But Dárja knew what they were all thinking. She was thinking it now. *Please let Lejá return safely from her Origin. We can't lose another.*

"Have you chosen a guide mother?" Birtá asked, her voice overly bright.

Lejá raised her head. She wiped her eyes, nodding quickly, then glanced at Tuá and smiled. "I chose you."

Tuá hugged Lejá, holding her for a long time. When they separated, tears shown in Tuá's eyes as well. "We will all love her!"

Dárja thought she'd go mad if she had to sit there one moment longer stuck between Úlla's resentment and her own fears of what might happen to Lejá.

"Thank you for your kindness," Lejá said as fresh tears welled. She scooted to the edge of the cushion in an embarrassed rush. "I am expected at the Chamber of Passings."

Tuá, Ravna, Birtá, and Ello all helped Lejá to her feet. Only Úlla sat still with her arms wrapped around her waist, her sooty hands grasping tightly the folds of her loose tunic. As the goodbyes stretched into more hugs and tears, Dárja jumped up, bumping into Ravna's back. She saw the stunned expressions of the nieddaš, but she didn't care. She didn't care what they thought or what they'd say. She had to get away. She had to find some air. She couldn't breathe.

Dárja ran as fast as her feet would take her. She ran until her full heart pounded and her empty lungs burned. And then she ran some more, thinking she could outrun her worst fears.

~

By habit, Úlla's feet carried her back to the forge, but her thoughts remained with Lejá. Her gift had been neither kind nor sweet, like Tua's or Ravna's. But she meant it with goodwill and a longing to see Lejá return with her baby. They had heard the whispers. How the Song would no longer hide them at long distances. At first, she had dismissed the rumors because few had gone Outside since the battle, and none at any significant distance. Then the first two nieddaš had left for their Origin, but neither had returned.

A cold sweat broke out on Úlla's skin, as her stomach revolted against the little food she had managed to eat today. Panic vied with regret in each hurried step she took. She should have become a biebmoeadni when it was offered to her. *But Kálle was gone*, she thought, her misery growing. *I could not love a child and grieve his loss*. But now it was too late.

Úlla entered the forge, stopping at the threshold, her stomach churning, her thoughts dark and unbearable. The other smiths had left for their evening meal, but Marnej stood with his back to her. His arms arced up high with an axe before he swung down upon an upended log. The sight of him put her teeth on edge. Úlla swallowed back the sickness that threatened to erupt, then wiped sweat from her brow and her neck. She had gone from cold to hot as her panic turned red with enmity. *Why does he persist on coming each day when he knows I do not want him here?* she demanded of the gods.

Úlla reached out for her leather smock, ready to find fault with Marnej. She regarded the wood pile beside him that reach as high as his shoulder, then looked to the coals that glowed yellow and red. Irritated, Úlla slid a leather smock over her head, then tied it about her waist, uncomfortably aware of the snugness. Fueled by anger, she stuffed her left hand into a thick gauntlet and drove a misshapen iron rod into the fire. With surety born of practice, she waited until the end glowed. Then she placed the rod upon the anvil where she brought down her short, stout hammer on it. Turn. Strike. Turn. Strike. Each blow released a bit of her anger, a bit of her anxiety.

When the tapering rod cooled, Úlla stuck it back in the fire again, eager for the glow to return, desperate for the chance to pound something. To shape something. To have control over something.

"I've finished," Marnej said, coming to stand next to her. "There's no more wood."

Úlla looked up, flushed and bitter. "So, the forests have been cleared of wood," she sneered, pushing the rod further into the coals as she glanced over to the woodpile to see that Marnej had indeed chopped all the wood.

"The forester hasn't returned with a fresh supply of logs," he said.

And before Úlla could think of another a task for him, Marnej said, "Why don't you teach me something useful? I'm happy to chop wood for charcoal and lay the fires. I even welcome working the baffles. But if I'm to be your apprentice, shouldn't I learn something?"

Úlla pulled the rod from the fire, bringing it close enough to the maddening Olmmoš that he jumped back.

She picked up her hammer. "Apprentice." She snorted. "It takes four or five seasons of snow to learn what you need to know to be an apprentice." She struck the rod, shouting over her pounding. "Smithing is not some task to do. It is the heart of us. Every nail, every bolt and latch, every cooking pot is born here in this fire, shaped by my hands and the hands of the other smiths." Her hammer punctuated her words. Úlla stopped to push the rod back to the fire.

"Teach me," Marnej said. "I'm here to learn. If I can't, then you can cast me aside. But if I can, aren't we all served by my work?"

Úlla shifted her attention from the coals to Marnej, ready to meet his smug Olmmoš face with a scowl. But his sincere expression caught her off-guard. There was none of his usual arrogance. She eyed the rod. It glowed, even as her anger cooled.

"Fine," she said, worn down by this Olmmoš and the inevitability of her future. "We'll start with the nail. The winter cold will swell the wood and come spring, repairs will be needed on doors and sleds and hand carts." When Marnej made no objection, she pulled the rod from the coals. "You'll pound the iron I narrowed. Turn it a quarter each strike to form a tapered square." She demonstrated her point with powerful strokes. "Cut the sharpened end from the rest of the iron. Then shift that piece into the head mold." She moved swiftly. "Pound the top to form a flat head. Remove it and leave it to cool."

Bang. Shift. Clang. Snap. Hiss. She repeated her movements.

"I want you to form six in the time it takes me to form twenty. If you succeed I will consider you worthy to continue."

Marnej donned a smock and gauntlet. Úlla handed him the rod and hammer, then gestured for him to start.

She pulled out another stretch of iron and her own hammer. "Temperature is the most important thing," she said. "Too cold and nothing happens. Too hot and the metal becomes brittle. Look for the colors yellow and red. White is too hot."

Úlla was about to add some further instruction, then decided against it. If the Olmmoš could succeed with what he had observed, then he had a natural skill. She was not going to waste her time training someone who lacked ability. Returning to her own task, she found comfort in the reverberation of metal upon metal—the sound of rock turned to ore, turned to iron, turned to whatever she wished to create.

When Úlla had completed her twenty nails, she looked up. Marnej worked on, but she noticed he had surpassed her expected count by one, and was about to finish another.

"Do not grin like some nattering Billy goat," she warned him, coming around her anvil to inspect his work. *Surprisingly good*, she mused.

"Acceptable," she said.

"So, you can look forward to another five seasons of snow with me," Marnej said, handing the nails to her before pulling off his gauntlet.

Úlla accepted them, saying, "If we live that long."

"The war's over," Marnej said, replacing the hammer he had been using. "You're safe here."

Úlla grunted. "We are safe here. But out there?" She pointed toward some unknown place. "We are not safe."

Marnej's expression darkened. "No. You're right. It's dangerous. The Olmmoš and the Piijkij are both armed. And . . ."

"And the Song will not hide us," Úlla interrupted, tossing the nails into a bowl.

Marnej shook his head. "Dárja and I traveled within the Song to return."

"Well, Dárja's blessed with skills beyond us all," Úlla said, her dislike for that nieddaš like a splinter under the skin.

Marnej's eyes narrowed. "If you mean that to be unkind, you

miss your mark. But you're right when you say that she's skilled. I know. I've matched metal with her. She's more than my equal."

The Olmmoš had kept his voice calm, but the tension in his body told Úlla he harbored stronger sentiments.

Her reserve shattered like brittle metal.

"Dárja struts around with pride. Cherished by the healers. Acclaimed by the Elders. But what about Lejá, who is leaving us and will never come back? And do not tell me she will return, because then I will call you a liar and a killer. Dárja is not special. I know she has prayed her time will never come just as I have. Just today, she ran from the gathering hall when Lejá spoke of the Chamber of Passings. She may wield a sword, but she is a coward nonetheless."

"Her time will never come!" Marnej's booming voice cut off the rest of Úlla's tirade.

~

The farther away Marnej drew from the forge, the more enraged he became. He'd taken to heart Kalek's suggestion and made himself useful, and promised himself he wouldn't let Úlla goad him into a bad mood by her capricious orders. And, for a moment, it seemed they were able to work together companionably. He could tell she'd been impressed. But she couldn't keep a civil tongue in her head, even when he agreed with her. He hadn't thought it possible, but Úlla was even more adept than Dárja at bringing out the worst in him. Whatever Dárja's faults, she didn't deserve Úlla's scorn and ill will.

Without considering the possible consequences, Marnej turned on his heel and marched back to the forge where he found Úlla by her anvil, pounding on a thick piece of iron.

"It's my fault," he shouted at her.

Úlla stopped what she was doing. Her head snapped up, mouth open. *Ready to argue*, he thought. But Marnej didn't give her a moment to gather up her spite.

"Dárja will never travel to her Origin because of me," he

continued shouting. "So, while you may return from your Origin an almai and hand over your mánná to her guide mother, Dárja never will. Think on this when you feel it necessary to cast scorn upon her. Whatever Dárja is, it is because of me."

Marnej paused breathless, his body trembling with spent rage.

"What do you mean?" Úlla asked, her confusion genuine.

Weighed down by a truth he could no longer bear, Marnej sagged. Looking directly at Úlla to make sure she heard him, he explained, "To bring me back from death, my father placed me in the spirit stream meant for Dárja and her oktoeadni. Her mother died because of it, and Dárja only received a part of what was meant for her. I am alive and she will never be an almai."

His confession made, Marnej turned to walk away, but then the last spark of justice flared within him. He met Úlla's stern gaze.

"And before you call Dárja a coward, imagine yourself riding into a screaming mass of men and horses, to fight, knowing you'll die. She did that. She survived her wounds. She escaped her jailors, bringing me with her. What you called cowardice is the will of one who's lost everything and can't bear others to know."

~

Marnej fell into his bunk, the smell of hay and wool and dust filling his nose. His cooling anger had turned his sweat sticky on his skin. He strode to the icy water bucket where he scrubbed his chest and shoulders with a piece of felted wool. When he was done, Marnej dried himself with enough force to smooth timbers. Clean and dry, he dressed in haste. The pressure he felt within him was building once again. He needed to talk to someone—someone with enough reason—preferably Kalek, but Okta would do.

Descending from the sleeping loft, Marnej moved with purpose. As he passed through the gathering hall, Ello waved to him. He waved back but didn't stop. He couldn't stop, not when his apprehension gained traction with each step. Marnej was certain now that he'd made a grave mistake in revealing Dárja's truth to

Úlla. He'd been so angry. So frustrated. *But what kind of excuse is that?* he thought derisively, knowing that it was a rationale he'd begun to rely upon. *I need Kalek's advice.* Kalek knew Dárja best. He could help Marnej sort out the mess he'd created.

Remembering earlier warnings to not barge in, Marnej knocked when he reached the door to the apothecary.

Dárja's voice rang out to enter.

Marnej groaned. He took a cautious step away from the door, then glanced up and down the hall, deciding on which way to run. But if Dárja opened the door and saw him running, she'd track him down and grind him like a millstone until she had the truth. *No, I'll go in and face what I must*, he thought. Squaring his shoulders, he pushed open the door. The unoiled hinges protested.

Dárja shot a hasty grimace in his general direction, then returned to her work.

"I'll oil the hinges later," he said, unable to think of anything else to say.

With her back to him, Dárja continued to work.

Marnej cleared his throat. "Are Okta and Kalek here?"

Dárja shook her head but didn't look up.

"Will they be back soon?"

She shrugged.

Pulled by guilt, Marnej took a step forward. "Are you feeling unwell?"

Dárja shook her head again.

Marnej waited for her to say something. When nothing distinct came out of her hunched figure, he breathed a sigh of relief.

"I'll leave you to your work then," he said.

Dárja's whirled around, her eyes were swollen and red. "No! Don't go."

The cold, clammy feeling returned to Marnej, creeping up his spine. Without really wanting to, he found himself asking, "What's wrong?" He then cringed inwardly, knowing there'd be no escape for him now.

"I can't do this," Dárja said.

"What? Mix herbs?" Marnej asked, hoping the problem were that simple. "I'm sure you can do it. It just takes practice."

Dárja waved the suggestion away. "No. I can mix herbs. I'm surprisingly suited to be a healer if you ask Kalek and Okta. But I can't do this." She motioned to where she stood.

Marnej found himself praying Dárja would go no further, that she would stop with the last statement. But an inescapable certainty suggested it couldn't be that easy. So, he waited with mounting dread for Dárja's explanation.

"I can't just stand here mixing herbs when Lejá's about to go Outside and face dangers for which she's not prepared."

"Oh. Lejá," he said, wishing this were a casual conversation where an amusing story was about to be told. But it wasn't that kind of tale and Marnej knew it. He knew because Úlla had already assailed him with the outcome.

Dárja's brows furrowed. "Do you know her?"

Marnej shook his head.

"Then how do you know of her?"

"Úlla mentioned her today."

Dárja's eyes narrowed further. "What did she say?"

Marnej felt the walls closing in on him. "She said Lejá was leaving for her Origin and that she was worried."

Dárja leapt around the work table to stand directly in front of him. "Exactly! Lejá's vulnerable. The dangers are even greater now. She won't know what to do. But I do."

Dárja seemed to radiate an unnerving recklessness. And when he didn't answer right away, she went ahead, undeterred. "I've been there."

She pointed in a direction that had no meaning to him.

"I've traveled outside the Song," she said. "I can protect her."

"You mean, to escort her to her Origin and back," he said, finally grasping her intention.

"Yes!" Dárja's dark eyes blazed with intensity. "I can't just offer Lejá herbs and tinctures and let her walk out there alone. I've fought—you've seen me—I can protect her."

"But . . . Kalek? Okta? The Elders?" Marnej sputtered every objection he could imagine.

"It's the only way to ensure we'll survive," Dárja said with such ferocity that Marnej dared not object.

"Then I'll go with you," he said, his feeling of responsibility overriding his better judgment.

Dárja shook her head. "No, this isn't for you to do."

Marnej stood rooted as guilt hardened into insult. "So you're saying one blade, your blade, is better than two?"

"This is something I must do," she said resolutely.

Marnej threw up his hands, stalking the corners of the apothecary. "Are you so stubborn you don't see what's offered?" He circled back to face Dárja. "I was trained to kill your kind. Don't you think that I'm capable of protecting them as well? It's my world out there, as you so often like to point out."

A crack in Dárja's determined expression gave Marnej hope that she was beginning to understand and he pressed his point, "My blade served the Brethren in training and in war. We both know it's wasted here. I can work with Úlla and the other smiths, and I can learn to forge a blade, but it would be better for us all if I were using my weapon instead of learning to craft one. It's where my true skill lies."

Without warning, Dárja shot forward and embraced Marnej, squeezing him tightly about his ribs. "Thank you," she said, her voice thick and muffled against his shoulder. "We can protect them. I know we can."

Stunned by the sudden change in Dárja, Marnej stood frozen for a moment, then he awkwardly brought his arms around her and returned her hug. Her hair smelled of herbs and smoke.

Uncomfortable in the embrace, he felt like he should say something, but the right words eluded him. Instead, he wondered how many times Dárja had embraced his father like this. Part of him wanted to be jealous of their connection, but another part, the bigger part of him, just wanted to be held a little longer.

~

Úlla stood alone in the forge long after Marnej stormed out. She had not tried to stop him because her mind reeled in shock. For so many seasons of snow, Úlla had resented Dárja's blind love for her Olmmoš bieba, Irjan. She had imagined Dárja to be proud and disdainful of the rest of the neiddaš, those older than her and deserving respect. When Dárja had disappeared with their warriors, Úlla had celebrated her absence, while others worried and fretted over her. The fawning concern had made Úlla despise her even more.

When Dárja returned from the battle and Kálle had not, Úlla had wished upon her the darkest evil. How could it be that Dárja walked among them, while Kálle lay rotting in some Olmmoš field? Úlla pictured her beloved, as she often did. His soft, dark eyes had held the promise of happiness, of a long life lived together. She wished a thousand times to see those eyes once more.

Úlla slumped against the wooden post next to where Kálle's smock hung—the smock she wore each day, hoping to find his strength. She sank to the ground, her arms crossed tightly against tender breasts. The pain of examining her loss, her fears, was too much for her to bear. Úlla spent her days working in this forge, working with tools Kálle had used, showing the other smiths that she was worthy to take over for him. But as much as she wished she could be as strong as the iron she wrought, she was still just flesh and bones and blood, and all of her ached. She had lost so much. Tightness gripped her chest. *Kálle, my sweet one. How can I do this without you?*

Part Three

WE SING TOGETHER
AS ONE

CHAPTER THIRTY-TWO

COMPARED TO THE FROZEN practice ground, the heat of the apothecary felt stifling. Dárja shrugged off the outermost layer of her furs. Marnej came after her, tugging her arm to make her stop, a sheen of sweat upon his face.

"I don't think it's wise to talk to Kalek today," he whispered, looking over her head toward the work area.

Dárja pulled her arm free. "Why not?" Her eyes narrowed. "Have you lost your nerve? Because I can travel with the nieddaš by myself. I don't need your help."

Marnej held up his hand to make her stop. "I haven't changed my mind. It's just . . . Kalek isn't well disposed to hear this today."

"How do you know?" she demanded.

Marnej fumbled for an answer, not wanting to reveal Kalek's recent embarrassment at the forge. "I just know, Dárja. Can't we just leave it at that?"

Her eyes narrowed further. "No. Nothing'll improve by waiting longer."

Marnej lunged to catch her arm, but Dárja slipped free and entered the workspace. Marnej trailed, a step behind.

Kalek stood bent over the fire, stirring something.

When he heard Dárja call out his name, he turned to them. His face was flushed with the heat from the fire, but there was something else about Kalek's expression that Marnej couldn't quite define. The last time he'd seen him, the healer had been upset and embarrassed. Now he looked as if his world had not only righted itself but perhaps even held some light.

Yes. That's it, Marnej thought. The frown Kalek normally wore had been replaced by what Marnej could only call light.

Dárja cast a fleeting glance back at him, her eyebrows arched with condescension. Then she returned her attention to Kalek, saying, "I need to talk to you."

Kalek held up his hand. "I need to take this to Ávrá. She is ill and this will ease her discomfort."

"Marnej can take it to her," Dárja promptly suggested.

Marnej elbowed her in the side with a warning look. She winced but went on undaunted, "I need to talk to you."

"No. I prefer to take it myself," he said, ladling a strong-smelling tea into a pitcher. "I will speak to you when I return."

"I can go with you." Dárja edged forward, her eagerness barely contained. "We can speak along the way."

Kalek offered her a brief smile. "Thank you, Dárja, but I prefer to go by myself."

Marnej grabbed Dárja's hand. "It can wait."

Dárja snapped her head around to Marnej. "No, it can't!" she said, turning back to Kalek. "I wish to travel with the nieddaš on the way to their Origin—to protect them."

The light in Kalek's eyes vanished along with his smile. Concern pushed Marnej to step forward between Dárja and the healer.

"She wouldn't travel alone," he said, trying to divert the healer's attention. "I'd go with her. Together we can protect the nieddaš."

"Is this your idea?" Kalek asked, his voice tight and whittled to the bone.

Marnej hesitated. He'd succeeded in attracting Kalek's bitter focus and now thought better of it. But before Marnej could speak, Kalek answered his own question.

"No. This is your idea," he said, peering around Marnej to Dárja. "It has your marking on it—rash and ill-advised."

The healer's icy tone made Marnej shiver, but he didn't dare turn to gauge Dárja's reaction.

"Perhaps this isn't the best time to discuss this," said Marnej.

"You are right," Kalek said. "This is not the time for discussion." He turned on his heel, grabbed the ewer's handle, and stalked out of the apothecary, liquid sloshing over the ewer's lip.

Marnej released the breath he'd been holding.

Dárja rounded on him, her face splotched with fury.

"Is this some revenge for something I've done to you? Or are you so weak that you cannot stand up for what is right?"

She moved to follow Kalek.

Marnej blocked her way, contempt vying with anger for control of him.

"For the first time since I've been here, Kalek seems to be at ease. Maybe even happy. And you've ruined it," he said, failing in his efforts to keep his tone even. "Don't you understand? He doesn't want to lose you. You're all he has of your mother. All he has of Irjan."

My father, he silently added.

Dárja met his gaze, her whole being alive with disdain. Marnej reached out to grab her shoulders to shake her, then stopped as she visibly stiffened. His hands paused mid-air, balled into fists before dropping to his sides.

"He thought you were dead. Now you're telling him you want to risk your life again. How do you think he feels?"

"This is more important than feelings," Dárja said with contempt, as if he were blind to what was important. "We're talking about the survival of our kind."

Marnej took in the set of her shoulders. So like she'd been in the Brethren's cell—smug and careless of all the love gifted to her. Given the same he would've cherished it—fought for it. His envy gnawed at him, hungry and spiteful.

Dárja continued to talk, but her voice became a distant murmur amid Marnej's turbulent feelings. When he'd heard Dárja tell Kalek her plans, he knew what the healer felt because he'd felt it too, and it had unnerved him. He feared losing her. Her idea was no longer some noble abstraction, and he wouldn't be able to change her mind. When had he ever been able to do that?

In that moment, Marnej hated her. He hated her because he cared about her and there was nothing he could do to change that.

Dárja paced in front of him. Her arms waved as she mouthed something he'd no desire to hear.

"No, Dárja." Marnej shook his head. "You're wrong."

She stopped her pacing.

"Right now, there's nothing more important than feelings," he said, his voice a brutal whisper.

Dárja's face reddened, a rebuttal ready on her lips.

Marnej left her standing in the middle of the apothecary, sputtering. He had neither the time to argue nor the inclination to absolve her for her singlemindedness. He needed to find Kalek, and stop Dárja from making the same mistake she'd made with Irjan. Most of all, he needed to get away from her.

Marnej made his way through the gathering hall unaware of those around him. At the stairs to the northern quarters, he bounded up the steps two at a time, his mind rehearsing what he would say to Kalek. On the landing, he paused to catch his breath, and it occurred to him that Kalek might take this intrusion badly.

I am like some startled moose charging ahead, he thought, berating himself. But that was what Dárja did to him. She made him crazy. Reckless. Marnej slumped down to the floor, his eyes intent on the shadow cast by the flickering torchlight. His brooding outlook shaped the outlines into an ominous sign. Although Kalek had treated him as a friend, Marnej wasn't sure he actually was one. Kalek had been close to Irjan, but friendship wasn't something passed from father to son like land or a trade. And, friend or not, Marnej doubted Kalek would find what he had to say any more palatable than Dárja's words .

Kalek will never want Dárja to go, he thought. The chance of losing her again was too much to consider. Marnej understood that. *We all want to hold on to the gifts that we are given*. He didn't want to give up the life he'd built among the Immortals. He wanted to safeguard his feeling of belonging, as tenuous as it was. But without Dárja what connection did he have?

Marnej briefly wondered what his father would've done. Maybe Irjan would've been able to talk some sense into her. But he doubted it. He recalled how she'd come charging after Irjan the one and only time he had encountered his father.

On one of the rare occasions when they were not at odds, Dárja had explained the circumstances of their unforeseen meeting. But, even now, Marnej questioned whether the gods had been testing him. That day, he'd heard the voices and felt the presence of something beyond his vision. But he'd never expected to see an Olmmoš ride out of the air on a binna, trailed by Immortals.

Dárja had said that they had been traveling north to the Pohjola to escape the Brethren when Irjan had bolted from her side. Marnej had never shared with her the fact that he had been actively seeking out the Immortals. Instead, he let her believe that chance or the gods had brought them all together.

Marnej closed his eyes, conjuring Irjan's likeness as he had on so many sleepless nights. His long, dark hair streaked with grey, eyes pleading even has he widened his stance to fight.

The weaver's door opened, startling Marnej awake, the unnerving memory of his father's soft, fierce voice in the forefront of his thoughts.

I cannot undo the past, but I beg you to believe that I have only loved you and tried to protect you.

Kalek emerged, his disapproval evident. "If you have come to convince me of Dárja's plan, you have wasted your time." He walked past Marnej without waiting for a response.

Marnej jumped to his feet and ran after him. "I don't want her to go either," he said, speaking to the healer's back as they descended the stairs. "But she's determined to carry out this plan. Isn't it better to support her than to let her go on alone?"

The stairs protested under Kalek's weight.

Marnej followed on his heels. "You know that's what she'll do. And, she won't be alone. I'll be with her."

At the bottom of the stairs, Kalek rounded on Marnej. "You think you can solve our problems by venturing out?"

Marnej was ready to repeat the words he'd practice. But facing the despair he saw in Kalek's eyes, he couldn't give voice to them. Nor could he back down. "Is there another way?" he asked, frustration coursing through him.

Kalek shook his head, but Marnej couldn't tell if it was to deny the possibility or register his disgust.

"Why do the nieddaš even need to travel to their Origin?" he asked, feeling like a badger who has been cornered. "Can't they just give birth here?"

"It is our way," Kalek said, turning to leave.

Marnej stopped him with an outstretched hand. "But why?"

"It will take more time to explain than I believe you have patience for," the healer said, pulling away.

Marnej jumped in front of Kalek. "Fine, then," he said. His need to find a solution had made him rash. "Can the nieddaš and the old one travel together?"

"I do not know, Marnej," Kalek said, his exasperation shattering his calm demeanor. "What do you want from me? This has been our way for untold generations."

"I don't know," Marnej admitted, his desperation brimming over. "But Dárja can't just sit here and watch her friends go out and never come back. It's like watching the condemned. She was trained to fight. And honestly, it's all I know how to do too."

"And you will fight your people?" Kalek asked, looking doubtful.

"Who are *my* people, Kalek? There's only Dárja!"

～

Dárja muttered to her herself as she picked up her furs and readied herself to go out into the woods where she could find some sense and order.

"What is all the noise?" Okta called out behind her.

Dárja considered leaving without answering, but she had no quarrel with Okta.

"I'm going outside," she said, sliding her arms into her furs.

Okta picked up his writing materials. "Not before explaining why you are clomping about my apothecary. You are talking to yourself as though you disagreed with your own answers."

Dárja's anger flared, then gradually faded away. She'd wanted to speak with Kalek before bringing the matter to Okta and the Elders. But Kalek refused to listen, and Marnej's accusation that she was thinking only of herself had stung.

But what did he know? She knew she could help.

Okta scanned the vellum before him, then looked expectantly at Dárja, "Well?"

Dárja laid her furs down. She took a deep breath as she straightened. "I wish to escort the nieddaš to their Origin," she said. "I want to protect them." Dárja stood still, wound tight like a rope, waiting for the old healer's reaction.

Okta placed the vellum aside. His lined and weathered face was inscrutable.

"I told Kalek. I had hoped to enlist his help in convincing you and the Elders," she said, sounding more confident than she felt.

Okta's bushy brows drew together. "What was his reaction?"

"He refused to listen," Dárja said, her exasperation barely restrained by her desire not to anger Okta, who, at least, seemed willing to hear her out. "He called my idea rash and ill-advised."

Okta snorted. "The mark of Irjan remains."

Dárja started at her bieba's name. "Irjan would have understood," she blurted out, silently daring him to contradict her.

The healer raised his hands in surrender, then sat down, and regarded her. "Tell me then."

"So you too can say it's ill-advised?" she challenged.

Okta shook his head. "No. So I can understand and share my insights."

"You'll listen and help me?" she asked haltingly.

"I will listen and tell you what I think," he corrected her.

Dárja came and sat opposite Okta by the fire. The warmth worked its way into her taut muscles, entreating them to relax. "I wish to travel with the nieddaš to their Origin," she said. "I think the strength of two voices can keep us hidden within the Song of All. It worked with Marnej and me. Even at great distance." Dárja paused, doubt sidling in as she considered the other possibilities.

"And if that fails," she said, "my blade can protect us on the journey."

Okta rubbed his gnarled hands together, then held them before the fire. "But the nieddaš is only half of the pair," he pointed out, not unkindly.

"Marnej will travel with the boaris." Dárja instantly assigned Marnej the role, even as she doubted his commitment. Maybe another almai or Taistelijan would stand in his place if he proved unwilling. "He can protect the old ones."

Okta sniffed as if insulted. "He has agreed to this?"

"Yes. He told me he was better suited to wielding a sword than hammering on one," Dárja said, crafting as truthful an answer as served her purpose.

Okta let out a mirthless laugh. "I do not doubt his words."

"Well?" she asked, her knee bouncing as she waited for the old healer to continue.

Okta sighed. One hand absentmindedly stroked his short grey beard.

Dárja was on the verge of leaping to her feet and declaring she didn't care what he thought, what any of them thought. She would protect the nieddaš.

"My selfish heart tells me to agree with Kalek," he said finally. "Your plan is incautious. We risk losing more than a nieddaš and a boaris. We risk losing you and Marnej."

"But we are already losing more than just a nieddaš and a boaris," Dárja argued. "Every time one of them leaves, never to return, we lose another piece of our future."

"Yes, Dárja," Okta agreed. "We are losing our future. But

it is not your future, nor is it Marnej's. You both have destinies beyond what any of us can see, maybe even imagine."

This time Dárja did rise to stand. "I have no future outside of those who are around me!"

Okta placed a hand on her arm, his touch gentle but firm. "I have told you what my selfish heart thinks, the one which wishes to keep you and Marnej safe. The one which wants, more than anything, to protect Kalek from further heartbreak." The old healer spoke with weariness flagging each word.

Dárja faltered as she saw Okta clearly for the first time since her return. This was not the conspiratorial healer who slipped her honey-in-the-comb. Nor was this the voice of the hard truth she had railed against. Okta was a boaris, wise and worn by measures of time. Dárja didn't even know how many times Guovassonásti had shined upon him or how many seasons of snow Okta had seen. He'd always just been there.

"Okta, you know this is the right thing to do," she said, as the healer's gaze slowly turned away from her. "It's the only way."

When he did not respond, she offered her final gambit. "It's what you would've done."

Okta looked back to her. His milky eyes glinted with firelight and indignation, "Once, maybe. But look at the price we all have paid."

Dárja fought the urge to shrink back from the old healer's rebuke.

"You believed you were doing the right thing! Just as I do," she said.

"And what price are you willing to pay?" he challenged, his voice harsh and ragged. "Have you thought of that?"

"I'm willing to lay down my life," she said, her body alive with the urgency of her calling.

"But what of Marnej? Are you willing to lay down his life as well? Because if he journeys out he does so for you."

Dárja froze. She had no answer. She'd never considered Marnej's actions to be anything other than of his own making.

"And Kalek. Are you willing to break his heart? Are you willing to feel yours broken again, just as it was with Irjan?" Okta continued. "You are more than an apprentice to Kalek. More than some memory of Aillun. You are a piece of his soul. I watched him struggle to live, believing you were dead."

"I can't live like this, Okta," Dárja interrupted. "I can't live knowing that Lejá is out there on her own. And one day Tuá, Ravna, and the others will follow, likely never to return. I can't remain safe while they are not, and I can't remain here when I have the skills to protect them."

Okta released a long, slow breath. To Dárja it seemed as if he were letting go of something deep within him. For a long while they sat quietly. Dárja had no more arguments to tender.

"You are right," he said at last. "This is something I might have done. I cannot stand in your way."

"But will you help me?" she asked, her voice yielding and uncertain.

"I will not try to change Kalek's mind. If that is what you want of me," he said. "But if Kalek agrees, I will help you speak to the Elders."

The tension that had kept Dárja coiled and anxious drained from her body. She had fought and won a major battle.

Inhaling the scent of warmed herbs, reminded her of her reasons, she said, "You know you couldn't have stopped me."

Okta nodded. "Just as we could not stop Irjan, and it almost cost Kalek his life." Okta pushed himself up to stand. His bones popped along with the fire. "Do not make that same mistake."

CHAPTER THIRTY-THREE

BÁVVÁL STOOD WITH HIS arms outstretched. Deft hands fitted him for his ceremonial robes. Advisors and supplicants milled about, alternately presenting reports and vying for the High Priest's favor.

"I am done listening to these matters," Bávvál said, stepping off the dais. The acolyte serving as his dresser followed and fussed. Bávvál shooed him away with an impatient wave. "Rikkar, you will remain."

The room quieted. All eyes turned to the man singled out. Envy and scorn flashed across some faces, then vanished behind facades of piety and disinterest.

Bávvál enjoyed these moments of insecurity he witnessed. A touch of discord proved useful among those who sought further power.

"Usher them out," Bávvál ordered the fresh-faced acolyte standing by the door, then met his spy's gaze briefly.

Áigin slipped into the stream of exiting notables. He would report anything he heard, if only to show off his skill at unearthing well-guarded secrets.

When the door closed behind the last shuffling petitioner, Bávvál raised his arms to allow his dresser to tie a thin band of red around the waist of his yellow robe. *The red of man's blood encircles the gods' golden light*. The High Priest mused upon the truth of this middle line of the Believers' Verse as he dropped his arms.

From the corner of his eye, he observed the lone counselor. Rikkar had looked back to the door more than once.

Bávvál wondered what preyed upon the man's soul. *What is he hiding?*

"Rikkar."

The counselor flinched at the sound of his name, then he bowed his downy head.

"My Vijns," he greeted the High Priest with deference, but his eyes scurried about the room like a frightened mouse.

Bávvál said nothing in return, choosing to scrutinize his counselor as he made him wait. He knew the man's thoughts ran between possibilities of reward and punishment. Bávvál had always been able to see right through Rikkar. Even when they were both young acolytes. Rikkar, the child of faith. Himself, the child of ambition. His counselor finally looked up from his pious examination of the ground to meet the High Priest's frank appraisal. Even after all these seasons of snow, Bávvál still found Rikkar's icy blue eyes disturbing. They were the last remaining vestige of the fanatical priest he had once been.

Bávvál shifted under the weight of his fur-lined robe to hook the silver clasp at his throat. *The blue sky. The white clouds. The Ten Stars of the Bear*. Quite unlike him to feel the words of the Believers' Verse stirring his heart. But he had spent a sleepless night. Vivid dreams of hungry gods wanting to taste his flesh had woken him.

Bávvál dismissed his dresser with a curt, "The gods thank you."

"As I thank the gods," the acolyte replied, bowing before leaving the High Priest alone with Rikkar.

Bávvál stepped onto the dais. He noticed the ink stains on his counselor's robe. Rikkar usually dressed with more attention to his appearance.

"We have not spoken at length in some time," the High Priest said, surprised to find within himself a true desire to speak with the man. "I am in need of your particular skills."

Rikkar nodded, then smiled hesitantly.

"We have a long history together," Bávvál began. An image of the sharp-toothed gods flashed into his mind. He shook it off, focusing on this man who had known him longer than any other. "You were once the best among all of us, you know."

A slight quiver about Rikkar's mouth betrayed his otherwise placid countenance.

Bávvál continued, his curiosity verged on sincerity. "None rivaled your oration for rousing the faithful. I imagine you miss it."

"My duties satisfy me," Rikkar said primly. However, his pugnacious chin rose ever so slightly.

"Come now," Bávvál chided. "We both know you miss the dais."

Rikkar's birdlike arms fluttered as he smoothed the front of his robe. "I might miss the preaching," he said. "But I do not miss the village."

Bávvál laughed heartily as he sat down in his chair. "Your wit has sharpened over these many seasons of snow." He waved Rikkar over to a hardbacked seat across from him. "Sit and share your wellspring of inspiration."

Rikkar approached with a smooth step. Once seated, his fleshy fingertips were white points of suspicion as he gripped the arms of his chair.

"It has been almost eighteen seasons of snow since I last stood to address believers," he said. "I would not know what to say."

"Has your faith ebbed?" the High Priest asked with none of his usual cutting delight. "I remember it as a shining, if not grating, example to all us acolytes."

"My faith is resolute," Rikkar answered hastily, but with a hint of reluctance.

"But . . ." Bávvál supplied.

Rikkar sat a little straighter, as if he had resolved himself to some course of action. "The defeat of the Jápmea has removed a great evil from our world," he said, reminding Bávvál of the supercilious acolyte he had once loathed and goaded. "We have been relieved of the pressure to preserve our faith."

"It appears you have become quite pragmatic," Bávvál said with a note of amusement. "Your time among the Brethren was not wasted."

Rikkar stiffened. "The Brethren taught me that a common enemy unites." He paused, then added almost wistfully, "But that enemy is now gone."

"And so are the Brethren," Bávvál said.

Rikkar's drawn features became pensive. "Yes. And perhaps that is to our detriment. Now we have nothing to inspire fear in the hearts of the believers."

Bávvál choked upon a laugh. "You are jaded as well, it would seem."

Rikkar shrugged. "Observation has served its purpose."

Bávvál leaned forward. "You do not believe in faith alone?"

Rikkar shook his head. "We have relied upon fear for countless generations. Fear of evil, fear of death, fear of the Jápmea. Without fear, I wonder if there is faith."

True interest prompted Bávvál to ask, "What do you fear?"

"The loss of my faith and death's eternal darkness," icy-eyed Rikkar said. "Once, I believed that I had a great calling—that I could instill faith in the hearts of those who listened. Now, I wish only to find mercy in the gods' judgment of my actions."

Bávvál leaned back in his chair, adjusting the clasp at his neck. "Take heart, Rikkar. The gods know we strive to act in the best interest of those we guide. That is why we have been given power. It is sublime service to take the harder path of questionable action and save others from that same dilemma."

Rikkar made to rise. "I am afraid I have not been of service to you in this conversation."

"On the contrary, Rikkar," Bávvál reassured the man. "You have given me counsel I can use. The gods thank you."

"As I thank the gods," Rikkar said with a bow. His shoulders remained sloped as he stood, as if he carried some unseen burden.

Too much introspection about the man, and it is leading to a dangerous place, Bávvál thought. But, Rikkar had clearly stated the dilemma the High Priest faced. Faith needed encouragement, and fear was the key.

～

Bávvál rested his gaze upon the smoke-blackened rafters as he rubbed his hands together under the cover of his cloak. The temple braziers had been lit in the morning, but did little to lift the stony chill. When the muffled din of those gathered quieted, he cleared his throat.

"My Brothers in faith," he began, letting his words drift toward the heavens before continuing. "I stand before you, not only as your Vijns but as a true Believer. It might be said that, as the breath of the gods, I stand above you all, but I say, I stand with you." Bávvál paused, taking in the faces of the men before him. Some were familiar to him, and he nodded to them.

"Not long ago we raised an army of pure hearts to deliver our people from the evil that has long cast a blight upon our world. At last we can walk freely without fear of the Jápmea. Our victory is a testimony to our faith and its righteousness. But while we celebrate our triumph, we must not let our elation turn into complacency. Because, in complacency lies the gradual chipping away of faith. Until we find ourselves godless and judged for it."

A murmur of agreement rippled through the solemn crowd.

"That is why I turn to you, my brothers. You, who are at the heart of every village and every crossroad. Vigilance must start with you. The souls in your care require it. Be wary of folly and waywardness. Be firm with your admonishment. And be forthright in your moments of doubt."

Bávvál caught Rikkar's eye in the front. The counselor lowered his gaze to his hands, clasped piously in his lap.

"While it is true we no longer need fear the Jápmea, death still abides. A worthy life is rewarded by the gods' embrace. For those who do not honor our ways, the agony of eternal darkness awaits. The faithless shall be buried in the earth, trapped and howling."

The High Priest waited while the image registered in the hearts and minds of his priests.

Conscious that he held sway over this gathering, Bávvál let his voice deepen as he went on. "A true Believer sacrifices much in this life. Our guidance is not meant to soften this harsh truth. Instead, like sound parents, we must use a firm hand to ensure all make their way as the gods demand."

Bávvál opened his arms to encompass the hall, feeling the power of his final exhortation surge through him. "I send you back to your podia. I ask you to honor the gods with your faith, your vigilance, and your governance. Speak to the souls in your care as I have spoken to you. Impress upon them the acts of worthiness. Remind them all of death's waiting call. My brothers, the gods thank you."

The gathered priests stood. The rustle of cloaked bodies muffled the groan of unburdened benches.

"As we thank the gods," the voices of many answered as one.

~

In the High Priest's personal chamber, his dresser carefully removed the last piece of the vestments. Bávvál lowered his arms, shivering in his linen shift. An acolyte held out the green robes of everyday wear with reverence. Bávvál slid the garment over his head, the rough wool scratching his shorn crown, before slipping down over his shoulders and hips. The dresser cinched a leather belt about his middle. Bávvál had not allowed himself the kind of indulgence that bloated many of his bishops. He cared for himself as he cared for the ministration of the souls entrusted to him by the gods.

As Bávvál waited for the chains of his office to be placed over his head, an unctuous voice called out, "A moment of your time, my Vijns?"

The High Priest turned to see a young man attempting to push his way past a protective acolyte.

Bávvál's satisfaction with his oration let him overlook this breech of decorum. "Let him enter," he said, bowing to receive his ornate bronze chains.

"Your words today were inspired," the young priest said, freeing himself from restraining hands.

Bávvál accepted the compliment without comment, surprised to see the priest was a mere youth.

"I minister to the souls of Hassa," the man-boy stated, striving for an air of dignity, achieving something closer to comical. He stopped, as if waiting for a sign of recognition.

Bávvál's critical eye fixed on the angry spots covering the boy's forehead and beaky nose, then drifted down to the patched robe with soiled hem. His benevolence waned. "Your purpose here?"

The young priest swallowed. His large farmer's hands knit and re-knit themselves. "No doubt, it's come to your attention that, with our temple burned, we've no refuge for the faithful."

Bávvál's eyes narrowed on the youth, but he kept his tone even. "Brother, worry not that you repeat news. Unburden your heart. Speak to me as you speak to the gods."

The young man's worried expression bloomed with relief. "It's been a grievous time for us. I was quite unprepared to take on my priest's ministrations, what with our temple burned to the ground and our priest taken from us." This last part he said with such haste that Bávvál barely made sense of the mash of sounds.

"Tell me about your late priest," he encouraged.

The spotty face before him drooped. "He was like a father to me. His passing is a sorrow of which I can scarce speak." The young man bowed his head, gathering himself. He sniffed. "He never recovered from the wound inflicted upon him by the Brethren." The boy raised his eyes, red rimmed and indignant. "They cut through his heel to hobble him. He only just reached the outpost, crippled and in terrible pain. Our healer couldn't save him. I'd be dead too if he hadn't sent me to tend the sickbed of one of our farmers."

"This is indeed a hard loss to bear," Bávvál soothed as he

inwardly seethed. "You are certain it was the Brethren?" he asked with the beguiling tone of one trying to coax a frightened animal.

The young man nodded vigorously. "My priest was certain of it."

Bávvál placed a hand upon the youth's sloping shoulder. "I will personally see to the matter of your temple. For now, return to your village, and remember my guidance. Vigilance is needed. We cannot be idle in the face of such threats to our faith."

"I thank the gods," came out in a rush of gratitude as the young priest bobbed his head.

"As the gods thank you," Bávvál said, leading his young visitor to the door with no hint of the impatience that twitched within his tightening muscles. To the guard stationed at the threshold he said, "Make sure this priest returns safely to his village."

"I'm most grateful, my Vijns," the young man whispered in awe.

"Your devotion to your priest and village is most worthy," Bávvál said, straining now to maintain his composure as the guard led the man away. When they were finally gone from sight, he rounded on the other guard. "Get me Áigin."

Bávvál strode back into his chambers, slamming the door with a resounding bang that punctuated a string of invectives. Bávvál paced his quarters, muttering to himself, promising the gods to pull the skin from Brethren bodies while they watched.

The knock upon the door paused a litany of other imagined punishments.

When Áigin entered the room, Bávvál exploded, "Why am I hearing from a spotty-faced, newly advanced acolyte that not only has the Hassa temple been burned, but his priest maimed and now lying dead? At the hands of the Brethren!"

Áigin's thin lips pressed into a slit.

Bávvál took the man's silence as defiance and it drove him to greater volumes. "I just reminded all my priests to be vigilant. Yet, I am the one who is made to feel a fool when a runny-nosed priest of some three-hut village says to me, 'that no doubt it has come to my attention that with their temple burned and they have no refuge for the faithful.'"

Áigin remained silent as the High Priest finished his imitation of the sniveling youth.

Bávvál's chest rose and fell with trembling fury as he stared at his spy. "Have you nothing to say?" he asked, but before Áigin could answer, he found further outrage. "And if this whelp-of-a-priest had not sought my audience, would you have even brought these events to my attention?"

"It has been taken care of," Áigin said with a finality that both brooked no doubt and also needled like an unwelcome thorn.

"Taken care of?" Bávvál questioned. "Meaning the Brethren are dead?"

"Niilán's regiment is headed for Skaina," Áigin said, shifting his lithe frame. "He'll have the Piijkij in due course."

Bávvál stepped within inches of his spy. "In due course is not the same as taken care of." He looked up into the man's face, searching for signs of treason. "Do not make the mistake of assuming a power which is not yours. You gather information. I decide." Bávvál returned to his desk, then fell into his fur-lined chair. "Now, tell me everything you know."

◦

Niilán took his regiment west around the Great Valley. The new recruits grumbled that they had been denied the chance to see the site of the Olmmoš's greatest victory. So far, Niilán had kept his tongue, conscious of a need for unity. However, it took practiced effort to tamp down his growing resentment of the empty boasting of those who had not been there. *A leader does not fall to the low and mean*, he reminded himself countless times as he rode through the ranks. Then came that one unguarded moment, that one braggart who made it impossible for him to keep silent.

Niilán rode up to two milk-fed youths whose misfortune it was to be the last in a long line of voices grousing at the lost opportunity.

"You feel you've missed something?" he shouted at them from astride his horse. All those around the two young soldiers came to a halt.

Niilán was distantly aware of the uncertain silence that had rippled out around him. But he could not stop himself, nor did he want to in that moment.

"Well, you have. You have missed adding your limbs and guts to those now lying in rot in the Great Valley. If you wish for us to walk across the bones of those who died so that you might breathe this air, then, by all means, let us go back and trample the corpses of our heroes."

The two cornered soldiers cowered. But Niilán's satisfaction of finally saying his piece proved momentary. He had no sooner unleased the full force of his anger than he cursed himself for losing his temper. Disgusted with these young recruits and his own behavior, he circled his horse around to ride ahead. *They are just young. Young and ignorant*, he reminded himself, adding, with even more regret, *like most of this regiment*.

Niilán joined Osku near the front, asking, "Have the scouts returned?"

"Skaina is prepared for our arrival," Osku assured him.

"How many leagues?"

"One. Maybe two."

"Will we have room for this lot to camp?" Niilán indicated the regiment with a curt nod to the rear.

"Not within the garrison," Osku said matter-of-factly. "But there are broad fields directly to the west where we may camp."

Niilán nodded, his disquiet manifesting in curtness. What he secretly hoped for was a proper meal and cup of juhka and perhaps time by the fire to warm himself. At least these were his hopes for Skaina. It was possible the village was so far north that the courtesies of life were not considered important. If that was the case, he would have to console himself with the fact they had at least reached the beginning of the Brethren's trail.

Niilán looked back at the long stretch of weary men straggling into the distance. He felt like a salmon with his tail stuck in the bear's mouth.

"Come Osku, let us ride ahead to Skaina," he suggested impulsively.

Surprise registered on the soldier's face "Who will lead the front ranks?" Osku asked.

"Matti can lead, Joret and Jonsá are middle and rear." Niilán looked around for Matti. When he saw the giant of a man, he hailed him over.

"But what about the Piijkij?" Osku hedged.

"Fine. Bring a dozen men for our safety," Niilán conceded as he awaited Matti's looming presence.

Upon his approach, Niilán briefly wondered how Matti's squat horse could carry him. The man's legs very nearly touched the ground when seated in his saddle.

Matti nodded, but behind his respect, Niilán sensed a timidity that was at odds with his size.

"Osku and I will take twelve men ahead to Skaina. You will take command in my absence. Let Joret and Jonsá know. When you reach Skaina, make camp in the western fields. Have my lavvu set far enough away from the other tents so that I will not hear men piss during the night."

Matti smirked in spite of himself, then regained his deference. "I'll take care of it," he said, signaling to the men who served him.

Anxious to feel free, if only momentarily, Niilán spurred his horse ahead. "Come, Osku!" he called over his shoulder as his horse galloped away unrestrained, for once, able to act as he pleased.

~

The uncharacteristic optimism that had carried Niilán to this northernmost outpost disappeared the instant the commander of the Skaina garrison offered him juhka but no food. Sipping the overly spiced drink as he listened to the man's report, he thought, *At least the fire is warm.*

"Three messengers carrying supply requests and offerings to the Vijns traveled out beyond the village and were ambushed," said the outpost commander. "Two bodies were found stripped of their belongings along the road, their throats cut."

"What type of offerings?" Niilán asked.

The commander poured himself a cup of juhka, then leaned back in his chair, steam rising from the mug he held. "Some pelts and a bit of coin from what little trade there is."

Niilán considered the man. He thought him to be older by a few seasons of snow, but the far north was a hard place to live in. Niilán took a sip from his cup. "Any sightings of strangers?"

The commander shook his head.

"The messenger who survived made it to the Stronghold of the Believers," Niilán prompted, curious to see if the commander had anything to add. When he did not, Niilán continued, "He said he had been attacked by Piijkij. He recognized their swords by the one held to his throat. He said they gave him a message to carry back to the Vijns. That we should expect more of the same."

The commander nodded. "Like the fire in Hassa."

"They burned the temple and maimed the priest," Niilán said, drawing small comfort from the fact the commander was at least informed.

"Not surprising, really," the man said with a shrug. "We kill them. They kill us. But, all the same, I hope you brought reinforcements in case they return this way."

Niilán sipped his rapidly cooling drink, reflecting on the commander's offhanded acceptance of the situation. "I have brought men to bolster your ranks, but men alone will not be enough."

The commander drained his cup. "The sooner you find and kill the Piijkij, the easier we will all rest."

"To that end," Niilán broached the topic that held his interest, "do you have a thought as to where they might strike next?"

The commander grimaced, as if he had not given the matter any thought until this point, which to Niilán's mind was part of the problem. *Let someone else handle the Brethren. Someone like me*, he thought dismissively.

"They attacked Hassa, which is closest to us," the commander said. "The next village is hardly more than a couple of rotting goahti. There is nothing to be gained there."

"A place to hide perhaps?" Niilán wondered aloud.

The commander shook his head. "I doubt it. They would stand out like the fifth teat on a cow."

Niilán smirked. "Where else is there that might attract the attention of men intent on striking at true Believers?"

"Perhaps Oso to the west. Mehjala to the east. But they may avoid them entirely and head south."

Niilán considered the possibility. "There is that chance," he said. "But the farther south they go, the closer they bring themselves to more-fortified villages with larger garrisons." He paused and thought about where he would go if he were in their place. "No. I would stay in the north. Far from the reach of the army, and close enough to disappear into the Pohjola." Niilán handed his empty cup to the outpost commander, then stood. The commander did likewise, and the two men clasped arms.

"Thank you for the warm fire and the juhka," Niilán said, appreciative of the respite if not the fervency of the company. "I am sorry for the loss of your messengers. I hope the men I bring will make up for them."

Outside, Osku waited for him, mounted and ready to ride. Niilán took the reins offered him with a twinge of guilt for the warmth he had enjoyed in the commander's quarters. But he balanced the small pleasure afforded him with the unenviable position in which he now found himself. To be sure, he had traded three masters for one, but that one master was the Vijns. Niilán did not want to consider the outcome if he failed in his assigned task.

"Let us see if camp has been made," he said to Osku, without so much as a look back at the warmth the billeted soldiers would be enjoying that night.

CHAPTER THIRTY-FOUR

Dárja left Okta working alone in the apothecary. The healer's quarters felt oppressive, as if the familiar sights and smells accused her of betraying happy moments she'd shared with Okta and Kalek.

Outside, in the barren herb garden, Dárja could breathe again and she inhaled deeply. The icy air stung her nose and eyes. Underfoot, the soft, new snow squeaked. Her boots, however, stuffed with dry grasses, protected against the cold. She looked beyond the barren garden to the woods and shivered, but not from the chill, which she found bracing. Rather, it was the prickle of doubt that trailed her confident steps.

She'd sounded so sure of herself when she spoke to Marnej, Kalek, and Okta. But now her inner voice wavered, shaken by all the quiet moments of secret shame she'd gathered and kept hidden like an accursed treasure.

Dárja walked out through the gate which, not that long ago, she'd rushed through into Kalek's arms. She'd made it home. Now she wanted to leave. Run away, if she were truthful. Dárja looked up at the blackened wood of the walls that sheltered the place she called home. The cracks and chinks were fitted with lichen like fine embroidery upon cloth. Dark spires rose, dizzyingly, as if reaching for the stars hidden beyond the ominous sky above.

Home. Dárja repeated the word to herself until it sounded strange to her ears.

But this wasn't her home. She'd not grown up here. They'd come here, fleeing the Olmmoš with the hope of preserving peace. Dárja snorted at the thought. They'd been foolish to believe peace with the Olmmoš was possible. She was barely passed her second measure and it was clear to her the Olmmoš would never stop until they'd killed the last of her kind.

They won't have long to wait, she thought dismally as her feet carried her onward.

Snorts and breathy grunts disturbed Dárja's bleak vision of the future. She looked up from her feet toward the corral adjacent to the stables, teeming with dozens of binna. In their midst, Tuá spread out forage. The nieddaš nudged aside curious snouts with a firm, but gentle push, ducking to avoid the antlers of the mature reindeer.

Dárja drew alongside the corral fence, smiling at the antics of the furry-nubbed juvenile binna. She placed a foot upon the lower rail and leaned her forearms on the upper. A few of the reindeer came to inspect her. Their warm, snuffling breaths filled her nose with their musky scent. Dárja drew back to avoid the growing press and knocking antlers, and began to laugh. It was a foreign sound and felt so strange. She couldn't remember when she'd last felt lighthearted.

Tuá stood up and waved to Dárja as she climbed over the corral railing. Dárja waved back, noticing that Tuá's hood had fallen back, revealing her red, felted hat. The nieddaš swept aside her two long braids. Dárja felt a pang of loss. Her hair only now reached the nape of her neck.

As Tuá approached, Dárja became suddenly anxious. But she couldn't just leave, not without offending the nieddaš who'd always been kind to her. Even when Dárja was a boisterous child, running when she should've been walking and shouting when she should have been quiet, Tuá never had a harsh word for her. She'd only raised her brows to encourage Dárja to change her behavior.

She'll make a good biebmoeadni, Dárja thought, then her heart sank. Lejá had left for her Origin three days ago. Dárja looked to the woods where the trees swayed as if beckoning, but her feet refused to move.

Tuá hailed her.

Dárja tried to smile back, saying, "I needed to get some fresh air."

Tuá squinted up at the sky. "Storm's coming."

Dárja sniffed the air, realizing she was right. "A little ways off, but not long now."

Tuá frowned, and Dárja imagined she was thinking of Lejá, wishing she was safe. Dárja shrank under the weight of her growing guilt. She had chosen to go Outside. Lejá and the others didn't have a choice.

As if reading her mind, Tuá said, "She'll come back."

Dárja's head snapped up. "I know she will," she stuttered, swallowing back the welling despair that proved her a liar.

Tuá's smile conveyed her hopes. It was like a delicate web of promise, held together by dreams and plans. But this was the season of snow when darkness reigned.

"Next time, I want to go," Dárja blurted. "I can protect them."

Tuá's smile faded. Dárja knew she'd made a mistake.

"It is not your burden to carry," Tuá said quietly as the wind picked up.

Dárja looked away, repeating to herself every reason and argument she'd crafted for Marnej, Kalek, and Okta. When she finally spoke, her voice wavered. "It was my choice to go Outside. Lejá didn't have a choice."

The touch upon her shoulder made Dárja start.

Tuá's expression was patient and understanding, like a kind bieba. "It is something we must all face," she said.

But it wasn't true. Dárja would never return to her Origin like Tuá and the others. It was what set her apart, even when she couldn't see the full scope of her future. Yet, she couldn't admit this to Tuá, who'd always sought to include her.

"What of Kalek?" Tuá asked when Dárja failed to continue. "You are training to be a healer."

Here again, Dárja wanted to unburden her heart and share her doubts about becoming a healer. But how could she say that training with Kalek reminded her of being with her bieba—Irjan. She and Kalek worked well together, but there was something missing. Rather, there was *someone* missing, and that was Irjan.

"I'm not sure I am what Kalek wants," she said softly, a thread of truth slipping through.

Tuá took Dárja's gloved hands in her own. "You will be a fine healer. You have nothing to fear."

But I do, Dárja thought, nodding, worried she'd never find her place among her own kind.

~

"How'd you get him to change his mind?" Dárja asked, standing in the hall outside the apothecary door.

"I didn't," Marnej said.

Blocking the door, she pressed him about the news he'd shared. "But Kalek's agreed to talk with Okta and the Elders," she said.

"He's agreed to talk with Okta and the Elders about the possibility of another solution," Marnej said, then held up a hand. "That doesn't mean they'll agree to your idea."

Dárja crossed her arms in front of her. "As long as he's considering it. That's what's important."

Her rehearsed confidence, however, did not dispel the worry clouding Marnej's eyes. Standing this close to him, she could feel his tension.

"I know it seems like folly to venture out when we barely made it back here. It's just that, in my heart, I know it's the right thing to do," she said, wanting to reassure him. Putting her hand on his arm, she added, "You don't have to do this."

Marnej drew back from her as if her touch had burned. "Of course I do. Don't you see? I can't lose you. You're all that I have."

Dárja staggered back at the force of his biting reproach. And before she could gather herself, the door to the apothecary swung open. Marnej took an abrupt step away from her.

"Come," Kalek said, standing aside. Dárja glanced apprehensively at Marnej, who stood rooted, his face a cold mask in the flickering torchlight. Dárja took a hesitant step forward, followed by another, more-determined one, then walked past Kalek, convinced she didn't care whether Marnej followed. She'd already made it clear that he didn't have to go. Still, she found herself listening for his footfalls behind her. When she finally heard his heavy, even step she exhaled, her shoulders relaxing.

Inside the apothecary, Okta sat on a stool beside his work bench. His face was impassive beneath his gloomy brows. Somewhere behind her, Dárja sensed Marnej shifting his weight back and forth. She clasped her hands tightly behind her to hide their twitching. Dárja looked from Okta to Kalek, who now stood like a grim sentinel beside the ancient healer.

"We will escort you to the Council of Elders to bring forth your proposal," Okta said. His weary tone hinted at acceptance, if not approval.

Dárja stepped forward to hug Okta, but stopped, aware that Kalek had turned his back on her.

"I want you to know that we are looking for another solution. One that will serve us all," Okta continued. "Do you understand?"

Dárja nodded, fearing her voice would crack. She looked to Marnej, who ignored her, asking instead, "When will they see us?" His words pulsed with restraint.

Dárja turned back to the healers, her heart skipping a beat.

"Now, if you like," Kalek said calmly, though the etched lines around his mouth and the dark circles under his eyes hinted at his real feelings. It seemed to Dárja that he'd aged in the brief time she'd looked away, yet she couldn't own her part in it. Not if she was to present her plan to the Elders.

Kalek helped Okta to his feet, and the pair walked toward the door, one towering over the other, but both somehow hunched in on themselves.

Dárja hesitated, momentarily unsure of herself.

"Are you coming?" Marnej asked, an edge to his question. "After all, this is for you."

Dárja flushed red with anger. She strode past Marnej, humiliation prickling her skin. Trying to outrun this new reluctance within her, Dáraj walked briskly ahead until she found herself on the heels of Kalek and Okta. Out of respect for the healers, she slowed her impatient step, half-expecting Marnej to draw up beside her at any moment. His long stride had always been a match for her quick ones. Dárja slowed further as she crossed the gathering hall, conscious of the eyes upon her. But Marnej continued to lag behind.

Well, I'm not going to stop, she thought, refusing to look back over shoulder amid all the inquisitive looks in the latnja.

At the end of the corridor, beyond the gathering hall, Okta stopped. He placed his hand upon the paneled wall, then slid it to the side. He walked on, followed by Kalek, then Dárja, and last, Marnej. As she entered, Dárja looked up to see the night sky above their heads. She blinked away the illusion of twinkling stars, but they remained above her, shining even brighter.

Although she'd been around the Elders her entire life, she'd never had the occasion to visit their chambers or seek their counsel. She'd made her own choices. Now, facing the Elders, with the stars above and the gods beyond, Dárja shrank back. The urgency of her request withered, eclipsed by the vastness of what she sensed around her. Dárja willed herself forward into the Elders' circle, keeping her purpose in the forefront of her mind. The closer she got to the center, however, the harder it became for her to concentrate.

Voices and songs she'd always found comforting now clamored. They demanded more than her attention. They wanted all of her. She couldn't stop them. She couldn't deny them.

We are the Jápmemeahttun.
We are the guardians of the world.
Our memory stretches back to the start of days.
Our vision reaches beyond all tomorrows.
We sing together as one so that our one may always survive.

Dárja's heart pounded to the beat of each word. Her blood pulsed in time with the chorus. Her legs felt as if they might collapse, and yet she didn't care.

We are the Jápmemeahttun.
We are the guardians of the world.
Our memory stretches back to the start of days.
Our vision reaches beyond all tomorrows.
We sing together as one so that our one may always survive.

The refrain repeated, as intimate as her own breath. Her own voice rose to meet it.

I am daughter of the gods.
I am sister among the Jápmemeahttun.
I started my life at my Origin, with sadness and joy as my companions.
I braved dangers and met enemies, and can see the truth of friendship.
I go into the world to meet my destiny, knowing that the stars watch
over me.

As Dárja sang, it was as if she were hearing her song for the first time. What she'd taken for granted, or ignored in the past, came to the fore. She'd awakened to something new within her, and felt reborn within her song, emboldened.

I will go out into the world to meet my destiny, she answered the unspoken question. Her body was alive with a purpose and new meaning.

And just when Dárja thought she would break wide open from the fullness of her heart, the chorus subsided. It pulled her back from the precipice of her future into the substance of her present. Her knees trembled, and her breath came in gulps. But her heart beat as steadily as it always had. A new low chant began to envelope her, filling her ears.

We are the Elders.
We are chosen to guide.
We listen to the voices of the gods.
We seek to avoid the mistakes of the past.

Dárja focused on the Elders, who rose as one and came forward to stand before her.

She wanted to turn and run, but she was held in a trance.

"We greet the Elders and ask for their audience," Okta said.

Dárja jolted, remembering now that she wasn't alone. Okta and Kalek and Marnej stood with her. The realization comforted her until she looked back to Marnej, who stood, feet apart, fists clenched, as if ready to do battle.

"We are ready to hear you," the Elders said as one.

Dárja turned to them, meeting the direct, unwavering gaze of the Noaidi.

Drawing on her song for courage, Dárja resisted the urge to flee. "We wish to travel with the nieddaš," she said. "To protect them and ensure they return as almai."

The clarity of her voice came as a revelation to her. Dárja had worried she would sound weak and unsure in the face of such power and authority. She stood a little straighter. "We cannot remain blind to the fact the life bringers confront great dangers, more so now than ever before."

The Noaidi raised his hand to stop her.

Fearing her chance to speak slipping away, Dárja jumped ahead. "The last two nieddaš who journeyed to their Origin haven't returned. If this continues, none will be left."

"It is not our way," an Elder near the back intoned.

"Is it our way to simply die?" Dárja challenged, her heart racing.

A firm hand gripped her arm, breaking her concentration. She glanced back. Kalek held onto her, his eyes imploring her to stop. But she couldn't. She couldn't stop and still honor her song as she now understood it. She pulled her arm free. "If we're content to die, why did we fight the last battle?"

Before any could recover from the affront, Marnej sprang forward. "Maybe the life bringers can travel together . . . or maybe they don't have to go to their Origin. Can't they bring life here?"

Dárja's outrage threatened to spill over until she saw Marnej's anxious expression, and recognized that he wanted to help.

"To be Jápmemeahttun is to transform," the Noaidi said to Marnej.

The others joined in, their solemn voices filling up the room.

Once we believed ourselves to be like the orbs in the heavens, permanent.
Our self-deception brought tragedy. But the tragedy helped us hear the
*   true voices of the gods, and we changed.*
We learned the power of transformation.

Marnej opened his mouth to speak, then shut it as the Elders continued as one.

Our renewal began with the first old one and the first oktoeadni.
They were two of only a few souls clustered together for survival.

Panic surged through Dárja. *This is the end*, she thought. *They won't listen.*

One soul prepared to leave the world, the other to bring a new soul
*   into it.*
The instance of birth and death intersected.

They're just going to recite the story, fall back on "our ways," she thought, wanting to scream.

The old one died.
His life force joined with the soul of the waiting unborn, but its power
did not stop with the waiting soul.

A sidelong glance at Marnej told her he'd given up on the prospect of interrupting again. In fact, he appeared to be listening, rapt, as though he were hearing some vital truth. And then it occurred to her that Marnej was, in fact hearing the truth for the first time. One to which she'd long ago become deaf.

The Elders went on in their measured retelling of the story of their kind.

Instead, the spirit of the old one suffused all of the Jápmemeahttun.
But not all were strong enough to absorb it.
Those too weak exploded in a burst of light that filled the night skies
for all time.
When we look to the heavens of the dark time, we are reminded of the
power of transformation.
We see the true meaning of the Jápmemeahttun.

With an audible sigh, the spell that held the room broke.

"But this could be another transformation." Marnej's thick Olmmoš accent cut the silence.

The Noaidi shook his head. "You are not accustomed to our ways. You must trust that we listen to the gods. We answer their call."

"And they call for us to die?" Dárja interrupted, shaking off their reasoning.

"Dárja . . ." the Noaidi said her name with stern kindness.

"No," she said, ignoring the Elders' censorious mutterings. "Your song speaks of our survival. We sing together as one so that our one may always survive. You can't speak those words and just accept our end."

The Noaidi shook his head. His disappointment showed in the deeply etched lines of his face. "You are more the child of Irjan than of us."

"Gladly so!" Dárja said fiercely. "Look at what he did."

"Enough, Dárja," the Noaidi commanded. "I do not impugn your biebmoeadni. I say that your vision is beyond what we have experienced for lifetimes."

Dárja tried to regain her calm as she stood her ground. "I understand. But if we don't change, we will die."

The Noaidi regarded Dárja and then Marnej. "Are you so willing to risk your lives after you only just returned to us?"

"Yes." The two answered as one.

"And Okta, do you agree with their plan?" the Noaidi asked.

"I believe it is Dárja's destiny to find her own way," he said.

"Kalek?"

Dárja peered over her shoulder to see Kalek's mouth set in a severe line.

Her breath caught.

Finally, Kalek nodded.

Dárja faced the Elders once again, this time feeling as if she now answered to all the souls who'd passed and all those yet to come.

"We will consider your proposal," the Noaidi said, turning his back on Dárja to rejoin the others in their circle.

Dárja continued to stare at the Elders, wishing they would agree, anxious they wouldn't. Then someone took hold of her hand.

"Come," Marnej said. He nodded in the direction of the door where Okta and Kalek stood waiting. "There's nothing more you can say."

~

"Are we to consider the young nieddaš's proposal?" one of the Elders asked when they were alone in the council circle.

"Her words deserve reflection," Einár said.

"It is not our way," another objected.

"Is it not?" Einár wondered aloud. "When we counsel the boaris who are about to leave, we speak of transformation. We tell the story of our early folly; how we believed ourselves to be everlasting, like the sun and the moon."

"We exist to counsel against the mistakes of our past," yet another Elder pointed out.

"Are we not presently confronting folly?" Einár asked, looking from one Elder to the next.

"We have always traveled to our Origins," the first Elder pointed out.

"Yes, yes," Einár agreed.

"Our souls are tethered to this world at our Origin," another added.

Einár nodded again. "Valid points. But what of Dárja's offer of protection?"

"It is meant to be a test of our survival," said the Elder closest to Einár.

"It was a rite of passage perhaps when our numbers were great," Einár said, "when we were protected by the power of the Song."

"As our Noaidi, your duty is to honor our ways," said the Elder who had first spoken.

"So I shall," Einár met the challenge with more sharpness than he had intended. He paused, taking in the worried faces before him, and softened his tone. "We should remember that, though we have lived by our ways for countless generations, our ways were once a break from tradition. We changed once to survive, and I believe we may need to do so again."

A murmur of discontent moved through the Elders.

"I do not make this suggestion lightly, nor do I advocate a reckless abandoning of our rituals," Einár said. "But we may gain a way forward if we let these two do as they believe right. We have only our steadfast adherence to custom to lose. But we stand to gain life returned to us, transformed."

This time, Einár's argument was met with the sense of some willingness to consider the proposal. For the Noaidi that was enough.

"I thank you all for your counsel," he said, "and for the opportunity of contemplation."

The other Elders stood, recognizing their leader's desire for seclusion. Einár grasped arms with each Elder as they left the room. He wanted to make sure they all felt the sincerity of his promise to honor their ways. Change, however necessary, was not easy or straightforward. Then again, neither was survival.

~

"Do you really think they'll agree?" Dárja whispered to Marnej as they sat by the fire in the apothecary.

Marnej glanced over at Kalek and Okta, who worked quietly. "I don't know," he said, keeping his voice low. "The Elder said they would consider it. I believe he will honor his word. He wouldn't be the Noaidi otherwise."

"There's no other way," she whispered hoarsely.

"If you two must talk," Kalek spoke up, eyeing them over the powders he mixed, "then do not whisper. What you have to say will not harm either of us."

Marnej doubted the healer's assertion, but he spoke aloud as instructed. "If they do agree to Dárja's idea, how much time will we have before we must leave?"

Okta laid down his ink-stained quill. "Are you asking who will soon be life bringers?"

Marnej didn't know if that was his question or not. He looked to Dárja for assistance, but she shrugged.

"I guess I don't understand," he confessed. "I know how we have children, but I don't know . . ." Marnej stopped himself, heat rising to his face. He hadn't intended to ask such a delicate question.

Okta laughed loudly. "Determined to save us, but you cannot face the simple fact of life."

Marnej shifted his eyes from Okta to Kalek, hoping for a way out of this increasingly embarrassing discussion. The almai, however, busied himself with the powders in front of him, spilling most, obviously ill at ease.

"Gods be blamed," Kalek muttered, drawing Okta's attention.

"Kalek, would you mind explaining to Marnej our ways?" Okta asked. A grin played across is lined face.

"What?" Kalek said, harried and concerned.

Marnej choked back a laugh, then pretended not to notice the young healer's discomfort.

Dárja snorted next to him.

Okta cleared his throat, "Marnej, if you would like an explanation . . ."

Marnej shot his head up, "No! I just wanted to know if we would be leaving soon."

Dárja masked her amusement with a cough.

"Dárja might need to hear an explanation though," Marnej said.

Her face fell, and she shook her head, but her mop of dark hair was not long enough to hide her blush.

"Do you know if we would be leaving soon?" Marnej rephrased his earlier question.

Okta's mood darkened. "It is likely."

The ancient healer's pronouncement sobered them all. They sat in silence, each engrossed in their own thoughts, until Kalek cleared his throat.

"I must go and check on Ávrá," he said, almost knocking over the mortar and pestle in his haste to leave the apothecary.

In Kalek's absence, an oppressive stillness settled over the room. Marnej briefly thought to say he was needed at the forge to make his escape. But that was a lie, and he'd no taste for lies at that moment.

CHAPTER THIRTY-FIVE

Ello, Tuá, and Úlla sat beside the fire while Ravna rested on the pallet beside Ávrá.

"You need not worry," Ávrá said. "Kalek said I will be fine."

"Oh. Kalek said," Ello teased.

Ávrá blushed.

"Ello, you are the worst," Ravna scolded, patting Ávrá's hand.

Ello laughed heartily, her eyes shining with merriment. "What of Marnej, Úlla? You can't keep him to yourself, you know."

Úlla scowled. "I don't keep him. He tries to be useful, though he rarely succeeds." She poked at the embers in the hearth as she if she was in her forge.

"I would say he's useful. Did you know Tuá brought her knives for him to sharpen?" Ello asked, winking at Ávrá. "Úlla, you might want to wear something other than your grain-sack tunics if you want to catch his eye."

"Enough, Ello," Ravna said. "Tuá, sing for us. Otherwise, Ello will continue with her silliness."

Ello stuck her tongue out playfully.

"Yes, sing, Tuá, you have the prettiest voice among us," Ávrá encouraged before a cough racked her chest. She leaned back on her pillow to rest. Ravna brushed the hair from her forehead.

Tuá's face glowed in the firelight. She smiled.

When darkness descends
Upon the heavens
And fair eyes look to the sky.

Do not mourn
The sun's passing
Like a lover left to cry.

Wait hopeful and humble.
Wait patient and pure.
You will bask in the warmth once more

When rays of sun
Refuse to set
And scarlet blankets night.

Do not mourn
The hidden moon
Like a child gone to fight.

Wait willing and welcome.
Wait steadfast and strong.
You'll be cradled in moonlight 'ere long.

Tuá repeated the verses, then let her voice trail off when she came to the end.

Ávrá sighed from her bed. "That was beautiful."

The others readily agreed. Only Úlla remained quiet.

She stood abruptly. "I must go," she said, her voice wavering.

Aware that all eyes were on her and she dangerously close to tears, Úlla forced herself to find just a little more strength.

"I'm tired," she said, walking to the door. She was conscious that she held herself as stiff as the rods she forged. Before leaving, she said over her shoulder, "The song is beautiful, Tuá."

Úlla slipped into the hall, then raced down the stairs, unable to get away fast enough. On the bottom rung, she caught her foot, tumbling to the floor, to land with a thud that knocked the breath from her.

From around the corner, Kalek appeared, an ewer in his hands. The healer rushed over to her, ignoring the sloshing contents of the pitcher.

"Did you hurt yourself?" he asked, kneeling down beside her, freeing his hands to help her to her feet. "Are you all right?"

A tremor ran through Úlla. "Yes. I'm fine," she said, swallowing back her tears. "Please excuse me. I'm sorry, Kalek."

Úlla broke free from the healer's hold, and ran away before he could ask another question. She needed to be alone, but she could not return to her quarters. She shared bunking with three others and their children. *Outside*, she thought. She could be alone there. But Tuá's song drifted back to her. *No.* Her heart would break to see the sun's passing. *Like a lover left to cry*.

Habit took hold of her, and Úlla ran to the forge. Her soft, padding footfalls upon the earthen floor betrayed none of the urgency behind them. Mercifully, she encountered no one before she reached the dark contours of the forge's fading embers. Disappearing into the blessed darkness, Úlla's familiarity with the forge allowed her to move without injury until her eyes adjusted to the deep shadows. Her heart pounding, a sob escaped her as her body began to shake.

This time, nothing could temper her anguish. "Oh, Kálle," she cried out.

Úlla covered her mouth to stop herself from repeating his name again. The name alone was enough to rend her anew. But an image of him as she had last seen him still formed in her mind. His eyes, deep like the night sky and fringed with dark lashes and his expression so soft and kind.

"Stop," she whispered in fierce denial to the unseen forces. "I cannot."

"Úlla?" a voice asked behind her.

Úlla whirled around. Marnej stood holding a torch that lit his angular profile in planes of light and dark.

He came forward. "What are you doing?"

Úlla wiped her eyes roughly. "Nothing," she said, stepping away from the encroaching light.

Marnej fitted the torch into a bracket by the furnace trough. "It can't be nothing. You're crying."

Unable to hide, Úlla shrank back. She hugged herself tightly, her hands wrapped around her middle. "What do you want, Marnej? Is it not enough that you are like a thorn in my boot? Can't I be free of you and your endless questions?"

"Maybe," he said warily, coming closer. "If you tell me what's wrong."

The concern in his voice reminded her of Kálle. *Gods, make him stop*, she silently pleaded as new, treacherous tears welled in her eyes.

Marnej reached out to her.

"No!" she recoiled. "Do not touch me."

His hand fell. "Tell me, Úlla," he commanded, sounding more like the rude Olmmoš he was. "I won't leave until you do."

"Gods, do you have to know all my pain?" she cried out, trapped between him and the wood pile he had stacked just days before.

"Úlla, I want to help."

She glared at him through her wavering vision. "So like you. Your arrogance masquerades as pity."

She laughed. Her timbre was thin and fragile even to her own ears. "You cannot help. You cannot bring Kálle back. And you cannot change the fact that I must leave for my Origin."

As soon as the words flew from her mouth, Úlla regretted them.

Marnej stood staring at her.

"I thought not," she said bitterly, pushing past him.

Marnej caught her arm. "Wait. Úlla!"

"Wait for what?" She spun to confront him. "Wait until everyone knows what I already know." Úlla stretched her linen tunic taut around the unmistakable bulge of her belly.

Marnej gawked wordlessly, then recovered himself. "You're right. I can't bring Kálle back," he said savagely. "I also can't change that you're going to give birth. But I can protect you." His tone softened. "You don't need to go to the Outside alone. I'll be there. Dárja'll be there. We'll protect you to your Origin and back."

Úlla snorted. "That is not our way."

"We've spoken with the Council of Elders," he said, letting go of her arm.

Úlla did not move. She stared at him, deciding if what he said was a joke, or worse, a lie. She shook her head. "I do not believe you."

Marnej placed his hands upon her shoulders, and looked her directly in the eyes. "We won't let you face danger by yourself."

Úlla's whole body began to shake. She wanted to hold on to her anger, her memories, but relief betrayed her, and her knees threatened to buckle.

Marnej pulled her into a rough embrace, and Úlla let him, recalling what it felt like not to be alone.

~

Okta knew he had put off this moment for far too long. Still, he was not sure he could go through with what needed to be done. As a courtesy to an old friend, Einár had informed Okta of his decision to allow Dárja and Marnej to escort the life bringers. However, there would be rules to follow, to make sure the ritual was preserved. Nevertheless, a major shift had occurred. Thankfully, Einár had not asked him whether he had told Kalek yet. But the visit made it clear that he could wait no longer.

Okta went to the work bench to find a task but the surface was clear and clean. Kalek had already seen to everything before leaving to tend to the sick. Okta regarded the jars neatly marked with Dárja's script, deciding that he should make something, anything, to distract himself. A tincture. A poultice. A tea. But the recipes ingrained in his memory over the countless measures of his life eluded him. Now that he had decided to tell Kalek the truth, every moment of the almai's absence tested Okta's resolve.

He banged his fist on the work table, scattering Kalek's weight stones across the worn wooden planks. The healer swore under his breath, then gathered the burnished stones together again. Their cool heft in his hand was soothing. They had been given to him by his master when he had finished his training. Okta had given them to Kalek when the almai had recovered from the wounds he had sustained aiding Irjan's failed rescue of Marnej.

Foolish and foolhardy, Okta thought, shaking his head at the memory. He had almost lost Kalek. But he could not hold it against the young almai for helping a friend. If any should carry the blame, it should be Okta. He had been the one to involve Kalek in the first place. He could not fault the almai for the bond that had formed with Irjan. Okta rolled the smooth stones in his hand as he paced the room.

Back and forth he measured the distance from hearth to sickbed, his heart finding reasons not to tell Kalek, while his mind argued to tell the truth. *Gods help me*, he thought in silent exasperation. He had not been this conflicted since he had sent Kalek out to find the newly born Dárja and had not told Einár nor Mord. *Mord.* The name clung to his thoughts like a burr. He and Mord had fought together in the early battles against the Olmmoš. They had both been young almai recently returned from birthing. When the Elders asked them to become Taistelijan, they had not hesitated. Inexperienced but eager to serve their kind, they had fought side by side until the battles ended and their lives diverged.

Okta had been grateful to be apprenticed as a healer. Violence and death had taken a toll on him. But Mord remained a warrior at heart until the end. Now he was gone, as were most, if not all, of the Taistelijan. Killed in the last battle.

So many lost, he thought, wondering if he could have done anything to change the outcome.

With a bang and a clatter, Kalek entered the apothecary, interrupting Okta's pacing and ruminations on a past he could not alter.

"Gods be cursed," Kalek called out, "Who placed the chair so close to the door?"

"I am sorry, Kalek," Okta apologized, moving toward his limping assistant. "I must have done it when I stood up."

Kalek rubbed his hip, promising Okta he would be fine. Then he smiled, but the dark circles beneath his eyes haunted his features. "That will teach me to come charging in here with speed behind me."

Okta pulled his chair closer to the work table as Kalek began to scan the jars.

"How were your visits?" he asked, searching for a way to broach the true topic that preoccupied him.

"They are improving, with the exception of Ávrá," Kalek said, seemingly distracted.

"Do you have pressing matters at the moment?" Okta asked, almost hoping the almai would say yes.

Kalek turned. "No. Why?"

Suddenly, Okta could not make himself speak. His mind raced for a suitable answer. "I need you . . . I need you to help me forage for ránesjeagil."

Kalek reached for the jar. "Do we not have enough?"

"We have some," Okta interrupted. "But gathering more now while the weather is mild would be prudent."

"I will go then," Kalek said, turning. "There is no need for you to go out in the snow." He started for the rack that held his furs.

Okta swore under his breath. His ruse was going all wrong. "I have not seen you much in the past few days, and I would relish your company."

Kalek eyed him from the far corner of the room. "Well, make sure to take an extra layer. I do not wish to add you to my list of the sick."

Okta took the furs Kalek held out. "No. There is no time for sickness now," he agreed, putting on one set of furs and then the other.

Once outside, Okta breathed in the freezing air. It cleared his mind of any lingering doubts. He'd had a long, full life. One with regrets, but, then again, who did not have regrets? He had also experienced great happiness, primarily due to his calling as a healer and his friendship with Kalek. But his end approached, and that too was part of being a Jápmemeahttun.

"Kalek, I had another purpose in wishing to be out here," Okta began, observing his apprentice with a sidelong glance. "I wished to speak to you without interruption."

"Hmm." Kalek answered, scanning the snowy ground for the grey, reindeer lichen.

"Our time together has made me happy," Okta said, though each word pulled him apart a bit more. "There is no one I value more in this life than you."

Kalek's head shot up. "What are you trying to say, Okta?"

The old healer hoped his eyes reflected his acceptance, his willingness to fulfill this last role. "There is no easy way to say this. I will be going to my Origin soon."

Kalek stopped. "Soon? What does that mean?"

"It means I will visit the Council of Passings at the new moon. I expect to leave before the quarter moon." Unable to bear Kalek's stunned expression, Okta turned his attention to the distant horizon, where the sliver of the wintry sun was already setting.

"How long have you known?" Kalek asked.

Okta winced. The question was a dagger to his heart. "Too long," he admitted, then paused, summoning his courage. "I told myself I feared hurting you. I feared your reaction. The truth is, I feared my own heartbreak, having to admit that I will no longer wake to see your face."

With growing sadness, Okta watched Kalek's broad shoulders droop, and his head bow. Okta said, "I thought, if I told you earlier, the knowledge would be a burden," he endeavored to explain. "You have been in brighter spirits since Dárja's return. I did not want to darken your days needlessly."

Kalek kept his head bowed as Okta struggled on. "I am sorry for making that decision, one which so deeply affects you. I have made too many of those in our time together. I hope you can forgive me for all of them."

Kalek drew a shuddering breath. He looked up, opening his arms to Okta. "There is nothing to forgive. You have given me the chance to watch Aillun's mánná grow and to know the love and friendship of an Olmmoš."

Okta lingered in Kalek's embrace, its solace as profound as any he had experienced in his long life and his many loves.

He stepped back to hold his apprentice at arm's length, knowing more needed to be said.

"You have neglected to mention the sadness and the heartache of which I am also party to."

Kalek shook his head and smiled weakly. "There would have been sadness regardless."

CHAPTER THIRTY-SIX

THE NOAIDI WAITED UNTIL the Elders had settled before addressing the two before him.

"Dárja, the eighteen seasons of snow you have experienced are but a small part of your life," he said. "Yet you have made those of us who are many measures older stop and reflect. You were right to challenge me. To be Jápmemeahttun is to transform. But our ways make us who we are. You and Marnej are too young to understand the importance of ritual and practice."

Seeing the nieddaš's readiness to argue, Einár raised his hand avoid a debate. "I do not say we must follow our traditions to our end, but their value cannot be overlooked. Neither you nor Marnej are truly Jápmemeahttun and so perhaps you cannot fully understand what that means."

The unequivocal tone of the pronouncement had an immediate and sobering impact on the young petitioners. Dárja's once-eager expression now matched Marnej's grim determination. Einár had no wish to hurt these two before him, but he needed them to acknowledge their place among their kind.

Turning from the chastened pair, Einár glanced to the other members of the Council of Elders. They nodded their approval. He was mindful of the concessions they had made, and the tenuous nature of their support.

He cleared his throat. "You may escort the life bringers," he said, catching the sidelong look Marnej gave Dárja.

"But you must adhere to our traditions," he continued. The other Elders murmured their agreement.

"Dárja, you will escort the nieddaš, and Marnej, you the boaris. You may not travel together. You will see the life bringers to their Origin and then withdraw. The life force of the boaris is powerful. It is meant to assist the nieddaš to give birth and transform to almai. The ritual is sacred and not meant to be shared."

Einár addressed the frowning Marnej directly. "You had no part in what happened with Aillun and Djorn, but here you do. Our ways must be respected."

The young Olmmoš nodded, his mouth a hard line.

Einár looked to Dárja, "Do you understand and agree?"

She met his gaze unwaveringly. "Yes," she affirmed, then asked, "Will we leave soon?"

"That is for the Council of Passings to decide," Einár said, perplexed by this unlikely pair in front of him. They looked like mánáid to him, yet much had happened already in their short lives. More than what many of their kind experienced in ten measures. They were linked in ways few would understand, in ways that perhaps even they did not realize.

Dárja and Marnej moved to leave, prompting the Noaidi out of his thoughts. "You both risk much. Let us pray the Song holds you and all are returned safely."

⁓

"They agreed," Dárja said, sounding surprised. "I'd hoped . . . but I didn't think. . ."

She mumbled something Marnej couldn't hear.

"It's what you wanted," he said.

Dárja didn't register his comment. She shook her head. "I didn't think they would agree," she said. "I wasn't . . ." she began, then stopped, seemingly lost in thought.

Marnej wanted to point out that she'd gotten her way, just as she always did, but there was something about Dárja's eyes and how they'd lost focus that made him stop. She'd barely been able to contain herself before the audience with the Elders and now she stood motionless.

For his part, Marnej was relieved to have the Elders' support. It saved him from having to choose. If they succeeded in this foolhardy quest, Marnej hoped he might be welcomed back among the Immortals. He wanted to make a life for himself as his father had done. *But Irjan had Dárja*, he reminded himself. *And I have the forge*, he thought, claiming his place, even if Úlla complained about his presence.

The thought of Úlla chased away any notions about his future. She would be leaving at some point to give birth. He couldn't imagine working in the forge without her. She was as much its heart as its fires. *If she doesn't come back* . . . he began to worry, then reaffirmed that she would come back. They would *all* come back.

"There's much to do before we leave," Dárja said.

Marnej returned to the present, realizing they still stood outside the Elders' chambers.

"What?" he asked.

"I said there's much to do before we leave," Dárja repeated. Her voice had regained some of its confidence. She'd fixed a smile upon her face but it didn't reach her eyes. "I'm glad the Elders saw reason. I know we can protect the life bringers."

Dárja began to prattle on that they were doing what was right. How the only thing that mattered was protecting the nieddaš. How this was the only way. All the while, Marnej studied her.

Her hair had grown out from the shearing he'd given her on their journey north. However, it would be some time before she could braid it again. Right now, her short, wavy tresses bounced along with her insistence. And this, more than anything the Elders had said, drove fear into his heart.

Suddenly, he needed to get away from her as quickly as possible, before the dread and worry drove him to say something he couldn't take back. "I need to go. Úlla's expecting me. We have a lot of work to do today."

"Oh," Dárja said. The single word stretched out in disappointment. "I thought we would tell Kalek and Okta together."

Marnej looked away. "Later."

When she didn't answer, he was forced to look back. The lines around her mouth had hardened. Her smile was gone.

"I should go," he said, taking a few steps away from her, before breaking into a jog. Then, when he was sure Dárja could no longer see him, he slowed to a walk.

Marnej didn't really want to go to the forge. It was true there was a lot of work to do today, but he was reasonably certain Úlla had no wish to see him. She'd been avoiding him since the night she'd shared her secret. And now, he felt torn as to whether or not he should tell Úlla that Dárja would be her escort. If Úlla didn't want to think about returning to her Origin, then he didn't want to be the one to remind her.

Gods! Why can't it be easy? he agonized. It was never this difficult with the Brethren. They'd been cruel and demanding, but he'd never had to worry about another person's feelings. Here, among the Immortals, he was trying to balance everyone's feelings and failing. *Kalek's angry because Dárja wishes to leave. Úlla's upset because she must leave. Dárja's disappointed that I'm not excited. And me?* What did he feel? He no longer knew.

Marnej walked on, blaming himself for something he couldn't control or change. His feet, by habit, carried him to the forge. When he realized where he was, he stopped. Úlla stood by the grindstone, a scythe in her hand.

"I was beginning to think I would need to do all this work myself," she said, without looking up.

Marnej took a smock from the peg, then slipped it over his head, tying the leather strips in the back as he moved to the forge. The fire was out.

"Should I get the fire started?" he asked.

Úlla picked up a smaller whetstone, "Yes. The others will be here after their meal." She honed the scythe's edge, not bothering to look at him.

Marnej began to load the furnace with wood, layering it as Úlla had instructed him. He used pine and pitch to get the flames burning high and hot. It would take time for the wood to die down to coals, and he was grateful that he would need to watch it. The task would keep him occupied and away from the apothecary.

Marnej piled more logs by the forge. He hefted as much as he could carry each time. The effort helped to consume the anxiety that had been building within him since leaving the Elders. He stacked more wood on the fire, then shifted around to work the bellows. The flames roared upward, forcing Marnej to jump back and shield his face.

"Have a care or you will lose your brows," Úlla said, coming to stand beside him.

Her proximity made Marnej uncomfortably aware of the heat within him.

"More air," she said.

Marnej worked the bellows again.

"Good," Úlla said, her eyes on the flames.

Marnej moved to get more wood, but Úlla's calloused hand stopped him.

"Have they decided?" she asked.

Without meeting her eyes, Marnej nodded, then he faced her, knowing that Úlla deserved more. "They've agreed to let Dárja and I escort the life bringers."

Úlla's grip slackened. A long breath escaped her.

"I didn't know if I should say anything," he said, unsure what was expected of him. Frustrated by it all. "You've been avoiding me. I didn't want to upset you."

Úlla's head shot up. "I haven't been avoiding you."

"I haven't told Dárja you will be traveling," he interrupted. "I haven't told anyone. The Noaidi said the life bringers are to travel separately and withdraw once the ritual has begun. I don't understand why. And please don't say it's 'our way.' It makes no sense to me. We'd be safer if we all stayed together." Marnej hesitated, aware his hand was now on Úlla's arm. "No one knows that I share your secret."

Úlla started to say something, then pulled away when the other smiths entered the forge. As she passed her work bench, she grabbed a sheathed dagger and began to fasten it around her waist, then stopped. Úlla looked at Marnej, her bearing both defiant and imploring, then turned away. Her long braid swayed against the back of her leather gilet as she strode out of the forge.

Marnej bit his cheek. He couldn't call after her, and he didn't want to go running after her. He sat down before the bellows, kicking an errant ember which sparked, then sputtered and died. Despite the heat of the forge, a cold chill ran down his spine. He tried not to read it as an ill omen.

⁓

Dárja walked slowly back to the apothecary. Marnej's reluctance to tell Kalek and Okta had added to her disquiet. She wanted to be angry with him for his inconstancy but couldn't quite coax the resentment required. Particularly when doubt gained more ground with each step she took. It was more than confronting Kalek and Okta. She'd already spoken to them about her intention. It was something the Noaidi had said that shook her to the core.

Neither of you is truly Jápmemeahttun.

Dárja had always had misgivings about her place. She'd always felt different than the other nieddaš, but she'd had Irjan and Okta and Kalek and she'd never doubted she was Jápmemeahttun. She was born of Aillun, who had given her a part in the Song of All. She'd fought alongside the Taistelijan, her heart as determined to defeat the Olmmoš as any of her kind. She'd known she wasn't like the others, but she'd always considered herself Jápmemeahttun. And yet, the Noaidi had said she was not. He'd said it with a surety that made its impact all the more wounding. It was as if the

Elder had witnessed all the moments where she had felt herself at odds with the others and had tallied them against her.

A sinking sensation took hold of Dárja. She halted midway through the gathering hall, her knees shaking. Conversations swirled about her. Dárja looked around at faces she'd known her whole life.

"Is it true?" someone asked.

Dárja reeled, almost losing her balance, her heart racing. A cold sweat had broken out across her chest. Her hand instinctively went to her belt until she focused on Ello's wide-eyed expression. Dárja dropped her hand at once, aware she'd been reaching for a weapon she didn't carry.

Ello's gaze slid down to where Dárja now flexed her fingers. "Is it true?" she asked again. "You will travel Outside with the nieddaš?"

Dárja nodded, not trusting herself to speak. Her mind, all the while, struggled to understand how this news could already be known. If Ello knew, then it would soon be common knowledge.

Ello rocked on her heels. A sad smile trembled on her lips. Then she jumped forward and hugged Dárja as if she meant to crush her.

Taller than Ello, Dárja felt more than heard the nieddaš's fierce, rushed words. When Ello released her, Dárja swayed unsteadily. Ello's eyes shone with tears, and her cheeks were as red as her hair. "Thank you," she said, then abruptly walked away. The scent of damp earth and herbs lingered in her absence.

Aware that whispers had replaced conversations, Dárja straightened. She glanced at these faces she'd known her whole life, convinced they judged her as the Noaidi had done. Then she resumed walking toward the apothecary, careful to hide her uncertain step with an affected swagger.

～

Dárja found Kalek and Okta working quietly, side-by-side. However, she could tell by their rushed movements that both were anxious. In an effort to temper her own fears, she smiled. But the muscles of her face twitched, and she could feel the lump in her throat forming.

They both stared at her as she approached the work table.

"They have agreed," Kalek said, more a statement than a question.

"Yes," Dárja said, keeping her voice from wavering.

Kalek turned to Okta, obviously displeased.

Then something unspoken passed between the two healers that Dárja could not decipher. Kalek pushed the gathered lichen toward the old healer. He took up a satchel bundled next to him. "I must tend to the sick."

He was out the door before Dárja could say anything. The sight of the door closing on his back had a finality that nearly drove her to run after him. Only her fear of further rejection kept her rooted.

"He's mad at me," she said, her words sounding hollow.

Okta looked up from sorting through the lichen. "No. Dárja. He is not mad. He is hurting. You are not alone in disappointing him. I am afraid I also hurt him today."

Okta's painful expression made Dárja hesitate before asking, "What did you do?"

The old healer shook his head. "Nothing I care to discuss. It is something which can never be undone."

Without waiting for an invitation, Dárja sat down beside Okta. Her bones felt as old as the stones in the hearth. She sensed Okta's looming questions, but her own were more pressing.

"Why did you send Kalek to find me?" she asked.

"Because," Okta started and then stopped, as though the answer eluded him. He cleared his throat. "At the time, I told myself it was to save lives: yours, Irjan's, maybe all of ours. The Noaidi had set into motion plans with which I did not agree. I stood against him for the first time in my life." He paused again. A heavy sigh escaped him in a single long stream. "I think I did it for Kalek as well. He and Aillun had parted poorly and I knew enough to believe that he would never forgive himself. I thought, if he could find you, then some of his guilt might be assuaged."

"What did the Noaidi do when Kalek showed up with Irjan and me?" Dárja asked.

Okta snorted. "He very nearly banished the lot of us. But I persuaded him that Kalek acted innocent of my interests and that you were a faultless babe and Irjan, well . . . Irjan was Jápmemeahttun. At least, in part."

"In part," she repeated, adding to herself, *But not truly Jápmemeahttun.*

"He proved himself," Okta said as if to convince her.

"But sometimes there's nothing you can do to change what they think of you," she said.

Okta regarded her, his bushy brows nearly touching. "What do you mean?"

Dárja shrugged. "I mean, it doesn't matter what I do, I'll never be truly Jápmemeahttun."

There, I've said it, she thought, feeling like a weight had suddenly been lifted from her shoulders.

"Where did you get that notion?" Okta blustered, his expression suspicious.

"The Noaidi," she said, feeling no anger toward the Elder. He'd spoken the truth.

"Einár said that?"

Dárja nodded. "He's right."

"He has never been more wrong," Okta huffed, shifting his weight to stand.

Dárja put her hand out. "No, Okta. Don't."

The old healer settled himself again, muttering in displeasure.

"He must know," she said, feeling foolish for only now realizing what she should've figured out the moment she'd learned the truth from Irjan. "He's always known," she said with more certainty.

When Okta didn't reply, she suspected she'd hit upon something else the healer would rather not discuss. "It's not like before," she said. "I know the truth."

Okta nodded but she could tell the subject bothered him.

"If he knows the truth, then why did he accept me when I returned from the battle?" she asked. "Why wasn't I cast out?"

Okta grimaced and appeared to age before her eyes. But she had to go on. She had to know.

"If I'll never give birth . . ."

"We do not know that," Okta interrupted, a shadow of his warrior-self coming through. "None of us do, not even the Noaidi."

"So we'll just wait?" she wondered aloud.

"Yes," the healer said decisively. "We will wait."

Dárja looked at Okta, at his gnarled hands that shook. "And if that time never comes?"

"There's more to you than giving birth," he snapped.

"But I will never become an almai."

He waved away her objection with a contemptuous gesture. "If you need to be almai, be almai."

"But my body will remain nieddaš."

"The body is not all that we are," Okta said so fiercely that Dárja stopped forcing the matter. Though she was far from convinced.

Okta winced. A moan escaped him. To Dárja sounded as if his very soul was being taken from him. And then she understood. In her time running around the apothecary, she'd seen and heard enough about the boaris to know what was happening.

"Your time . . ." she said, but could get no further.

Okta nodded, his eyes shut tight.

Panic grabbed hold of Dárja. It twisted her gut and then her heart. "What can I do? Should I get Kalek?"

Okta shook his head. He said hoarsely, "No."

"What am I supposed to do?" she asked, frantic in the face of his agony.

Okta slumped against his chair, panting, his body limp. He reached out for her hand. Dárja felt heat radiating through his papery grasp. She wanted to ask him again what she should do, but she feared he'd said all that he could.

~

Kalek had raised his hand to knock on the weavers' door when the door opened, and one of the clothmakers moved past him carrying a large spindle. He started to speak his purpose, but the nieddaš spoke first, "I am off to the woodworkers. Ávrá is at her loom. Do not scowl at me, Kalek. I told her to rest, but she did not listen, and I am not her guide mother." The weaver hurried off across the landing and clumped down the stairs.

"Hello," Kalek called out through the clacking looms. "Ávrá?" The clatter stopped. Ávrá stepped out from behind a pair of large woolen looms.

"Kalek, I didn't expect to see you," she said, smoothing her tunic.

"I see that," he said, feeling out of sorts.

Ávrá's thin face reddened, highlighting its strong angles.

"I am sorry, Ávrá," he said, immediately ashamed of his tone of voice. "My words were ill-considered and undeserved." He smiled hesitantly and reached into his satchel. "I brought this for your cough. I did not like the way it sounded this morning." He handed her a ceramic jar with a neatly fitted wood lid. "Rub this on your chest before going to sleep and again in the morning. It will ease your breathing and help your discomfort."

Ávrá took the jar, beginning to cough as if on cue.

"I will leave so you can apply it," Kalek said. He stepped back toward the door, regretting that he had spread his agitation and foul mood.

Aware of Ávrá's scrutiny, he said in a rush, "I would rather you rested. You may feel improved, but rest will serve you far better than work."

"Lying down has become tedious," she said, with a shrug, then added shyly, "Perhaps if you stayed and talked to me for a while I would be more inclined to rest."

Luckily Ávrá had lowered her eyes so Kalek's blush went unnoticed. He turned to leave, then stopped. "You are right, Ávrá," he said, recognizing the reprieve she had offered him. "Resting can be tiresome."

Ávrá looked up and laughed a full belly laugh that ended in a fit of coughing. Concern for Ávrá's welfare made Kalek slow to reflect upon the odd choice of his words.

He smiled tentatively, saying, "Perhaps I can bore you with my chatter until you fall asleep." Kalek tucked Ávrá under the woolen blankets, then sat on the stool beside the pallet, finding himself unable to think of a suitable topic.

"You don't have to amuse me," Ávrá said, arranging the furs around her. "But, perhaps it will help you to speak of what troubles you."

Kalek felt the floor shift under him, and he tried to recover his composure by adjusting the stool.

"I may have a cough," Ávrá said with a kind smile, "but it does not cloud my eyes or my reason."

Called out for his pretense, Kalek flushed and looked away. As he wondered where to start, he felt Ávrá's slender hands on his.

He took their warmth as a sign of a fever and promptly retreated to the role of healer.

"You feel warm," he fretted, loosing his hands from hers to touch her forehead. It was deceptively cool to the touch. Kalek shifted to stand, his mind already reviewing which herbs might be needed. A firm tug brought him back to himself.

Ávrá lay upon her pallet. Her pale eyes were patiently expectant.

Kalek continued to stand, the need to leave rising along with his discomfort. But he found he could not take a step under the nieddaš's watchful gaze. The weight of the burdens he carried in his heart pulled him down, guiding him to sit once again.

"I feel like everything I love has been taken from me," he managed to say, then the truth of his confession overwhelmed him.

Ávrá said nothing as she waited for him to make his way through the tangle of his emotions.

"Okta . . ." he started to explain but knew instantly he could not begin with this loss. Instead, he said, "Dárja has received the blessing of the Elders. She will protect the life bringers. She and Marnej both. I know she believes this is the only way to help us, but I cannot accept it." Kalek faltered, his fear squeezing the breath from him.

"You are afraid to lose her," Ávrá said.

Kalek nodded. "When Dárja ran away to the battle and did not return . . . I could not survive that again." *First Irjan. Now Okta. And soon Dárja. No. I will not survive*, he thought. Aloud he said, "I am not her bieba, but . . ."

"She is Aillun's mánná. You love them both." Ávrá drew herself to sitting. The furs slipped from around her narrow shoulders. "I remember Aillun well. We were close as mánáid. When she began training as a healer and I as a weaver, we drifted apart. Our lives did not often cross. But my memories of her are sweet. I am sorry for your loss."

"And Irjan," Kalek said without thinking.

"True," Ávrá said. "I did not know him. There was not much occasion for me to cross paths with him. Although I did see him often."

"He was Dárja's guide mother," Kalek said.

"And your friend."

"Mmm," he agreed, leaving the rest unsaid. "And now Okta will shortly leave for his Origin."

"I am sorry, Kalek," Ávrá said softly.

Kalek looked away, certain her pity would crush him. "Part of me refuses to believe it is true because my life will never be the same when he is gone," he said, his voice quivering like birch leaves in a cruel eastern wind. He paused, feeling his despair about to crest. "I will be alone."

"You do not need to be alone," Ávrá whispered.

Kalek nodded, hearing little over his fearful reflections. Then he felt the warmth of Ávrá's hands upon his. Through his welling tears, Kalek made out the shape of her fingers as they intertwined with his. His heart skipped a beat, aching from both hope and sorrow.

CHAPTER THIRTY-SEVEN

THE MEN SAT SHIVERING in the cave as the wind howled, their horses outside, too large to be brought further into the sloping recess. Beartu withdrew the rabbit from the smoky fire. Prying off a small piece of flesh, he blew on it, swearing all the while as the meat burned his fingers.

"Ready," he said to anyone listening.

Beartu laid the rabbit on a low flat rock, then pierced its charred flesh with his knife. "Hand me the cups."

The men passed forward the few cups they had stolen. Beartu cut the rabbit into meager portions, adding it to the stew that remained to them. He waited for Válde to decide who would eat first.

"Redde, Mures, Edo, Feles," Válde said, staring down the others who hungrily awaited their turn. When the first four were done, they handed their cups back to Beartu. But they held on to their bones.

"Gáral, Herko, Daigu," Válde said, raising his hand to wave off the cup Beartu held out to him. "You eat. I will go last."

Beartu did not need to be told twice. He pulled flesh from bone with his teeth, then took a swallow of the stew.

Mures cracked his bone between his forefingers and thumbs, then sucked on the marrow.

Between bites, Beartu barked, "Don't throw those bones into the fire when you are done. Put them in the pot and I'll make bone broth for us all."

Redde tossed his bone into the iron pot by the fire. It made a tiny plink as it landed. He handed his cup to Válde, who scraped the remnants of the meat from the rock where Beartu had carved it. He chewed slowly in an effort to make each morsel last.

"That wasn't enough for a mouse," Herko stated, cracking his bone and taking his knife to it. "Not even marrow for me." He tossed the bone in the pot.

Feles cracked his, then handed half to Herko. Herko took it with an appreciative mumble.

Feles resumed scraping out the center of his half, saying, "It is better for all of us if you do not bellyache."

Herko opened his mouth.

"Leave it, Herko. Save your energy," Gáral said.

Beartu stood hunched, and using the edge of his cloak, he took hold of the iron pot.

"Any more?" he asked.

Válde reluctantly added the bone he had been sucking on to the pot.

"The rest of you can add yours when I am back," Beartu said, heading toward the horses and the snow beyond.

"Does anyone have a leather cord?" Daigu asked. "I need to tie off my boot. The cold's edging down my leg to my foot."

"You're better off than me," Redde snorted, "I haven't felt my feet for days."

"Listen to you," Gáral sneered.

"The only time I've felt warm is when we set fire to the temples," Herko added, and then grinned. "They do burn nice and hot."

Beartu came shuffling back, the iron pot heaped with snow. He knelt and placed the pot upon the coals.

"Speaking of fires," Edo said, cleaning his knife on his pant leg before putting it back in its sheath. "Do we continue?"

"Can't we find somewhere safe to hide until the snow ends?" Daigu asked, then yelped. He turned to glare at Gáral, rubbing the back of his head.

"Listen to you," Gáral said again, his voice dripping with disgust. "Have we grown so weak that we cannot survive a season of snow without running to our mother's bosom?"

"That's easy for you to say, Gáral," Mures complained. "You've had respite in travelers' huts. We haven't."

"We cannot exactly walk into a village and ask to stay," Edo pointed out.

"No, but none of us are known by our looks," Daigu said. "A couple of us could scout the next village for an abandoned farm."

"And when a passing trapper sees smoke rising from the chimney? Do you not think it will raise suspicion?" Feles asked.

"We know a regiment has been sent to hunt us. If we sit cozy in a cabin we will be vulnerable for ambush," Válde said. "Our best strategy is to keep moving. The snow is as hard on them as it is upon us. But we can gain ground faster than they can. Our best chance of success is to keep striking as we have been doing."

"Maybe there's a better way," Beartu said, stirring the rabbit bones in the melting snow. He sat back on his haunches. "If we were disguised as soldiers, we could move as we wanted and stay where we pleased, without question or bother."

"Until some commander pulls us into their unit," Herko objected.

"Or we're seen burning a temple," Redde added.

Beartu shook his head. "Don't you see? It's a perfect disguise for burning a temple. It'll turn all the eyes and suspicion onto the army. They'll be so busy crawling through their ranks to find traitors, they won't have time to look for us."

Válde scratched at his growing beard. "It is a risk to seek out soldiers."

"Those scouts proved no obstacle," Beartu pointed out. "Nor any others we encountered."

Edo shook his head. "Nine uniforms? That is a lot of men to dispatch at once without anyone taking note."

"Perhaps we only need one or two to begin with," suggested Beartu. "With a couple of uniforms we could gain access to a garrison, where there are more for new recruits."

"You propose that we infiltrate a garrison?" Válde asked.

"Yes," Beartu said. "We would gain access to not only the uniforms, but also information. It's not enough to listen to gossip from farmers and merchants."

"The risk is high," Válde hedged.

"I would rather gamble my life in action than have my bones freeze in a cave," Gáral said.

Válde shifted, a plan forming. "Mehjala is the closest village east of the Great Valley."

"They might be prepared after the fire in Hassa," Edo worried.

Mures clapped him on the back. "Don't fret, Edo. If it doesn't suit our needs, we can always burn their temple by our old methods and look for another village."

~

Niilán stepped outside of his lavvu, letting the leather tent flap fall back into place. Fresh snow blanketed their encampment, softening the peaked outlines. In the gloom of what constituted morning this far north, men and horses huddled together, both desperate for warmth. He exhaled, his breath like steam. Niilán clapped himself about his shoulders, fighting off the cold that dug through his layers as if it searched for his flesh. The previous day's storm had prevented their departure from Skaina, convincing Niilán they could not succeed traveling as they had been.

Awake long before the others, he'd had time to make up his mind. Now that they were no longer obligated to supply reinforcements, he would divide what men remained to him and spread out, increasing their chances of capturing the Piijkij. Niilán strode out to the cooking fire where Matti, Joret, Jonsá, and Osku stood close to the smoldering flames, waiting for him.

Coming to stand beside Osku, Niilán accepted a cup of broth, sipping it gratefully, before moving ahead with his plan.

With the exception of Osku, the others stared at the fire. They no doubt wished they were somewhere else. *But here we are*, Niilán thought, wiping his short beard with the back of his hand in a futile attempt to keep ice from forming a crust on his face. He had not forced them to become soldiers. Nor had he been responsible for their being part of his unit. They were, however, his responsibility now, and Niilán reminded himself that his plan was designed, at least in part, to serve them. The sooner they found the Piijkij, the sooner they could return south, where they would not freeze their puohtja every time they took a piss.

"I have decided to divide the regiment," he said. "We stand a better chance of success if we spread out."

Three of the four men looked ill at ease. Reading their thoughts, Niilán said, "It will not be like before. You will each have enough men under your command that the Piijkij will not be a threat. We will fan out and sweep across the terrain. They will not escape."

Matti looked down from his towering height, doubt written across his broad face. The others shifted uneasily, avoiding Niilán's gaze. Undeterred, he unsheathed his sword, then used its tip to draw in the muddy snow.

"We are here. We know they have traveled to Hassa. From there, they could have spread out in any direction. It is possible they headed to the Pohjola, but I doubt it. Their message to the Vijns spoke of more action to come."

Niilán waited to see if his men had anything to add. When they did not speak, he went on.

"We will divide the regiment into four equal units," he said. "Joret, you will head north and east along the border of the Pohjola. Matti, I want you to head to the western border and then south. The rest of us will fan out in the middle. I will travel to Hassa with Osku and from there to Mehjala and then south toward the Stronghold. If you find their trail, follow and attack.

They are well trained, but their numbers are few. If you are smart and stay vigilant you will remain at an advantage."

"What if we don't encounter them?" Jonsá asked, stomping his feet against the cold.

Niilán squinted through the shifting smoke. "Return to the Stronghold. Seek out Áigin, and tell him of our plan."

"And if none of us succeed?" Joret pressed.

"The burden of failure rests with me," Niilán said. When silence, thick as any snowfall, descended, Niilán endeavored to think of something encouraging to say, but, to his mind, the only thing that really mattered at this point was action.

"Have the men break camp," he said to his new commanders. "Osku will divide the regiment into units. When you have your men, head out." Niilán felt all eyes on him now. He knew his men needed more than direct orders. They needed hope.

Niilán cleared his throat, searching for heartening words. "May the gods favor us all," he said finally. It was not enough, but it was the best that he could do.

Niilán waited until his men were about their duties, then returned to his tent. Throwing back the ice-heavy flap, he ducked inside. The pine branches he had laid down on the ground to prevent it from becoming a quagmire creaked under his weight. The sound hit the wrong note in Niilán's ears, reminding him of his own inadequate words. He had not lied to the men when he told them the burden of success rested with him. However, he had not shared his doubts about the future, nor had he voiced his regrets about the choices he had made in the past. A true leader should have neither doubts nor regrets.

Perhaps that was why most leaders were men with more ambition than sense.

CHAPTER THIRTY-EIGHT

MARNEJ AND ÚLLA STOOD beside the cold forge. The day's work had not yet begun. Úlla pulled her furs tighter around herself. Her curved belly, however, poked through in spite of her efforts. Marnej had accustomed himself to seeing Úlla as his equal in strength, swinging her hammer, bending metal to her will. But in this moment, with her breath labored, he'd never seen her look so vulnerable.

"I leave today," she said, glancing about the forge as if taking it all in to preserve the memory. "I began working here to be close to Kálle. He was a master. He could take the toughest piece of ore and turn it into a finely honed blade or the most delicate piece of jewelry." Úlla shifted aside her furs, revealing her dagger, slung under her belly. She pulled it from its sheath, then ran her fingers along the flat of the blade, before tracing the curved filigree of the bone hilt. "Kálle made this. He was the best bladesmith we had."

"You learned from him?" Marnej asked when Úlla's voice trailed off.

She returned the dagger to its sheath, then wrapped her furs around her. "I learned much from him."

"You can teach me when you return," Marnej said, a feeble smile breaking through.

Úlla snorted. "I liked you better when you were a Piijkij and not spouting wishful notions."

Marnej laughed. Úlla appeared now as hard as the metal she forged. *And yet*. He thought about the challenge she faced—that all the Immortals faced. "You're right," he said. "I wasn't making light of what you're about to do. I'll do everything in my power to see that you make it back. Especially if you'll teach me to make a dagger like that."

Úlla shoved him, but without much force. The hard lines at the corners of her mouth curled up into a reluctant smile. "We'll see if you have the skill for it."

"I'll hold you to that," Marnej warned. He leaned back against the anvil and looked around the forge. "It won't be the same here without you."

"That's true. No one will keep you in line," Úlla said, then added, "But you won't be here either." Her expression softened into remorse.

"No. I'm leaving soon," he agreed. "I'll see you at your Origin. You'll have the whole journey back to remind me of all my short-comings."

"You make it sound so simple," Úlla rounded on him. Her pensiveness was gone, replaced by her usual challenging nature. "I've never been Outside. What if the Song fails us?"

"If fortune is with us—" Marnej began, then hesitated. The truth seemed cruel, but he needed to honor it, to honor Úlla.

"If fortune is with us," he said, "your Origin will be close, and the Song of All will keep us safely hidden. But if we must travel farther south, I don't know if we can sustain the Song. We may all be traveling like the Olmmoš." Marnej held up his hand, pre-empting Úlla's next question. "I can't tell you what that feels like. It has been my world from birth. But you should take heart that Dárja has experienced the Outside. She knows what to expect. She'll guide you and keep you safe."

Úlla pushed herself up from the post she leaned against.

Marnej couldn't tell if he'd convinced her or just himself with his reassurances.

Úlla held out her hand awkwardly. "I will see you at my Origin."

Marnej clasped arms with her. He felt the ropy muscle of her forearm beneath the supple skins of her sleeve. "I'll see you at your Origin," he said, hoping he sounded confident.

~

Dárja would not slink off into the woods without a word this time. She'd learned enough about loss to know that she didn't want to repeat the mistake.

"I'll be back before you realize I'm gone," she said.

Kalek nodded, his mouth set in a bloodless line.

Dárja bit her lip. "I know you don't approve . . ."

"It is not that I do not approve," Kalek said, speaking for the first time since Dárja had entered the apothecary to make her good-byes. "You believe you are doing what is right. Maybe you are. But I do not want to lose you. You are more to me than an apprentice, Dárja." Kalek faltered. "I love you like . . . a father."

The Olmmoš word sounded strange to Dárja's ears.

"I do not seek to replace Irjan," Kalek said, his broad brow knit with concern. "He will always be your guide mother." He took her hands in his. "But I am your father, and I love you no less than Irjan."

This time, the foreign word came out easily, with force behind it.

Dárja's reserve crumbled. She wrapped her arms around Kalek's waist, and pressed her cheek against his rough wool cloak. She inhaled deeply the scent of bitter herbs. She never wanted to forget it.

"I know you do," she whispered hoarsely, recalling the countless times Kalek had soothed her when she couldn't be with Irjan, or had healed a cut or gash when she and her bieba had sparred.

Irjan had always sat beside her as she'd sniffed back tears, but it was Kalek who had carefully cleaned her wounds and applied the tinctures before wrapping her arm or leg or shoulder. Irjan had made her strong, but Kalek had made her whole.

"I'll come back," she said.

Kalek's hand brushed the hair from her forehead, curling it around her ear.

"I know you will," he said, kissing the top of her head. "You are the very best of us."

~

Dárja closed the door to the apothecary. She swallowed hard. It took all her strength of conviction not to turn around and go back in. A part of her longed to remain safe in the apothecary with Kalek, Okta, and Marnej. But Marnej would be leaving soon too. They hadn't had much time together since their meeting with the Elders. Marnej was always busy at the forge with Úlla. Dárja felt a spark of jealousy flair. Dárja knew she was being petty, but she couldn't help it. At least where Marnej was concerned.

If someone had asked her, Dárja would've been unable to say exactly when her feelings for Marnej had changed, but they definitely had. He still drove her mad with frustration, but there was something more to their interactions. She no longer blamed him as she'd once done. In fact, she'd often sought out his company. She enjoyed their sparring practice. But more importantly, she took pleasure in their conversations afterward. Marnej had shared much about his life with the Brethren, careful to spare her feelings whenever possible. He'd described his loneliness and his isolation, his desire to prove himself and his anger toward Irjan.

For her part, Dárja spoke a great deal about Irjan. She shared her memories of growing up with the man Marnej had called his father, but had hated all the same. There were times when she'd hurt him. She could see in his face that he wondered, "Why her and not me?" But recently, she sensed he'd made peace with not only with his past, but also with his relationship to Irjan. He'd relaxed. He sulked less and joked more. She doubted if any of the others would believe her, but when they were alone, Marnej would tell stories, make faces, and mimic Okta's gruff scoldings. He made her laugh until her sides ached. Then he would smile. *His smile*. Dárja's breath caught at the image. It was like a sun breaking through the clouds after a storm. The echo of the storm's power remained but the promise of warmth was so inviting.

Of course, that was before he'd accused her of being blind to the feelings of others. She wasn't blind to these feelings. Perhaps that's how it looked to him. But it wasn't true. It was just that she didn't know how to express her own. They made her feel weak and vulnerable. She hated that. Maybe if Irjan had not been her guide mother, or maybe if she'd been more like the other nieddaš, she would've been truly Jápmemeahttun. Dárja had wanted to tell Marnej all this and explain herself, but he'd been avoiding her. Now, time was running out, and she was about to leave for the Outside. She'd told Kalek she would return, but she knew there was a chance she might not. She couldn't leave matters as they were. She needed to find Marnej and tell him the truth.

Dárja picked up her pace, conscious of not drawing attention to herself. But she could not ignore the morning greetings of those she passed. Once the news had spread that she and Marnej would escort the life bringers, everyone had begun to take new interest in her. Some offered advice and opinions. Others reprimanded her for interfering in the traditions that had been handed down. This morning she didn't have time for any of it. She needed to speak with Marnej before she left.

Once across the gathering hall, Dárja ran toward the forge. It was the only place she could think Marnej would be. At the threshold, she came to a stop, feeling the hammering on metal jar her body and thoughts. The furnace blazed to life, the fire fed by the bellows. *Marnej*, she thought, relieved to find him. She rounded the pillar, convinced she could say what needed to be said. Seated at the bellows, however, was an almai she knew only by sight. He nodded as he eyed her, his scrutiny distressingly skeptical. Likely, everyone who worked in the forge had feelings about Úlla leaving for her Origin.

Dárja scanned the forge, careful to stay out of everyone's way, then she called out to a nieddaš on the sharpening stone, "Where's Marnej?"

The nieddaš looked up, shrugged, and then went back to her task.

It was just like Marnej to make her run after him. Úlla was waiting for her, and she couldn't leave without speaking to him.

Dárja spun on her heel, breaking into a run when she reached the hallways. She didn't care now who saw her or what they thought. At the apothecary, she burst through the door. Without stopping to explain herself, she ran past the startled healers, and out their garden door. Outside, Dárja's feet slipped in the icy snow, but she kept running. At the small clearing where they'd sparred and practiced, Marnej stood, looking up at the dark sky.

Dárja ran to him, reaching him breathless. All along the way, she'd rehearsed what she would say. How she would tell him her feelings, but now, when confronted with the opportunity to do so, she froze.

Marnej stared at her. Falling snow caught on the edge of his fur-rimmed hood and his lashes.

Dárja was certain her mouth moved, but no words came out.

Marnej began to walk past her.

"Wait," she called after him, tripping over her feet to grab hold of him.

He reeled around to face her. Dárja flailed like a fledgling perched on the side of a nest until he steadied her.

"I know you think I don't understand other people's feelings," she said, catching her breath. "But I do. I really do. It's just that . . . up until now, I didn't understand my own feelings. I couldn't leave without telling you—telling you how much I . . ." Suddenly her thoughts and her words were like rabbits, running off everywhere.

Dárja reached up her hands. She cradled Marnej's face, tipping his head toward hers. As she kissed his cold lips, the snow of his hood fell upon her nose and her cheeks. Marnej's searching eyes closed, and then she felt the pressure of his arms encircling her. He crushed her to him, kissing her, his mouth drawing up a fire within her. Dárja pulled back. Her heart pounded in her chest. She watched his eyes slowly open, momentarily lost in the light she saw pouring out. She leaned forward and kissed him lightly on the lips, then pressed her forehead against his.

"You have my heart," she whispered.

CHAPTER THIRTY-NINE

UNACCUSTOMED TO RIDING ON a binna, Marnej bumped alongside Okta. He missed the even, trotting gait of a horse.

"Do not fight the animal, Marnej, "Okta said over his shoulder. "Listen to its Song. Bring it into you. The binna will guide you."

Marnej squirmed in the saddle. Trying to get comfortable, he accidentally pulled back on the reins, halting the reindeer's forward motion.

"How am I supposed to stay centered on the Song of All if I also have to pay attention to this beast's song?" he complained, encouraging the reindeer to start moving again.

"They are one and the same," Okta replied enigmatically.

Marnej mimicked the healer behind his back. They were six days out on their journey and he felt defeated by the difficulty of even the simplest things. After living with the Immortals within the Song of All, traveling Outside and having to maintain that link was frustratingly hard.

"I thought it would be easier," he grumbled.

"What would be?" Okta asked.

"Traveling in the Song," Marnej said, shifting in the saddle again. "I thought after all the time I spent with your kind it would be easier for me."

Okta tsked loud enough for Marnej to hear the disapproval.

"It was never easy. Much less so now. With few of us remaining to hold up our part of it, it takes focus and diligence."

As the two rode on in silence, Marnej resolved to practice his concentration. But as he tried to center himself, other ideas and questions bubbled up through his mind, pulling his attention in one direction and then another. In the midst of ideas flitting here and there, Marnej alighted on the fact that, while he'd spent time alone with Okta, it had never been for this long, nor under this kind of circumstance.

Dárja had framed their efforts as protecting the nieddaš about to give birth. But Marnej was escorting the ancient healer to his death. And, even though he knew he had no control over Okta's life, and respected that the healer's death would bring a new life to the Jápmemeahttun, he still felt like an executioner.

"Are you afraid?" Marnej asked, shattering the snow-hushed quiet.

"Afraid of what?" Okta murmured, as if lost in his own visions. "Traveling out here?"

"No," Marnej said, then felt his next words stick in his throat. "Your death," he croaked.

Okta faced him, but the hood of his furs shadowed his eyes as if death was already claiming him, piece by piece.

"No. I do not fear my end," he said. Then he paused as if he were considering the matter further. "No. My fear is for the future. I worry for you and Dárja and Kalek. I want the lives of the Jápmemeahttun to continue long beyond me. But I am not sure how that will come to pass."

"That's what we're trying to do," Marnej said.

"It is a noble sacrifice, and it may yet succeed," Okta said. "But we are a closed circle."

"What do you mean?" Marnej asked, reminded once again of how little he knew about the Immortals.

"Our numbers are set. I leave and another will take my place. We will not grow." Okta took a deep breath, then released it in a long ribbon of steam. He seemed to shrink before Marnej's eyes, as if the ancient healer had only ever been made of the air he held inside himself.

"This order saved us in the past, when our numbers had become so vast we overran the land," Okta said. "It was the gods' way of preserving a balance among all of their creations. But the wars with the Olmmoš took many of us and I am afraid the last battle has sealed our fate."

"There are still almai and boaris," Marnej pointed out.

"Yes, yes. But so few, and there will never be more."

"But you changed once. You can change again."

"Perhaps the gods will gift us once more. But I am afraid we have squandered their mercy on wars with the Olmmoš."

"You didn't choose the wars," Marnej argued

Okta shook his head, his grey beard peeking out, flecked white with snow. "I chose to ride into battle, as surely as any other almai."

"No, I mean . . . my kind pushed you into it. We came after you. We hunted you."

"True. But looking back, I can see we were not blameless in what came to pass."

Marnej felt a rising sense of frustration. "What about my father and me?"

Okta shrugged. "You are special. Like Dárja."

"Maybe that's the future," Marnej insisted.

"Let us hope," Okta said, sounding weary. He faced forward again, letting silence descend.

～

Okta was thankful for a reprieve from the boy's questions. He knew Marnej sought only to help. Still, he felt doom's mocking presence within each of his own answers. Once, he had advocated the possibility of change, but that was before the last battle. Before they had lost so many. Okta did not believe they would ever recover from it. Whatever small strides they made now only served to prolong an inevitable decline.

However, he admired Marnej and Dárja their youth and bravery. They reminded him of Djorn and the others who had fought on after the rest had withdrawn into the Song. They had honored what they believed to be right. While Okta had not shared their convictions, he respected their valor. Djorn's memory reminded Okta not only about the choice he'd made, but also about the more fateful choices made by Irjan. Both Dárja and Marnej shared Djorn's life force and lived because of it. But there was a deeper connection. One which Okta had often considered when he contemplated the gods who had shaped and spared them.

It had been Djorn's mánná, Mare, who had birthed Irjan. When Irjan found Djorn and Aillun, he unknowingly brought together a bloodline in his attempt to save Marnej. Okta wondered if this union was an act of the gods or the result of one man's frantic effort to save his child. So many times he had believed himself capable of changing events, only to discover he had been powerless. Maybe this was different. Maybe the gods had acted through this one Olmmoš to help their kind find a new way forward?

"You may be right, Marnej," Okta said, finding a sliver of hope in this new understanding.

Startled, Marnej pulled back on his reins, causing his binna to stop.

"About what?" he asked.

"About you and your father," said Okta.

Marnej's proud features furrowed in concentration as he nudged his reindeer to keep moving.

So unlike his father's gaunt, brooding countenance, Okta thought.

"I don't understand," Marnej said, still unable to get his binna to respond.

Okta stopped himself from reminding the boy to not fight the animal, asking instead, "How much did Einár tell you about Irjan?"

With the binna moving again, Marnej settled back into his saddle. "Well, he told me of my father's time with your kind. I think it was his way of warning me not to make the same mistakes."

"No. No. I mean about your abilities," Okta said.

Marnej shrugged. "He said we shared the same ones."

"Did he ever speak to you of how Irjan came to possess those abilities?"

"No."

"You did not ask?"

"I wasn't about to question the Elder," Marnej said, huffing in disbelief.

Okta pushed back his hood. The cold brought a fresh ache to his ears, but a frank discussion could not be carried on while cloaked and hidden. "What do you know about our life cycles?"

"You just said yourself it's closed—one birth for one death."

"Yes. But, what else?"

"Are we talking about how you create life?" Marnej asked warily.

Okta laughed. "Yes, in a manner of speaking. But I am not asking about the workings of it."

"Good," Marnej said, relief apparent in his relaxing shoulders.

Okta watched the youth resist the sway of the binna beneath him. *He will learn*, Okta reminded himself.

"You have lived long enough with us to have noted the differences between your kind and ours," Okta said, hiding his question within the statement.

"Yes."

"Well?" Okta prodded.

Marnej twisted in his seat. "I don't know?" he said. A hint of annoyance edged his voice.

"What about the mánáid?" Okta asked, wanting Marnej to come to his own understanding.

"What about the children?"

"What do you notice?"

"They're all female."

Okta nodded and searched Marnej's shadowed face for comprehension. *Gods, this boy will wear me down before I have a chance to ascend*, Okta thought unkindly. But he persisted in his method. "What about your father? Tell me his story as you know it."

"When my father was a little boy," Marnej began, "the Jápme-meahttun killed his family and burned his house . . ." He stopped.

"Exactly," Okta said. "We are born female and . . ."

"He was born male," Marnej said. He pushed back his hood. "But how is that possible?"

Okta steered his binna around a rangy spread of birch trees. "There are stories from the days before the Olmmoš and the Jáp-memeahttun were at war of the coupling of our two kinds."

Marnej's mouth twitched. Okta found the boy's discomfort amusing. "We are not that dissimilar."

"No. It's not that," Marnej protested, his cold-reddened cheeks flushing even brighter. "It's just that if it's possible, then why aren't there more like me and my father?"

"When the Olmmoš arrived among us, we believed the gods had given our kind the duty of biebmoeadni. We were to be guide mothers of the Olmmoš, not make more of our own kind."

"But it did happen," Marnej said, latching on to the idea.

"Yes. It did. And that led to the Olmmoš casting off our guidance to seek war," Okta warned.

"And after the war? My father was the only one?" Marnej sounded dubious.

"Perhaps there were others," Okta said. "But none of them entered the Song."

"What about me?" the boy asked.

Okta shook his head. "I am not sure, Marnej. Perhaps you are one of a kind. Perhaps you represent something we might become. I cannot say."

~

Okta and Marnej rode for the better part of three days in the silence of the Olmmoš realm when the Song of All deserted them. Marnej had sworn bitterly, but Okta had remained serene, as if the shift had not affected him. After the initial shock had worn off, Marnej had assumed that it would be a relief to be back in a world he understood. But the absence of the songs had left him feeling hollow and lost. In particular, he wished he could still hear Dárja's song. He prayed to the gods that she and Úlla were still safe.

With no song to concentrate on, Marnej's mind began to obsess on what Okta had shared with him. There had to be a way to save the Immortals. *It happened before*, he reasoned. *It could happen again*. But it would be madness to approach the Council of Elders to suggest that their kind might be saved if they interbred with the Olmmoš. They would think him a traitor. They would never consider joining with the people who'd hunted them into extinction. And even if they did agree, how would they approach the Olmmoš? The blood lust of his kind hadn't changed. They were rejoicing that the Immortals had been wiped from existence. *So what could they do? Steal away some Olmmoš and enslave them?*

"It's all madness," he said out loud.

"What is madness?" Okta asked.

"Nothing," Marnej said hastily, focusing his attention on his surroundings for the first time that day. So far, he'd been content to follow Okta's lead. Ahead, to the south, he now saw a familiar stone gorge. Even blanketed in snow, there was no mistaking the fissure that allowed men to pass through rock.

Marnej looked uneasily at Okta. "You know where we're going."

The statement probably sounded more like a question because the healer answered, "Yes. I have been there before."

"So have I, Okta. Tell me we travel beyond it." Apprehension had crept into Marnej's voice.

"I am afraid not," the ancient healer said placidly, refusing to make eye contact.

Marnej's anger flared. "You've known this whole time. You just didn't tell me."

"It is my Origin. I traveled here as a nieddaš and gave birth here." Okta turned to him. His eyes looked tired. "If I told you we were going to the Great Valley, would that have changed your mind about coming?"

Marnej gritted his teeth, feeling trapped. "No. You know I'd still be here. It's just that . . . I would've been prepared."

Okta sighed and nudged his binna toward the hills in the distance. "Believe me, if I could have chosen another spot, I would have."

CHAPTER FORTY

Herko and Gáral sat in the musty corner of the travelers' hut outside of Mehjala. They sipped juhka from rough wooden mugs, listening to the joiken of travelers. Some chanted of the hardship of their lives. Others sang of the freedom of the wind. All the while, the two Piijkij watched the comings and goings of visitors. Only one soldier had come in, but he had been too small to interest either Herko or Gáral. They would have looked like boys who had outgrown their winter woolens if they had tried to fit into his uniform.

"My beard has grown while we've been waiting," Herko complained.

Gáral scanned the newly arrived. "You can go and send in another who might appreciate the warmth."

"All right. All right," Herko grumbled.

The door to the travelers' hut swung open. Gáral tensed at the sight of two soldiers. He nudged Herko and nodded his head in the direction of the door.

We just need to wait until these two have had their fill of cups, he thought, still listening to the conversations around him about the mold in the barley stock, the aches in the joints, and the recent rain that had turned snow to ice.

Herko signaled to the hutkeeper for more juhka. The woman gave him a brusque nod, then went to see to the soldiers.

When she returned with their drinks, Herko gulped his, then fell back into a slouch, his eyes slitted as if asleep. Gáral knew his comrade still watched the soldiers. As did he, noting that although both men sat, they had not taken off their cloaks. When handed their cups, the soldiers drank the warmed juhka without comment, then called for a second round. Resigned for a long wait, Gáral was surprised to see the soldiers drop a coin in the woman's palm when she refilled their cups. With a gusto worthy of Herko, the two drained their second round, then stood to wind their way through those gathered by the fire pit. As the soldiers passed, Gáral leaned back into the shadows, his hand upon his discarded furs.

Herko was already on his feet, downing the dregs of Gáral's cup. "What?" he muttered. "That might be my last drink for a long while. "

"Come on," Gáral hissed.

Herko hurried after him.

Outside, the two soldiers cut through the trees and into the darkness.

"Follow my lead," Gáral said, padding silently after the soldiers, Herko on his heels.

"Excuse me viel'ja," Gáral called out, "did you drop this pouch?" He lifted a leather purse in the air, jingling it.

The two soldiers turned.

"Who names us?" one of the soldiers called out as they walked back toward the waiting Piijkij.

"I will take the one on the left. You take the one on the right," Gáral whispered.

Herko grunted, standing back.

When the soldiers reached them, the one on the left held out his hand for the purse. Gáral dropped it into his palm. The soldier hefted its weight, then turned and grinned at his comrade. When he shifted back around, he met the full force of Gáral's fist, just as Herko leapt forward, skewering the other with his dagger.

Herko immediately lugged his dead soldier into the woods, where he began stripping him.

"You should not have killed him," Gáral admonished, picking up the fallen purse.

Herko glanced up. "You're suggesting I should've left him alive?"

Gáral rolled his moaning soldier onto his stomach. "At least until you got the clothes off him. The uniforms are no good to us with blood all down the front of them."

Herko patted his dead soldier's face. "A little blood never hurt anybody." He yanked the man's boots off, then rolled the breeches down, letting the man's legs fall back in the snow with a powdery thump.

The soldier Gáral had punched groaned again.

Herko looked over. "Dead ones don't make so much noise," he pointed out, grinning as he pulled off a woolen tunic.

Gáral straightened and kicked his moaning soldier in the head. The man fell silent.

Herko gathered up scattered clothing, saying, "Much quicker when they're dead."

Gáral ignored the taunt, tugging off his soldier's tunic. When the man was lying naked in the snow, he unsheathed his sword, then plunged it through the man's chest. Withdrawing the bloodied blade, he was careful to run it through the snow before wiping it on the man's pale, fleshy thigh.

"That is how you avoid bloodstains on your clothes," he said to Herko as he rolled his dead soldier into the tree well of a broad pine. Gáral kicked snow onto the body, then stood back. "Hurry up or I will cover you as well."

Herko heaved his soldier into the tree's round gulley. He scooted out of the way just as Gáral batted the snow-laden branches. A deluge of powdery snow covered the bloody slush below. From beyond a tight copse of larch, the rest of the Piijkij emerged, bringing their horses.

"You succeeded?" asked Válde.

Herko and Gáral held up the uniforms.

"Herko stained his," Gáral announced.

"He usually does," Mures teased.

The others joined in as the two Piijkij finished lashing their uniforms to their saddles.

"Seven more to go," Redde said.

Válde smiled. "I know just the place to find them."

∽

Herko tugged at his tunic. The faded yellow was stained a dull brown with dried blood. He tied the red woven belt of a foot soldier around his waist. "Lowest rank," he mumbled in disgust.

"You look just like a true Believer," Redde beamed, batting his eyes at Herko, who took a step forward, but was held back by Edo's hand.

"You wouldn't want to split those seams," Mures added.

Válde stood by Gáral as he adjusted the soldier's black felt cap down over his ears.

"We can offer no aid this time," Válde said in a hushed tone.

"We will not need it," Gáral declared, shrugging himself into the crudely embroidered cloak. "Herko is a natural thief and spiteful enough to take down anyone who stands in his way."

"All the same . . ."

Gáral cut him short. "Save your speech for when we have returned."

Válde inclined his head, his self-control irritatingly unflappable.

Gáral signaled to Herko, who then handed Feles the reins to his horse. "I trust you to take care of her," he said, then turned a mean eye toward Mures and Redde who snickered.

"Herko," Gáral called out, drawing away from the group.

Theirs was a straightforward plan. The two of them would walk into the garrison, locate the stores, take what they needed, and ride out on stolen horses. Simple enough, but with room for much to go wrong. Still, the plan suited Gáral's mood. He was tired of hiding. He wanted to stand in the open. Also, the thought of wreaking havoc while wearing a True Believer's uniform appealed to him.

Herko caught up, scratching at his sides. "I think this mother's cur had fleas," he groused.

For a moment, Gáral wondered if he had made the right choice in choosing Herko. Aloud he said, "Do not make me regret bringing you along."

Herko pulled his cloak tightly about him. "Don't think you could do this without me, Gáral. You may've served the Avr personally, but he's gone. You're no better than any of us now."

Gáral bit back his response, letting Herko's affront go unremarked upon. If they were to have any chance of success, they needed to work together. But the comment rankled, and though he focused his attention on winding his way through the snowy landscape, Gáral relived the anger and shame he had endured by not being able to protect the Avr. He should have convinced Dávgon of the danger the boy posed. But he could not countermand his leader. *If only I had killed Marnej*, Gáral thought, allowing the rest to remain unsaid. It was in the past. Nothing could be changed. All that remained was their plan, and whatever came of it.

Emerging from the trees, Gáral was surprised to find they were on a cart path. He had been prepared for a long and tedious slog. But it was barely first light, and to the east, rose the outpost's palisade wall, and beyond that the defense tower. Even at this distance, Gáral could see that guards posted at the gate had slowed horse and cart movement to a trickle.

"We are in the gods' graces," Gáral enthused. "It is a large garrison and not some goat-shed outpost."

The two picked up their pace as they crossed the white expanse before the garrison. Gáral recalled an old rhyme taught to them as boys by an elderly brother who'd had a keen interest in fortified defense. "Keep the forest at bay and your enemies away," the old man had counseled, wagging a finger. As if any of the boys he taught would ever oversee the building of a fortress. Still, as Gáral stepped over steaming piles of dung to weave his way through the mounted soldiers, he reflected on the fact that sometimes a forest was not made of trees.

Keeping a relaxed and confident stride, Gáral approached the gate.

"You there, viel'ja," the sentry called out.

Gáral stopped. From the corner of his eye, he saw Herko draw back. He looked over at the guard, prepared for a fight.

"Lead these men to stable their horses," the sentry said. "Then have them presented to the commander."

Gáral nodded, like a good soldier, then took hold of the bridles on either side of him. Keeping his eyes lowered, he glanced over his shoulder as he started walking. Herko had followed his lead. As the two of them guided the mounted riders forward, Gáral scanned the area ahead, spotting the stables at the northwest curve of the palisade wall.

Outside the stables, he waited as the lead riders dismounted. Handing the reins to Herko, he whispered, "See what you can find out. I will meet you back here," before adding aloud, "Make sure these horses are groomed and fed."

As Gáral gestured to the dismounted riders to follow, he caught the eye of a weathered soldier. The man's brooding stare unnerved him, but Gáral kept his voice even as he said, "This way."

Stopping at the base of the defense tower, Gáral felt the soldier still watched him. He feigned a casual look over his shoulder, as if he were making sure he had not lost any in his charge. The man who had taken such an interest in him rubbed his stubbled beard, observing the outpost around him. *I have become as nervous as Edo*, Gáral thought, climbing up the steps, the man now forgotten.

At the top of the sloped wooden causeway, two guards stopped him.

Gáral said, "Riders here to see the commander," hoping he had guessed correctly where the outpost leader had sequestered himself.

"What name do I offer?" the sentry asked.

The riders came forward, pushing Gáral out of the way and nearly off the top of the walkway.

The weathered one said, "I offer the name Niilán."

As the guard escorted the riders into the defense tower, Gáral descended the causeway. From his vantage point, he saw that, far from being a worthless errand, his commission to deliver the riders had brought him to the ideal spot to survey the entire outpost. He took a moment to watch the comings and goings, his attention resting on a cluster of three long huts with snow-covered roofs. Smoke rose from two. One likely served as the cook hut which meant the store rooms were nearby. Gáral bounded down the causeway, mindful of the soldiers milling. They had cloaks but no furs. They were common soldiers. No men of rank. Still, Gáral was conscious to not make eye contact as he walked with the airs of a man who had his orders.

When he arrived at the stables, Gáral found Herko inside, picking out the hoof of a grey mare.

"What are you doing?" he asked.

Herko looked up, letting go of the horse's hoof. The animal snorted. "Picking shit out of hooves. Have your eyes failed you?"

Gáral flexed his hand. He dearly wished to hit Herko. Hard.

"Save your energy," Herko said, nodding at Gáral's poised hand. "I've no fight with you." He stretched his back until it cracked in a quick succession of pops. "As soon as you left, the guards from the gate approached. I couldn't pass them without rousing suspicion. I've been here, stooped over, caring for these brutes. But I can tell you which are in the best health, and I overheard the guards mention that the riders we brought in came from Hassa."

"Word of our deed must have spread," Gáral said, his flush of anger cooling. He clapped Herko on the back, enjoying the man's wince.

"Let's find what we need and leave these soldiers with something else to talk about."

~

Niilán and the Mehjala garrison commander stood to clasp arms.

"I wish you good fortune in your hunt," the commander said.

"We will camp on the outskirts and travel tomorrow," Niilán answered, turning to leave.

With a rush of wind, the door to the commander's quarters flew open. A breathless sentry entered. "Fire at the stables, sir!"

Niilán suddenly found himself at the back of a crowd pressing through the room's door. Outside, he saw smoke rising from one of the squat structures. Soldiers ran in all directions as the garrison commander clattered down the causeway, shouting orders. Those soldiers who had their wits about them had organized a bucket chain leading from the well to where the flames licked up the structure.

Finally free of the men blocking his way, Niilán raced ahead. His one thought was their horses. He could not afford to lose a single one.

When he reached the stables, the shouts of men were drowned out by the frightened screams of animals. A handful of soldiers ran out from the black interior, coughing, leading out wild-eyed horses who reared and fought to run away. Niilán charged inside, his nose and mouth covered by the crook of his arm. Thick smoke stung his eyes. He squinted as he moved further in, but could see nothing beyond the smoke and the voracious glow of the fire as it devoured the wooden walls and the hayloft above.

A tumble of rafters crashed down, spreading a fresh wave of heat. Niilán drew back. His flesh felt crisped, as if he were roasted upon a spit. He ran from the building, his chest burning.

Outside, Niilán dropped to his knees, gasping, choking on the fresh air. He grabbed at the nearest soldier.

"The horses?" he croaked.

"They're out," the soldier said, tearing himself away to rush off.

Niilán scrambled to his feet, his eyes watering. Through the blur, he saw the horses corralled together near the gate. He staggered to the makeshift enclosure, searching for Osku, silently berating himself for not bringing Matti. Standing a head above any man around, Matti would have been easily spotted.

As Niilán neared the corral, men rushed past him shouting, "Close the gates!"

He grabbed one of the gatesmen. "What has happened?"

Before the man could answer, the horses broke free as a new panic swept through them.

The soldier shoved Niilán back, but Niilán held on. "What has happened?" he shouted again.

The man wrenched himself free without answering.

Jostled on all sides by men scrambling to catch the horses, Niilán heard Osku's deep voice berating a soldier. Niilán made his way into the tumult of men and beasts and found his man, holding firm to the reins of his horse and another. Niilán grabbed hold of one set of reins, surprising Osku, who rounded on him with a ready kick and a curse. When he saw that it was Niilán, he shouted above the din, "They set fire to the stable and stole horses!"

In an instant, Niilán knew who *they* were. Fury clouded his vision. He mounted his frightened horse. With Osku beside him ready to ride, Niilán shouted at the gatesmen. "Open these gates or I will kill you where you stand!"

❧

"Of all the stupid things, Herko," Gáral yelled as they raced away from the garrison.

"You won't be complaining when we use these bows to pick off soldiers from a distance," Herko shouted, shifting the hefty quiver of arrows onto his back.

"We were to get uniforms! Not weapons," Gáral fumed.

Herko leaned closer to the horse to lessen the jolting gait. "What good's a uniform without weapons?"

Gáral drove his horse on, leaving the damnable Herko to his own fate. He threaded the sparse trees. Branches snapped his face. Gáral's eyes watered in pain, but he kept riding, all the while blaming Herko. When he reached the meeting point, Gáral brought the horse to an abrupt stop, almost tumbling head-over-ass onto the pointed rocks.

"Válde, get out here. Now!" Gáral yelled. The cold wind pulled the words from his mouth, leaving quaking silence in their wake.

"Válde!" he yelled again.

The others emerged from the thick forest just as Herko arrived.

"Do you have the uniforms?" Válde asked.

"Yes," Gáral almost spit the word out, "but the alarm was raised at the outpost. We are followed."

Válde tensed. "How?"

Gáral snarled at Herko. "Do not ask."

"Here," Herko grunted. He handed out two bows with a pair of full quivers. Edo took one, Feles the other.

Válde looked to Gáral for answers.

"Do not ask," he repeated. "There's no time. We need to put distance between us and the outpost. Now!"

Válde signaled. The men mounted.

"What direction?"

"The Great Valley," Gáral said. "At least there we will have the advantage of a lookout if we need to shoot those arrows."

CHAPTER FORTY-ONE

VÁLDE CAME TO A stop, surveying their location. The darkening sky gave no sun marker, but he knew by the hills they were east of the Great Valley.

"Pull out the uniforms," he said, dismounting. "If they catch up, the uniforms may prove useful."

"If we keep going, they won't catch up," objected Herko.

"Herko's right," Gáral said. "We should keep going."

"That is fine for you and Herko," Edo said. "You already wear your uniforms."

"The animals need a break," Feles said, wiping ice crystals from his horse's neck.

As the men dismounted, Válde looked to Gáral. He expected to see defiance and disdain. Instead, he was surprised to see resignation. Gáral untied the roll of tunics and cloaks from his saddle. He handed them down to Válde. "Hurry up, Herko," he said. "The sooner these uniforms are on, the sooner we can get moving again."

Herko grumbled, but unstrapped the roll of clothing behind him, handing out the stolen uniforms. The men shivered as they stripped off their outer layers to replace them with the soldiers' tunics. Donning the thick cloaks, some of the men thanked the gods for the warmth, while others bemoaned the need for the disguise.

While the men tightened belts and refastened weapons, Válde said, "If we are followed, I want to lay a false track from here."

"And what if they hunt you down?" Gáral asked pointedly.

"Then I will have succeeded in drawing them away."

"No. You'll only have succeeded in getting yourself killed. That would leave us short on horses and Gáral to lead us," Herko said, disgusted. "I will ride with you."

"So, two swords will make a difference?" Gáral scoffed.

"No, but three might," Feles said, taking a step forward.

Gáral's hand shot out to stop Feles. His expression darkened. "You lead the others to the ridge," he ordered, meeting Válde's appraising look.

"We will lay tracks to the south, then come up into the valley through the southern gap," Válde said.

"That shit-cursed place," Herko spat.

"You can stay behind and practice your skill with a bow," Gáral said.

Herko rose into his saddle. "To let Válde meet the same fate as the Avr by relying on you alone?"

Gáral lunged forward, ready to pull Herko from his horse, but Feles blocked him.

"You think I would not change that day if I could?" Gáral fought to get free. "I would gladly have sacrificed myself if I could have stopped the Avr from trusting Marnej." He pushed Feles aside. "I should have killed that boy when I had the chance."

"It was the Avr's choice!" Válde boomed. "He knew Marnej was a traitor's spawn. He chose to listen to him anyway. Now, the longer we stand here arguing among ourselves, the closer we are to our end. Come with me, Gáral, or go with the others. Either way, mount your horse and ride."

To Feles he said, "If we do not meet up with you within the day, take it as a sign of your leadership. Ride for the cave."

～

When the gates finally opened for Niilán, he shouted to the sentries, "Which way did they go?"

The soldiers pointed south.

Niilán knew he could not follow the tracks by himself without risking a confrontation with an unknown number of Piijkij. But in the time it would take him to reach his men and return, he might lose the fresh horse tracks. Niilán's own mount pawed the ground. Any riders who came from the south would easily obscure the tracks he wished to follow.

"Gods plague the lot of them," Niilán swore and spurred his horse west to where his men were camped.

~

Less than a league separated Mehjala from what remained of Niilán's regiment. Thirty men was a group small enough to move quickly and large enough, he hoped, to rout the last of the Piijkij. Niilán pushed his horse faster along the cart path, feeling as if each moment were a lifetime.

When he reached the edge of their encampment, the relaxed movement of his men drove him into a fury. There was no way for them to know of the events at the garrison. Still, he had expected them to be ready to ride. Niilán heard the sound of a horse behind him. He spun to see Osku draw up short, his horse snorting.

"Get the men ready to ride," Niilán shouted. Not bothering to dismount, he continued to bellow orders. "Have someone commission a cart from the garrison and pack what remains. Have him head south. If fortune rides with us, we will be at the Stronghold to greet him with Piijkij heads on the picket."

Niilán rode up and down the ranks of rushing men. His exasperation drove him to crude threats and snarling epithets.

"Hurry," he growled at a young soldier who had dropped his saddle and startled his horse. "You had better be on that horse the next time I look your way, boy, or you will wish that your mother had drowned you at birth!"

Finally, with the last of his men mounted and Osku by his side, Niilán galloped back toward the cart path heading south. As they neared the garrison, Niilán slowed. He looked back to reassure himself the others still followed, even though he knew he could rely on Osku to keep the men apace.

In the fading light of the already-gloomy day, Niilán turned his attention back to the cart path. His eyes swept to either side. They had already ridden at least two leagues beyond the garrison, and as he had feared, the tracks he had seen earlier had been trampled into an unrecognizable mush of snow and mud.

"Keep an eye out for signs of horses veering off," he yelled back to his scouts, hating every moment of the struggle to balance lost time with the chance of losing the trail.

"Here," called one of the scouts.

Niilán joined him and was emboldened to see two sets of tracks leading southeast through lightly forested ground.

"Follow them," he ordered the scout, bringing his own horse abreast.

Now that they had clear tracks again, the plodding pace of the scouts made Niilán want to skin them alive. Still, to rush might mean losing the trail.

"They stopped here," one scout called back to Niilán.

Niilán rode forward, then dismounted to examine the tracks. The snowy ground was a mash of prints. Both men and horses had trampled the area. There were, however, several sets of clear tracks leading south. Niilán circled the area, scanning the hill to the north. Just beyond his waiting men, he noticed several trees with green, low-slung branches. The surrounding trees were still plump and white with snow.

Niilán pushed his way through riders and shying horses.

Trudging up the incline to the trees, he saw that branches had been cut. "They've tried to cover their tracks," he shouted, looking to the ridge line.

Niilán ran back to his horse. "Osku, take half the men and ride to the ridge. Then make your way into the valley. I will take the rest and head south. Meet at the southern entrance to the valley if you have not encountered the Piijkij. Sound the alarm if you do."

CHAPTER FORTY-TWO

THE SLED CARRYING DÁRJA and Úlla shushed along the overhung path. Dárja felt the menace of the snow-laden pines. To keep her growing sense of unease at bay, she delved deep into the Song of All, taking comfort in the familiar choruses, as she searched for one in particular.

Dárja had heard Marnej's song not long after she and Úlla had begun their journey. She listened for him now. Though she could almost sing his song as her own, she couldn't find the refrain within the chorus. Beside her, Úlla sat as imperious as always with her hands resting upon her belly. The very likeness of a mother bear. Úlla's song was now strong beside her own, but it had wavered at times. And that gave Dárja cause for concern.

"How much farther must we travel?" she asked Úlla, unable to ignore her growing disquiet. "Can you tell?"

Úlla gave her a long look before she closed her green, ermine-like eyes. The crease between her brows deepened. After a moment her eyes fluttered open. An odd half-smile graced her lips, as if she couldn't decide the true measure of her feelings.

"Not far," she said.

"You're sure?" Dárja asked, anxious that she didn't know where they were headed.

Úlla puffed with indignation. "I know what my body tells me."

Dárja looked ahead to the thick, murky woods. Fighting back memories that threatened to consume her, she brought an image of Marnej to the forefront of her mind, to find his voice within the Song. But what rose unbidden was Irjan's face. And Kalek's. Faces of disappointment and hurt.

Úlla gasped.

Dárja pulled back on the reins. "What is it?" she asked, her heart beginning to race as she took in Úlla's expression. "Is it the baby? Has the birthing begun?"

Úlla shook her head wildly. The whites of her eyes showed full around their glazed centers. "I do not know. Something is wrong. My body feels strange and . . ."

"Oh gods, no!" Dárja cried, dreading what was about to happen. She didn't understand how Úlla had lost her connection to the Song of All, because she still felt the Song's pull. But how or why no longer mattered. Úlla was all that mattered.

Dárja filled her mind with all manner of competing thoughts and desires. Letting her own song lapse into silence, she banished the internal chorus. Her body stiffened. The weight was suddenly too much for her to hold as she sat. In an instant, the sonorous Song disappeared, replaced by the horrifying, thick silence of the Olmmoš side.

Dárja fought to open her eyes. Her lids felt heavier than the ore that Úlla turned to metal. Úlla sat bent over the side of the sled, retching into the snow. Dárja moved to comfort her, but could barely shift her limbs.

"You'll feel better soon," she promised, her voice like a lone echo in her head.

Úlla sobbed. "What is happening? Everything is silent. Heavy."

She retched again. This time, Dárja was able to reach her. She pulled the nieddaš back from the sour contents of her stomach.

"We are outside the Song," Dárja said, looking around the woods to reassure herself that they remained unobserved. "We need to move," she said, resting the still-sobbing nieddaš across her lap. Reaching over Úlla's shaking body, Dárja took hold of the reins, giving them a snap. The reindeer, seemingly unfazed, moved with a start.

Dárja used one hand to guide the binna and her other to pat Úlla. "The feeling will pass. You'll be able to move again."

Muffled by her fur hood, Úlla's voice sounded small and distant. "The silence." She hiccupped, then began to cry once again.

"You'll get used to it," Dárja said, trying to soothe her.

She felt Úlla's head shake in her lap before she heard her whimper, "I do not want to get used to it. I want to be back in the Song."

"Then concentrate, Úlla," Dárja encouraged. "Concentrate on your part and listen for the others. I'll do the same." Dárja drew her mind back from the problems they faced and the plans she'd been crafting. She slowed her breath and forced her Song out beyond her. She listened deep within herself, hoping to hear something—anything. All she heard was Úlla crying. Panic welled within her. *It's held until now. Why is it failing us?*

"Try again, Úlla," Dárja said, her tone like a command.

"Everything is silent," the nieddaš whined.

Barely managing to hold back her own fears, Dárja concentrated on how hard she'd fought to be here. She took a breath to prepare herself. "We knew this might happen and it has," she said. "But, Úlla, I can't do this without you. You're the only one who knows the way."

Dárja slowed the sled. "We need to keep going, but we must leave the cart paths."

Úlla pushed herself up. Her face was blotched and her eyes were swollen. Even so, traces of her contentious spirit shone through.

"Why?" she demanded, sounding more like a petulant child than a nieddaš about to give birth.

"Úlla, we need the woods to hide. But we can't travel with the sled through thick forest," Dárja explained, praying the nieddaš would see reason—*at least once in her life*. "We'll tuck the sled by those trees, and reclaim it after the birthing."

Before Úlla could object, Dárja slid out of the once-cozy sled, and whatever confidence she had scraped together crumbled. Her knees wobbled as she sank into a deep pocket of snow. Feeling fear take hold of her, Dárja grabbed onto the binna's yoke, using the sturdy reindeer to pull herself upright. For a long moment, she stood panting, unable to move. But then the sound of Úlla's crying became unbearable. Dárja took a hesitant step forward. Relying on the reindeer's surefootedness, she led the laden sled toward a stand of tall spruce.

At the trees' edge, she beckoned Úlla to step out of the sled, offering the nieddaš a steadying hand until she could hold herself upright. Dárja then unharnessed the binna, murmuring to the animal that their journey still continued. She handed the reins to Úlla, who held on to the reindeer as if it were her last connection to their lost world. Dárja unloaded their supplies, placing them by Úlla's feet.

"I'll cover the sled with branches, then saddle the binna for you," Dárja explained in a soothing voice. "I'll carry what supplies I can. The rest will be left behind."

Dárja waited to see if Úlla would respond. She needed the nieddaš to regain herself because she couldn't be both a crutch and a protector and hope to succeed.

～

Úlla swayed astride the saddled binna as Dárja walked alongside her up the snowy slope.

"I'm sorry you must walk," Úlla said, catching Dárja lost in her thoughts.

"It's better this way," Dárja said. "I won't need to dismount to defend you."

Úlla's grimace made Dárja regret her unguarded response. It was true, but hardly comforting. Had she had her own binna, one she'd trained with, Dárja would've happily fought astride the animal. *But, with an untrained binna, whose own fears and emotions took precedence* . . . No, she preferred being on her own two feet.

Silence reclaimed the two nieddaš as they continued to climb the hill. One was intent on her steps and the other sat quietly astride the snuffling binna. When they reached the ridge, Úlla gasped.

Dárja looked up to see Úlla smiling down at her. It was perhaps the first time she had ever smiled at Dárja.

"It's there," she said, gesturing excitedly downhill.

Dárja turned to where she pointed, and her bowels loosened. She had been so intent on her footfalls she'd failed to notice the direction in which Úlla led them. With sick horror, she gazed upon the expanse of the Great Valley.

"My Origin," Úlla said, urging the reindeer forward.

"Wait," Dárja called after her, but to no avail. Úlla's faster pace forced Dárja to skid and slide down the slope, only just avoiding trees and branches.

Reaching the base of the slope, Dárja paused, unsure her legs would hold her. Then she took her first tentative step onto the valley's wide-open field. She shuddered. She thought of the battle and of Irjan, lying dead somewhere in this vast whiteness. A groan escaped her lips before she could stop it.

Úlla turned. "Are you all right?"

Dárja bit down on the scream within her. She bobbed her head as she drew even with Úlla. The nieddaš smiled, her relief palpable. Úlla cleared her throat. "I want to thank you for coming with me, Dárja."

"Of course," Dárja said, surprised by Úlla's sincerity. Her heart swelled with the enormity of it. "We all want you to return safely with your baby in your arms."

"I have not always been kind to you," Úlla said, casting an uncharacteristically shy glance at Dárja. "I know this can't be easy for you."

Dárja looked around at the valley, now so peaceful. She waited until she was sure her voice would not break. "The battle's long over," she said, reassuring not only Úlla but herself as well.

"The battle?" Úlla brows knit in confusion. "I don't understand." The look in her eyes was one of guilt. "I thought . . . I mean . . . Marnej said that you'll never see your Origin."

Dárja staggered back as if she'd been hit. She gaped at Úlla as her mind reeled. *He told her*. Marnej had told Úlla what she'd never told anyone. *He'd betrayed her confidence. With Úlla*. She had trusted him. She had given him her heart-pledge. Anger took hold of Dárja. There Úlla sat upon the binna, looking down on her, her expression so full of pity. Well, she would tell the insufferable nieddaš that they stood on the very ground where her beloved Kálle died. *We'll see who deserves pity then*, she thought. But before Dárja could utter that harsh truth, Úlla's head snapped up, "Someone's approaching."

Dárja looked to where Úlla pointed, her hand going to her blade.

～

As Marnej rode behind Okta, he thought about the last time he stood in the Great Valley. They were more than halfway through the sun's turn, yet everything about that day in the valley was fresh in his mind. The horrifying sounds of men and beast, shattered and dying. The sickening slosh of blood and mud below his feet as he swung his sword in all directions, killing almai—perhaps even Úlla's Kálle. Who knew? They were faceless Jápmea to him then. Their death at his hands was a way to prove himself worthy to the Brethren of Hunters.

Irjan had fought and died here. And Marnej wondered, not for the first time, if he'd unknowingly faced his father. He dismissed the thought, telling himself, as he often did, that he would've recognized him, even in the blood-frenzied state he'd been in. *I would've known*, he thought, *I would've known my own father*.

Marnej shook his head to clear the image of Irjan. A vision of Dárja rose in its place. Marnej's breath caught. What would've happened if he and Dárja had faced each other on this battle-field? They'd crossed swords before. He'd given no quarter then. But now. . . He shuddered to think what might've happened. He would have nothing without her.

"I hoped I'd never see this place again," he said, riding through the north end of the Great Valley. He glanced up at the steep walls on both sides of him. "Is your Origin near?"

"Yes. We are close," Okta said, with no hint of emotion.

"Please tell me it's not out in the open," Marnej said, looking around at the flat expanse.

~

On the eastern side of the valley, Okta guided his reindeer to the forested edge where dense pines opened into a small clearing. He dismounted as if the movement caused him pain. Marnej slid off his mount to run forward and help the ancient healer. Okta leaned on him, yet he felt as light as a bird, as though part of Okta was already gone from the world.

"Do you think Dárja and Úlla are close?" Marnej asked, worried about what was to come.

Okta's head shot up and Marnej realized too late his blunder.

"How did you know that Úlla travels with Dárja?" Okta demanded, his weariness seemingly forgotten as he stepped back to scrutinize Marnej. "Did Dárja tell you?"

"Dárja didn't tell me," Marnej protested as he contemplated lying. But his respect for the ancient healer required the truth. "Úlla told me. She didn't mean to . . . but . . . why does it matter anyway? We all end up here together." Marnej gestured to the clearing. His frustration with this needless pretense preempted his desire to honor Okta.

"It is our way," Okta said forcefully.

"But it makes no sense!" Marnej argued.

Okta's stern gaze met Marnej's emboldened one. "The importance of our traditions goes beyond an Olmmoš's understanding of reason. Our traditions connect us to our past, to our gods, to our purpose."

Marnej shook his head in defiance. "You yourself said the Jápmemeahttun may be at their end. Why continue with a ritual that serves no purpose?"

Okta closed his eyes. His bushy brows knitted together for a long moment. Without opening his eyes, he said, "Because the meaning behind our traditions is all that is now left to us—all that is left to me."

As the silence lengthened, Marnej felt guilty for wrenching such a sorrow-filled confession from someone he had grown to care for. He put a hand upon the ancient healer's arm and squeezed lightly, hoping to convey the depth of his remorse.

"Are you well enough to stand on your own while I tether the binna and make camp?" Marnej asked.

Okta nodded his head as he looked up. A weary smile had replaced his frown.

Marnej took the reins and led their reindeer to forage. After caring for their mounts, he glanced back at the ancient healer. Okta stood still, staring off into the forest beyond their clearing, his expression unreadable. Marnej had not wanted what little time was left to them to be overshadowed by regret. He vowed to himself to do whatever was asked of him, regardless if he understood why. He owed Okta this and more.

Marnej unstrapped the saddle bags in preparation for making camp. He wished they'd brought more supplies to make Okta comfortable. But in light of the purpose behind the healer's journey, perhaps the Immortals didn't consider it necessary. Still, he had his hatchet and he could at least fashion something for Okta to sit on, as it was getting increasingly harder for the healer to rise from the ground. Walking back toward the birch trees bordering the valley floor, movement caught Marnej's eye. He stepped out in the open, squinting to make out two figures. One mounted. The other on foot. The mounted figure waved.

Bittersweet gratitude filled Marnej as he called out over his shoulder, "They're coming." Marnej's news was met with a grunt of pain. He turned in time to see Okta crumple to the ground. Marnej ran back to gather the ancient healer in his arms. Holding Okta as a spasm racked his frail body, Marnej feared the healer would not have the strength to do whatever was needed for Úlla and the baby.

"They'll be here soon," he said, unsure if these words were of any comfort.

The healer grimaced, then nodded, gripping Marnej's hands.

~

"Put your hand down," Dárja hissed.

Úlla looked confused, "Why? It was Marnej."

"You don't know that."

"But it is my Origin," Úlla pleaded. "I can feel it. The pull is so strong. You cannot understand."

Dárja stopped, stunned by Úlla's words. When she'd gathered herself, the nieddaš was ahead of her, swaying atop the reindeer.

"Úlla, wait!" she shouted after the foolhardy nieddaš, her resentment giving way to panic.

"I can feel it," Úlla shouted.

Dárja dropped everything she carried. She began to run, but deep snow slowed her down.

Ahead, Úlla shouted a greeting. A figure emerged from the trees. Dárja pushed herself to move faster. It could be Marnej, but it could also be some other Olmmoš. Dárja's legs and lungs burned with effort. Then another figure emerged, stooped and bare-headed.

"Okta," she spoke his name aloud as relief washed over her. Dárja slowed from the run and strode forward with new purpose. As her fear receded, her anger came charging to the fore. Each step through the sticky snow fueled it.

When she reached the trio, Úlla stood beside a smiling Marnej.

"Dárja," Okta greeted her, his voice like a sigh.

She looked past him, her rage focused on Marnej. "You told her!" Dárja's words lashed out like a whip. Marnej's smile disappeared, and Úlla drew back.

"Dárja," he said.

His thick Olmmoš accent made her grit her teeth. "Who else did you tell?" she shouted.

Marnej took a step toward her. Her hand went to her knife. She heard him say, "No one," his eyes pleading, big and round like all of his kind. "I'm sorry."

"Liar!" she screamed. "I should never have trusted you. An Olmmoš." She spat.

Dárja relished the fear she saw in Úlla's eyes as the nieddaš cowered next to Okta.

"Dárja, stop this!" Okta bellowed. "You dishonor yourself."

The rebuke stripped Dárja of her words. She looked at Okta and saw him as the formidable warrior he'd once been. Her shame tore at her from within. "I'm . . . sorry, Okta," she whispered.

The ancient healer seemed not to hear her. "This is a sacred rite," he roared. "You have pledged service to the life bringers, yet you stand before us snarling like a wolf gone mad." Suddenly Okta sagged, moaning. Úlla rushed to help but could not hold him up. Dárja lunged forward to bear the weight of both life bringers.

"Help us," Dárja called to Marnej, who stood staring into the valley.

"Riders are approaching," he said, glancing back at her.

CHAPTER FORTY-THREE

MARNEJ REALIZED IMMEDIATELY THE terrible mistake he'd made riding out from the cover of the forest. They could've all remained hidden and perhaps gone undetected. But the moment he'd seen the riders, all he could think about was Dárja. He couldn't just hide and hope for the best. He had to do something. He knew now that he'd lost Dárja's trust, but maybe he could still atone for what he'd done. He could give her a chance to protect Úlla and the baby when it was born. Perhaps the child was already in the world. He'd ridden out moments ago, but he knew nothing about how long the birth would take. How many times had he heard it said that this was a sacred ritual? Marnej's frustration died. He didn't need to know. He was an Olmmoš. Just as Dárja had said. She didn't need him. She would take them back. Úlla would return to the forge, and the baby would go to a guide mother. But Úlla would be an almai. Marnej briefly wondered what she would be like as a man.

At this distance, Marnej recognized the soldiers' uniforms. There were three of them riding up through the valley. He hoped they'd come to honor their fallen from the battle. Or maybe they sought a shortcut. But experience told him they were likely scouts. They were three men to his one. The odds were against him but not formidable, unless an army loomed beyond sight. Marnej spurred his reindeer into a run, knowing he would not be able to pass for an Olmmoš. His people did not ride reindeer. They rode horses. Only the Immortals rode the binna. Marnej drew his blade. He wouldn't waste his time on subterfuge. He would attack and hope to catch the soldiers unprepared for a fight.

When he got close enough, Marnej saw that the three soldiers rode with their weapons drawn. There would be no element of surprise. Marnej charged, then broke left, raking the outermost rider. The soldier's horse screamed. Marnej brought his reindeer around to charge again. The remaining two soldiers rode directly at him. Marnej broke left again, but the soldiers intercepted him, hacking at him from both sides. Marnej blocked on the right, then slashed left, but he couldn't pivot fast enough to stop a blow from unseating him. His reindeer staggered. He fell off the beast, tumbling over the animal's prodding antlers. He felt the burn of cold metal cut across his arm, then saw blood blooming through the cut in his furs.

Marnej rose to his feet, his blade ready. He heard the sound of his name an instant before a soldier tackled him. Marnej's long blade was useless to him in close quarters, but he fought the soldier off with his fists.

Then he saw the man's face clearly.

Marnej stared, stunned. "Gáral."

"I thought I had lost my chance to avenge the Avr when you ran," the man growled, squeezing Marnej's throat.

Marnej clawed at the man's hands. Then stuck his thumbs into his former comrade's eyes.

Gáral howled and released his hold, allowing Marnej to roll away, gasping.

"Leave him," a voice commanded.

Marnej's vision cleared in time to see Válde pulling Gáral to his feet. Herko sat astride a horse. A smile twisted the man's thick features.

Marnej scrambled to his feet. He pointed his blade at men he'd once called brothers. "The Avr betrayed me!" he shouted.

"Lies!" Gáral lunged for him, spittle flying from his mouth.

~

The hillside to the west erupted in shouting. Válde looked up to see colors flash through the trees.

Válde yanked Gáral back. "Leave him. We must go!"

"Let me kill him," said Gáral, breaking free. "It will be quick. I promise."

"This is no time to defend your honor," Válde said, rising into his saddle. "Honor is useless if we are all dead. Now mount up or we will leave you."

Before Gáral could take a step away from the traitorous Marnej, a young boy astride a reindeer rode at Herko. Válde hesitated for an instant, unable to fathom what he saw. Then the boy raised a blade and rode as if born in the saddle. Válde shouted Herko's name. It was the only word he could get out before the boy set upon Herko with vicious blows. But the Piijkij came back with powerful sweeping strikes that toppled the boy from his mount. The boy landed ass-over-shoulder with a scream that made it clear it was no boy. It was a girl. Válde gaped as she leapt to her feet, her blade ready.

Marnej charged between the girl and Herko, Gáral on his heels. "Get out of here!" Marnej shouted, then turned to parry Gáral's attack. The girl stood her ground, moving around him.

"Leave!" Marnej implored.

"I'm no coward," she said, blocking Herko's assault. Before Válde could act, the thunderous sound of hooves drew his attention. He turned to face a mass of soldiers riding toward them. It was impossible for Válde to tell if any among them were his men. But with both Herko and Gáral on foot they could not ride away. They would have to fight. Válde swore at the gods who seemed hungry for their souls that day. Then the onslaught was upon him.

From the corner of his eye, Válde saw a blade flash. He spun to attack and narrowly missed Herko's head. The man's bald pate ran with sweat and blood. At Herko's side Gáral fended off another. As Válde pushed his way forward into the fight, two soldiers collided in front of him. He lurched to one side to avoid them, but a pair of rough hands unseated him. Lying winded on the ground, Válde fought against the relentless pressure that pushed his face down into the snow—into his grave. He arched up, desperate for air, and managed to push off his attacker. Lurching forward, he grabbed a sword in the slurry of blood and icy mud, then felt the sting of his flesh being cut open through the quilted layers of his clothing. He turned to block, but was too slow. His sword flew from his hand. His attacker raised his blade to slice through Válde's belly, then the soldier dropped to his knees, his eyes wide and unseeing. Over the top of the soldier's head, he saw the girl's menacing sneer. In that instant he recognized her. It was that Jápmea girl who had escaped. Then the moment passed and she was a blur, moving, fierce and deadly. Válde grabbed a sword, ready to fight once again. But the question of why the Jápmea girl had saved him continued to plague his thoughts.

A voice shouted, "More soldiers to the south!"

Válde spun to see at least a dozen mounted soldiers riding toward them. He tugged a slumped soldier out of his saddle and pulled himself up.

"Brethren. Ride!" he bellowed, heartened to see that a few men were riding north already. Válde circled, looking for more of his men. Herko had his hand out to Gáral to lift him up onto his horse. Then he saw the Jápmea girl. She fought beside Marnej. In her blood-streaked furs, she looked like a wild animal. The two stood against five. The girl fended off two at once. Válde glanced to the south. The riders were nearly upon them. He did not care about Marnej's fate, but the girl . . . she had saved his life.

Válde rode into the fray, swinging at any uniform in his way. He heard Marnej yelling for the girl to run. She ignored the plea. Instead, she parried and blocked, moving forward, heedless of his words. Válde did not doubt she could hold her own, but with fresh soldiers bearing down upon them it was hopeless. He brought his horse between the girl and soldiers. He hacked at the men's heads, then circled again, holding out his hand to her. "Take my hand or you will die here."

"I will die fighting," she snarled.

"Dárja, no!" Marnej shouted. The boy's warning was cut short by a cry of pain.

The girl spun to him, just as a soldier charged her, knocking the blade from her hand. Válde seized his opportunity. He grabbed her by her outstretched arms, and pulled her awkwardly off the ground. Her legs dangled and kicked as he spurred his horse toward Marnej.

The boy rose to his knees to block Válde's escape but then collapsed backwards into the bloody snow.

～

Dárja squirmed against the man that held her. The horse's withers pounded into her ribs and gut.

She looked back to the spot where Marnej had fallen, willing him to get back up. "Let me go!" she shouted into the wind.

"So you can die on that field?" a voice growled and elbows dug into her.

Dárja felt the reins snap across her back. The horse lurched forward, gathering more speed. She arched, breaking the Olmmoš's grip on the reins, and, for one brief moment, both she and the rider were suspended in the air, then a branch caught her in the head. She fell back into something else hard, then tumbled to the ground.

Lying on her side, Dárja attempted to take a breath through the pain. Snow filled her mouth and nostrils, cold, wet, and suffocating. She clawed at the ground, her hands raking through the snow as she tried to move. Somewhere beyond her, she heard men shouting, "Don't let the Brethren escape."

Dárja rolled under the low spread of a pine tree, and lay still, her breath returning slowly as the sounds of men and horses faded north of her. She didn't know what it meant that Olmmoš soldiers fought among themselves, but she didn't have the time to look for reasons. The soldiers were gone now. She needed to get back to Úlla and Okta. Úlla may have already had the baby. If that was the case, they could ride and regain the sled. Then she could make Úlla and her mánná comfortable for the journey home.

Dárja crawled out from under the tree. Her body screamed in protest as she pushed herself to her feet. Then her head exploded in pain and she crumpled to her knees again. A piercing scream cut through the air, followed by another.

Terror gripped Dárja in the silence after Úlla's scream. She had to get back to her. She had to help her. Dárja scrambled to her feet, stumbling headlong back the way she'd come. When she broke through the trees into the valley, it was blanketed by sickening stillness. Mounted Olmmoš soldiers surrounded the place where she'd left Okta and Úlla.

Dárja stood, dazed, her head pounding with blood and defeat. Each inhale was a knife through her ribs. She looked across the valley to the dark rise of scattered bodies that marked the spot where she'd last fought alongside Marnej. Nothing moved there. She ran forward, toward the gathered soldiers. To where she'd last seen Okta. To where Úlla was to give birth. Her hand went to her belt, but she had no weapon. She had nothing.

Dárja's footfalls slowed. The wind picked up. It was like a howl in her ears. Then she realized the plaintive sound was coming from her. In some distant part of her mind, she registered the sound of horses growing louder. She turned her unseeing eyes away from the death before her and half-ran, half-staggered into the cover of trees, heedless of the branches that lashed her. She accepted their sting like a penitent, thinking, *They're all dead*. She'd been so sure. She'd convinced them all that she could protect the nieddaš. Now Marnej was dead. What did it matter that he'd shared her secret with Úlla? What they'd shared together had been greater than one broken promise.

Her foot turned on a rock. She stumbled, and her other foot plunged through the ice of a hidden stream. Dárja stood breathless, looking up at the sky, as cold water seeped into her boot. Above the snow-topped trees, the just-waning moon shone, casting shadows, even in darkness. There, beyond the moon, was the bright and unwavering North Star. It pointed the way back home. *Home*. She thought of Kalek, how he had held when she'd returned from the battle. She longed for that comfort now. The warmth of his embrace. The scent of herbs. She had promised she would return. He had called her his daughter. But she could never be that now. She could only hope to be forgotten, even if she would never forget herself.

CAST OF CHARACTERS

Olmmoš

Áigin	Order of Believers	spy/agent for the Vijns
Bávvál	Order of Believers	High Priest/Vijns
Beartu	Brethren of Hunters	Piijkij/rogue
Daigu	Brethren of Hunters	Piijkij/rogue
Dávgon	Brethren of Hunters	leader/Avr
Edo	Brethren of Hunters	Piijkij/rogue
Erke	Order of Believers	member of Court of Counselors
Feles	Brethren of Hunters	Piijkij/rogue
Gáral	Brethren of Hunters	Piijkij/rogue
Herko	Brethren of Hunters	Piijkij/rogue
Ivvár	Soldier	killed at Brethren introduction
Irjan	Brethren of Hunters	Piijkij
Jonsá	Order of Believers	soldier
Joret	Order of Believers	soldier
Marnej	Brethren of Hunters	Irjan's son
Matti	Order of Believers	soldier
Mures	Brethren of Hunters	Piijkij/rogue
Niilán	Order of Believers	soldier/commander
Osku	Order of Believers	soldier
Redde	Brethren of Hunters	Piijkij/rogue
Rikkar	Order of Believers	Apotti/Priest of Hemmela
Selen	Order of Believers	soldier/guard at Ullmea
Válde	Brethren of Hunters	Piijkij/rogue

Jápmemeahttun

Aillun	nieddaš	oktoeadni to Dárja
Ávrá	nieddaš	weaver/Kalek's love interest
Birtá	nieddaš	cook
Dárja	nieddaš	Aillun's daughter
Ello	nieddaš	farmer
Einár	boaris	leader of Council of Elders/Noaidi
Háral	almai	Kalek's lover before Aillun
Kalek	Healer	Aillun's mate/Okta's assistant
Kálle	almai	blacksmith/Úlla's lover
Kearte	nieddaš	Kalek's guide child
Lejá	nieddaš	about to give birth
Okta	Healer	former Taistelijan
Ravna	nieddaš	tanner
Tuá	nieddaš	butcher
Úlla	nieddaš	blacksmith

ENGLISH TERMS GLOSSARY

Brethren of Hunters: group whose original function was to hunt and kill the Jápmemeahttun.

Chamber of Passings: ceremonial group charged with overseeing the Jápmemeahttun life bringers.

clasp arms/clasped arms: greeting and parting gesture.

Council of Elders: the guiding group of Jápmemeahttun.

Court of Counselors: advisors to the High Priest of the Believers.

end time: the period of time where the Jápmemeahttun boaris experience the change in their body that signals their end.

Fortress of the Brethren of Hunters/Brethren's Fortress: Fortified encampment of the Brethren of Hunters.

handmate: spouse for the Olmmoš.

heart-pledge: to be "in love/monogamous/together as an understood partnership" for the Jápmemeahttun.

High Priest of the Believers: leader of the Order of Believers; theocratic/military leader of the Olmmoš.

Hunter: English term for a Piijkij; capitalized to distinguish for an ordinary hunter.

hutkeeper: wayside Olmmoš tavern keeper.

league: measurement approximately equal to three miles.

life bringer: term used by Jápmemeahttun to refer to the individuals involved in the birthing process.

moon cycles: how the Jápmemeahttun and Olmmoš mark the passing of a month.

Northland: geographical term associated with the Pohjola and the Jápmemeahttun.

Order of Believers: religious hierarchy developed by the Olmmoš after their rebellion against the Jápmemeahttun; became a theocracy.

Origin: birthing area for individual Jápmemeahttun.

Outside: Jápmemeahttun concept of everything "outside" the Song of All; the Olmmoš world.

quickening: Jápmemeahttun concept of pregnancy.

season of snow: how Olmmoš and Jápmemeahttun mark the passing of one year.

spirit stream: the energetic force released at the death of a Jápmemeahttun boaris as part of the birth process.

Stronghold of the Believers: fortified temple for the religious seat of power.

travelers' hut: wayside tavern.

weight stones: measuring weights for the healers

JÁPMEMEAHTTUN GLOSSARY

Many of the terms used in The Legacy of the Heavens trilogy are derived from various Saami dialects spoken in the northern regions of Norway, Sweden, Finland, and extreme northwestern Russia. The definitions in this glossary reflect the meanings as related to the books and are not intended to be a dictionary of Saami dialects.

almai: male Jápmemeahttun
Avr: leader of the Brethren of Hunters
bieba: short form of biebmoeadni; term of endearment like "mom"
biebmoeadni: guide mother
bierdna: bear
binna: herd of reindeer; used as singular and plural for the animal
boaris: the old ones among the Jápmemeahttun males
chuoði: regiment
chuoði olmmái: commander
chuoika: mosquito
duordni: sea buckthorn berry
Geassemánnu: summer month (June/July)
goahti: hut
Guovassonásti: Life Star; its cycle marks the ages of Jápme-meahttun individuals
Jápmea: Olmmoš name for the Jápmemeahttun (slang pejorative)
Jápmemeahttun: tribal name for the original inhabitants of the area
jogaš: stream
joik: personal song (chant); story of an Olmmoš individual (plural: joiken)
juhka: alcoholic drink

latnja: gathering hall
lavvu: leather tent
mánáid: children
mánná: child
Mehjala: name of a village
miehkki: sword
mihttu: measurement of age
niibi: knife
muorji: berry
návrrás: turnip
nieddaš: female Jápmemeahttun
Noaidi: head of the Jápmemeahttun Council of Elders
oktoeadni: birth mother
oarri: squirrel
Olmmoš: name for the "human" tribe; man or men
Oso: name of a village
Piijkij: title for a member of the Brethren of Hunters
Pohjola: Northland
puohtja: penis
ránesjeagil: grey reindeer lichen
Skaina: name of a village
Taistelijan: title for Jápmemeahttun warrior
Ullmea: name of village
uulo: plant tea used for medicinal purposes
urtas: angelica root
viel'ja: friend
Vijns: High Priest of the Order of Believers
vuodja: butter
vuodjarássi: dandelion

ACKNOWLEDGMENTS

While writing is often a solitary endeavor, publishing a book is an act of community. I am deeply grateful to all who have been a part of this journey. Special thanks are due to Cory Allyn, Jeremy Lassen, Oren Eades, Paula Guran, my marvelous editor, and Mark Gottlieb, my agent. I am indebted to Sita Saxe, Melina Selverston-Scher, and Benjamin Thompson for their invaluable comments. Finally, I offer homage to the Muse for gifting me this story and letting me share it with readers.

TINA LeCOUNT MYERS is a writer, artist, independent his-
torian, and surfer. Born in Mexico to expat-bohemian parents,
she grew up on Southern California tennis courts with a proph-
ecy hanging over her head; her parents hoped she'd one day be
an author. Tina has a Master of Arts degree in History from the
University of California, Santa Cruz. She lives in San Francisco
with her adventurer husband and two loud Siamese cats.